I0773242

SAVIOR
TIME DETECTIVE
(BOOK 1)

BY

KENNETH L POWELL

First Edition
Cover design by Melody Harbison
Edited by Kenneth L. Powell and Andrea Nordahl

ISBN 978-1-969130-01-4

Published by
Kenneth L. Powell
Molalla, OR
www.kennethlpowell.com

Printed in the United States of America

Acknowledgements

Good day, reader.

Usually, I list the people I'm thanking, giving each their own space. This time, I want to speak directly to you while honoring those who helped shape this book.

Andrea Nordahl—your candid feedback meant everything. I poured over your comments, and every suggestion that resonated made its way into the manuscript. The first chapter, especially, would not be what it is without your insight.

Matthew Wright—thank you for always carving out time to read my work before it's even finished. Your thoughts directly shaped how Sylvester's friends and Savior's clients came to life. Your input mattered more than you know.

To both of you: this book would not exist in its current form without you. I am deeply grateful.

Now, to *you*, dear reader...

If you've made it this far, thank you. What you're about to read marks the first time I've partially intertwined two of my series. Don't worry—*The Hybrids* isn't required reading to understand the crossover chapters. But I will say this: the sequels to *Savior: Time Detective* and *The Hybrids* will be tightly connected, sharing characters and arcs across both narratives.

This story is part of a greater saga I call Fàisneachd Caora, or *The Prophecy Saga*. It began with *Dawn of Prophecy*, my first published novel. And though this saga spans millennia—yes, even stretching back ten thousand years—everything is connected. It *will* all come together. Especially once *The Wolf's Dragon*, the fourth *Dragonkind* book, is released.

To answer the questions you might be asking:

Scholar of Duplicity is slated for release later this year—likely November, just like *Herald of Heresy* was.

The Wolf's Dragon will follow next year, in the second half of the year.

So...

Thank you for your patience. Thank you for reading. Thank you—for everything. This is a career that I could not be more appreciative of, and all of you make it happen. So without further jabber jawing, yes I like odd phrases, I present to you... *Savior Time Detective*.

Table of Contents

Kenneth L Powell

Part One

____

Where Time And Space Meet Mediocrity

Chapter One
Infected

Stars shone heavily over the empty cornfield. A twenty-two year old man floated above the bed of his truck as an orb of yellow light engulfed him. His entire plan that night was to watch the night sky as streaks of light crisscrossed the black veil of the galaxy beyond. When the cloud of yellow appeared high above him, he was awed. Never had he seen anything quite like it. As it rushed toward him, fear overwhelmed his senses. His life flashed before his eyes, and every memory was surrounded in a yellow aura.

Most of his evenings were spent in the Cedar Vale diner, doing exactly what he was doing now, reaching for something he could never have. In this case, what he couldn't have, was a woman named Ira. Strange choice by her parents, especially since the only other Ira he knew, was a wrinkly old cashier at the local grocery store. Usually, he only spent a minute or two even glancing at the old woman. It felt as though something burrowed deep in his brain, pulling memories and thoughts forward.

Ira—the Ira he admired—was a five-foot-six blonde who worked on her daddy's farm before the economy wasted away, and threatened to take it from them. She waited tables, pouring coffee and serving folks lunch or dinner, to help pay the bills. A warm smile crossed her face whenever he sat in her section. Jolts of pain and excitement filled him when an image of the woman crossed his mind.

His name was Sylvester. It was another odd choice of parents who were raised in a different time. As he worked his way through school, his classmates often teased him with questions like, *where's Tweety*, or *how many lives you got left*? It had been three years since he graduated, after being held back an additional year. He never had the desire to continue his education at the community college thirty miles away. Now, he would never have that opportunity. The light burned into his every orifice as it picked apart everything about him.

It was truly amazing that Sylvester could even finish school. The diploma he received felt like it was just to shove him out the door so he could move on with his forever life down on the farm. He didn't care then, because he didn't have to go back, and that was all that mattered. His final year was harder, because Ira, and his best friend Tommy, were no longer in school with him. She graduated on time with everyone else in his class.

His place was on the farm with Ma and Pa. He knew nothing of leisure, only the hard work of life on a dusty old plot of land where they barely made ends meet. The truck he lay in, pondering the many paths of his life as he stared at the big black sky above, was his sixteenth birthday gift. He worked every day and rarely took time off. All for a weekly pay of fifty dollars. Not enough to do much aside from put gas in the truck and buy a few cups of coffee. It was enough for him.

I wish I could be more. His mind screamed at the yellow mist delving deep inside of him. No one up there ever seemed to listen, this time was clearly different. The longer he remained in the yellow mist, floating above the bed of his truck, the more his life ran through his mind. It seemed to pull everything he loved, and hated, about himself forward. That he even considered to be more than just a farmhand, had never occurred to him until this very moment.

What could *he* be? It was a hard decision. It was one of those that needed more than a night of drinking and watching the stars, to decide. An old forties detective story he watched a few evenings before ran through his mind. He had an affinity for detective stories and considered the profession as something he could do. At least, as something he could have done. As quickly as the thought came, doubt overwhelmed him, and he knew that he could never be a detective, even if he were to live beyond this moment.

Stories about private investigators were the only thing that really helped push him through the hard nights. Most of the books involved crime in the nineteen twenties and thirties. They were dime store novels at best. Usually, they ended with the detective uncovering the truth, and the dame falling head over heels in love with the man. Rarely did he read Sherlock Holmes. Books written by Sir Arthur Conan Doyle truly required a certain level of skill when it came to reading, and his was not what it needed to be. As the yellow light bore deeper behind his eyes he realized it never would.

The yellow light reflected within him and the face of his oldest friend flashed before his eyes. With Tommy around, life was mostly filled with hard work and easy times. Sylvester really only had one heart-breaking moment in his life. He and Tommy were driving around, hootin' and hollerin' at anyone and everyone they could in such a small town. They were both sixteen. That night, Tommy wrapped his Mustang around a pole trying to avoid a deer. He was paralyzed from the waist down after that.

Currently, Tommy lived in a home a hundred miles away for people who had no one to take care of them. Back then Sylvester begged his parents to let Tommy stay, but they refused. They couldn't afford another mouth to feed, not to mention the special needs they, and the farm, couldn't fulfill for him. Both Tommy and Sylvester were heartbroken. Sylvester watched as the bus drove his best friend away. Tommy's face was buried in his hands, hiding the feelings of doubt and shame that filled him. These days, Sylvester didn't see him enough to count as more than an acquaintance, but they would always be best friends in his mind. Sylvester cried for his friend, not for the first time.

Deep down, he really only wanted the old Tommy back anyways. The guy who laughed at every joke, regardless of content, and had a lust for life. Tommy would have shoved him into Ira on a dare, which may have ignited both their passions. That version of Tommy pushed Sylvester to be better than he settled for now. When Tommy was gone, Sylvester's grades slipped, and depression was an everyday companion.

Before the accident, Tommy helped at the farm every chance he had. He wasn't an orphan, but had a drunk for a father at home. Tommy's mother walked out when he was five. For a while, his father held it together. It wasn't long before the hooch filled the void Tommy's mother left behind, and he drifted from job to job.

When his father heard about the accident, he tried to overcome the addiction, but it was a difficult road. Eventually, the state intervened, and Tommy was taken away. His dad had finally hit rock bottom. Not long after, he swallowed a bullet. Sylvester's family was the closest thing the crippled boy ever had to a real family. Everyone turned their backs on him when he needed them most.

Sylvester's parents were right. Tommy would have had a hard time on the farm. They would have had no way to feed the extra person who couldn't help, let alone take care of his own daily needs. Tommy never understood the trials and tribulations that Sylvester's parents were already going through. Back then, it was hard to feed everyone around the table, though they always made sure Sylvester ate. His parents would alternate nights during the rougher months, where one would eat more than the other.

"I hate you!" Sylvester yelled to no one in particular. One would think that he was yelling at the yellow light, but it seemed to be a self-reflection more than anything. Whatever the light was, made him question everything he knew about himself. "Why'd you have to take away the one person who helped me?"

As the last word fell from his lips, he opened his eyes. The yellow light had changed colors while it invaded his body, and the pain had softened. A teal light now surrounded him. Everything that popped into his mind had an ethereal teal glow. The light continued holding his body suspended in the air above the bed of his truck as it continued to mesh and meld within him.

See, this is why I don't like crashin' down from space into someone. They get all scared and expect something big to happen. Especially when they start floatin' and they always start floatin'. A voice suddenly spoke in his head.

6

Don't get me started on the life flashin' before yo' eyes thing. Every time they're like 'oh I'm dyin'.

"What's happenin'? Where are you?" Sylvester yelled at the voice.

Dummy, I'm in ya head. You can call me Tempus, and I can read ya thoughts. That way ya don't sound too crazy talkin' to me in public.

Sylvester's eyes widened. He heard stories of people who could read other's minds. They were all fake. At least, he thought they were. Some *thing* was reading his thoughts though.

Idiot. I'm literally inside you. You're my host and I'm about to become your best friend in the entire universe. Now listen, I only saw what happens to this point and what's about to happen is going to knock us both out. Don't be afraid. You'll be fine when we wake up.

Sylvester craned his neck, muscles in his body spasming and pulling of their own accord. The teal light released him as it dissipated, and he slammed into the bed of his truck. An old country song played on the radio, Patsy Cline, or Dolly Parton, Sylvester couldn't tell over the ringing in his ears. His last thought, before unconsciousness found him, was of Ira. Then, he closed his eyes and fell into a deep sleep.

Chapter Two
Introductions

Sylvester woke to the blazing heat of the sun. It was the strength of an electric oven, or maybe even one of those tanning booths he'd heard about over the years. Either way, he woke up hot.

The voice was silent in his head. He couldn't remember drinking as much as the plethora of cans laying in the bed of his truck implied. A flash of the strange glowing emptiness revealed itself to him. "I must've drank way more than I thought," he said, in a hoarse whisper. He felt his jeans for the lump that was his truck keys and smiled, remembering he left the truck on for a bit of music as he watched the stars.

As quickly as his smile appeared, it faded when he realized he couldn't hear the music. *How long was I out?* he questioned himself as he slowly scooted his butt toward the open tailgate.

The sound of rusted hinges bending as he closed the tailgate was as bad as nails across a chalk board. Not only did he have a headache, but his throat was sore, and his body was hot. He thought he must have caught a cold, or the flu, from sleeping outside in jeans and a t-shirt.

The key turned in the ignition, chugging slightly as it struggled to turn over. The telltale clicks of a dead battery followed. He hung his head, irritated he had done something so stupid. His body groaned and ached as his stomach started to turn with every click of the ignition.

This wasn't his first time falling asleep in the back of his old beat-up truck, but this was the first time his battery jumper failed to start it as well. It was only two hundred dollars, but he saved for a year. He used it two dozen times in the two years he had it. *Ol' Reliable* he called it.

He rested his head on the hood, looking down at the small rectangular box and pursed his lips. His head thudded as he softly smacked it against the metal. *Two dozen times and it's dead. I swear it was fully charged,* he reminisced.

Oh, my achin' head. Two dozen times and what's dead?

Sylvester looked around, Ol' Reliable falling to the ground. The voice really was there, clear as someone speaking directly in his ear. It was flat all around him as he stood in the empty field of the old Rollin's place. Not even a rock popped up from the dead weeds.

"Hello?" he called out in his thick southern drawl. *I swear these fields are haunted,* he thought.

How can you be from this part of the country and have that kind of accent? You've never even spent time in Georgia.

Again, he heard it, and again, no one was around to say it. The only figures in the field were Sylvester and his shadow. "Who's out there playin' a prank on me? Willy? James?" He knew his friends didn't have an eastern accent, but they would fake one to have a little fun at his expense.

Idiot. Though he couldn't see it, his mind told him the owner of the voice was shaking its head. **Listen to me, you dumb hick. You're hearing me in your mind. I am your permanent guest. At least 'til you die.**

Sylvester turned pale and his eyes widened in shock. His body ached more than it had, and he shook violently. The way his body convulsed was almost like he was having a seizure. He had seen people experience a seizure, and though they convulsed like he was, they were non-responsive.

The thought of this killing him, alone in the middle of nowhere, filled him with dread. Death at the hands of a seizure, and not the long nights of drinking. Grammie Jean died of tumors in her brain. Was this what the voice was? A tumor that made him think he heard voices.

Whoops let me get that for ya. The voice rang through his skull.

Sylvester's skin regained its golden shade. Farmers tan most called it, everyday tan for farmers he supposed. His aches and pains were all gone, even the ones he felt from working the fields day in and day out. *It's a tumor, but one that saves lives?*

That's right, I'm a tumor and I save your life instead of...what's cancer?

"I don't really know," he said aloud. He was unaware whether the voice could hear his words when spoken.

Well, we're going to have to find some way of finding out. I don't know if I am a cancer or not, just that I live in you. Also, if it's an insult I'll make you, the voice paused for a second **piss yourself.**

It could hear his thoughts and his voice. "How did you make me feel better?"

Simple. I adjusted the receptors in your brain to increase the T-cell response. I just made it so you'll never get sick again.

His mouth hung open. If that were true he would only die from old age, or someone else causing his death. "I can't get sick from anything?"

Now I didn't say that...necessarily. Sick and dying are two different things. Your common cold will never bother you again, neither will other parasite issues.

His family had a history of several life-threatening illnesses. Diabetes was his uncle Ken's affliction. It wound up being his downfall, because he refused to look at it as a serious concern. Cancer took his grandmas, Jean and Pearl. They were both such loving people, he was devastated at each loss. Dementia and Alzheimer's took his grandpa on his dad's side.

How can you say took? He's still alive.

"You'd understand if it happened to you," Sylvester stated, realizing how idiotic the statement sounded.

So, explain it to me.

"Tell me your name first." While he walked, Sylvester rubbed his head.

The voice was silent for a while. Every step the man took, reminded him, he was at least five miles from town, and thirty miles from home. With any luck he would find his pa in the *Pickin' Go* looking for something he needed for the farm. It would be an extremely long walk after the strangest night he could somewhat remember.

Y'know what, your people can't say my actual name. My species is known as Tempus-Parasita, in your language. As I said last night, call me Tempus.

"Fine...Tempus. What I mean by *Dementia and Alzheimer's took him* is that he was a different person when I grew up. He loved everyone and made sure they were all taken care of. Pa got the worst of him, but he really only wanted what was best for his son." He stumbled on a raised section of the asphalt as he walked the broken road, lost in his conversation. It had not been paved for at least ten years, and the raised section was one of many.

"He'll always be my grandpa. I'll be sad when he passes, but the man I loved is no longer there." Small splashes fell to the ground as he walked and refused to acknowledge and wipe the tears away. He hadn't thought of the man in a long time. "Anyways."

Too bad you don't have the ability to time travel. Then maybe you could say your goodbyes a little differently, or maybe you could travel forward until society finds a cure. The voice was snarky and not the least bit sarcastic.

He stood on the side of the road, lost in thought. "How?" Sylvester never invested his time in science fiction anything.

Time is vast. I can see certain events. You'd need somethin' special, somethin' a hundred fifty years in the future on a ship somewhere out in space.

"Shut up." Sylvester laughed. "You can't travel through time. That's just too much. 'Sides if you could, you'd have moved us from here to my house already."

Pressure built inside of him. It was almost too much for Sylvester to bear. He closed his eyes as he dropped to his knees. The pressure continued to increase and so did his grumbling and groaning.

As suddenly as it started, it stopped. Everything was okay. When he opened his eyes he stared at a house. His house. Painful tears fell from his face without a hint of emotion behind them. He felt across his body for any sign of damage or blood.

Nothing.

Yeah that was my fault. I forgot to prepare you for that. Your species is better at traveling through space than I expected. Other species would have turned to dust had I forgot to flip the right switches.... Yeah let's say switches. Tempus' laugh echoed through Sylvester's mind.

"Funny for you maybe." He wiped away the tears and looked around, eyes wide and veiny. The yellow siding was faded from years of sun exposure. Each step creaked as his weight pushed down on them. The wood boards, once stained dark brown, were weathered and old. "You really did it."

Boy you ain't seen nothin' yet. We've got so much to discuss. Though to be honest, probably shouldn't speak out loud to me here. May make ya seem crazy and get ya thrown in some sort of correctional facility. This one time on Cralaplex Thirty-Three, my host just wouldn't shut up. Could've saved 'im, but I chose to let him rot. Tempus language was taking on the familiarity of the English language.

The parasite waited for a response. When Sylvester didn't say, or think anything, the parasite thought maybe it was time to be quiet. He watched through the tear-filled lenses of Sylvester as the man walked through the door. Years of knicks and scratches covered the white surface. He hugged an older woman, who looked at him with a quizzical smile. Then he walked upstairs and plopped into his bed.

That may have been too much, Tempus thought to itself.

Chapter Three
Details

Twelve hours passed. Tempus was used to silently waiting while its host slept. The parasite itself only slept when it absolutely had to. It knew the future, at least until it joined with Sylvester. What was coming was all new. Tempus floated in space for ten thousand years before finally arriving at this point in time. There were always two possibilities of where it would end up.

The first was of course Cedar Vale, Kansas, where it was to be hosted by Sylvester, which clearly happened. It still wasn't sure what they were destined to do together, but it was sure this was the better option. The other possibility was that it would be sent to a planet that the earthlings called Mars. Once there it would rest on the surface. In this reality, Tempus would experience the feeling of being run over dozens upon dozens of times by machinery sent from Earth.

The first real human host would have been decades later when the humans from Earth finally decided to colonize the red planet. Tempus was ecstatic that Sylvester was its destiny. For centuries it thought the Mars option would be its fate. Tempus passed planet after planet, some destroyed, others flourishing with life.

About three thousand years after Tempus separated from the Tempus-Parasita colony, it was passing a planet with weird translucent beings of different color and size. They hovered around, waiting for some inevitability that it would never understand. Tempus assumed they were preparing to invade the teal globe. A large, six-sided, rectangular, black stone, rushed from the planet, carrying a large grouping of the translucent beasts with it.

The stone, and its colorful entourage, rushed silently over the parasite. At first, Tempus looked at the incident with disdain. It was angry that the ship had pushed the parasite toward its destiny even quicker. Tempus floated for nearly six and a half thousand years after that, to the inevitable crossroad that would push it to either Earth, or Mars.

Then it happened. A blue box created a vortex that shoved the parasite away from Mars. The pilot of the crazy blue ship, opened its doors, and stared at the spot where Tempus was. The person hanging out of the doors, was seemingly aware of the being floating there. He looked like what Tempus expected a human to look like.

The man mumbled something, Tempus only slightly heard the words *"not good"* as the blue box continued along its own path. Tempus understood what the blue-suited man meant by those two words. Whoever Sylvester was, it was possible that their pairing could in fact, not be good.

It never had morality, so it depended heavily on its host to decide what was right and what was wrong. The only thing that it controlled was what they could and could not change. Tempus would list all of those things for Sylvester, when the man eventually woke up.

Often, Tempus-Parasita caused their hosts to sleep for long periods after first contact. It wasn't surprising for the beings to sleep for weeks. In those situations though, they wound up in some form of a hospital in a coma. Sometimes, the treatments would kill the host, and the parasite within. Tempus was hoping this wouldn't be the case.

It waited, reflecting on its long life. It was no longer connected to the hive knowledge that the Tempus colony learned with every connection. Most other Tempus were connected until they died, which was usually eons after they departed. They would send information from their host, updating the hive on their activities, and the dos and don'ts of their own abilities.

This Tempus didn't miss the connection. It was constant feedback about the same old things that it was tired of hearing about. Tempus-Parasita existed for eons before the start of the universe. They were a being living safe between non-existence and the beginning of time. The most recent transfer of rules, before Tempus lost contact, was bound to be its final communication with the colony.

★★★

Sylvester woke with a start. He remembered what happened this time. Even if he didn't, the sudden and annoying Bronx-accented parasite, wouldn't let him forget. It was only seconds after his mind woke that the being living within him announced itself.

Goooood mornin' sleepyhead.

The voice was loud and obnoxious. It slightly sang the phrase to him. Sylvester didn't respond right away. He took in his surroundings, recalling where his truck was as well as how he had arrived at his home. Sylvester blinked a few times looking around the darkened room, then at his clock.

Three in the morning on Monday. He slept through his last day off and it was time to start working the farm. He rubbed his face with both hands, hoping to arouse the sleep that had yet to leave his weary body. Still, the parasite, or as it may as well be known, his new *buddy*, sang on—and loud.

"Dude shut up," he whispered.

Tempus went silent and returned to its waiting state. Sylvester was still wearing the jeans and t-shirt he wore Saturday night before *it* came. Normally, Sylvester didn't shower first thing in the morning, but his clothes felt moist and damp with sweat. He hoped the moisture was nothing else.

The hallway was already lit outside his room and the whole house was moving about their normal daily routines. Sylvester exited, with clothes in one hand, and hat in the other. The smell of bacon and sweet hot cakes filled the air. His stomach growled uncontrollably as he made his way toward the bathroom. The door was closed, and Sylvester knocked.

"Mornin' son." An older grizzled voice rang through. "If you're tryna use the toilet, I'd suggest goin' out back."

"Alright, pa." Sylvester returned to his room, defeated, and stripped the dirty clothing from his body. He put on fresh clothes, and a healthy amount of deodorant, and left his room. Steps echoed every time his boots hit the ground. The stairs opened to the living room, followed by the kitchen where it smelled like his ma had whipped up quite the feast. He hung his hat on a hook and sat down.

"Mornin' sweetie. How'd you sleep?" the woman asked as she flipped a pancake.

"I slept alright," he replied.

"You feelin' okay? You don't typically sleep a whole day away." She turned to look at him for the first time that morning.

He really didn't. Most of the time he was lucky to sleep past six in the morning. Sylvester smiled at his ma. "I'm fine, thank you. Just needed some extra sleep I guess."

The woman smiled and took his answer at face value. Sylvester knew that it was nothing to do with the need for sleep. Instead, everything was caused by the thing that now lived within him. He considered telling her the truth as he sat down at the table, but chose not to.

She set a plate down in front of him: two eggs, three pieces of bacon, and three pancakes. Then she returned to the stove and prepared for the man occupying their only bathroom to come down and eat his breakfast.

"Thanks, Ma, that was great," he announced only a few minutes later.

"Sylvester Pemberton you ate that far too fast." She turned and frowned at him.

"I haven't eaten since Saturday's dinner," he offered as an answer.

"That's no excuse young man, you shouldn't eat so fast. It's not healthy for ya." She flipped an egg with ease as she lectured him.

"Sorry ma. I'm gonna get to work. Think you or pa can run me out to pick up my truck? It's at the old Rollins place."

"What's it doin' out there?" the older, deeper voice asked with authority as his pa entered the kitchen.

"I was havin' a few beers in the back, listenin' to music, and passed out. Batteries dead. Ol' Reliable was dead. Was gonna take care of it yesterday after I woke up, but we all know what happened after I went back to sleep." Sylvester stood up, taking his hat from the hook.

"I'm busy all day, got that field to work. You headin' into town at all, Ma?" Using gas for something like this wasn't taken lightly.

"Nope, you'll just have to walk it." The woman set a plate on the table. "Now sit and eat your breakfast, hun."

The burly man sat down and slowly ate his food. He was in his late fifties, but he was built like a man in his early thirties. He looked at Sylvester, pausing a moment as he swallowed. "If things change I'll let you know, but don't count on it. You've got a full day ahead of you too. Make sure that thing's charged before you head that way either way."

"Already charged it," he replied.

Don't worry about it. We'll get that thing later, the voice interrupted.

Sylvester smiled at his parents. "I'm gonna start my day. Let me know if you need help in the east fields."

"I'll send you a text," the old man grumbled.

"Sure, and I'll start shootin' smoke signals as a reply," Sylvester joked. They couldn't afford cell phones; they could barely afford the landline they did have.

The older man laughed, stopping the fork an inch from his face. Sylvester always liked leaving him in a good mood. As he left the house he returned his hat to his head and walked to the barn.

He was in charge of ensuring all of the animals were fed and tending to the west fields. They grew mainly hay, but had to rely on old, worn-down machinery, and the power of the two oxen they owned to till and cut the fields. Sylvester threw a feed bag over his shoulder and carried it to the first pen.

Is now a good time to talk to you? Tempus had a lot to go over with the man.

"I suppose it's as good as any," he replied as he spread feed for their chickens. "Beat you to your crowin' you son of a bitch," he announced to the bird staring at him.

You have a problem with that bird? Tempus was clearly confused.

"Nah, he's just a dick. Always wakin' me up when I'm not out feedin' him, or his flock, early enough." Sylvester shook the feed bag for the birds.

Alright. Tempus figuratively shook its head. ***We have a lot to go over, but there's some basics that I really need to tell you.***

"Well, you have until lunch. I don't like the whole speakin' in my head thing and that's the next time we'll be around anyone else." He managed to get used to the idea of no longer being an "I" and instead being a "we".

The Pemberton farm had a total of three employees: Al Pemberton, Janet Pemberton, and Sylvester Pemberton. Al exclusively worked the fields to the east. He didn't handle the animals any longer, that was a job for the younger, more agile, and flexible, Sylvester. Janet handled the finances, and the selling of crops or herds. Essentially, she was management, but rarely checked on either of the men. By lunch she would have something put together for both of them.

Alright, then here's your basic rules of our newfound abilities, Tempus announced.

Chapter Four
Rules

First thing. You can't change events that will alter the course of all your people. The parasite considered whether it should take questions first, or wait until after it finished listing the rules.

"So don't go assassinate Hitler before he takes over Germany...gotcha." Sylvester moved from one pen to the next. It was a surprisingly knowledgeable response for the man.

Tempus had seen plenty of animals in its time. Most of its knowledge of the beasts was because of the connection it had with its host, or the colony. As far as the parasite could tell, none of its people were ever in contact with anyone from the planet Earth. *Then again I lost my connection to the colony, maybe one of the others did too?*

Sylvester returned to the barn and put the chicken feed away, then picked up one with a fat creature who had a snub nose. ***What's that?***

"What?" Sylvester absentmindedly asked.

That thing on the bag.... Tempus had never seen anything as strange as whatever *that* was.

"It's a pig. We raise 'em and use 'em for meat." Sylvester shook his head as he hefted the bag into a wheelbarrow, followed by another...and another. By the time he finished he loaded six bags and was pushing it out of the barn with little trouble.

So, what's a Hitler?

20

"Look, I don't have time for all of those types of questions. I suppose that I'd have to ask you a ton too though. Then again, I'm not connected to your brain like you are to mine." Sylvester stopped in front of another pen.

Tempus looked at the animals through Sylvester's eyes. They were different colors and sizes, but it supposed they were the same basic shape of the one on the bag. ***So, you're saying I can rifle through your memories?***

"Yeah sure. I don't see why not. Actually, I'm surprised you haven't yet." Sylvester cut open the bag and started pouring it in a trough for the animals.

Tempus quieted and Sylvester felt strange. It was like he was free of the parasite, but he knew he wasn't. Regardless, his mind was silent, and he focused on pouring bags of feed into bins.

For everything they didn't have, the animals on the farm had plenty. These days they ate just fine. Back in his preteens, the animals' lives were no different. The family, however, struggled to put food on the table.

They were what paid the bills most of the year. Pa branched out and, instead of just dealing with Cattle and the farm, added sheep and pigs. It was a busy place and only Sylvester worked with the animals. They had the land which was in the bank's possession.

Would be paid off if he'd just stop buying more. Sylvester thought to himself. His pa was notorious for having an idea and needing more land to expand on it. *God forbid he ever hired someone, or I don't know...stopped buying land for ideas that barely pay for the extra.*

Sylvester loved his parents, but as with Saturday, he was thinking about what else he wanted to do with his life. He didn't want to work a farm, or ranch, until he was well into the twilight of his life. The world was filled with so much more, all he had to do was take it.

Most of the time he watched stupid detective shows that, while entertaining, couldn't possibly have been what really happened to a detective. Then he thought of Tempus and what the parasite claimed it could do.

It already proved it could move him from one place to another with little effort. A slight sickness was nothing in comparison. *Maybe that was only the first time?*

I'm trying to work through your innermost thoughts and dreams...not to mention the databank that you call a brain. Could you speak out loud and not overrule your mind with these thoughts?

Sylvester's mind went silent. "What a jerk."

I change my mind, can you just not think, or talk? And for your information yes...that was just the first time. You shouldn't feel sick every time and the pressure will fade.

Sylvester was silent. He no longer protested and only pushed his wheelbarrow to feed the animals. His chores moved at a quick pace when he wasn't thinking about anything else. The sun was just breaking the horizon when he finished feeding the horses, the last of the animals that he had to worry about. At least, until later when he would have to do it all over again.

He went into the house. "Hey Ma, any coffee left?"

It was silent.

"Must be off doin' somethin'." He walked to the coffee pot. Empty. Instead of brewing a new batch he simply filled a glass with water and drank.

Each room was empty when he checked for the woman. She wasn't downstairs, nor was she upstairs. He finally submitted that she was likely out, though she had claimed that she wouldn't be going anywhere that day.

His next job was in the west field. Pa was somewhere in the east, working the corn. Sylvester worked the wheat. When the time came to harvest pa would rent a harvester, freeing Sylvester for the days it was in use. Then, after the harvester was cleaned and returned, he would start the process over again.

Sylvester was just going out to manage the crop, which would be another six hours of his time. After that, he would be able to fix his truck. He trudged along to the field, the same wheelbarrow being pushed in front of him. His job, pretty much every day, was checking the soil, pulling weeds, and spraying for insects.

Alright, now I know what a Hitler is…and a whole lot more about your species than I ever wanted to know….

"It's good to hear ya. I was thinking, after I'm done with the field, that we could zap over to the truck. That alright with you?" Sylvester expertly traversed the field and avoided the many humps and divots in the soil with ease.

Yeah, sure, whatever. In response to ya question, no, you couldn't do that. Hitler created the world you live in. By removing him you could remove yourself from the present.

"Huh?" Sylvester was trying to remember what they were discussing, slowly recalling the actual question. "Sorry, it's been hours. I guess I forgot what we were talkin' about."

Tempus rolled its figurative eyes as Sylvester inspected plant after plant. *Anyway…. The point is you can't change events like that.*

"How will I know what the events are that I can change?" Sylvester dug down into the dirt and tried to pull the root of the weed he was trying to extract.

Simple…I'll tell you if it can be done. Next rule, you can't teleport to a place you've never been. Let me clarify that even further. You can't teleport into a place you've never been, or I've never been.

That said, you can teleport to a place another person has been simply by allowing me to glean their memories. This requires a longer period of time where you hold their hand, or really any other body part. During his time sifting through Sylvester's brain, Tempus had become familiar with the human body. More so than it ever would have wanted to, but memories were all useful.

"So, I could be transported to a place my pa's been, but not one I've never been." Sylvester was understanding things quicker than Tempus thought he would.

Yeah, but it may be a long interaction that you and he aren't used to having. I'm talkin' a few minutes of touching the man somewhere. Even Tempus, before interacting with Sylvester's mind, understood how awkward that could be.

"Does that mean you invade their mind like you did mine?" he asked.

Pretty much.

"Does anything happen? Like do I glow, or is it just me standing there touching the person?" The weed finally pulled loose, and he tossed it into the wheelbarrow.

Nope. You're just the creep standin' there touchin' 'em.

Sylvester was back at it and pulling another weed. "Can we change things about me?"

Like what? Tempus laughed.

"Like can we make me smarter, or rich?" Sylvester was struggling with the weed. It broke and he tossed the broken bit into the wheelbarrow, then used a trowel to dig the rest up.

I mean...I guess so. The problem is if you want to be smart, we have to travel to a time where you could be affected. I'm not sure how we would do it though. Probably better if you just try to work on that yourself instead of drinkin' beer and watching TV in your down time.

"TV can make you smart...if you know how to make it work for ya. What about being rich?" Sylvester was walking with his wheelbarrow and looking for other weeds that needed taken care of.

I mean yeah. We could make you rich. The problem is you'll need to choose how you'll do it. I could take you back in time and have you interact with someone where they could take advantage of the stock market, though I can see that being a slippery slope. Could rob a bank, or something, but that would probably get you in trouble.

"Well, if I'm in trouble what's it matter? You can just buzz me out of there to a safe place, right?" The wheelbarrow continued to roll over the dirt with ease and no other weeds could be found.

Yes, and no. Do you know where the money is kept in the bank in town? Have you been inside of the place it resides?

"I suppose I haven't." Sylvester rounded another row.

Well, that'll violate the second rule.

"How many rules are there?" he asked.

That's basically it. I'll let you decide the moral ambiguity of your decisions.

Then a thought ran through his mind. "Could we fix Tommy?"

I'm surprised that question took so long to come up. I would have to meet him, and you would have to let me scan him, but we could definitely save him.

Sylvester thought about it. He hadn't seen Tommy for over two years. Last time Tommy said he never wanted to see Sylvester again. For the most part he had abided by his wishes, but had sent a few letters, with no response. "I'd have to drive for three hours in order to see him."

Have you been to this place before? Tempus already knew the answer. Sylvester had been to Kansas City many times. Even to the facility where Tommy currently resided.

"Yeah, but that's not why. I'd want to collect my thoughts." Sylvester paused as he looked at the sky and wiped his brow.

And you would need gas money to do something like that. That beater of yours doesn't really go far does it?

"I suppose you're right. I would need gas money. Last time I had to save for three months to have enough money for the trip there, and back. I couldn't even afford food for the ride. I made stuff at home so I wouldn't starve, but that's not the point." Sylvester took a deep breath, inhaling the scent of manure, then coughed.

Out of curiosity, why are you always so broke, and your parents aren't?

The question was strange. Sylvester wanted to look Tempus in the eye, but since the parasite resided within him, he chose to look to the sky. "What do you mean exactly?" he asked exasperated.

When you hugged your Ma the other day, I kind of gleaned information from her that they weren't worried about money.

"I didn't hug her that long." Sylvester recalled the moment as he came in the house on Sunday. He embraced the woman for thirty seconds, not much more than that.

It seemed like you hugged her for at least an hour. I don't know, maybe my inner clock is off. Earth has such a weird feeling.

"Okay." That relieved one bit of stress over what the parasite could do. "Then what did you find?"

Well, apparently, there's a secret room in your basement. Your Ma spends most of her time in there managing finances. Tempus had no idea the impact of what it was saying to Sylvester would be.

"So, there's a secret room? Could you help me find it?" Sylvester stood up straight and started walking toward the house.

Of course I could. I assumed you knew about it. Though I guess it wouldn't be a 'secret' room then.

"Alright, let's go see what they're hiding from me. Maybe that's where Ma is now anyway." Sylvester quickly returned to the house. The door to the basement was always shut. He opened it and walked down the creaking steps as quietly as he could. At the landing, he looked around.

How could they hide anything down here Tempus? He was trying not to reveal that he was talking to someone inside his own head.

Very easily, go past the washing machine and push on the wall to the immediate left of the racks.

Sylvester followed the instructions. He passed the washing machine, the dryer was running, masking some of the noise from his movements. At the racks, he looked at the wall. Something was different about it, though he never noticed anything strange before.

He touched the wall behind the rack. The basement walls were always cool even in the summer heat. The place Tempus claimed there was a secret room was warm, hotter than the rest of the wall.

Just push it, Tempus said.

Sylvester pushed the wall, and it gave, opening silently on well-oiled hinges. Inside, startled by the suddenness of the opening door sat his Ma. Around her were stacks of green bills.

Sylvester had never seen so much money in his life. The woman stared at him wildly, arms flailing as she tried to cover the money that her thin frame couldn't possibly hide.

Sylvester reached out to a small stack of twenty-dollar bills. The money fanned in front of his wide eyes. There was at least fifty bills there, if not a full stack of one hundred. He looked at his Ma with confusion and anger. Sylvester spent his whole life working the farm with his Pa, only receiving a small, dire salary. They had plenty of money to use for whatever they wanted. The stack slid easily into his pocket.

She didn't say anything as it disappeared. There was no sign of remorse either. They stood there playing chicken. Neither wanted to speak to the other, though Sylvester wanted plenty of answers. Words refused to leave his mouth. He stared dumbly at what had to be tens of hundreds of thousands of dollars.

"All you could get me was a beat-up truck for all the hell you put me through. Tommy couldn't live with us because we couldn't afford to have a cripple livin' here?" Sylvester was shouting.

She still said nothing. The woman saw the pain and anger raising, as his life truly opened before his eyes. "Does Pa know?"

A devilish smile filled her face. "Oh, he ain't even your Pa."

Chapter Five
Revelations

The shock of the answer ran through him. "Are you at least my Ma?"

The smile covering her face spoke volumes. "I ain't your Ma either. We found you in our field when you were just a baby. Long-term investment we thought."

She's not wrong. You've saved them thousands of dollars according to her thoughts.

Sylvester ignored the parasite. He was shaken to his core. "I'm leavin', and you can't stop me."

"I wouldn't count on that," Al Pemberton said from behind him.

Sylvester turned around and saw the man, whom he always thought of as his father, holding a shovel. "So, what, you're just gonna kill me?" he asked.

"What we've done ain't exactly legal. You're not really my kin. I've always kept my distance, at least enough so I wouldn't have any moral complications." The shovel raised behind his head and came down.

Sylvester cowered at the blow, expecting it to come, only to find that nothing happened. He unshielded his eyes and looked at the man. It was like someone had pressed pause on a movie. Al was frozen in place, the shovel inches from Sylvester's arm.

You're welcome. Tempus' voice echoed through Sylvester's mind.

"Thanks Tempus." Sylvester backed away from the man, only to bump into the woman. He looked at them. "How long can we stay like this?"

As long as you want, Tempus said.

Sylvester moved around the man and walked toward the stairs. Every step felt like he was wading through a shallow pool of water. While there was resistance to his movements, nothing stopped him completely. He walked to his bedroom and grabbed his backpack.

He didn't have much. The truck, clothes, and a jump starter. Nothing tied him to them. He pulled on the drawer to his dresser. It moved, but it felt like the rollers needed to be oiled and the drawer needed to be shimmed. The bag was still mostly empty after he loaded his clothes.

He carried it to the basement, moved past Al, and stood in front of Janet. There were dozens of stacks of bills, consisting of hundreds, fifties, and twenties. Stack after stack loaded into his bag until it was completely full. Money was heavier than he thought it would be. He thought about the amount of money he was taking, adding numbers together in his head. There was at least four hundred thousand dollars if he was right.

He looked at Janet again, then the bare counter space around her. The thought that he was taking from them bothered him slightly. Sylvester never imagined this was the way he would leave home. Then he considered the way they held him there. Every day they used his emotions and loyalty against him. "Can you teleport us to my truck?" he asked.

I can, but is that going to be far enough? Won't they chase you? The amount of concern in Tempus's voice was admirable, but Sylvester wasn't worried.

The Pembertons would chase after him. They would want their money back, but he wouldn't give it to them without a fight. He looked at the stairs, then back at Al. He couldn't damage the stairs enough, especially with time frozen, to prevent them from following him.

"Gimme a minute," he said.

He walked back upstairs with the bag and closed the door. It never had a lock on it, but there was plenty in the kitchen he could use to block the door. The space between the door and the other wall was roughly four feet. Neither Janet, nor Al, would be able to escape from a tiny gap in the door.

"Alright, Tempus, go ahead and release it." Sylvester picked up the bag.

As time started flowing again, things began feeling and moving like they should. A dull thud could be heard in the basement, followed by wailing. Sylvester smiled and looked around the room.

"Janet," Al yelled through his sobs.

Sylvester realized what he forgot. With him out of the way, Janet was the next target for the falling shovel. Sylvester froze, unsure of his next move. "Tempus...I didn't want to hurt either of them physically."

I'm sorry pal, but that's what's happened. Going back now would be devastating, a time traveler shouldn't interact with his own timeline.

"Does my time still move while everything else is frozen?" Sylvester asked, ignoring what any sci-fi fan would know of time travel.

Tempus was quiet for a moment as the parasite considered what the young man was asking. *Yeah, your timeline is still flowing while time itself is frozen. I know what you want to ask.*

"Do you? Cause I haven't asked it yet, not sure I've even fully thought it out." Sylvester was not being quiet about his conversation.

You're going to ask if you can go back to just before you asked me to return time to its normal state. Then you're gonna ask if I'll also teleport you to the basement where you can make things happen differently. Do I really need to remind you that they were going to kill you?

Sylvester shook his head. "Didn't you tell me I would be the person who decides what's right and wrong?"

Fine. Is that what you want to do?

Sylvester nodded absentmindedly.

Even though the parasite couldn't see the action, it knew what he meant based on the electrical connections firing in his brain. *Last chance. By doing this one of two things will happen. You and I will either exist in an alternate reality or be completely erased from reality.*

"Shouldn't you know what happens?" Sylvester asked.

I suppose you think we can still communicate with other realities. Or that the person who's erased from existence is able to get some message off beforehand... Doesn't work like that kid. Are you absolutely sure you wanna do this?

"I couldn't live with myself if I left things the way they are now." Sylvester felt the pressure again as he was teleported back to the basement. He looked around and saw Al once again in position to drop the shovel. Upstairs he could hear himself moving around, preparing to block the door.

He moved quickly toward the bigger man. The bag of money felt heavier this time. Moving a man that outweighed him by a hundred pounds was a different matter altogether. He could hear himself upstairs and it was getting closer to normal time flow again.

Sylvester hesitated only another second before grabbing the shovel. Al was big, Janet was small. They both could handle Al falling into Janet. A couple of bruises were far better than severe injury.

He pulled with all his might, but the man had a superior grip on the handle. The intention to kill Sylvester could be felt as he pulled on the shovel. Sylvester shook his head, looked at Al, then noticed the rope dangling from the ceiling. It was easier to move and could still be wrapped around the tool.

Quickly, he looped it around, tied a knot, and tugged. The rope was taut, and the shovel wouldn't budge, unless Al dropped the handle. Sylvester smiled, backed away and imagined himself somewhere he'd never been before. A picture he'd seen in a magazine at some time. A place called Tahiti. "Let's go there for our final moments."

You've never been there, Tempus stated.

"And? You also said I shouldn't do this." Sylvester shook his head.

The disgust of the parasite was evident. **Ugh** was all it said before Sylvester felt the pressure and they disappeared.

★★★

"Alright, Tempus, go ahead and release it." Sylvester picked up the bag. Time released and he waited. He wanted to know that time was once again moving before trying to move the table.

"What the hell?" Al yelled, followed by an audible tumble.

"Get off of me, you fat bastard!" Janet replied.

A few seconds of tumultuous movement passed. "Where's the money?" Al asked.

"Was here a few seconds ago." Janet paused a moment. "Where's Sylvester and why's the shovel hangin' there like that?" Sylvester thought nothing of the comments, only laughed as the table moved swiftly in front of the door.

Tempus had a different reaction. It recalled seeing the shovel and the tool was neither tied to anything nor in any way capable of floating in the air if Earth's gravity were taken into account. It said nothing, but suspected something that shouldn't have happened, did. *Sylvester's going to be a lot,* the parasite considered silently to itself. The advantage of their connection was that, while Tempus could understand all of Sylvester's thoughts, the same wasn't true for Sylvester.

"Let's go to my truck Tempus," Sylvester said.

Before they blinked out of existence and arrived at his truck, he heard Al say one more thing. "We're in trouble. This is all your fault." Then he was standing in front of the patchy blue beat-up truck, staring at it.

He considered his next few actions. Jumping the truck only bought him a little time. Afterward, he would be running in something they could easily track. "No," he said out loud.

Whad'ya mean? Sylvester's mind hadn't put the thought together and Tempus wasn't sure what he meant.

"I mean this isn't gonna work. We were going to help Tommy, right?" Sylvester asked.

Yeah. Tempus was having a strange sense of déjà vu. ***Doing anything to change the past would affect your future though. Consequences exist, but for some reason I'm not worried about them as much as I should be. Not anymore.***

"Let's go to Tommy's then. You read him and we'll see what we can do." Sylvester disappeared again, leaving barely a footprint behind.

Chapter Six
Tommy

Sylvester stood at the stoop to Tommy's group home. The outside wasn't as depressing as television shows would make it seem. He walked up the stoop and hesitated as he pushed the button for the speaker.

What if Tommy didn't want to see him? It was always a possibility, and they were fighting last time he saw the man. He closed his eyes and waited.

"Hello?" the voice box squawked back at him.

"Hello, this is Sylvester Pemberton. I was hoping to see Tommy today," Sylvester replied.

The box didn't answer back. Sylvester realized there was something wrong when the door to the home didn't buzz either. He waited two minutes, looking around, then pushed the button again.

"Please wait," the voice returned quickly to the line.

Sylvester nodded to no one in particular. He turned around and leaned against the rail. The staff didn't make him wait any of the other times. Tommy, regardless of his mood, usually met with him.

"Are you still there?" the voice rang through.

"Yes, ma'am," Sylvester replied.

"When you come in, please go to admin. Tommy's doctor will speak with you." The door buzzed.

Either Tommy got himself into trouble, or something else happened. His breath caught as he subconsciously held it. Sylvester walked down the hall. It was well-lit but smelled of urine. Tommy had moved from facility to facility. The rooms never smelled the same as the other areas of the building, but the halls and common rooms all gave off the same putrid smell. The clerk at the counter directed him to sit down and wait for the doctor. Sylvester sat and waited patiently.

A man in a white jacket and scrubs walked up to him. He was tall and his hair was greying on the sides. His face was clean-shaven, likely earlier that morning. "Sylvester, right?" the doctor asked.

He nodded.

"Why don't you follow me to my office," he said in a pleasant tone.

Sylvester walked through the hall, a feeling of dread slowly creeping over him. *Couldn't be that serious, or they woulda called me.* Would he have gotten any messages, though? He was a hardworking and integral part of the farm. Maybe *they* didn't tell him something bad happened, because *they* didn't want his performance affected.

The doctor showed him into the office, then closed the door behind him. "Water, coffee?" he asked.

"No, I'm fine," Sylvester replied.

"I know you're here to see Tommy. I wish I could comply, but he took you off of his emergency contact list. I know you visited him a few times a year, so I'm going to tell you this." The doctor leaned in.

"Tommy's dead," Sylvester said before the doctor could reveal the secret.

"Yes." The doctor's eyes fell to the file before him. "He left you a note. Though I'm not sure I should let you read it based on the content."

Sylvester's eyes welled up. "How?"

"It was suicide. Tommy suffocated himself with his pillowcase." The man leaned back. "Would you like to read the letter?"

Sylvester shook his head. Tears fell and his breath became a stutter as he sobbed. As much as he wanted to, Sylvester couldn't pull himself together. He tried as best he could. Tempus waited patiently and silently in the background. The parasite was aware enough to understand it wasn't the time for words.

"How about I give you a few minutes," the doctor said. It was clear that Sylvester needed time to mourn his friend. The doctor stood and left the room.

Once he was alone, Sylvester let all of it go. His head fell to the desk, and he cried. At first, it was sobs, then the anger and pain escalated, and he was smashing his fists into the desk. It was solid wood, and he wouldn't hurt anything except his hand.

He stood up and started pacing, fists being thrown around as he did. Anyone nearby could hear the pain and frustration as he spoke to himself. *Why would he do something like this?* Sylvester was devastated.

An hour passed and the doctor came back. Sylvester was once again sitting in the chair, head tilted back. The doctor returned to his own seat, shuffling papers on the desk as he waited.

"When did it happen?" he asked through exhausted breaths.

The doctor hesitated. "Two days after your last visit."

"Selfish son of a bitch." Sylvester shook his head. "Lemme guess, blamed me in his letter."

The doctor nodded.

"All because he was driving stupid when we were kids. If he only..." Only what? Tommy was just cruisin' and looking for girls to holler at. Sylvester was glad to join him. Really, it was the deer's fault. Tommy wasn't driving in excess of the speed limit.

"Unfortunately, we can't change the past," the doctor said. That was exactly Sylvester's plan. He looked at the doctor, smiled and thanked him for his time.

"I wish I could say his estate would be going to you, but it's in the hands of the state now." The doctor closed the office door behind him. He walked Sylvester to the entrance and said his goodbyes, leaving the man to ponder.

Sylvester walked the streets, silent in both mind and voice. He wasn't at a point where he could make good decisions, and he was smart enough to understand that. Did he care if they were smart decisions though?

Hey, bud. You doin' alright? Tempus asked.

Sylvester nodded. "I'm just fine. Take me back to twenty sixteen," he said.

Before I do, is there a specific day and time? Tempus could feel the shift in the man's mind.

The time and date were burned into his memory. It happened at ten thirty-six on October twenty-fifth. The streets were cold and wet. Rain poured that day, but there was no rain in the forecast for Halloween.

Tommy picked up Sylvester at the diner where Ira was already working. Sylvester was staring at her the same as every other time he went in. His truck was parked outside. He had been at the diner for an hour, eating pie and drinking coffee while admiring the love of his teenage life.

"Tommy picked me up at about eight fifteen. I was at the diner, and that's where we're gonna go, but about forty five minutes earlier." Sylvester smiled as he finished.

Alright, comin' right up, Tempus replied.

"Wait," Sylvester said abruptly, staring at the front of Dick's Sporting Goods. "I need something first."

He rooted around in his bag and pulled out a few twenties, then walked into the store. He navigated himself to the hunting equipment. Purchasing a gun would take three days before he could pick it up. A big sharp knife would be an over-the-counter transaction.

He looked in the glass case at all of the different options. "How can I help you?" the attendant asked.

"Goin' huntin' with my pa. It's been a while and I need a good solid blade," Sylvester said. "Preferably fixed, don't want to worry about joints and all that."

The attendant walked him down the cases, pointing at different options. "Are all of these pre-sharpened?" he asked. "I don't want to have to worry about sharpening until after we get that buck and have already cut 'im up."

"These are all fairly sharp, but you'll probably want to sharpen it anyway, if you want a good clean cut." The attendant smiled at Sylvester.

"How about a sharp point at least?" he asked, looking at a blade in the case. "How's that one?" The blade was black and had a fine tip on the end.

"Kershaw spear-point. I mean...it'll do the job." The attendant shrugged his shoulders and smiled at Sylvester.

"Great, does it have a sheath?" Sylvester smiled.

The attendant nodded.

"Wrap'r up," he replied.

He walked to the men's section and found a heavy jacket with a large hood. Sylvester left with the knife, the jacket, and his pack was just under one hundred dollars lighter. He walked to a trash can outside and unpackaged the blade, placing the sheath at his belt with the knife inside. The jacket covered the blade. *No point in causing a scene,* he thought. Finally, he looked in a display window at his reflection. With the hood up, no one would recognize him.

"Alright, Tempus, do it." Pressure built up within him and the man suddenly disappeared.

Chapter Seven
Changing The Past

The sun was setting outside of the diner. Younger Sylvester sat at a table, a piece of pie sitting on his fork for longer than it should have. Ira waited on a table of truckers passing through town.

Older Sylvester was sitting at a booth in the corner, waiting for his friend Tommy to walk in and sit down. The hood of his jacket was hung down enough to cover his slightly older face from view. He watched his younger self with an embarrassed smirk on his face.

Alright, this is gonna be a bit difficult. Make sure you don't talk to your younger self.

"But I can talk to Ira or Tommy, right?" he asked.

Of course, but I'll say this much…disguise your voice. You sound too similar to you at that age. Sylvester could feel the parasite gesturing toward the distracted version of himself.

Why wouldn't I sound similar? Sylvester wondered. That Sylvester was already using his adult voice. "I will. How's this?" he whispered in a deep voice.

Fine, just stop talking to me. You look crazy. Tempus wasn't wrong. The people two tables away were looking at the man while he spoke.

Ira finished with the truckers and walked up to him. "Will that be all, hun?"

Sylvester thought about the question. He looked at her, then at his younger self and smiled. "See that young man over there," he whispered in a husky voice reminiscent of Elvis.

"Oh Sylvester?" she asked. "He's in here all the time."

"He likes you. Maybe you should try to talk to him?" She saw the hooded man's smile, but that was all.

"Really? I just thought he liked our coffee and pie. It's all he ever orders." Her face blushed slightly.

"Trust me, I've seen him hold that fork up and just watch you. Are you interested in him?" he asked.

Her blush reddened. "I don't know. Not a lot to do in this town, but maybe I'll suggest he take me for a ride in that rusty ol' truck o' his. Course...if he does like me, why hasn't he said anything?"

Sylvester's smile broadened. "He's a young man infatuated with an equally young, but beautiful woman. It's expected. You will definitely have to make the first move with that one. What's my total?"

She handed him a check as the door to the diner opened, ringing the bell above. "Better do it quick, before his friend interrupts him," he said as he reviewed the check.

She rushed off, holding a hand up to Tommy, who stopped in his tracks. The younger version of his now dead friend watched as she sat down across from Sylvester and quickly started a conversation.

Subconscious tears rolled down older Sylvester's cheek as he looked at the young man. Tommy was standing on his own feet, which seemed to open the floodgates even more. He hung his head and hid the tears that fell.

This change isn't big enough to affect much as it is, Tempus said. ***Better make whatever you're doin' quick though, once things change permanently we'll be gone.***

"What do you mean?" Sylvester quietly asked, clearing his throat as he did so.

Do what you planned and if there's time I'll tell you...again.

Sylvester dropped three hundred dollar bills, then stood up and walked out the door. Ira looked only briefly to be sure there was money on the table, then turned her attention back to the younger Sylvester. Tommy, after hesitating only a bit longer, joined in.

The time was already eight seventeen. Tommy and Sylvester's timelines were rapidly changing. Older Sylvester stumbled as he walked. It felt as though he were dying, a different type of pressure building up inside of him. He walked to the car that he was as familiar with as he was his truck, but hadn't seen in six years. It was a classic and an overwhelming since of longing filled him. The last time he saw the vehicle he was being wheeled into an ambulance. It was totaled then.

His new knife slid easily from its sheath, and he knelt down, stabbing the wall of the driver's-side tire. He moved on to the next, performing the same task and sneaking his way around. Older Sylvester looked through the window as he neared the front passenger side. Tommy was deep in conversation with both Sylvester and Ira. They showed no signs of moving or stopping and the streets of the dusty old town were dead.

Okay, things are moving really quickly now. Here's what's about to happen. Tempus explained the consequences of Sylvester's actions. To Sylvester's credit he only nodded and accepted his fate.

"Great," Sylvester replied. "So, every time I change the past, I disappear?"

Only if it changes your life. If you change the timeline for someone who doesn't have an effect on your life, then it doesn't affect you.

"Are we dying?" Sylvester asked.

Like I said, I don't know, Tempus replied. ***This is a pretty substantial change. I suspect we'll be movin' forward in an alternate timeline, or simply not existing at all. So not quite the same as dyin' either way.***

The final tire deflated, and he snuck back to the other side of the car. Tommy never locked the Mustang, though he probably should have. Sylvester opened the door, laid down a stack of twenty-dollar bills for the damage, then shoved the bag of money on the other side of the car.

"Will that still be there?" Sylvester asked.

I'm sure it will. Inanimate objects don't have an exact timeline. They're created and destroyed. There's no change of fate for them. They'll always be in one state or the other.

Tommy always kept a pen and paper inside the car and Sylvester swiped it, quickly writing a note, then throwing it on top of the stacks of money in his bag. He closed the door and stepped away from the car in time to watch Tommy and Sylvester stand up. To younger Sylvester's surprise, Ira hugged him long and deep. Older Sylvester smiled, vanishing just before the boys exited the diner.

★★★

Tommy and Sylvester were distracted by the state of the car and missed the vanishing act. "The hell happened to my tires?" Tommy yelled.

No one was around, though the damage was clearly there. Tommy had only been inside for a few minutes and knew that there was no way anyone would have gotten away. He looked inside and saw the stack of twenty-dollar bills and his eyes widened.

Sylvester looked in the passenger side, unaware of Tommy's discovery. "My bags in your car. That's weird. I thought I left it at home." He opened the door and took it. "Guess I'll give you a lift home then?"

Tommy nodded. "I'll lock it up and talk to John, make sure he doesn't have it towed." He shoved the bills into his pocket, intent on counting the money later. "Least one of us has a date, never thought it'd be you."

Sylvester smiled as he threw the bag in his truck and started it. It roared to life and hummed as it idled. He opened the bag and stopped in shock. Inside was money...a lot of money. A folded note sat on top of the pile and said *read me* on the outside. Sylvester unfolded it, recognizing his own handwriting.

Sylvester,

You wouldn't believe me if I told you the truth about who I am. This money is rightfully yours. It's somewhere in the range of $400,000 dollars (probably more) and should be used to start a new life for yourself when you're twenty two. Before you set out on that life you need to continue like this doesn't exist. Go into town and put it all in a savings account only you know about. Then don't touch it. Try to make it a high interest one if you can.

Be sure that you're at the Old Rollins place on July 25th, drinkin' beer and hangin' out. After the next two days, you can use the money, but until then **don't** touch it.

OS

He refolded the note and closed the bag. It was his handwriting, but he pushed that to the back of his mind. The drive to Tommy's place took fifteen minutes, then he was off to his own house. The money pulled at his mind, and he knew he wanted to spend it. The note was clear about what he should do though.

Six years is a long time. He thought as he lay down after stuffing the bag under his bed. When the bag with the money touched its twin, the empty bag disappeared. Unbeknownst to Sylvester, a theory had been modified regarding inanimate objects.

A book lifted above his head, *Shadwell's Confession*, and he read into the night. Eventually the detective novel, set in the nineteen-forties after World War Two, fell to his chest. Soft snores escaped him as he fell into a deep sleep. Sylvester would never know the pain of the car crash, nor the loss of his best friend. All seemed right with the world.

Chapter Eight
Where We Left Off

For the most part, things went in a similar direction to his other life. Sylvester was once again in his truck, fleeing from his supposed Ma and Pa. This time, he had nowhere to go, and Tommy sat in the seat next to him. "They said you weren't their kid?"

Sylvester shook his head as he drove, once again with the same bag full of money from his supposed parents. Tempus was also in tow. The note Sylvester read never mentioned Tommy shouldn't be present when Tempus arrived.

That night, only a few nights ago, Tommy and Sylvester lay in the bed of his truck, drinking beer and having fun. Tempus's planetary arrival was met with shock for the parasite, as well as both Tommy and Sylvester. They both rose above the bed of the truck, bathed in light, crashing down and passing out afterwards.

Tommy seemed unaffected. All he would say was it was strange as he walked with Sylvester all the way home. Tempus was quiet since arriving. It wasn't until Tommy left that Tempus introduced itself.

Everything else played out the same: Working that day, discovering the secret money room and traveling back to change the fact that Ma Pemberton had been killed. The only difference was Sylvester's truck was running, and his first stop was Tommy's. They were best friends, and Tommy was his planned best man.

He and Ira dated since that night at the diner. They lasted through the rest of high school. Sylvester was smarter than he would have been otherwise. She pushed him to be better in all manners of life. He didn't graduate valedictorian, but he did pass with a solid 3.2 GPA, and with his class.

They were headed to pick her up so he could explain everything. Tommy had a cell phone and called her. "Ira, it's T, how you doin'?"

She said something that Sylvester couldn't hear. "Man, just tell her we'll be there in a little bit. Tell her to call out of work, and pack a bag."

Tommy relayed the message, then hung the phone up. "Where we goin' anyway?" he asked.

"Anywhere we want, but as far away as we can until I can wrap my head around everything." The truck's tires squealed as he took a right turn a bit too hard. "I gotta stop at the bank too," he said.

"Why?" Tommy asked.

Sylvester never revealed anything about that night to Tommy and followed the note's instructions to the letter. "I've got a savings account with a lot of money in it, I need to either drain the account, or somethin'."

They came to a stop outside of her house, honked and yelled at her to get in as soon as she came out. Tommy stepped out, taking and throwing her bag in the back. She sat in the middle. After Tommy was back in, Sylvester stepped on the gas.

"What's goin' on?" she asked in a fright. She had been working on a college application when Tommy called. It had yet to come up with Sylvester, but she intended to go to college and earn a degree.

Sylvester explained everything, except anything about the parasite residing in his head. By the time he finished his story, they were pulling up outside of the bank. "Hold on a minute, I'll be right back," he said as he grabbed the bag and ran inside.

Tommy and Ira sat in his truck, confused about what was happening. They discussed what had been said. Forty minutes passed and Sylvester ran back to the truck.

"What'd you do, rob the bank?" Tommy asked as the bag full of money was shoved into his lap.

"Nope, just switched my savings account to a checking account. No one else's name is on it, so I shouldn't need to worry." The truck darted off, toward the gas station. "Hand me a hundred," he said as he pulled up.

Tommy opened the bag. For the first time since Sylvester picked him up, he believed the story that Sylvester told them. His hand sifted through the stacks of hundreds, fifties, twenties and so on. Ira looked inside and had the same reaction.

Tommy handed a hundred to Sylvester, though his hand was still in the bag. "Can we go inside and get a few things for the trip?"

"Yeah, take fifty and get drinks, snacks and whatever else you think we may need." Sylvester handed the attendant the hundred and waited for the pump.

Tommy snagged two fifties and walked inside with Ira. They returned with three small bags filled to the brim with junk food they normally wouldn't buy. Sylvester looked at the pair, then at the bags. "Keep the change, buddy, everything's on me until we figure out what we're gonna do."

Sylvester drove the truck north, eventually merging on to I-70 and heading west. He drove ten miles over the speed limit, weaving and bobbing through traffic. He explained to his companions that he didn't have a plan, other than the timeless classic...run.

The Pemberton's couldn't say he was a runaway. They had no access to any bank accounts that he had. Cops wouldn't be involved, but it didn't stop them from coming after him, and their money, themselves.

He didn't need the money either. Sylvester knew that when he took it, but everything that happened since that night at the diner, made complete sense now. He, not necessarily this version of himself, but another version of himself, traveled back in time and cut Tommy's tires, leaving money for the damage, and the rest for him.

Sylvester wasn't sure why he chose that specific time. What he did know was Tempus told the truth about its ability to travel in time. He took the money to hurt them, much like they hurt him. There was no shame. Fear overwhelmed him at the thought of the Pemberton's finding him.

"Are we going back?" Ira asked softly as she leaned against his shoulder. The unfinished application to the nearest community college, sixty miles away rested at the forefront her mind.

"I have no plans to," he said.

Tommy looked at them both. "So, you're kidnapping us?" he joked.

"Really? Takin' you from a life where drinkin' beer in the back of my truck was the highlight, is kidnapping?" he replied.

"Well, he may not have had much going on, but I have a job. My parents are expecting me back sometime." Ira looked at Tommy. "No offense."

Sylvester hadn't thought about it. He didn't want to leave her behind and wasn't sure what else to do. "Would you have preferred to stay?" he asked.

She thought about it. "No, not with everything that's goin' on with you." Her answer was soft, almost inaudible. In her mind it was an answer given from necessity. "I just would have liked to let the diner know I wasn't gonna be back. Parents too."

"Tommy can she use your cell phone?" he asked.

Tommy handed her the phone. She called the diner first and explained to John that she was leaving town and apparently wouldn't be coming back. To her surprise, John didn't sound mad from the tone in his voice, he actually sounded relieved. She hung up the phone and held it for a minute, then looked at Sylvester.

"He was closing the diner at the end of the month. Said he was too old to keep it up and no one wanted to take over, or could afford it." A tear rolled down her face as she realized John was closing the diner because she was leaving to make something of herself. "I told him to make my last check out to my parents and mail it to 'em."

Such was life in a small town. All of the businesses one thought would be there forever eventually disappeared. Both Sylvester and Tommy were quiet. The diner meant as much to them as it did to Ira.

"Let your parents know," Sylvester said.

She dialed the number and waited. When it picked up she explained the news and said she was leaving town for a while. They lectured her about the decision, and she grew angry. "My last check will be in the mail in your name," she yelled in the phone and hung up.

"Everything okay?" Tommy asked as she tossed the phone back at him.

"Oh peachy. Didn't it sound like such a pleasant conversation?" she retorted to Tommy. "They know…" she began but quickly stopped.

"What do they know?" Sylvester asked, confused.

"That I'm an adult," she lied and folded her arms across her chest. She was done talking.

They drove in silence until the moon rose high above their heads. Tommy stared out of the window, watching as scenery blurred by. Ira sat in the middle stewing over the conversations.

"Anyone hungry for some real food?" Sylvester asked.

To his relief, both Tommy and Ira agreed they could eat. It had been hours since Sylvester picked them up and they had only eaten chips, sweets, and jerky during their drive. A sign read *Denver 30 Miles*.

"Where ya wanna eat?" he asked.

"Anywhere's good for me, buddy," Tommy replied. "How 'bout you?"

"I want pasta," Ira said. "Can we stop for the night?"

Sylvester thought about it. Denver was a big enough city they could stop, and it would be safe to stay for a few nights while he sorted out what they were going to do next. He nodded.

"Can we have our own room?" she asked, smiling at him. Ira wanted to tell Sylvester about her plans, hoping that he would move with her.

"Sorry buddy. You're gettin' your own room tonight," he said to Tommy.

"Long as I can have a few bucks to go to a bar and unwind myself, that's fine by me." Tommy kicked his foot on to the dashboard, rolled down the window and hollered like he was sixteen again.

Chapter Nine
Goodbye Old Friend

Sylvester and Ira spoke into the night. At first the conversation was all about what happened to him that caused such overwhelming foresight. After he explained, in full, she lay there quietly. He hadn't really told Tommy everything, just as much as needed to be said, really. She was the first to have a full look into what was happening within him.

Tempus was quiet during their conversation. *It's been quiet since I picked up Tommy,* Sylvester realized. Tempus was lost within itself for reasons it hadn't explained.

It was lost inside its own thoughts about its journey through space. The entire time it floated through the void it remembered thinking it would only be Sylvester when Tempus made contact. When it actually made contact, it was different than the parasite had seen. Sylvester was less reluctant than it imagined. Tommy was there in the back of the truck with Sylvester. The whole thing felt like déjà vu, minus the extra person. That felt wholly new.

When Sylvester discovered the money the Pemberton's were hiding, he already had a bag in hand to carry everything. When Al Pemberton was swinging the shovel toward Sylvester and Tempus stopped time, he tied the shovel so Janet Pemberton wouldn't be hurt. It was like the man had done it all before.

Maybe we have done it all before. If Sylvester changed the course of his future, then maybe some of that knowledge is leaking through. Tempus was ignoring a feeling that nagged at it since it bonded with the man. It didn't feel whole but couldn't quite figure out why.

While Sylvester and Ira talked, it was calculating all of the different possibilities. It couldn't see into the future anymore, that much was expected at least.

It chose not to speak until it understood everything a lot more clearly. In its experience, hosts altered the past, but not in a manner that changed who they were. Mostly they used it for traveling to places and making themselves wealthy beyond belief.

Of course, the host always made enemies. This was different. Yes, its host had made himself wealthy to an extent, but there was a depth that no other being had shown. It was new territory for Tempus and the hive the parasite came from. While Tempus was sure others of its kind had hosts who changed their past, the colony had no information on what would happen in those situations.

Tempus listened to Ira snore softly as she cuddled to Sylvester's chest. While they spoke, Tempus could feel Sylvester's mind poking around, searching for the parasites existence. **What?** it finally asked.

"What's the matter with you?" Sylvester whispered.

Speak in your mind, not out loud. You're going to wake that girl up and then you'll have to answer more questions. Tempus was deep in the man's mind and its voice echoed.

Fine, this better? Sylvester responded.

The parasite grunted it's approval and considered how to answer the question. ***Tell me what you remember from when we've traveled in time.***

Thoughts and emotions started filling Sylvester. Tears fell steadily, but he couldn't understand why. ***I don't know what you mean. I don't think we've done much other than when you stopped time that one time.***

Then why'd you already have a bag, and why'd you tie the shovel up? Tempus understood the physical things that were happening to Sylvester. He had memories of other times but couldn't access them.

Sylvester thought about it. *I just knew I needed the bag. Same goes for tying the shovel up. I knew that if I didn't Ma...* Sylvester's thought stopped quickly. He had never called his *Ma* by her first name. Then again, she wasn't his Ma. *Janet would have been severely injured, and I didn't want that.*

Tempus was nodding, though it didn't think Sylvester could tell. *Alright, I think we went back in time and changed the way that went. Tommy feels off too, but in a good way. Like he wasn't always with us, but now he is. Does that make sense?*

Ira made a noise and rolled to her other side. Sylvester stopped to listen, making sure he didn't wake her. *Not really. Are you saying that we changed the past for Tommy and he's here because of it?*

You really need to stop playing dumb. Tempus stopped. Even Sylvester's intelligence seemed different. *I'm going to be quiet for a while, if you need me to do something just ask, but I've got to dig into this more.*

Okay. Do I just ask you to do something? Sylvester's question went unanswered. Tempus had completely shut itself off. "Jeez, just wanted to talk more," he mumbled to himself.

Ira lay there, next to him, in underwear and a tank top. Sylvester smiled, shuffled under the blankets, and cuddled back up to her. He kissed her neck and softly moved his hands.

"Hey there sailor," she said as she groggily woke up.

★★★

The next morning they sat at a table with Tommy outside on a bright, but cool day. He had a pair of sunglasses on, and his mouth hung slightly ajar. "Have a bit of fun last night buddy?" Sylvester asked.

"Dude, not so loud," Tommy replied.

Ira smiled at them. "What y'all havin' for breakfast this morning."

"Omelet with veggies and bacon," Sylvester replied. "Oh...and hash browns."

"Bacon, sausage, hash browns. Double orders of each," Tommy replied as he leaned forward and lay his head on the table.

Ira laughed. "So, a heart attack is what you want? How much did you drink last night?"

For the first time all morning Tommy smiled, though only half of it was visible. "I was out until about two hours ago, then I was with a girl I met in the bar. She's still in bed...where I hoped to be."

Sylvester looked at Ira, then at Tommy. "Sorry pal, but I needed to talk about plans." Sylvester looked around suspiciously, then leaned in. "I think they'll be tryin' to find us. I gotta get rid of the truck."

Ira tried to stay straight faced, but the joy in no longer having to ride in the middle overwhelmed her. The truck's seat wasn't the most uncomfortable, but she was sure it was a close second. It was about the same level as sitting on the high school bleachers for hours on end.

Tommy shared a similar response to the news. They drove for nearly nine hours, and he never wanted to sit in the truck again. "New or used?"

"Somethin' with a plate, or we'll need some way to get a plate," Sylvester replied.

Tommy nodded. "Go to the post office and sign up for a box," he replied. "You've got enough money to buy whatever you want, just make sure it can seat at least four."

Tommy spoke as though he wasn't going to be part of it. *Probably goin' back to bed,* Sylvester thought to himself. "I'll be sure it fits us all. Course I don't wanna get a box, nothing with my name on it."

"They'll probably be able to find us based on just that," Ira responded. "They aren't your real parents, think you could get some fake ID's? Go by something else?"

Sylvester thought about it. "I wouldn't know where to get something like that."

They were in a city that none of them had really been to. Likely, the Pemberton's wouldn't be able to find them, but the truck would be a sure sign of their presence. It was his only real gift from them, but it was time to let it go.

"Think we could be here a week or more?" Tommy asked.

"Money's not a problem, I'm not sure they'll find us if we get rid of the truck, though," Sylvester replied.

"That a yes or no?" Ira asked.

"Sorry, yeah, we could stay a bit."

"Get rid of the truck, we'll take taxis and such while we're here. Let me see if I can find a way to get us some clean ID's." Tommy smiled again as the waiter walked up to them. He rattled off his order. "Oh, and throw it all on the same plate with some biscuits and gravy if you have it."

Sylvester stared at Tommy, his own mouth now ajar.

"What? I gotta soak up all the alcohol somehow." Tommy smiled at the waiter, who clearly understood the feeling and jotted the order down.

Sylvester and Ira ordered, then sat in silence as they waited. Tommy was the only person Sylvester knew who could always find the seedier side of any city, or town. There was no doubt in his mind that his friend could find what they were looking for.

"What did you mean by us?" Ira asked.

"Well, I don't know about you, but I'm changing my name too. First name's gonna stay the same, but last name has got to go. I'm tired of being Thomas Howell the third." Tommy took a drink of water. "Ugh, I need coffee." It was the one thing he didn't order.

"What would you change it to?" Sylvester asked.

"I love my old man, but since he died I've been thinking about my mom. Her last name was O'Halloran. Thomas O'Halloran. Tommy O'Halloran. Has a nice ring to it." Tommy hung his head and rubbed his temples. "This headache is killing me."

"Maybe you shouldn't drink so much." Sylvester laughed. "I like O'Halloran. Not too many people would know that fact about your Ma. I don't think you would have to worry about legally changin' your name."

"I would need to change mine too, if I wanted to stay at your side." Ira wasn't questioning them. It was a deep dark realization that spread across her face. One she hadn't considered before packing her bag for the trip. In her defense, she also didn't know what had happened when she did. Still, the college application sitting on her desk at home rested on her mind.

A smile crossed her face, but both men could tell it was only on the surface. It was something that made Sylvester sure that, if she had known, she wouldn't have joined them. After speaking to her boss, then her parents, she was fired up, and angry. After a great night's sleep with the man she loved, and had loved for the past five years, things were different. Not changing her name meant she likely wouldn't be able to stay.

"I love you," Sylvester said as he turned to her. "If you don't want to change it, that's fine. We can make it work. They won't look for you." Sylvester knew that wasn't true. He had stolen a fortune from ruthless people, they would do anything to get it back. The Pemberton's would look for signs of anyone who fled with him, whether it be Tommy, or Ira.

She started crying, wiping away the tears in her eyes as the waiter returned with their breakfast. The meal was an awkward silence that none of them could break. Tommy finished his food, threw down a twenty, one that had been Sylvester's, and made his excuses.

Ira and Sylvester remained. He ate slowly, picking at his food. *If I just let her know I was leaving.* Then he thought about what would really have happened at that point.

If he left her behind he would have gone east, toward another Kansas town, not west toward Colorado. Because of her they were in the safest place they could be. She had never been to Colorado. Tommy and Sylvester had, once upon a time.

She understood everything now, aside from the decision to go to Colorado. "I don't want to change my name."

"You don't have to." Sylvester was thinking about traveling back and changing the flow of time.

"I don't want to leave your side," she said. "I wouldn't change a thing about being with you." Still, she couldn't bring herself to mention her own plans.

Sylvester smiled. "Then don't change your name to anyone you know. Just change it for those that don't know you."

"What happens if we get married?" A blush filled her cheeks, though she wasn't sure they would last after she left.

That was a thought that crossed his mind often over the past two years. Before everything happened, he was trying to find a way to earn more money and ask her to marry him, even though he was only two years away from a fortune. *She would say yes*. The thought felt like more of a fact, than a wish to him.

"Well, if we were to marry, you'd have to change your name, or I would. Either way, someone would be changin' their name." Sylvester thought for a minute. "Then again, it's not like anyone has to just because they're married. So maybe it'd just stay the same?"

She smiled. "I do love you." She leaned into him, and he wrapped his arm around her. His appetite returned, as did hers, and they finished their meals.

"What do you think of Eldritch?" she asked.

"For a last name?" He considered for a moment. "I think it sounds mysterious. Course Templeton feels proper and noble."

"Ira Eldritch," she said aloud. "You think I should change my first name?"

Sylvester smiled. "Nah. I love your name. It's far better than Sylvester. Feel like I'm supposed to be chasin' birds most the time."

They laughed as he paid the bill. It was a beautiful day and all he wanted to do was walk around Denver with her. For a while, that's what they did, but eventually they returned to the hotel.

"Anyway we could pay for two weeks on the rooms we got last night?" Sylvester asked the concierge.

He looked at his computer. "Well one of the rooms we can, but the other won't work out. The only other room we have is a two bedroom suite on the top floor."

Sylvester looked at Ira. "We'll take it."

The cost was extreme, but Sylvester only smiled at the concierge. At the moment, he only had ten percent of the cost of the stay on him. The rest was in his backpack upstairs. Sylvester said he would pay the balance after they gathered their things. "I'll have your key ready when you return," the concierge said.

Their first stop was Tommy's room, he wanted to knock, but the *Do Not Disturb* sign was up. "We'll grab him later," he said to Ira.

They gathered everything. Between them, only Ira really packed anything, aside from a backpack full of money and a few clothes that barely fit. Sylvester had a denim coat with a wool lining. At one point, the wool was bright white, but now it was tinged yellow from working the fields early in the morning. He put the coat on, shouldered the pack, and headed downstairs.

The concierge gave him three copies of the key and directed him toward the elevator when he paid. "Thanks, but would you mind showin' her up to the room?" Sylvester asked.

Ira looked at him, her right eyebrow raised.

"I got that thing with the truck to take care of." Sylvester had other plans as well, but he hadn't discussed them with anyone.

She smiled. "I'll see you when you get back. Until then I'll try to get Tommy up and movin'." She kissed him, and they parted. He kept one of the cards and twirled his keys on his forefinger. When he first started carrying the keys, he would pretend he was Billy the Kid, twirling his gun on his trigger finger. Even though he was an adult, he still did it.

He was heading to do something he thought wouldn't bother him. When he sat in the truck and started the engine, he paused. It was like an old friend to him, almost like Tommy. *Why would it be like Tommy?* he considered.

It had seen him through the best and worst times, but he, and the others, knew it was time to say goodbye. No trace could be left of the truck. He pulled onto the street and drove with no specific destination in mind.

Twenty minutes passed by the time he finally found a highway. He drove until the landscape changed from office buildings to warehouses, then to industrial metal buildings. It was the right area, and he took the first exit.

He was searching for a metal recycler but didn't know where one would be. He'd been to Colorado, but Denver was a short pit stop on a trip he took long ago. Eventually, he saw signs pointing him toward the metal recycler and he followed.

The truck roared in, chugging as it slowed. It sounded like it was going to die when Sylvester dropped the clutch and took it out of gear. The engine continued to run.

There was an attendant at the gate, scowling as he entered. "Whad'ya need?" he grumbled.

"I'd like to recycle my truck." He stuttered as he said the word *truck*. "Also, if you wouldn't mind callin' me a cab."

The attendant looked at him with a strange expression. "Why you recyclin'?" he asked. The sound of the engine, chugging and storing some unknown amount of energy somewhere, didn't leave too much to the imagination.

"Tranny's goin' out, engine's rustin' in places." Sylvester wasn't lying, but it wasn't the full truth. The transmission was slipping, but only slightly. Rust was there, but it was only on the surface.

"Gotcha." The attendant got on the phone and dialed. "It's Morty at the recycler, can you send a cab." There was a response, but Sylvester couldn't hear it. The man hung up the phone.

"All good?" Sylvester asked.

"Yeah, the cab'll be here in about thirty minutes." For the first time the man gave him a soft smile.

"Can I watch my truck get crushed?" Sylvester asked.

"That's not somethin' we normally allow," the attendant said.

"Would this change your mind?" Sylvester showed three one hundred dollar bills.

The attendant looked at his watch, then picked up his walkie. "Frank, head to lunch. I'll take the crusher 'til you're back." The attendant signaled Sylvester to pull forward as the pole arm raised.

"Roger that," the walkie replied.

The door to the security control room he was waiting in closed and locked behind him. "Move over kid. I'm gonna drive." The attendant hopped in as the arm lowered in place.

They drove forward and parked next to the recently vacant crusher. Sylvester grabbed his bag and stepped off to the side. The attendant entered the control area, moving the crane to the side, lowering the magnet, and picking the truck up with ease.

Sylvester watched as the truck lowered and then stopped. As the magnet moved back to its original position. His breath caught. He didn't think this moment would be as hard as it was. As the machines roared to life, he watched in awe as the truck, his only means of transportation for six years, cried and squealed as it compacted to a tiny cube of metal.

When the job was done the attendant joined Sylvester. "Everything alright?"

"Yeah, just feel like I killed an old friend," he replied.

"First vehicle?" The attendant was smiling with warmth and compassion. He had seen this before.

Sylvester nodded and handed the three one hundred dollar bills to the man.

"Thanks. Come this way." The man guided Sylvester back to the entrance. "Cab's here." He pointed to a yellow hybrid that sat waiting.

Sylvester walked to the cab.

"Hey kid..." The attendant yelled.

"Yeah?" Sylvester replied.

"It gets easier. You'll find something newer and better." Again the man smiled at him, then held up the money, and nodded at Sylvester.

Sylvester smiled at the man. *I hope that's true.* Even if it wasn't, Sylvester wouldn't need to do the same thing. Not for a long time...if ever.

Chapter Ten
New Beginnings

It was a long ride back to the hotel. Sylvester spent three hours searching for the recycler. Even with the GPS guiding the driver, it took nearly an hour to get back. They were in rush-hour traffic. Sylvester quietly contemplated his life and choices while he waited.

"Can we change course a bit?" he asked.

The driver looked in the rearview. "Where would you like to go?"

Sylvester thought about it a lot since they arrived. "I need a cell phone. So...a store that deals with that."

The driver nodded. "There's one just down the street, it's Verizon, a bit expensive, but worth it."

Sylvester nodded. "You prefer a specific phone over the other?"

"I've got an Apple. I love it, but some people prefer Samsung." The driver handed his phone back to Sylvester. "Have a look."

It was already open. "Just swipe and tap, right?"

"Have you never had a cell phone, sir?" the driver asked.

"My friend had one, but I've never been able to afford it, least 'til recently." Sylvester smiled at the driver.

"Very well. I would suggest an Apple for you." The driver turned a corner, barely looking at the road.

Sylvester played with the phone for a few minutes then handed it back. "Thank you."

They drove another half hour before the driver stopped outside of a Verizon store. Sylvester pulled out another hundred-dollar bill and looked at the tab. Twenty dollars didn't feel like a good tip. He reached into his bag and pulled out two twenties as well.

The driver looked at the money. "It's only eighty dollars, sir."

"I know, but you let me play with your phone, and were very helpful. I want you to keep the change," Sylvester insisted.

The smiling driver took the cash. "Thank you so much. If you need anything at all here is my business card. I would be happy to drive for you again."

Sylvester took the card and closed the door. He stuffed it in his pocket and walked into the store. The halogen lights burned into his irises as he walked in. Phones and screens blurred his vision.

He spent an hour and a half inside, talking to the associate who helped him. He walked out with an account under the name Sylvester Tempus. It cost him an additional fifty dollars to have the associate overlook the fact that he had no ID to give or an address to put in the account. In the end, he told the associate he would update the information as soon as he settled wherever they wound up.

He bought three brand new iPhones, all activated. The first thought he had was that he now had access to the Internet, and wouldn't struggle when finding places. He also bought AirPods, cases, and wireless chargers for each phone.

Tommy had a cell phone, but Sylvester was going to make him get rid of it. It was as much of a liability as his truck was, if not more so with its ability to be tracked. He knew Tommy would understand, besides, he was getting a brand new smart phone. Tommy would be thrilled.

It was nearing the end of the day, as the sun set somewhere over the mountains, but Sylvester couldn't see it. Streetlights lit up all around him, revealing a pretty, and clean city. He imagined not too many big cities were as clean as Denver. The city was growing on him, and he was even considering settling down with the woman of his dreams there. Ira could have her parents visit without stressing about the Pembertons finding them. That was assuming they would stay quiet about it.

He walked in the hotel, smiled and nodded to the concierge, then rode the elevator to their suite. It was quiet. All he could hear was the electronic murmur of the television. Ira smiled at him when he opened the door. He eagerly returned the smile.

"Well, hello handsome," she said.

"Hello to you too. I have a present for you." He set the bag down on the living room table. Two boxes were set on the table in front of her, both different colors. "Pick one."

She smiled. "You bought us phones?"

"All three of us," he said.

She picked the purple phone and smiled at him. "Take care of the truck?"

"I did," he said, busying himself with pulling the rest of the items that went with her new phone from the bag. "Tommy in one of the rooms?"

She pointed her thumb toward a door. "Been sleepin' since we got here."

Sylvester shook his head. "Too much drinkin'. Imma wake him up." He walked toward the room. "Then I want to talk about what comes next."

The door to the room opened and Sylvester stepped inside. Tommy's date left at some point, before they moved to the suite, and he was alone. His shirt was unbuttoned, and his pants were still on, but at least his boots were on the ground.

A smile rested on Sylvester's face as he kicked his own boots off and crawled in bed next to Tommy. His face was inches from Tommy's, his arm draped over the man's chest. Tommy smiled and snuggled up to the arm.

"C'mon you lazy slug. Time to get you cleaned up and movin'. I need food, you need food." Sylvester hadn't turned on the lights.

"Five more minutes," Tommy mumbled.

"Nope." He tightened his arm, then shook the man. "You've slept plenty. We have stuff to talk about anyways."

Tommy moaned, shoved Sylvester's arm off of him, and threw his own arm over his forehead. "Alright, can I shower first?" Like Sylvester, Tommy didn't have much with him. His car was back at home, his clothes left behind.

"Yeah. You need some new clothes." Sylvester sniffed the air, then his own clothes. "Damn, I need new clothes too."

"Yeah, I thought so too. Why don't we call for laundry service and just wear robes until it gets back?" Tommy said as he sat up.

"Great idea." Sylvester left the room, then tossed a robe in. "Get undressed and toss your clothes out."

Tommy emerged from his room a few minutes later, already dressed in his robe, and handed Sylvester a pile of dirty laundry. He disappeared into the bathroom shortly after. Sylvester threw the clothes in the laundry bag after Ira took note of the sizes, then called the concierge.

Five minutes later the bag was off and heading to be cleaned. "Well, looks like we've got about an hour to kill, according to the laundry lady."

Ira smiled. "That's perfect." Her face was buried in her phone.

"What do you think of Denver?" he asked.

"I think it's lovely. Why?" Ira barely glanced up at him, already consumed by the technology in front of her.

"Well, it's close enough to your parents that you could go visit. It's far enough that the Pembertons shouldn't find us, not to mention big enough they still wouldn't if they were here. Whad'ya think about livin' here?" He plopped down on the couch next to her.

"That would be nice, but what would we do?" Ira asked. Playing along at this point was all she felt comfortable doing.

"Yeah, and what about how I feel?" Tommy replied.

"I was thinking we would all live together if you wanted to. Didn't think you were done in the shower." Sylvester smiled at him.

"What would we all do?" Tommy reiterated Ira's question.

"What about a detective agency?" Sylvester wasn't thinking of traditional detective work. He wanted to save people from situations they had already been affected by. At the same time, he didn't want to charge for his services. "I'm thinkin' a free detective agency, one that relies on stocks and bonds to pay the bills."

Tommy sat in a chair opposite Sylvester and Ira. He looked at his friend. "You've got the money to do that, but how would you know what would pay out?"

"First, close your legs, we can both see your meat and two bits." Sylvester waited for Tommy to close his legs. "I've got a secret that I still haven't shared with you." He looked to Ira, then Tommy. "I can travel in time and space."

Tommy laughed at him and waved off the inane joke. "Shut up." He looked at Ira who sat there, but did not laugh. "For real?" he said after he realized she already knew.

"Yep. It's been a few days, but I contracted a parasite when we were drinking on Saturday. It's conscious, thinks, and I think feels. Because of it, I have the ability to jump to wherever I want, so long as I, or someone I'm in contact with, has already been there. Also, to whenever I want."

Tommy sat back, a look Sylvester didn't recognize covered his face briefly. As quickly as the look appeared, it disappeared. It was like Tommy was a different person in that brief span. "Is that why you have all that money, and how you found out about the Pembertons?"

Sylvester nodded.

"What would we do at this agency?" Tommy gestured to Ira and himself. The tone of his voice radiated anger and betrayal.

"I don't know, maybe help me in some way? Clearly, I haven't figured out all the details." Sylvester wandered off, thinking about Dick Tracy, Sherlock Holmes and Hercule Poirot. Since that night at the diner, where Ira asked him out, Sir Arthur Conan Doyle's work never seemed quite as daunting as it used to. "Be my sidekicks." He wanted to treat them both equally.

They sat in silence, waiting for the laundry to be returned. "I got this for you," Sylvester said to Tommy as he handed him the phone and accessories. "Gotta pull the battery and destroy your old phone though."

Tommy smiled in his usual manner, but his eyes still seemed off. "Gladly." He pulled the back off, removed the battery, and broke the phone in half. There were no saved contacts he couldn't live without. "What about my car? If you can travel anywhere you want, could we go get my car?"

Sylvester smiled. "New beginning's Tommy. I think until the heat is off for sure, we need to let go of past possessions. Is that alright?"

Tommy had the car since his father gave it to him. The smile faded and a flash of the other Tommy appeared for a moment. "You know what it means to me."

"Alright. How 'bout this...we rent a storage unit and store it there?" Sylvester watched Tommy closely.

"New beginnings will still work. I could paint it, have the VIN and plate changed." Tommy cocked his head.

"We'll go tomorrow. I've gotta talk to Tempus about bringing others along, but I don't think it'll be an issue."

There was a knock at the door. A fresh bag of laundry waited when Ira opened it. "Get changed boys. I'm starvin'."

Chapter Eleven
The Mustang

Tempus considered what Sylvester asked. Yes, we can bring others with us, either to a different place, so long as one of you has seen it, or another time.

"Is there a limit on how many people can come?" Sylvester asked.

As long as you're physically being touched by at least one person, I don't think so. Each person can hold another person's hand, and it should work. Tempus had traveled with one other being in the past. At the time, Tempus was unaware the tentacled monster rode it's hosts back.

Sylvester considered this. They had all been to Tommy's house, so having been there wasn't an issue. "How about inanimate objects?"

Like what? Tempus was curious what Sylvester's plans were. The parasite had largely ignored everything until this moment.

"Like a car or truck." Sylvester asked.

I'm not sure I can bring something that big, but we can try it. Go get in your truck and we'll try moving it to a different place. While Tempus was busy with its own machinations, it hadn't noticed Sylvester no longer had the vehicle.

"Let's just try it tomorrow when we go." Sylvester wasn't upset, but he didn't want to think about the vehicle that no longer existed.

Alright. I'll be waiting. Tempus once again disappeared to the background of Sylvester's mind.

Once again, Ira was cuddled up to him, sleeping while he had his conversation with the being in his head. They all discussed how they were going to get Tommy's car. Sylvester and Tommy would go, Ira would stay behind and do some shopping for the boys. They would try to transport the mustang to a deserted area they passed on the way in, but if they couldn't, they would simply drive back to Denver.

Sylvester squeezed her and closed his eyes. He fell asleep fast, though he dreamt of silly things, like walking around Denver with no clothes on. Nothing serious popped in his head. Overall, they were in a good place, and he didn't feel like there was anything to worry about.

★★★

Morning broke over the skyline. He and Tommy called the cabby who brought him back to the hotel. He took them to the outskirts of the city. When they arrived, Sylvester threw two one hundred-dollar bills to him, then asked him to take care of Ira. The cabby smiled and promised he would.

Two more hundred dollar bills lay in the cabby's hand after that. "Part of that is for the drive to wherever she goes, the other part is your tip." Sylvester winked at him. "She'll be callin'."

They were in an open lot, where cars passed at regular intervals. Dust kicked up as the taxi drove back the way it came. Tommy looked at him. "You've got to stop spending that much."

Sylvester smiled. If things went the way he wanted, they wouldn't have money problems ever again. "Alright, we've both been here. Tempus, you'll be able to bring us back here right, maybe behind that building so we don't just appear out of nowhere?"

Yep. Tempus hadn't really spoken much while Tommy was around. The parasite felt strange vibes emanating from him. The man just felt wrong.

"Alright then, Tommy, hold my hand." Sylvester smiled.

"You know I only swing that way for you big boy." Tommy laughed as he grabbed his friends hand. Whatever emotions the man felt about the parasite in his friend were gone, and Tommy was back to his old self.

"Alright Tempus, take us to Tommy's house." Sylvester closed his eyes and imagined the man's front door.

Pressure built within him. It was almost overwhelming. Then a gust of wind pushed both Sylvester and Tommy's hair. They both opened their eyes and looked.

The men stood on a wooden, greying porch. Their combined weight caused the structure to bend and creak at will. Paint on the door was fading into a pale, light green, and cracked all over.

When his dad passed away, he left Tommy enough money to pay off the house and taxes for the next ten years. Tommy also put money and work into the Mustang. It had been fully rebuilt. Sylvester helped when he could, but the paint job was all Tommy.

It was a beautiful teal that sparkled in the sun. A bright white racing stripe ran down the middle. The car was Tommy's pride and joy.

It sat in the driveway, dusty, but otherwise untouched. No cars drove past, and no one waited on the street, surveying the property. Overall, it appeared they were in a safe place. Sylvester wondered if the Pembertons had even come by. There was no sign that anyone had even been to Tommy's since they left.

"You got the keys right?" Sylvester asked when Tommy finally stood up straight.

Tommy's only response was a jingling sound as he held up the keys and wiped his mouth of the spittle that remained from their trip. They each walked slowly to the Mustang, looking left, then right as they did. His street was mostly empty. More people had moved to Topeka, leaving the dying town to wither and rot in their wake. Each step echoed around them.

Tommy opened the driver side door first, bending and peering in the back seat. No one lay in wait for him, or Sylvester. The passenger door squeaked and squealed, as Sylvester opened it.

"Man, you've gotta get that fixed," Sylvester said. "You wanna grab some clothes, maybe make sure your place isn't trashed?"

"Ira's grabbing clothes for both of us. I don't think I need anything." He had no medications to grab or keepsakes from his parents.

"Alright. Well get in." Sylvester sat in the car and held the door after it closed. "Better take my hand and we'll see if we can take this thing with us."

Tommy grabbed onto his door like Sylvester and took his friend's hand. He nodded, then closed his eyes. Sylvester took one more look around, making sure no one was sneaking up on them, then closed his own.

"Alright Tempus, give it a shot," Sylvester said.

The familiar pressure was there, though it was less overwhelming this time. They kept their eyes closed until it drained. The car was still parked in front of Tommy's garage when they both opened their eyes. Sylvester let go of the door and Tommy's hand.

"No go, Tempus?" Sylvester asked.

Too big. Traveling with you and Tommy, plus whatever is in your pockets, or in a bag on your back, wouldn't be a big deal. This thing is too much. Tempus sounded as though it had just run twenty miles in under an hour.

"No problem. We came with a backup plan." Sylvester pulled out a roll of hundred-dollar bills and handed Tommy three. "I'm not making you do the whole ride alone, but I have something I wanna do. Meet me at that gas station three hours from the border."

Tommy took the money, looked at him, then nodded. "I'll wait for ya, or I guess just call me if somethin' comes up." He wasn't used to Sylvester having a cell phone just yet.

Sylvester nodded, then opened the squealing car door. He shook his head, then backed away. The mustang rumbled to life, roaring as Tommy stepped on the gas. A smile could be seen broadening his face.

The man leaned out of the window and yelled. "See ya soon buddy!"

Sylvester nodded again. When Tommy peeled off, toward the end of the road, Sylvester's smile faded. He originally didn't intend to go back to the farm, but something was nagging at him to go and check things out.

He knew they could escape from the basement, but everything felt too easy. Escaping to Denver, retrieving the Mustang. It was just too simple, and he needed to know why.

"Tempus, take me to the farm." Sylvester closed his eyes, felt the pressure, then a pop.

Chapter Twelve
Consequences

Sylvester stared at the house from behind an outbuilding across a dusty walking path. He stared for an hour, waiting for any type of movement. It was like he had read in the books and magazines about detectives in real life...boring.

Al's truck was in the driveway, unusual for the time of day. His normal routine was to drive the truck to the field he was working, then work the field, and move on to the next. It was barely nine in the morning. With Sylvester gone, he would have to work longer hours. On top of that, Sylvester wondered why they weren't hunting him.

The lights inside the house were on. Another unusual sign. To conserve electricity and pass themselves off as poor, they always had the lights off when the sky was light enough to see. Sylvester looked at the shadows on the ground, the sun blazed down on him and his neck was hot to the touch. There wasn't a single cloud in the sky.

A final auditory signal made him wince. Animals that he was in charge of whinnied and whined. Al would have fed and watered the beasts of burden by now.

Still, no one moved inside, even with all the commotion outside. He shuffled his feet a bit, found a rock about the size of his hand, and picked it up. The distance between himself and the house closed quickly. Before he knew it, he stood on the front porch.

Sylvester crept toward the door, avoiding known spots that caused audible creaks. The handle turned with ease, clicking as it opened. They rarely locked the door. Something about the eerie silence surrounding him made him feel like they should have all along. The longer he remained, the more danger he felt closing around him.

Just bein' paranoid, he assured himself quietly in his head.

The front door led into the living room and its brown shag carpet. Over the years, Sylvester learned where not to step if you didn't want to get caught sneaking back in the house in the middle of the night. As with the porch, each step was silent, and filled with purpose.

He peeked around the corner into the hallway. Empty. It didn't smell like anyone had cooked in the last few days, but there was an odor that he couldn't quite place. It was too quiet for a house where two people should be fuming with anger.

As he inched deeper into the house, he recognized the smell. It was like someone left meat on the counter too long. Janet and Al wouldn't allow such a rank smell in their home. Even if it was just sweat from the day, Janet was intent that the house smelled good enough for company at all times. Sylvester was often ordered to shower when he was younger, though as he grew, he wanted to smell better...for Ira. The smell wafting into his nostrils was rot.

The door to the basement was open, though not smashed. Lying on its side, the table was moved out of the way. Sylvester wanted to save the basement for last. Like many of the books and articles he read over the years about being a detective said, never put yourself in a situation you can't escape from. The stairs in the kitchen were clear, and he snuck up, carefully avoiding creaking steps.

There was no noise, not upstairs, or down. His room was a disaster, someone tore it apart. Likely they had searched for the money that was safely in the suite with Ira. Even with all of the cash he spent, he still had over four-hundred-thousand dollars, not to mention the money in his account. Sylvester was sure they would want every penny, and more.

He stood upright while he walked the halls, concern over noisy footsteps no longer filling him. No one was home. His head poked into the Pembertons' room which was also trashed. Then he looked into the bathroom where the toilet had been torn apart, porcelain shards lying on the ground.

The shower hadn't been used that day. It was not uncommon for them to skip a shower in the morning until work was done, but this was something he took note of. He walked heavily down the living room stairs and noticed a few pictures missing from the mantle on the shelf. Pictures of him.

There was one place left, and his stomach churned at the thought of going back down into the basement. Though he liked to take the advice found in those books and magazines, he knew Tempus could get him out of any situation. His gut wrenched at the thought that all of his answers lay below.

Each step was slow and deliberate as he descended the stairs. The smell hung thick in the air, like a carcass lying on the highway in the mid-summer sun. Every step caused the scent to waft deeper into his nostrils until it was so thick he covered his nose and mouth to avoid gagging.

It was pitch black, but he knew where the string for the light was, and pulled it. Tied in two separate chairs were the Pembertons. Janet's face had been beaten and smashed. She was bruised and swollen to the point of being unrecognizable. Her arms had cut marks stretching from the elbow, all the way to her wrist. Fingers were missing from each of her hands.

Al wasn't any better. Sylvester thought he actually looked worse than Janet. There was a similar treatment done to him, but blood stained his mouth. His lips had been cut off and teeth removed with force, or broken. Sylvester looked at the situation, then immediately threw up.

His first thought was to call the police. Then he looked at the scene. There was no way he wouldn't be blamed and detained, at least until they realized he couldn't be the one who did this. He was the only other person known to live in the house, and would be the obvious suspect.

"Tempus what do I do?" His voice quivered as he wiped his mouth with his sleeve. He didn't want anyone to die because of what he did. Tears fell for the people who, for all intents and purposes, were his parents.

Find a corner and hide there. Make sure you can see. You said you wanted to be a detective, then you need facts. Tempus paused. ***Also, you can't change it. Just find out the who and the why, then we'll return to the present.***

Sylvester nodded, not thinking about what the parasite could and could not see. He didn't care about why he couldn't change the outcome, he just wanted to find answers. Sylvester searched the basement frantically, like time was going to eventually run out.

It was cement. There was no way to hide below, nor was there any way for him to hide upstairs to see what happened. The money room wasn't closed, so whoever did it knew it was there. The basement was clean, and though there were piles of boxes here and there, nothing would hide him.

The stairs on the other hand looked like the perfect place. If he covered himself and a few boxes with a blanket, he could easily hide there. No one would see him.

Carefully, he hid and covered his hiding spot, but left a slight crack so he could see the Pembertons lifeless bodies. Rancid air filled his lungs as he took a deep breath. "How do we do this?" he asked the parasite.

First we go back to when we closed them in. Remember, be sure not to change anything. After that we wait and see what happened. Ready? Whether he was or not, the world pressurized, then released.

★★★

Al finished his swing, though the shovel no longer rested in his hands. He stumbled forward and landed on Janet. She struggled beneath the man, mumbling wheezy words under his weight.

He returned to his feet, and looked at the shovel dangling in the air. "How the hell did that happen?" Then he turned to the money room to help Janet to her feet. He stopped when he saw all of the money was gone. "That damn boy," he said, fear filling his voice.

"Help me up Al, don't just stand there gawkin'," she said. When she was on her feet, she looked at the empty room. "Get after him," she yelled.

Sylvester watched as the older people labored up the stairs and pushed on the door. A slight crack revealed the kitchen, but it moved no further. Sylvester was nowhere to be seen.

Al shoved his shoulder into the door, intent on breaking it down. He ran down the steps, dust landing on top of Sylvester's blanket, and grabbed the shovel.

"Push it open and I'll try to pry," he said forcing his way into the gap between Janet and the wall. "Damn it, it's not goin' in."

"Well, just keep tryin'. He'll be here any minute." Janet sounded panicked. Sylvester wondered what the money was actually for.

They struggled for another ten minutes when they heard the front door open, and a group of people with heavy feet entered the house. Al and Janet were quiet for a minute. Sylvester imagined they were considering what their next move should be.

Footsteps walked into the kitchen, then dragging sounds could be heard, followed by a loud thud. Janet backed slowly down the stairs and moved quietly toward the money room. Al followed, but they both wouldn't fit inside. He started to move toward the stairs where Sylvester was hiding. Anxiety was building when the door swung open, and four men dressed in suits entered the basement.

"There you are," one of the men said. Clearly he was in charge by the quality and style of his suit. The others were just peons.

"Hey Micky." Al's voice trembled. "How's it goin'?"

"Why you hidin' from me? Where's that hag of a wife of yours?" Micky signaled one of his goons toward Al.

"I'm not hidin', I was just grabbin' somethin'." Al followed the man's direction and stood in front of the group. "Wife's out gettin' groceries."

"Really. Then she's the one who shoved the table in front of the door?" Micky leaned against the railing.

"Did she? I had no idea." Al was sweating.

"Open the room." Micky pointed to the corner and one of the men walked over. Shortly after, the door opened and Janet was hauled out, fear filling her eyes.

"Hey boss, there's no money in here, not even a single penny." His accent was thick. It reminded Sylvester of Muggsy from the Looney Toons cartoons.

Micky was turned away from Sylvester, so he couldn't tell what the man's face was doing. When he spoke, his voice was surprisingly calm, which made it even more frightening. "I ride in a car for nine hours to come and collect from you. My business gave you enough money to pay off this farm and all you had to do was hold some product and take payment. I even paid to have this hidden room built in your basement." Micky pointed at two of the men. "Go get a couple of chairs and bring 'em down."

The men ran up the stairs, only to return a few seconds later with the chairs the Pemberton's would die in. Sylvester was crying, though he wasn't aware. "Sit 'em down." Micky demanded as he grabbed zip ties from a shelf.

Janet and Al fought back as the men forced them into their seats. Micky tied their hands together with zip ties, then used several more to secure them to the chairs. Their legs and ankles were next. Micky paced in front of them, never looking away as he turned the other direction.

"Where's my money?" Micky asked.

"I don't know," Al said.

Instead of smacking Al, Micky slowly put a leather glove on, then punched Janet directly in the eye. She cried out in pain, her eye swelling immediately. Sylvester wondered why they were protecting him since he was only a work hand.

"I'll ask again." Micky turned to Al, leaning down and grabbing Janet's hair. "Where is my fucking money?" he yelled.

Al sobbed, tears rolling down his chubby cheeks, looking at the woman he loved. Sylvester had never seen her as frightened as she was in that moment. "I really don't know." He wasn't lying. All he knew was one second the money was there and the next it was gone. He sobbed, spittle falling from his mouth.

Micky smiled at Al, enjoying the torment. He pulled his fist back, and Micky punched Janet three more times. Each time a dull thud was accentuated by a yelp. Sylvester watched in horror as her face turned into a bloody mess. Though he wanted to look away, something inside forced him keep watching. He hoped it was Tempus, but feared it was his own sick curiosity.

"Maybe we try with you for a bit. Take over for me," he ordered one of the other men. "I ask a question and if I don't like the answer, you know what to do."

The man lumbered forward, smiling at the thought of beating Al. He grabbed his head and held him in place. Al's eyes darted toward Janet. She was sobbing, bloody tears rolling down her cheeks as her head lolled to and fro.

"Alright honey. Where's my money eh?" Micky's tone calmed.

Janet sobbed. "I don't know," she mumbled through broken teeth as blood dribbled from her mouth. "The boy took it, then he vanished right in front of our eyes. Next thing we know we're locked down here."

Micky smiled at the beaten woman. "Where's the boy?"

If she could have opened her eyes wider, she likely would have. "I don't know."

"See Janet, we've got a problem here. I don't let people who let me down live unless they help me out. I'm gonna ask you one more time. Where is he?" Micky knelt in front of her.

Janet sobbed again. "I don't know." She continued crying as Micky looked at his goon and signaled.

Al took a beating far worse than her own. The goon didn't stop until Al's face was broken. His nose hung limply, and his eyes were swollen closed. Al's mouth hung open and blood spurted with every strenuous breath.

Sylvester listened to the man. He was alive, but for how long? Micky signaled another goon and pulled a finger across his neck, then pointed to Janet. Only seconds passed when the knife rested on her throat, then slid easily across, digging deep into her flesh. Blood gushed as Micky took the knife and ran it along her arms. He enjoyed the chaos.

Sylvester started to move the blanket, ready to reveal he was there to the broken people. Janet must have seen him because, in her final moments, she shook her head and tried to smile at him. The slight movement went unnoticed, and Sylvester covered himself back up. A fully formed smile rested on Janet's face as her head fell forward.

Micky took the knife and cut one finger away from her hand. Then another. When she didn't cry in pain, Micky, and Sylvester, knew she was dead. One finger fell to the ground as the other entered Micky's pocket.

Sylvester cried as silently as he could, watching in horror at the scene unfolding before him. Hands covered his mouth so he wouldn't reveal his hiding place. Micky turned around and walked to a shelf, shuffling around the tools, then selecting what he wanted. He returned to Al, put something in his mouth, then pulled.

The man screamed in agony when the jagged tooth pulled free. "Hold his mouth open!" The pliers returned and extracted another, then another. When no more sound came from the victim, Micky raised the knife, throwing the bloody pliers at the nearby wall.

"They're dead boss, what else you gonna do?" one of his goons asked.

Micky looked at the man who spoke, not saying a word, his eyes filled with lusty rage. When the man raised his hands and backed away, Micky removed the dead man's lips, then ran the knife down his arms as well. Most of what had been done to them, was out of pleasure...sick, twisted, pleasure.

Sylvester squeezed his hands tightly around his mouth, muffling the heavy and ragged breaths. They disappeared up the stairs and crashing could be heard. His parents were gone, in the most horrible way possible.

They walked upstairs, then to the upper level. Sylvester heard them rifling through things in his room. Crashes signaled the destruction of what little he owned as they carelessly threw them around. There was nothing in his room that would lead to Tommy, or Ira's parents. Porcelain crashed against the ground shortly after. Then footsteps moved to the living room. Sylvester thought they were likely taking the most recent pictures of him. The door slammed, and an engine roared to life. It idled outside for a few minutes, then the vehicle could be heard pulling away from the house and down the gravel road.

He pulled the blanket off when he could no longer hear the vehicle rumbling nearby. They were both dead, none of what they went through was necessary, but it happened. Anger flowed through him. Not at the Pemberton's, but at the mobster who had slaughtered, and tortured them.

Janet's final protection of him brought back all the memories of his life with them. They were never unkind to him, though they paid him nothing, they kept him fed, housed, and clothed. Tommy was allowed to stay over whenever he wanted and didn't even make him work for the food he ate.

Ira's company always seemed a welcome distraction, though recent discoveries made him question their opinions. He walked to them, reaching to grab a hand, or anything when the familiar pressure occurred, followed by a pop.

They still sat there in front of him, their bodies now decaying. It all happened after he left, minutes after. Why hadn't Tempus seen the reason they had the money? Sylvester stopped reaching out and pulled out his phone.

"Hello. I just found my parents murdered. Please send someone," he said to the dispatcher on the other end.

"Stay right there. We'll send someone as quickly as we can," the dispatcher said. "We've got your location."

Ten minutes passed and sirens could be heard in the distance. Sylvester sat on his knees, holding his head in his hands. The sirens blared as they approached, then one by one, turned off. Groups of officers entered the house, finding him kneeling in the basement.

They looked at the scene, then at the man on his knees. Some officers shook their heads in disbelief, others mumbled between themselves. None of them seemed to think he was the one to blame. It was a scene that many had seen, or heard of, in the past.

"Son, let's get you upstairs. Then you can tell me what happened." An older officer took him under the arm and helped him up.

Sylvester was quiet. He answered questions about his whereabouts, gave credible witnesses in Tommy and Ira. He explained they had gone out of town for two nights, traveled to Denver and were staying at a hotel there. He only came back because he had to help at the farm the next day.

"Do you have somewhere to stay?" the officer asked.

"I'll...I'll go back to Denver with my friends," he replied.

"Alright, what's your number so we can get ahold of you, just in case there's a break." The officers forehead had wrinkled over time, and crow's feet made their presence known. He wore an officer's uniform, but the look he gave Sylvester told him he would only hear from the police if they caught the killer.

Sylvester opened his phone then looked at the officer. "It's new, I splurged." He found his number, then recited it to the man, who verified it worked.

"Alright, do you have someone who can drive you?" he asked.

Sylvester nodded, knowing Tommy would be waiting for him at the rest stop. "I'm gonna walk to my friend's, if that's alright." Sylvester wiped away a few tears.

"I understand. If you think of anything else, call the number that just called your phone." The officer walked him out of the house.

"I...threw up. That's my vomit down there. I've never seen anything like this." Sylvester's voice shook as the officer eyed him.

"It's alright, I'll make a note of that. I expect anyone who hasn't seen it would have done the same in your situation." A soft smile formed on the man's lips.

Sylvester walked down the road, then darted behind a building. "Alright Tempus." He sniffed and wiped his nose. "Take me to the gas station, behind it please." There was slight pressure. The more he used the parasite's power, the less he felt. Then there was a pop, and he knew he was at the gas station.

He walked from behind the building and saw Tommy leaning against his car. When Tommy saw his friend he smiled, then his face dropped. All jokes escaped the man as he rushed to grab Sylvester and hold him up. Sylvester fell limp and cried as Tommy caught him. After a while he walked him to the passenger side of the Mustang.

Chapter Thirteen
Driving into the Night

Tommy drove at his usual breakneck pace on the highway, while Sylvester explained what happened. "Why didn't Tempus let you do anything?"

"I don't know. It said it would explain things later, but that's all. Hasn't said a damn word since." Sylvester stopped crying shortly after getting into the car.

"Do you know who those guys were? All you got was Micky and he drove for nine hours?" Tommy focused on the road. "Think he came from Chicago, or Denver?"

Sylvester thought about the men in their business suits. Their accents placed them in Chicago in his mind, but that didn't mean they didn't have people in Denver, at least contacts. "They had to come from Chicago. They took pictures of me." Pictures...another thing that should have made him realize he was more than a hired hand to the Pembertons. "Either way, I really can't keep my last name."

Tommy smiled. "Yeah, that's for sure." He looked at Sylvester. "Do you think I need to hide my 'stang still?" He wasn't trying to be insensitive, he just wanted to drive *his* car.

Sylvester met his stare. "No, I don't think you'll have to hide your car anymore." Sylvester's head shook with overwhelming frustration.

Tommy looked ahead. "Sorry. I wasn't really thinkin'."

"It's fine," Sylvester snapped back.

"Anything I can do to calm you down?" Tommy asked. "I assume the plan is still to open a detective agency using your powers?"

Sylvester hadn't thought about it. He focused on the fact that two people he really did care for were now dead. All in all, he was a witness to their murder. The original plan was to save people who died from horrible accidents—things that could have been avoided otherwise.

Another thought that crossed his mind was saving people being accused of something they did or did not do. He would stop something from happening, or watch it happen, and help answer questions. What he wanted to do was everything he just went through and watched, but the cases he wanted to be part of, would never have been something that close to him.

Tempus protected him by buzzing him back to the present. He wanted to blame the parasite for not stopping their deaths. There was always an option to pop over to the bank, withdraw the money he stole, then put it back. Fate could have been changed, if not for the parasite.

It was silent, a trend Sylvester didn't like. He wanted the parasite to speak. Silence was deadly, especially when he didn't control the creature and could only ask permission.

"I don't know," he finally replied.

"Okay. We can just invest money and become millionaires," Tommy noted.

Like he's going to contribute to it? He thinks that I'm just going to do all the hard work and let him sponge off me, Sylvester fumed.

Don't take Tommy for granted Tempus butted in. **You did a lot to get him here.** There was a sense of understanding in its voice.

'Bout time you started talkin'. Why couldn't we change things back there? Sylvester asked, completely ignoring the comment about Tommy.

Thing is, if you had done anything to change the outcome...I don't know what would have happened to you. Tempus's voice was docile.

Meaning? Sylvester asked.

Meaning that you may have been erased from existence. If you could have touched them while they were alive, I could have told you, but you've been erased twice now. Tempus really didn't know what happened to the other versions of them. There was a bleeding effect, and the parasite finally understood what happened before.

Sylvester's mind seemed to halt. It was filled with shock over Tempus's revelation. ***Can I get more details? What do you mean I've been erased twice now?***

Tempus explained the lives he saw. One ended after changing the outcome of Al incapacitating Janet with the shovel. The other saved Tommy from a doomed future. ***If you change something that may affect you, you disappear and a different you takes over.*** Tempus finished.

Sylvester digested the information, then looked at Tommy. "You're my brother, maybe not by blood, but I would do anything for you."

Tommy looked at Sylvester, his brow raised. He wasn't upset about what Sylvester said, or how he was acting. When his own dad passed away Sylvester was there and took the bulk of his anger. "I know. You're my brother too." He smiled at Sylvester.

Sylvester returned the smile, then returned to his conversation within. ***So that's why you stopped me? Touchin' them may have changed my future, or stopping their deaths could have? Maybe not in the here and now, but sometime later.***

Yeah. I'm sorry things went the way they did, but if you're gonna change the past, you have to make sure it doesn't affect you. Tempus hoped Sylvester understood.

Is that why you're so quiet around Tommy? Though the conversation was within, Sylvester's facial expressions changed, and Tommy went out of his way to ignore the changes.

No. There's something weird about him, not just the fact that once upon a time he was dead. Tempus paused. Sylvester never heard the parasite breathe but could feel a huff escape its body in his mind. ***Just keep an eye on him, I don't want to aggravate anything.***

Sylvester agreed, then both parasite and host went silent. He closed his eyes, thinking about his parents' bodies sitting in the chairs before him, then opened them quickly. Worry that he would always see the scene when he closed his eyes overwhelmed him.

"Tommy, at the next gas station with a mini mart can you stop?" he asked.

Tommy smiled and nodded.

"Drinks are on me. What are you gonna do with the house?" he asked.

"Well, I figured I'd sell it and have you take me back in time to invest in something, maybe Apple before they were popular, or Google." Tommy shifted and turned on his blinker. "How 'bout you?"

Sylvester hadn't thought about it. For all intents and purposes he was now the owner of the farm. "Probably the same, though I'd take a whole lot more money with me," he joked with Tommy.

They stopped, got out, and bought a few energy drinks. The sun set in an orange and amber sky as they neared the Colorado border. Not a good day, but a day that Sylvester, and Tommy, would never forget.

Chapter Fourteen
Back in Denver

They entered the suite just after seven. Ira patiently waited for their return. When she saw Tommy she smiled, but at the site of Sylvester, the smile fell. She immediately knew something was wrong, rushed to him and grabbed the man she loved. He once again broke down and cried.

Sylvester explained everything that happened. Ira listened in shock. Tommy disappeared into his room, he didn't want to hear it again, it was too disturbing. Ira held Sylvester's hand as he spoke, bringing him in and holding him in the moments he started to stumble.

Nine o'clock rolled around and Sylvester stopped talking. He was cried-out. A flat energy drink was all he bought at the gas station. Confessions of his fear that he would relive the moment for the rest of his life left him. She smiled, then pulled him into their room.

Bags upon bags of clothes were piled on the bed. While they retrieved Tommy's car and discovered the fate of his parents, she purchased all of them brand new wardrobes. She handed Sylvester a new leather wallet.

"What's this?" he asked.

"It's new. Yours has holes and tears all over. I figured it would look good on you," she replied, laughing as Sylvester opened and folded the wallet.

"It's very nice. Thank you." He looked around the room. "Cabby help you out?"

She nodded. "His name is John Dwayne." She laughed. "I don't think that's his real name, but that's what he says. Also, what the license in the cab says."

Sylvester opened bags and looked through drawers. She filled them all. In the closet there were two bags hanging and a suitcase at the bottom. He questioned her, then opened the bag.

"Figured you'd look handsome in a suit. Course you'll need a haircut, maybe a shave." She opened the other bag. "I got you gray and black.

"Didn't think you knew my measurements that well." He smiled, then kissed her.

"Thank you." Tommy yelled at their door.

She pulled away. "You're welcome. Try on the suits and if they don't fit we'll get 'em fitted." She looked at Sylvester. "Same goes for you mister, 'cept I wanna watch." She winked at him and sat on the bed.

He smiled back, then looked down. "I love you, but...I'm just not in the mood for that tonight. I'll try 'em on, but would you mind me doin' it alone?"

Her smile faded slightly, and she stood up. "I understand. I'm sorry about the Pembertons."

He rested a hand on her shoulder, pecked her on the cheek and watched her leave the room. The black suit jacket lay on the bed as he slid the pants on. They barely fit as he forced the clasp together. Everything squeezed and bulged. He took them off again and lay them on the bed, a sigh of relief escaping when the clasp was opened.

Again, as he put the jacket on, he seemed to have to force it. The sleeves were too short, and the shoulders tight. He couldn't move, even if he wanted to. "Hey hun." He yelled through the door. "Are both the suits the same size?"

"Yeah." Her voice was muffled and hesitant.

He took off the jacket, then put it back in the bag. A robe covered his body. The bags rested in his hand as he walked out of the room.

"Too small babe. I think they're likely not going to be able to tailor 'em for me."

"Me either," Tommy said as he turned to leave his room. His pants bulged at the thighs and in between his legs. They looked like a pair of women's highwaters, only made of classier material. He had forced his arms in the jacket which held them straight out.

Ira laughed, and though he tried not to, Sylvester joined in. "I don't know how that happened. I gave them your pant size."

"We'll take care of it tomorrow, then Tommy...well I guess we don't need to change our identities. Least not you two. I think I still need a different last name. I guess I could file for a name change, not sure they would find me based on that." Sylvester looked at Ira. "What do you think?"

"I think we should all still change our names, but the legal way sounds way better," she replied.

Tommy nodded as he removed the jacket. "Always better to be legit. Besides I don't even know that I could have found that anywhere at home, let alone a big place like Denver."

"Alright, tomorrow let's go file the paperwork. Who's hungry? Think John Dwayne is still workin'?" Sylvester asked.

John Dwayne was not in fact working and they didn't want to interrupt his family time, though he adamantly claimed it was fine. They walked to the nearest restaurant. The meal was delicious. Each decided to try the most expensive items on the menu. They were old friends chatting merrily into the night, drinking until they all smiled and laughed as if nothing bad had happened that day.

That night Sylvester didn't dream. He slept next to Ira, a drunken smile resting on his face. She snored, he snored just as loudly. Tommy was loud for other reasons.

★★★

Their first stop the next day was to return the suits. Both men stood uncomfortably in their boxers as other men ran tape across their bodies. Neither had ever needed a fitting like this. Usually, it was a matter of trying something on, getting the next size up, or down, if they needed it, and checking out. Sylvester wondered how the new clothing was going to feel when he finally put it on.

They were shown fabrics and asked which they would like to use. Tommy chose brighter colors, odd for him, but it was a change that he seemed to like. Sylvester stuck with the grey and black that Ira had previously purchased. The fabric they were shown was softer than he had ever felt and he wondered how something like that would hold up on the farm.

Then they went to the courthouse and filed the necessary forms to change their names. Sylvester thought the others did it mostly out of solidarity, rather than want, or need. Ira became Ira Eldritch. Tommy was now Thomas O'Halloran.

Sylvester considered everything. He had already used Tempus to sign up for a cell phone. He wanted to acknowledge the parasite, who changed his life in more ways than Sylvester could understand. The name was easily written onto the form.

Sylvester Pemberton would no longer exist in six weeks to a year. He became Sylvester Tempus, new resident of Denver, Colorado. There would be some other way for him to properly acknowledge the people who took him in. For now, it would be a nice change. Someday their deaths would no longer haunt him when he closed his eyes.

The clerk looked over the paperwork and verified the correct information was there. He looked up at the three individuals standing before him, and smiled. "Looks to be in order." The forms were clipped together...separately. "How will you be paying?"

Sylvester looked back at the others. "Cash." He pulled out the amount owed. "Here."

The clerk handed him a receipt. "Go to that window to pay." The woman at the next window neither smiled, nor looked at anything except the receipt. She took his money and he took the change.

"Thank you, have a nice day," he said, trying to get a rise from her.

She simply grumbled something he couldn't understand and waived the next person through.

As they exited Ira asked them to wait while she went back inside, claiming to need the bathroom. Instead of turning to head to the restroom she met the clerk who took their paperwork. A few minutes later her papers were destroyed and she was walking to the cashier with a new receipt. The cashier counted the amount back to her, then returned to her duties. Ira pocketed the cash and returned outside with the boys.

They walked until just after rush hour. Sylvester was taking in the sights, enjoying the fresh, cool, mountain air. He was thrilled to no longer smell manure, though he should have felt guilty about leaving the animals alone, he didn't.

Then he really thought about it. They hadn't been fed for days and he was just enjoying his time in a new state. He shook his head and looked at the others, who also took in the sights like the newcomers they were.

"I've gotta do some stuff, time stuff." He looked at Ira. "Can't leave the animals to starve to death."

"We can all come help," she offered.

Tommy looked at her, then back to Sylvester. "I guess if you really need us."

Sylvester smiled. "No, you two have fun. Maybe look at cars, or houses. Get a sense for what we'll need for cash. Course I'll only be gone for a few minutes, so you probably won't have time to do much."

Then he disappeared. Tommy and Ira looked at the place he used to be, then continued walking as though it had always just been them. They didn't spend much time alone together, but they were on good terms.

"What would you want in a house?" Ira asked.

Tommy hadn't thought about it that much. Mostly he expected he would live in the house he inherited for the rest of his life. Eventually, he would have to man up and get a job, but mostly just to pay taxes on the property. He looked around the city, then back at her.

"I think I would prefer to live alone, y'know. In an apartment here, rather than a house. Course I'd wanna own the thing." Tommy smiled. He was thinking about all of the beautiful women he'd met in the last day and a half and was thrilled at the thought of living in the heart of the city.

"Maybe we could get an office down here for this detective agency he wants to open, and it can have an apartment attached, or something," she offered.

"That would be perfect. No getting up and driving into the office, just sleeping until I felt like rollin' outta bed." Tommy was lazy at heart, though he would work hard on things he actually wanted to work on. His Mustang had been rebuilt from the ground up, and he did all the work. The only barrier to finishing was the almighty dollar that he always seemed to have too little of.

"Wait up," Sylvester yelled behind them.

That was quick, Tommy thought to himself.

As Sylvester rejoined them, Ira noticed a smell. "What, you fed all those animals and never took a shower?" She held her nose.

"Yeah, sorry. I'm starvin', didn't eat nothin' either." Sylvester looked at Tommy, then at Ira. Each stepped away from him. "Alright fine, Tempus...to the hotel."

Again the man disappeared from sight. People gawked at the place he used to be, then at his companions. They smiled and waved, slightly embarrassed. "We'll have to tell him to stop doing that in public." Ira whispered to Tommy.

Tommy nodded and just kept walking.

"I think I'd like us to have a house, Sylvester and I that is." She was looking at a brick building with an artistically crafted display window. "Not that you couldn't join us, but you know." Of course, that would be a one day thing. Right now, she was just trying to make it look real.

Arms suddenly rested on their shoulders. "What'd I miss?" Sylvester asked.

"You missed yourself making a big scene," Ira said. "If you're gonna do that, you've got to make an effort to hide before you do it. Don't need any videos gettin' online, if they haven't already."

"Yep, that makes sense." Sylvester looked around. "It felt like I was gone for an entire day. About six hours of feeding, six more tendin' the fields as quickly as I possibly could. You wouldn't believe how many pieces of police tape are all over that house."

Tommy and Ira could though. It was the biggest crime to happen in Cedar Vale. The local police would likely have had a field day gathering evidence and trying not to contaminate the scene with their lack of experience.

From the look and feel of Sylvester he was in a better place. It seemed work, and keeping busy, was good for his mental health. Ira wrapped her arm around his waist and hugged him.

"Sorry to lecture you," she said.

"No need. I was bein' stupid. Any progress on the housing, or car?" Sylvester let go of Tommy's shoulder.

"For you it may have been a day, but for us it's been about five minutes," Tommy said. "We figured out that I want to live in an apartment in the city and she wants to live in a house."

Sylvester laughed. "Let's head back to the hotel and we can really sit and figure it all out." They were too far from the hotel to walk, but there was always another way.

Taking the advice Ira gave, he walked them to a deserted alleyway and took their hands. "Ira this'll be a first for you, so things are gonna feel...weird. You're not dyin', it's just travelin'....instantly."

The pressure built within Ira, then popped. They were in their suite when she bent over and grabbed her stomach, then ran to the bathroom. ***Sometimes that happens. It's weird at first. She'll get used to it,*** Tempus cut in, knowing that she wouldn't be around too long either way. That information was not for the parasite to share.

"Alright, hun? When you're done come on back and we'll look at houses m'kay?" The only noise that came from the bathroom was the sound of Ira heaving, then panting and repeating the process.

Both Tommy and Sylvester sat on the couch, then scrolled through their phones. Tommy looked at apartments and offices in the greater Denver area. Money didn't seem like it was going to be an issue for them, so he didn't look at prices. He looked for something that was both professional, for the business side, and stylish for his personal quarters.

Sylvester looked at houses. He wanted a yard, though not a big one. Farmwork had consumed most of the last twenty years of his life, he had no desire to do more. The houses he looked at, in close proximity to downtown, were worth millions. The one he liked the most, was nearly four million dollars. Money he didn't have...yet. The house had been on the market for two months.

Ira sat next to him, cuddled in close and looked at the house. "Don't think we need six bedrooms hun," she commented.

"No I suppose not, but it's pretty nice." He kissed her on the forehead. "Feelin' better?" He pulled up another listing on his phone.

"Yeah, just felt like crap at first. Went away pretty quick." She tapped a house on the screen. "Bout the same price, one less bedroom. I like it."

"Alright, let's go for that one." He looked at Tommy. "Havin' any luck?" he asked.

Tommy shook his head. "Not yet, but I'll find somethin'."

"Maybe I'll pay for another month here, then we'll get real serious about this," Sylvester said. It was more than twenty thousand dollars for two weeks, but he had plenty of money, and they would have plenty after he started investing in something.

It was like they didn't think it was going to happen. Ira leaned back as though the reality of the situation sunk in, then looked at Tommy. "We're really doing this." Until that moment she never believed they would go through with a move to Denver, as well as starting a detective agency. That meant letting go of her dreams.

Tommy looked straight ahead. "I love Denver, but I'm going to have to sell my place." He knew that was the case, but like Ira, reality smacked him in the face and he reiterated. "You're going to have to sell yours, once it's in your name."

Sylvester was the only one who was calmly scrolling through listings. "Yep." The reality of the situation sank in long ago for him.

"We should invest in Apple," Tommy said. "Then you wouldn't need to worry about money at all. You'd be a multi-millionaire."

"When should I invest?" Sylvester never paid much attention to things like that. He never considered financial anything before. Now he was an adult living on his own. There was no other option for him.

"You should go back to nineteen eighty six. Invest in apple, then come back. I'd say a million shares ought give us plenty of money, then again I'd say a million shares each would be better," Ira said. With that kind of money in her name she could do whatever she wanted and go to any school. It was a selfish thought, but one she felt she needed to have.

Sylvester looked at her with a newfound respect. "How do you know these things?"

"Google dummy," she said.

"Alright. Apple stocks, nineteen eighty six." Sylvester looked around. "If we're all getting' a million shares, then I am not goin' alone."

Chapter Fifteen
1986

"We can't use the money you've got in your bag," Tommy said. "It'll look like monopoly money to people back then."

Sylvester knew Tommy was right. American currency way back when only had one color, green. Even the pictures were the same size, there was no variation between bills...aside from the dollar amount and the image of the president. It was something they would need to address.

"On top of that we would need birth certificates and driver's licenses." Ira was thinking further ahead than Tommy or Sylvester considered. "To actually buy stocks." She looked at the market on her phone.

Sylvester paced the suite. It was going to be more difficult than he originally considered. Tommy and Ira dug through their phones, trying to find a way to buy cash that was no longer in circulation. Each of them seemed to sigh at the same time.

Ira looked at Tommy, then Sylvester. "Can't buy the money. The notes that are available are worth five times their face value. A million shares will cost about a hundred and fifteen thousand dollars for each of us."

Sylvester stopped. "What about fifty thousand dollars? We could buy that much if we can find it. A bit more for some planning would be nice."

Tommy smiled.

Ira was confused.

"We deposit the money into a really big bank. The bank manager'll show me the vault just to be sure that the bank is a safe place to keep my money. That night, I buzz in and take as much cash as we need." Sylvester was smiling with Tommy.

Ira scowled. "So we're bank robbers then?" Her legs were crossed and the leg on top bounced up and down quickly.

"You got a better way to handle things?" Tommy asked.

Ira scowled at both of them, while they continued smiling. "Call it a loan," she said.

They both looked at her with strained looks on their faces. Neither grasped what she was trying to say to them. She stood up, hands resting on her hips. "Find a bank that's still here today, rob the bank, purchase the stocks, and return the money when we get back and have the money to return."

"I mean...we could do that. Though if we're going to, I don't want to rob a bank in the same city that we buy stocks," Sylvester replied.

Tommy nodded his approval.

"Alright then." She beamed at Sylvester.

"Plan of action then. Ira you get the money. Has to be enough that they take me on a tour in the vault, not to mention we have to eat and sleep for a number of days. Tommy you find a way to get birth certificates that'll pass as real. As for driver's licenses, we'll have to get those in nineteen eighty six." Sylvester smiled as he sat down. "As for me, I'm gonna take a break."

★★★

A week passed. Sylvester placed the *Do Not Disturb* sign on the door. He was sure they wouldn't be gone for more than a few minutes, but wanted to be sure no one would come in while they were gone. He wore his back pack. It was a faded blue Jansport bag. None of them were sure if Jansport existed in the eighties, but they were sure it could pass for a bag of the time.

Tommy wore another pack and in his left hand carried a suitcase full of old bank notes. Old for them at least. Once they were in the eighties it would pass for slightly used versions of the notes. Tommy also carried a wallet with a few thousand dollars in it. He told Ira and Sylvester that it was better to be safe than sorry, hungry, and with no way to get where they needed to go.

Ira no longer wore jeans. She wore a dress and black flats. High heels could be managed, but she only had one occasion to wear them, senior prom. Black flats worked better with the flower dress either way. In her right hand she carried a bag with things Sylvester would need for the robbery.

She convinced Sylvester to let her buy a computer and printer to type two notes. The first note was an apology for taking the money and that it would be returned. The second, was a note meant to be used in the future. It was a thank you note that sat in an envelope in the safe, in hers and Sylvester's room.

"Ready?" Sylvester asked. He had returned from feeding the animals only an hour before and was showered and fed. They all wore clothing that could pass as something someone may wear in the eighties, though Sylvester and Tommy didn't change their look much. Sylvester wore jeans and a black t-shirt with his worn cowboy boots. Tommy wore pretty much the same clothing, only a white shirt instead.

Ira squeezed his hand and smiled.

"Guess so buddy," Tommy said as he put his arm around Sylvester's shoulder. Though Sylvester wasn't paying attention to his friend, once again that strange face made an appearance and disappeared soon after.

They all decided that they wanted to be on the dirt road outside of the Pemberton's farm. It was a main road that shouldn't attract much attention if people just popped out of nowhere. Tempus took the image in its mind, then Sylvester and the others felt the pressure. It was heavier than Sylvester thought it would be and forced all three of them to their knees.

The pop seemed audible. It was loud and relieved the tension that built up in their chests. They were still on their knees, holding hands, when gravel started digging cavities into their resting skin. One by one they opened their eyes and looked around.

It was a warm spring day. In the distance, people arguing about a tractor's condition could be heard. Sylvester looked toward the sound and saw something he never expected, though he probably should have.

A young Al Pemberton was working on a tractor with a white haired older man standing over him. They were heatedly speaking about the fact that it was once again broken down. Al didn't seem to understand why they couldn't just get rid of it and buy a new one.

Sylvester smiled, remembering the countless arguments that he and Al had over the years about the same exact tractor. It was something he never expected to see, but was happy to have seen none-the-less. He turned and started walking toward them.

What are you doin'? Tempus asked.

"Don't worry, I'm just gonna ask for a ride." Sylvester looked at the others then waved for them to join him.

When the footsteps grew loud enough for the Pembertons to hear, they stopped bickering, and turned toward the noise. Al stood and started wiping grease off of his hands with an old rag. The older Pemberton, John if Sylvester remembered correctly, raised a hand in the air toward them.

"Mornin', how're y'all doin' today?" His voice was deep and gruff, but lacked any sign of an accent. The mans hair was thin, though his thick white beard made up for what his head lacked.

"Mornin' sir, we're a bit lost," Sylvester said. "We're from Tennessee and our car broke down miles back. Would you mind givin' us a ride into town? Would be happy to make it worth your while and pay for gas." Sylvester walked quickly up to John, then reached out to shake hands.

John shook Sylvester's hand vigorously. "I'd say yes on most occasions, but my boy Al is struggling to get our tractor goin', and I never leave anyone alone with equipment that could hurt them."

Sylvester took off his back pack and set it next to Tommy. "Mind if I have a look sir? I'm quite familiar with this model."

John smiled. "You a mechanic?"

Sylvester took that as a sign that he could move closer and start looking at the engine. "In a way. My pappy had one just like this, though it was a bit worse for wear."

Al stepped to the side and let Sylvester look at the engine. "What's goin' on with it?" he asked.

Al looked at John, then to Sylvester. "Won't start. Checked the battery and the spark plug."

"When's the last time it was run?" Sylvester asked as his hands moved from part to part.

John looked at the ground. "Been since last season."

"New gas?" Sylvester asked.

Al laughed. "Nah, it's the same as the season before, but pa doesn't spend money on gas when he don't think it needs to be done."

"Checked the starter?" Sylvester asked, ignoring Al's comment.

"Was my next step." He handed Sylvester a wrench. "Go ahead since you're so good at it."

Over the last fifteen years of Sylvester's life he removed the starter, rebuilt it, and replaced it dozens of times. Al, John, Ira and Tommy watched in awe as Sylvester quickly went to work. Al's face was red as he turned to John. John's smile was wide and revealed a pleasure in his son's irritation.

"Don't look at me son, watch this young man work," he said to Al.

Al turned his gaze back to his future adopted son.

For forty minutes Sylvester pulled apart the starter and inspected every detail. When he put it back together, then reattached it to the tractor, he looked at John. "I think it's the gas. Starter looks amazing, must take good care of it." He was looking at Al.

"That's me, Al's never touched it," John replied.

"Well either way you'll need new gas," Sylvester said. He was sniffing the open tank. "Fumes're light. Used to always happen with our tractor back home."

John smiled. "Well I guess I can give you a ride into town then." He signaled toward an older truck. It was crème colored, though it had dents and dings from years of use. "Y'all can ride in the back 'til we're in town." John signaled to Al to get in the passenger side.

"Thank you sir." Sylvester signaled to Tommy for the wallet of money. He sifted through, looking for a ten. Finding it he handed the wallet to Tommy and the money to John.

"What's this?" he asked.

"Well we said we'd pay you to take us into town, plus gas," Sylvester replied.

John pushed the money away. "No need. It was enough to watch you work. Besides, turns out I had to go into town anyway."

Sylvester shoved the ten in his pocket. He, Tommy and Ira loaded into the back, their things resting on their laps. The truck roared to life as John drove slowly down the dirt road, a trail of dust in his wake.

They drove thirty minutes before arriving in town. John leaned his head out. "Here we are," he announced.

Sylvester, Tommy and Ira gawked at the town. It wasn't much different from their time. There were a few small changes, but all-in-all it was the same place they grew up in. Sylvester smiled. "Can we at least buy you and your boy lunch?"

John returned the smile. "Sure." He drove to the freshly painted diner.

"Think John's still the boss?" Ira asked excitedly.

Both Tommy and Sylvester shrugged at her.

They entered the building. In the future the seats and other fixtures in the establishment were old, dingey, and in some cases, torn. Walking into the Cedar Vale Diner in nineteen eighty six was a shock. Everything was brand new. Booths that people hated sitting in were fresh and still had plenty of spring for their patrons behinds.

They sat around the table. Sylvester and his group carrying their belongings, John and Al just relaxing. After they ordered they waited. John made small talk about farming in Tennessee, asking questions that Sylvester had to pretend to know the answer to. He had never been to Tennessee, but his answers seemed to please John. Most of the answers were from years of experience working the way John had taught Al and John approved of the methods.

When the food came, along with milkshakes, everyone dug in. Each person from the future looked at each other after their first bite. It was juicy and fresh. Everything had a richer flavor that none of them could quite explain. They had never eaten food quite like this before. Sylvester and Ira drank milkshakes with full dairy and fresh ingredients. Tommy drank coffee, with John. The coffee woke his mind up better than an energy drink could.

As hard as they tried to eat respectfully, their manners still slipped at times. John smiled and laughed. He was a jovial man, at least in public. Al told stories of John's anger to Sylvester when he was old enough to understand. Often, it was an excuse for his own outbursts, and the start to an apology.

Sylvester and the others reddened a bit. "Sorry sir. Normally we're better with the whole manners thing, but they don't make food like this in tw..." he paused, realizing he nearly said *twenty-twenty-two*. "Tennessee," he corrected.

"Glad to hear that things aren't much different, but we still beat out the competition with our food." John drank his coffee and looked at his son. Al was still working on his milkshake, though his burger and fries were gone.

"How old are you Al?" Ira asked.

Al set the milkshake down and wiped the impromptu mustache away. "Sixteen ma'am."

Sylvester smiled. When he was walking up to the house he thought he saw a man, but Al was only a teenager, big for his age, but a teenager none-the-less. "What do you do for fun?" he asked.

Al looked at John, who nodded. "Most days I work the farm. I get up early, feed the animals, then head to school. Not a lot of time for fun. I'm on the football team and I get to practice all the time. I guess that's what I do for fun."

Sylvester didn't know much about Al's younger life. It was refreshing to see the younger version experiencing life in a similar fashion to his own. Sylvester would have loved to play football when he was in school, but Al and Janet said they could never afford the fees, or the time he would be away from the farm. A twinge of jealousy passed, then he smiled.

"Must be fun." Sylvester finished his milkshake.

Al nodded. "Did you play when you were in high school?"

Sylvester smiled again. "Always wanted to. Pappy always said that sometimes the farm's needs outweigh the needs of the person workin' it."

John patted Al on the back. "He's not wrong. We have to get that gas and then back to the farm." John stood. "Thanks for the meal. The mechanic is two blocks that way. Can't miss 'em."

Sylvester tilted his head and looked at John.

"To get your car towed," John reminded him.

Sylvester shook his head. "Oh yeah, sorry wasn't even thinkin' about it. Thanks for all your help."

John and Al left the diner, then loaded into their truck. Sylvester had a newfound appreciation for the things Al had taught him. He never met John, the man died before Sylvester would have even been born. It wasn't a freak act of nature, but he went peacefully in the middle of the night. John was seventy five when he died in nineteen ninety eight.

A tear fell from Sylvester's eye, which he wiped away quickly. The bill came and all three of them were in for a huge shock. It was less than eight dollars for all of them. Sylvester smiled and dropped the ten.

When the waitress came back she took the ten. "Keep the change," Sylvester said.

The waitress looked at him, questioning why he would leave such a large tip. For Sylvester that was a small tip, he was used to at least five dollars. A hard tip when you received such a small salary.

They gathered their things and walked to the bus depot. Three tickets to Topeka were purchased, and they waited until the bus was ready to depart. Price was the highlight of their conversation, though they spoke of their next steps as well.

They would take the money they needed from a bank in Chicago. Topeka would be the first stop to get ID's and possibly a car. After that, they would deposit the large amount of money in the briefcase and scope out the bank. Finally they would drive to New York City, Sylvester would rob the bank, then invest the money. It was all going to be easy, and the best plan three adults from Kansas in twenty twenty-two could come up with.

The bus to Topeka called for boarding and they said goodbye to Cedar Vale once more.

Chapter Sixteen
Chicago

There were no issues with getting their licenses, nor any issues finding a vehicle. The car itself cost them more than they suspected, but there was still plenty of cash in the suitcase. After they left Kansas the trip was quiet. Mostly they chatted for eight hours about nothing in particular. Ira remained quiet on the subject she was still hiding from Sylvester.

After driving by the closed bank, they arrived at a shady motel just after dark, and each of them rented their own rooms. The idea behind each having their own room was to save them from any potential incarceration should things go awry. Sylvester rented his room first. Tommy entered after Sylvester left and Ira after Tommy left. Ira visited Sylvester for a bit after they checked in, but chose to sleep in her own room.

The next morning Sylvester put on a suit that they had tailored with a style from the eighties. It was big and flowy with shoulder pads that made him look like he was always perfectly postured, even when he wasn't. He put the shoes on and thanked god that at least the shoes looked like something he could wear in twenty-twenty-two.

Two knocks sounded at the door. Sylvester answered and found both Tommy and Ira waiting. He looked out, checking that no one else was on the walkway and ushered them in. The door was quickly locked and bolted behind them.

"How do I look?" He felt that he looked dashing, except for the shoulder pads.

Ira smiled and gave him a peck on the cheek. "Bank's open in thirty minutes, best get over there."

"You gonna drive, or are you gonna do your poppin' thing?" Tommy asked.

Sylvester planned to *pop* to the alley between the bank and the next building. Less attention would be drawn to him that way. He smiled at both of them. "You know it."

"We'll wait here and see what eighties TV is like." Tommy plopped on Sylvester's bed.

"I'm going to get some food, see if it's as good here as it was in Cedar Vale," Ira said. "Tommy, come with me to be sure I'm safe."

Tommy rolled his eyes and huffed a deep breath. "I guess I could eat. Want anything?" he asked.

Sylvester shook his head. "Nah, I'm thinkin' we hit the road as soon as I'm done with the bank, whaddya think?"

Each of them shrugged. They had a good night's sleep and by the time Sylvester was done they would be fed. Sylvester smiled and dissappeared.

★★★

The bank was the epitome of the eighties. Everything was large and sparkled with excellence. Sylvester didn't feel out of place walking in, his suit matched others in style, but not in color. Some people wore blue versions, or black, he wore light grey. The only other grey suit in the lobby looked nothing like what he wore.

His suit was expensive. Though the attendant was put together in a professional manner, her suit was something one would find in an average department store. Sylvester smiled as he walked up to her.

"How may I help you today?" She was bright and chipper, even for working in a bank.

"I'd like two things: a tour of where my money is gonna be kept, and an account to keep my money in." Sylvester softened his accent, to the point a person couldn't tell he had one, and accentuated his letters. His voice was deeper than normal as well.

"How much will you be depositing?" she asked.

"Enough to pay your salary for the next few years." They researched salaries of employees at the bank in the eighties. In order for Sylvester to be taken seriously he needed to act like a businessman.

The woman only smiled at his snide comment. "Very well sir, if you'll wait here I'll have someone assist you shortly." She directed him to a grouping of leather chairs.

Sylvester nodded.

It was only a few minutes and an important looking man walked up to him. Unlike the attendant, his suit was expensive. *Manager*, Sylvester thought to himself.

He wasn't wrong, the man was a manager. Sylvester stood and reached a hand out. They shook. "Great to meet you, Tom Phillips. I'm the manager here and I handle high profile transactions."

"Great. I've got just over forty grand and I'd love to make your bank, my bank." Sylvester flashed a bright white smile, then shook the brief case to signal where the money was.

"Excellent. I'm told you would like a tour of our facilities as well?" Tom asked.

Sylvester nodded.

"Very well, let's start with that shall we?" Tom walked Sylvester around the lobby. He explained all the finer details and pointed out the security features of the bank.

Cameras were placed in visible locations that were difficult to get to. At the push of a button safety glass would drop in front of the tellers, protecting them and the bank from any would-be intruders. Tom glowed over the cleanliness of the teller workstations and the fact that each teller could use the button at their workstation, just in case.

"What about people in the lobby?" Sylvester asked.

"They're not our concern. Once the button is pushed the would-be robbers could try and take hostages, but the tellers would be unable to reverse the situation." Tom smiled. "Once the button is pushed the only way to raise the safety glass is for an outside company to manually reset things. It's a lot of coordination from what I'm told."

"Never had to use it?" Sylvester wasn't concerned about a fancy protection system that only protected the bank.

"Only test runs, when we were closed. We know it works, we've seen the reversal process." He sighed. "It was a really long night. It took five hours. I was the one locked in and there was absolutely no escaping when the bank was locked down."

"Excellent. Where will my money be stored?" Sylvester asked.

"That's next on our tour." The manager walked Sylvester back to the vault where two armed guards waited. The door was open, revealing the interior caged door.

"Not too worried about people robbin' ya I guess." Sylvester commented, his accent showing a bit more than he intended.

"No. The door you see there is made of the highest grade tungsten. It's one of the hardest metals to cut." Tom ushered Sylvester past the guards. "If someone pushes the button out there, it triggers the vault door to close in here. Anyone caught between the vault door and the tungsten bars will not be able to do much. They'll live but they won't be able to move until the door is released, five hours later."

"What happens if the guy is extremely fat?" Sylvester asked.

A smile spread across Tom's face. "Well I'm not one hundred percent sure they would live. Someone yours, or my, size would be stuck." Tom's fingers quoted the air. "'Fat' people like that would be smashed into the bars."

Sylvester nodded. "Hopefully no one tries."

"If they do it's their own fault," Tom replied.

Sylvester wasn't listening. *Is that enough to get us in?*

Tempus seemed to take the area in. *Between the manager's knowledge and actually seeing the area...I think we can make it happen.*

"Very good. Shall we sign paperwork?" Sylvester asked.

Tom directed Sylvester to his office. For the next half hour Tom instructed Sylvester to sign here and initial there. By the time he was done his hand had cramped and he was looking at a high interest account that he would never use again. Sylvester considered what would happen to the account in thirty-six years, but decided not to worry about it either way.

Tom escorted Sylvester to the door and shook his hand. Sylvester was thrilled with the outcome. They had the information they needed and would be heading to New York later that day. He was ready to get back home and put all of this behind him.

Sylvester returned to the alley he arrived in, which was still empty, aside from the garbage that seemed to gather thanks to the wind. People walked by regularly, so he walked deeper down the alley than he needed to. He looked around then started to tell Tempus to go back to the motel.

"What're you doin' here?" A gruff voice asked from somewhere behind him.

Sylvester turned around and saw a man, dressed in rags, wth a knife. Tempus seemed to have frozen, though Sylvester was sure it wasn't out of fear. "Hey buddy. Sorry I didn't see you there." His southern twang returned.

"Well now you have. Gimme your wallet," he demanded. Sylvester started to reach into his jacket pocket. "Eh, not so fast. Put your hands up."

The bum walked up to him and shoved the knife into Sylvester's ribs. "Move and I'll plunge this deep inside ya."

You got any ideas? Sylvester begged Tempus.

Tempus remained silent

"Alright buddy, it's in the breast pocket. I've got a couple bucks, they're all yours." The point of the knife pushed against his jacket, reminding Sylvester who was in charge.

"Stay quiet," the man said as he pulled the money from Sylvester's wallet and threw it to the ground, jabbing the knife to accentuate his point. "You weren't kiddin'." The money disappeared into stained jeans. Sylvester thought they may have been blue once, but now they were faded and stained brown.

"Got more money somewhere?" the bum asked.

Sylvester shook his head.

"People gonna miss you if you're stabbed?" A smile spread reminding Sylvester of Micky the mob boss, though he assumed Micky had more teeth. The man was too old to be Micky, but he could have been a relative, Sylvester considered.

Sylvester stayed silent, waiting for the man to stab him, or Tempus to react. Nothing seemed to happen on either side. "Maybe I do, maybe I don't," he replied.

"Good answer kid." The knife moved from his ribs and hid somewhere behind the man. "Get on your knees."

Sylvester was a foot taller than the man and the threat was gone. "No." He shoved the man back and grabbed his discarded wallet. When Sylvester pushed, the man tumbled, but quickly regained his footing.

Sylvester ran, hearing the footsteps of the bum racing after him. When he exited the alley, he couldn't hear anything other than people walking with him. He looked around in the crowd, but couldn't see the man.

I don't care who watches me disappear, just make it... There was a sharp pain in the space under his ribs.

He felt every inch of the blade as it pulled back. People walked around them, either ignorant of the fact that one man had been stabbed by another, or trying to avoid involvement altogether. Sylvester felt the blade stab him again in a different spot, then again.

"Tempus...I need your help," he said quietly, barely mustering the strength to speak.

A second later he was standing in a dark room, alone. Blood pooled at his feet and he was thankful the stabbing had stopped. His head filled with pressure and he mumbled something that not even Tempus could understand.

Sorry. I don' know why, but I couldn't move us. It was so weird.

Sylvester didn't respond.

C'mon kid, don't die. I'm doin' everything I can to stop the bleeding, but it's not working. Tempus could control a lot of Sylvester's inner workings. The man would age, but would never get sick. Cancers would die if they tried to corrupt Sylvester's body.

Physical wounds were a different story. While Tempus tried to thicken Sylvester's blood to staunch the bleeding, Sylvester swayed, and fell to his knees. Panic filled the parasite as it sifted through all of his memories.

At one point he was taken to a hospital in twenty-ten. He was treated for mumps, whatever that was, and sent on his way. Pressure once again built in Sylvester, though he was unconscious and barely aware of it. There was a pop and then Sylvester was lying on the ground in front of Emergency Room doors.

As Sylvester started to drift from consciousness, he heard people yelling. His final, fleeting feeling, was that of his body lifting weightlessly into the air and something shoved over his face. Then all went dark.

Chapter Seventeen
Six Weeks Later

Sylvester opened his eyes and looked around the barely lit room. There was a heart monitor steadily beeping. Breathing equipment raised and lowered at an even steadier pace. He was alone.

Sylvester tried to remember what happened, remembering only the white hot pain of a knife jabbing into his back. He couldn't speak, or call out for help with the tube jammed down his throat. So he waited, panic slowly bubbling within his mind.

Oh good, you're awake, Tempus said.

Where am I? Sylvester's eyes darted wildly around.

I found a place to take you in your memories. It's twenty-ten and you're going under the name John Doe. The ID Sylvester had on him looked unreal to the people who took him in. Everyone decided he was an actor.

What about Ira and Tommy? Sylvester asked.

They'll be fine, just focus on you. We'll go back and link up with them just after I took you out of there, Tempus replied.

Sylvester waited in silence. A nurse walked by, glancing into the room, and passing. She poked her head back in only moments later and yelled for a doctor. "Don't worry, we'll get that out of you in just a minute." She started taking notes as a woman in a white coat walked in.

"How're his vitals?" she asked.

"Stable," the nurse replied.

"Alright take out the tube, keep monitoring." The doctor walked over to Sylvester and looked in his eyes, then ears and, once the tube was removed, his mouth and throat. "How are you feeling?" she asked him.

"I..." He started then stopped and tried to clear his throat. "Water?" he managed to croak.

The nurse handed him a cup. He drank it quickly then asked for more. She disappeared. "I feel like I just woke up from a deep sleep," he replied.

"Well..." The doctor considered her words carefully. "You've been *asleep* for nearly six weeks." She air-quoted when she said *asleep*.

The amount of time shocked him. "That long? Was there any serious damage?"

"The knife pierced your liver. We had to do some pretty extensive repairs, but you'll make a full recovery." She looked at a chart. "At this point it looks like your liver is fully functioning. You should make a full recovery in a week or two, now that you're awake."

"Where am I?" Sylvester didn't recognize the skyline from the hospital window.

"Topeka General." She put the chart down. "Sit tight, I'm going to order you a meal and here's the remote for the TV." She said as she handed it to him. "Haven't missed much in the last six weeks."

Sylvester smiled at her and turned the TV on. He didn't plan on staying to try and explain who he was, or why he was carrying around an eighties ID. "Where's my stuff?" he asked before she left.

She pointed to a bag in a chair.

"You mind handing me my wallet?" he asked.

The nurse returned with another cup of water. A few words passed between her and the nurse as she came back in. He drank the cup of water and took the wallet the nurse handed him. Sylvester smiled when she left to check on other patients.

Get us out of here, he demanded.

Shouldn't we wait to make sure you're okay? Tempus didn't want to rush anything when time wasn't really out of their control.

No, we shouldn't wait. Make sure everything is as normal as can be, then get us back to the motel, just after we left. Sylvester was afraid that he ran the risk of running into a forty-year-old Tommy, or Ira. He wasn't normally the jealous type, but he couldn't help worrying about what would happen if they were left in the past for four and a half decades.

I mean aside from the equipment, your body looks fine, Tempus said.

Sylvester prepared for the pressure and closed his eyes. There was a pop and he was lying in a dimly lit room. He looked at the door to find Tommy and Ira staring slack jawed at Sylvester in a hospital gown.

Chapter Eighteen
Explanations

"Are you alright?" Ira rushed to him.

For six weeks he wasn't, but he was now that she was fussing over his health and well-being. He smiled, then looked at Tommy. "Shoulda had you go with me," he said.

"Why not me?" Ira butted in.

"Because he got hurt, he wants to protect you." Tommy looked at her with a stare that screamed *duh*.

Sylvester patted her hand and rubbed her face. "It's been six weeks since I left...apparently," he said to her.

Tommy and Ira looked at each other.

"I went down an alley to try and avoid suspicion when I popped back here. A guy jumped me, I got away into a crowd of people and then he stabbed me like three times." He tried to sit up. "I don't know that I'll be able to help drive."

Tommy laughed. "You're more concerned about this plan than actually healing."

"Well let me help you up. I've got your other clothes here." Ira pulled him slowly.

"Tempus sent me to Cedar Vale Hospital and they sent me to Topeka when I was stable, in twenty-ten." Sylvester explained as he moved parts of his body that hadn't moved in over a month. His arms regained feeling quickly, his back followed shortly after. He rested a hand over his hip and winced.

Small bumps and a long scar crisscrossed under his fingers. He rubbed them, his mind coming to the understanding that those scars would always exist now. A sigh escaped him as he considered everthing that had happened.

"What's the matter?" Ira asked.

"I just...these scars.... No one can change the fact that they exist." Tears started forming in his eyes as realization of everything he had been through hit him.

We could, Tempus replied. **Like I said, you'll disappear and a new version of you will take over.**

Sylvester thought about it, looked at Tommy and Ira, then smiled. "I'll be right back." Tommy and Ira had no time to protest when he vanished.

The alley loomed before him again, though this time he was in an open backed hospital gown. The wind whipped and the fabric fluttered, revealing his back side. Sylvester looked at the spot where, once upon a time, the man stared him down. He hid and waited.

The scene in the alley unfolded before him. He watched the bum put the knife in between his belt and jeans, then watched as the other Sylvester shoved the man and ran. There was a quick and deliberate step to the man behind Sylvester. This wasn't his first time stalking someone.

The advantage to a hospital gown, even in the cold of Chicago, was that Sylvester could sneak up behind the man unnoticed. He grabbed the bums shirt and pulled him back by his dirty, worn, hole ridden collar. Sylvester shoved him to the ground, then rolled him over and stared the man eye to eye. Surprise and fear of the unknown filled his face when Sylvester, the man he just assaulted, who now hovered over him in a medical gown, smiled.

"What is this?" he begged.

"This is your worst nightmare. Someone who you tried to kill is coming back for revenge." Sylvester pulled the knife from the man's belt and flashed it inches from his face.

"What are you gonna do?" he asked.

Sylvester smiled. "I'm gonna wait until I know how this all ends."

Pressure started to build in his chest. Something was happening and he didn't need Tempus to tell him that he was safe. Those scars would never form in his back because of the man underneath him. "You get to live, but I'm taking the knife with me." Sylvester said, the knife floating above the man's eye.

For a moment Sylvester was partially see through, his gaze still intent as he stared at the man. The bum began to yell, scream and thrash as this version of Sylvester vanished. The knife fell from the no longer present hand, and pierced the retina of his bright-green eye.

★★★

Sylvester pushed through the crowd. The bum wasn't following him, but he was sure that he would catch him if he stopped, or slowed. ***I don't care how you do it, just get me outta here and back to the motel!*** Sylvester's mind screamed.

Damn thing's not workin', sorry kid. Tempus stopped talking briefly and a few seconds passed. ***Wait…nevermind, it's workin' again. That was weird.*** Pressure built up, and Sylvester, to the astonishment of no one in particular, vanished into thin air.

He stood in his motel room, looking around, completely bewildered. ***Why wasn't it working?*** he asked.

I don't know. Nothing was responding like I expect it to. Tempus spoke like Sylvester was a vehicle with buttons and switches the parasite could pull and push at will.

He was safe and he never had to return to the alleyway again. The sound of a key placed in the lock of his door could be heard. Moments later it opened as Ira and Tommy stood there. A greasy bag of food in her hand for him.

"I'm starvin'. You'll never guess what happened when I finished at the bank." Sylvester took the bag and sat on his bed. Crumbs and chunks flew from his mouth as he explained everything that happened. His stomach grumbled deeply as he ate, almost like he hadn't eaten in a long time. When he finished his tale of daring and danger, Ira hugged him and kissed him on the cheek.

"Next time bring me. Guy probably wouldn't have even tried had I been there," Tommy offered.

"Hopefully there won't be a next time," Sylvester considered and realized there most certainly would be a next time. That was a problem for the future though. Sylvester smiled while he chewed, never fully grasping what had happened.

Chapter Nineteen
New York 1986

The first shift of driving was taken by Sylvester. By the time Tommy took over, it was late afternoon. They flew down the interstate toward the towering city known as New York. Ira took the next shift. It was only around four hours for each and they would arrive in the Big Apple just after ten.

Ira wanted to explore the city, even if it was in a much different time. Tommy was interested in one thing, women. He wanted to hit the town and have as much fun as he possibly could.

Sylvester's only thought was the bank. He would be the one to rob it, and because of this his stress level was off the charts. Tempus discussed their plans as they drove. Sylvester said he would dress for the occasion, all black, which Ira packed along with a bag that would hold plenty of money to support their cause.

They passed through states they had never been to. The world around them changed drastically when they approached larger cities. Highways were congested in each big city they passed through or by. Still, they were calm. It was almost as if they had no cares or worries they needed to mull over. The normal risks for normal bank robbers didn't seem to exist for them. Their plan, and Sylvester's abilities, mitigated their concerns. Sylvester wondered if it was actually robbing a bank if they planned to give the money back.

Each of their stops, where food was purchased and enjoyed, made them realize how severe the restrictions placed on the cuisine of twenty twenty-two were. Coke tasted different, and far surpassed its competitor's flavoring. Tab was popular and something Sylvester grew accustomed to enjoying. He had a hard time deciding which soda he'd enjoy when both were available.

Every stop to purchase gas he would have a Tab, or Coke, and some obscure snack that he had never heard of. It was a journey of freedom that only he, and Tempus, could have made happen. Whenever he could, Sylvester mentally praised the parasite.

Tempus hadn't really wanted to talk much beyond the plan, it wanted to know more about Earth and the people who inhabited the blue and green bulb. It used Sylvester's eyes and watched everything when they weren't discussing the robbery.

Other planets had moving walkways and the Tempus-Parasita's host often just stood and waited as it was carted away toward it's destination. Some planets had flying vehicles, or teleportation as their main mode of transport. It wasn't often there was a species who enjoyed looking at the nature of the planet it inhabited.

There were times, but most of those people did little to propel the knowledge of the Tempus-Parasita. Earthlings had an uncanny connection with their planet. A love-hate relationship from Tempus' limited experience, at least in the time Sylvester and his companions came from.

They seemed to be trying to right the wrongs done to the planet by those of the past. Unfortunately, for the time they currently resided in, the relationship was more hateful than filled with love. Tempus watched Sylvester pump gallons upon gallons of sludge known as gasoline into the tank of the metal contraption called a Chevrolet.

Tempus' quiet reflection went unnoticed by its host. Still it could feel Sylvester's mind pulling toward what he would have to do later that night. He wasn't alone, and the parasite reassured him that their plans would go unnoticed. Except, possibly, for the missing money.

They pulled from the highway and entered a district that was best known to the humans as Wall Street. Wall Street would be their final destination in nineteen eighty-six. Their plans would have no affect on their lives as they knew it. No issues with their current existence would come up.

Most of the trip, as Tempus admired the surroundings, it pondered the issues it had with its ability to manipulate time. As they arrived in New York, it understood what had transpired. Sylvester was injured and, while it did everything it could to save him, he was left with scars from the encounter.

Sylvester's vanity over the look and feel of the scars, and his inability to do anything about it, wiped that version of them from existence. It wasn't only them, they were all different versions of the people they used to be. Subtle differences, but different nonetheless. To Tempus this wasn't a problem. There was nothing to worry about and nothing it could do, aside from obey the host and change things when it needed to. So long as the changes weren't big enough to break the rules, the parasite could rest easy.

They stopped outside of a tall building. Sylvester stepped from the car and looked up. It was the first time Tempus had a sense of how big buildings could be on this planet. It was enamored with what humans created without the help of robotic assistance. These tall structures put the human's own lives at risk as they rose higher, and higher, to the sky.

Money exchanged hands and keys were handed to Sylvester. They entered an elevator. Not the same as the moving walkways on other planets, these structures used weight, another concept Tempus had a tough time understanding, to move up and down the tall buildings. Tempus could feel the pressure of the quick ascent and sudden stop, just as Sylvester had. It was a funny feeling that could never be gotten used to, by anyone, or anything.

Bags were set down in the room. Only Sylvester and Ira were in this one, like usual. Tempus enjoyed watching what they did, though it felt the moments while they lay in bed were personal and only meant to be viewed by Sylvester and Ira. At those times it shut it's own mind off to what they were doing.

In those moments it seemed like an eternity passed. Time was a funny and fickle beast to the parasite. It may have been three minutes for all it knew. Either way, by the time it opened it's mind back up, the couple were usually cuddling and, at times, fast asleep.

Sylvester paced. They arrived at the hotel three hours earlier than expected. Likely this was due to Tommy's incessant need for speed. He looked at his watch then looked at Ira. "I should wait til at least eleven tonight, midnight would be better."

She smiled at him. "That's fine. Let's go see a show. Seems like we have enough money to live like kings for the next few days."

It wasn't going to be days though. They would return to their time the next evening, if Sylvester could help it. He smiled at her. "I suppose we could do something classy like that. Maybe the guy downstairs could get us some tickets?"

Ira shrugged.

"Either way, Tommy's probably going to be findin' someone to do things he shouldn't be." Sylvester plopped into a soft chair. He looked at the arm of the furniture, and the rest of the furniture in the room. Velvet felt nice, but he was used to less shiny furniture.

"If he's lucky he won't get some woman pregnant. I guess it doesn't really matter to him. I'd feel guilty," Ira replied.

Sylvester smiled. "Can you imagine Tommy as a dad? Oh the habits that child would inherit." He laughed as there was a knock at the door.

Tommy stood on the other side as Sylvester opened it. "I think those habits would probably be just fine."

"You're probably right, but why don't you save the mating rituals for when we're back in our time?"

"Now why would that be any fun?" Tommy took Sylvester's chair. "What's the plan tonight then?"

"Ira wants to see a show, I've got to wait til later to do what we came to do." Sylvester shrugged. "Dinner and a show?"

"Works for me. We've got a couple thousand left, I don't think it'll affect our situation." Tommy smiled. "What are we gonna see?"

With that they went back down the elevator. Sylvester popped into the room, threw the latch, then popped back into the hallway. The elevator ride once again jostled Tempus and the other inhabitants. It was starting to like the feeling and wondered what else humans created that could cause such a reaction.

The concierge smiled as they approached. "Good evening. How may I help you today?"

Sylvester cleared his throat and practiced his professional accent. "Well, we'd like to catch a show and some dinner. Any suggestions?"

The concierge smiled. "Well what kind of show are you looking for?"

All three of them shrugged.

"Have you seen the film *Singin' in the Rain*?" he asked.

"Oh I love that..." Ira started to say movie, but paused long enough to reflect the concierge's diction. "...film. Is that a broadway show as well?"

The concierge laughed. "It most certainly is, though I think you'll want to change." The concierge was gesturing to Tommy and Sylvester, who wore their standard attire of jeans and a t-shirt.

"Great, can you get us three tickets? Best seats in the house?" Sylvester returned the smile.

"I'll make a call if you'll do me the favor of changing into a suit and tie." The concierge shifted his gaze to Ira. "Miss you are perfectly dressed for the occasion."

Ira blushed. "Thank you. Boy's run upstairs and change. Tommy be a dear and leave this nice man a nice tip."

Sylvester shook his head as Tommy pulled out a twenty, hesitated, then handed it to the man. His face broadened in a wide smile. "Thank you very much sir. I'll have the tickets waiting at the box office for you. As for dinner you'll find a nice little restaurant just outside of the theater and once you change you'll meet the dress code."

"Have a cab waiting for us when we come back down," Tommy announced. The concierge smiled again and hurriedly dialed the phone.

Both men dressed in their tailored suits, black for Tommy and grey for Sylvester. When they rejoined Ira, they looked sharp and ready for any meeting, or professional situation. Sylvester smiled, he was starting to enjoy the professional look and feel of a suit. Tommy looked uncomfortable.

They exited the hotel and entered a cab. Dinner was fancier than any of them had the opportunity to enjoy before. By the time they finished, the chef had brought them ten courses. Six were on the house. As the concierge said, the tickets were waiting for them. Ira always wanted Sylvester to take the time and watch the movie with her. It was one of her favorites, but he never did. Tommy had never seen it either. Both were content to see a live show and finally see something she'd wanted them to for many years.

It was exhilarating for both men. The minute the actor on stage ran his lines, they were hooked. Every scene caused their hearts to drop, or skip a beat. It was by far the most dramatic stage experience that either of them had. A spark was ignited within their respective minds for Broadway, and plays in general.

There was something different about seeing a performance like this in person, rather than on a screen. It was more personal, more vibrant. They were enthralled. When the curtains fell they, and everyone else, stood and cheered *Encore!* Ira smiled and squeezed Sylvester's hand.

She stood on her tip toes and pecked him on the cheek. "Thank you," she whispered.

He looked at her as he clapped for the cast. "Thank you, this was amazing. We have to see every show we can!" His clapping increased and whistles escaped him.

It was over. Sylvester, at least, didn't want to go, but knew he had other things to do. There was still an hour until he would move forward with the plan. His excitement over the new experience was overwhelming.

"Buddy, I'll see you in the morning." Tommy said as he showed up with his arm around a random woman's shoulder.

Sylvester shook his head. "Alright, I'll see you in the mornin'."

Ira shook her head as she entered the cab and directed him back to the hotel. Sylvester shook Tommy's hand. "Keep a hundred, give me the rest."

For a moment, Tommy looked at Sylvester with an accusing look on his face. His smile slowly spread. "Hundred's gonna cover a lot of drinking in nineteen eighty-six."

"Great, just make sure you're back in the mornin' so we can get outta here. Not to mention don't get her pregnant," he whispered in Tommy's ear.

The smile was all Tommy returned as he and the woman walked down the street. Sylvester shook his head and entered the cab. The engine rumbled and backfired every few feet until they arrived at the hotel.

Ira lay out the clothes and bag for him. Sylvester looked at the clothing. All black. The only uncovered part of his body was going to be a small slit where he could see enough to get the job done. He looked at Ira and smiled. "Don't think any less of me for this."

She returned the smile. "As long as we return it, it's fine." She handed him the envelope. "Don't forget to leave this behind, just in case you can't come back for some reason."

He stripped and dressed for the occasion, sticking the envelope in his bag. "I love you," he said.

Time stopped. Ira stood before him, her eyes big and blue, though there was a sadness behind them that he only barely saw. The back of his hand ran down the soft skin of her cheek. A smile spread across his face.

The plan had always been to stop time, then transport himself to the right place. He wanted to avoid any cameras that may catch him in the act. Pressure built, then popped. It was easier than it had ever been before.

When he materialized in the vault of Fidelity Trust Central, it felt like his body was filling the space inside Jello. It took him a minute to reacclimate to the feeling of time being stopped. His arms moved more freely as he worked them more, and more. Before long his body moved unhindered.

Tables stacked with money surrounded him. The bills were new, but the same style that he had purchased in twenty twenty-two. The bills were stacked and wrapped in similar amounts. A range of stacks were laid before him. Those with the hundred dollar mark were his target.

When they talked through the plan it was always a better idea in their minds to steal the money that looked older. He lifted and pulled the stacks against the weight of stopped time. It was hard work, but work that he could do for as long as he needed.

The numbers ran through his head as he added each stack to the bag. When he reached their goal, he pulled the note out. Sylvester considered whether he should bother leaving it at all. The plan was to return the money a minute after he left in a neatly stacked pile.

Just in case you can't come back. Ira's words ran through his head.

Is it possible that I won't be able to come back? Sylvester asked.

Tempus considered. **Anything's possible, but I don't think we'll have any trouble this time.** Tempus spoke as though it knew this wasn't going to be a special circumstance, like before.

The envelope bounced in his hand a few more seconds. He looked around, then set it where the money had been. *Better safe than sorry,* he thought to himself. He looked at his watch, which had been configured to Eastern Standard Time in nineteen eighty-six.

Once again he transported himself away from the bank. Ira still stood frozen in time. The bag of money was set on the bed, though it took extra effort to cut through the thickness of frozen time. The mask was removed and Sylvester smiled at Ira. **Alright Tempus, unfreeze time.**

"All done?" Her eyebrow raised and the sadness was immediately gone.

He nodded and pointed to the bed. The bag was closed, but it was clearly full. She slowly walked to it and poked it, then unzipped the bag.

Her eyes opened wide when she saw the money. It was almost as much as Sylvester had in their time. She hesitated, leaned down and took a deep breath. Sylvester smirked, but let her do what she needed to.

"It's real," she said, though she had no way to really tell.

"Of course it is. Tomorrow, we'll have our meeting, and then return home." He smiled and considered asking if everything was okay.

She walked to him, looked him in the eyes, and hugged him. Sylvester couldn't be sure, but the way she looked at him felt...different. It was a look that seemed to say she loved him, but wasn't in love with him any longer. Sylvester shook the urge and feeling away, leaned in, and kissed her deeply. The returned kiss felt as though she were saying goodbye. He couldn't quite put a finger on why everything felt so different with her now.

Chapter Twenty
Change in Fortunes

Morning broke through grey clouds. The city shined with a newly glossed surface. Rain poured from above as Sylvester, Tommy and Ira, all dressed in their finest clothing, waited for a taxi.

Ira once again said she loved Sylvester, and this time he felt she meant it. When the taxi pulled up the bellhop opened the door and ushered them inside. They chose a small company to make their purchase. It was run by a businessman who was still alive in their time, and still running the company. It was still small and inconspicuous, though. Ira wondered how this purchase would change things for the owner. The others didn't think twice about it.

Tommy and Sylvester each carried a suitcase of money. Sylvester held Ira's share, though it wasn't lost on him that he was the only one doing all of the work to this point. He didn't care. They were the people he cared about most. Tempus only resided within him, so he could do the work when they couldn't.

Financial Investments Association was on the second floor and housed one employee. James Johnson had only been out of college a couple of years, worked with one of the major investment companies, then decided he could do better on his own. In twenty twenty-two he still seemed to barely get by according to Ira.

James had done what he could, and his company was floating on lucky investments that actually paid off. He only had three clients, even though he started with seven. The desk he occupied was littered with past due notices and red final notice paperwork.

The door to his office opened, barely phasing him as he massaged his temples. He opened his eyes at the uncomfortable feeling of someone staring at him. Three people in his office caused him to jump and clutch his chest. "Sorry I, I wasn't expecting anyone," he stammered as he ran his hand through his thick dark hair.

For a moment he sat there, staring at three potential investors, then realized he was being rude and shot out of the chair. James smiled at them and took the trio in. "How can I help you?" He positioned himself so most of the desk was covered, but the damage, if there would have been any, was already done.

"Pleasure to meet you," Tommy said.

"Business been light?" Sylvester asked, not caring how rude the question was.

James' bright white teeth bared in a toothy smile. "It's the eighties, who's not strugglin'?"

The fat cats at any of the other investment firms, Sylvester thought. "We're here to buy stocks. You think you can manage us?"

"Sure! Of course, I'm happy to help!" James turned and started shoving all of the paperwork into one bundle. It disappeared into a drawer near the bottom of his file cabinet. "What were your plans?" he asked as he turned around.

Tommy and Sylvester looked to Ira. "She's going to handle the negotiations," Sylvester said. This too had been discussed. She was the smartest of the three of them.

James hesitated, then gestured for her to sit at the desk in front of him. When she was comfortably seated his smile broadened even further, which none of them thought was possible. "Alright little lady..."

"Kindly refrain from referring to me as little lady, hun, or any other gender stereotyping. I'm the boss between the three of us, and we have a lot of money to invest. If you don't want our business because I'm a woman, then we would happily go to your...ahem...competition." She knew that the *competition* was an investment firm with hundreds of employees. He wasn't a threat to them, but they were a threat to him.

The smile fell. "Alright, ma'am?" His hand rose as if to ask her to calm down and beg his pardon.

Ira nodded approvingly.

"How can I help you?" He pulled out a notepad.

"We each want to buy a million shares in Apple," Ira said. "And that's each...as in three million shares total."

James' mouth dropped. He took a second to look back at the computer sitting on a counter behind him. "You want to purchase a million shares of that company?" He gestured to the computer.

"Three million." Ira's face didn't change.

"Are you sure you don't want to invest in their competitors? IBM and Xerox have been doing fantastic in the market in comparison. Apple's only eleven cents a share." James pointed his thumb at the computer again. "That things worthless to most people."

Ira smiled. "Computers such as that will rule the world one day."

James broke out laughing. "You're not serious....Lady you are funny."

Ira's smile disappeared again. "I'm not jokin'. Boys show him our money." She raised a hand in the air as though ordering them to do her bidding.

Sylvester and Tommy set their briefcases down, one on each side of the woman. The clasps made a satisfying snap as they opened, and revealed neatly stacked bills, no longer sporting the Fidelity Trust Central currency strap. Instead, each stack was wrapped with rubber bands.

"This is our life savings. We are choosing to try and make money for our children and grandchildren." Ira watched as James wiped his upper lip with his sleeve.

"Sorry, how much is there?" James asked.

"Enough for three million shares of the stock. Three hundred and forty thousand dollars." Ira smirked as James leaned back.

"Alright, let's sign you up, but I have to tell you...I don't trust that stock is going anywhere." James pulled out forms. He lifted the receiver of his phone, dialed a number and waited.

"Yeah Harry, it's James. Kid's are good, wife's the same as ever." Harry said something the trio couldn't hear and James laughed.

"Yeah you know it. Listen I have a group here who wants to buy three million shares of Apple stock."

There was a long pause while James waited.

"Yeah I'm serious. I'm looking at the cash for it right now, so I'm good on my end. Can you buy me those shares?" James smiled and gave Ira a thumbs up. "Fantastic. I'll get the money over by the end of the day."

James hung up the phone and looked at them. "Well deals done. Money will go over today and the stocks will be in your names." He began filling out three separate forms. "And those names are?"

Ira leaned forward and handed him her driver's license. "Amanda Wallace." Then he filled out the rest of the information.

Sylvester waited as Tommy handed him his license. James held his hand out, gesturing for Sylvester's as he wrote Tommy's alias, John Stapleton, in the name field. Sylvester's alias was Christopher Clarendon. The forms took no time to fill out. James leaned back. "Is that all the money you have?"

"Three hundred and forty thousand dollars isn't enough?" Ira asked.

"I take a commission of ten percent." James lied. In most cases he took home one percent of the total transaction, but he was feeling lucky.

Ira smiled at the man, then snapped her fingers. "I expect this will suffice," she replied as three stacks of hundred dollar bills were placed in her hand.

James' eyes widened. "It's a little short, but I'll make an exception this time." He smiled.

Sylvester leaned in and lowered his voice. "I know you only take one percent you greedy son of a bitch." Sylvester smiled as he leaned back.

James' smile dropped and his head hung down. "I'm sorry. You're not wrong. Things have been lean."

"We'll forgive you on two conditions," Tommy said. "One you take half of that money and invest in the same stock we just invested in. Two, you fill out a transfer form and set the date for July twenty-ninth, two-thousand twenty-two."

James looked at them, his brow furrowed and an eyebrow raised. He thought they were crazy at first. A new light seemed to dawn when he really took them in. The fabric of their clothes was designed like the clothes he was used to seeing, but it looked softer, and yet the quality seemed worse.

"What do you mean?" he asked.

"I mean that you're going to buy over a hundred thousand shares in Apple as well. Trust me, you'll be fine with it...one day. As for the other thing, you'll just have to wait and see." Tommy closed his briefcase. "Unless you'd rather we went elsewhere?"

James's hand quickly covered the three stacks of bills. He picked up the phone again and waited. When he hung up he was also a shareholder in Apple. He pulled out another form and filled it out in his name.

"Fine, here's the transfer forms, fill 'em out and I'll be sure they're executed." James eyed them cautiously as Ira pulled out similar forms and filled in the information. She then pulled a trio of envelopes out of her purse and wrote *Sylvester Tempus* on one, *Ira Templeton* on another, and finally *Thomas O'Halloran* on the last. Sylvester and Tommy did not notice that she didn't use her alias.

"They're filled out correctly. Don't open them. These people will be expecting them at the time listed on the envelopes, not a minute before." Ira gave James one last smile, then gestured for Sylvester to lean down. "Give him one more stack, we still have plenty after that."

Sylvester set the stack of hundreds down. "This is for your silence on, and execution of, the matter. Understood?"

James nodded. "Thank you."

She smiled as Sylvester held his hand out to help her stand. "Have a nice day mister Johnson. Do not sell our stock."

They left the office, a stunned man following and locking the door behind them. The money still sat in the briefcases on his desk. He piled the bills into one, turned off the lights, and left the office.

James was only a few minutes behind the strange trio, but they were nowhere to be found. They were gone, though he didn't care too much. He would uphold the bargain and take the money where it needed to go. Whatever they knew about Apple, he didn't care. He only knew they were either the dumbest hicks he'd ever met, or the brightest young minds of his generation. Either way, he was twenty thousand dollars out of the hole.

★★★

The feeling of pressure released and they were back in their Denver hotel room. Ira still felt quesy, but it passed quickly. In nineteen eighty-six, after they left James's office, Sylvester transported them to their New York City hotel where they grabbed their things, checked out and paid their final bill. Now, they were back where they belonged.

It was as Tempus said, nothing changed. The bags hit the floor with a dull thud and they all sat on the couch...waiting. A knock rang across the door and Sylvester looked at both Tommy and Ira smiling. "Well sounds like he kept his word."

Sylvester answered the door and stared in shock at the man standing before them. James Johnson, older with a lot more white than grey, waited on the other side. Sylvester was frozen.

"Are you going to let me in Christopher?" James wasn't affected by the fact that he was staring at the same man who stood in his office thirty six years prior. "Or should I say..." James grabbed his chin and thought for a moment. "Well I know you're not Ira Templeton, but I can't decide if you're Thomas O'Halloran, or Sylvester Tempus." James assessed the others behind him, his eyes resting on people he hadn't seen for three decades. Sylvester stared at the man, but wondered how he knew Ira's original name. "I'm going to go with Sylvester."

Ira was the first to react. "Hello mister Johnson." Her tone was more personal than it had been in his office.

"You, my dear, showed me something that day that I needed." He smiled at her. "A woman who could take charge. It's because of our conversation that my middle daughter has taken over the firm."

Sylvester finally moved out of the way and let the man in. James sat and laid out three envelopes. He eyed them then smiled. "I'm too old to change my past, but apparently you young people are capable of so much more."

Ira smiled. "Actually, it's Sylvester who's able to do what we did."

"Why aren't you more shocked by it?" Sylvester asked.

James leaned back and laughed. He went into detail about everything that happened. The first few years he watched the stock raise and return a dividend. He still wasn't sure what happened and how the trio understood what was going to happen at the time. Then he was far too busy to worry about it.

After the bold investment, others started coming to his office and investing with his firm. The company exploded with business and he had to move buildings and hire staff. By the end of the nineties FIA was one of the world's leading firms. If it weren't for the good fortune the company had, not to mention the forced investment that made him a millionaire, he would have left the crazy transfer request behind.

The more the stock grew, however, the more intrigued he became. He announced his retirement two days before, his daughter happily taking over. She was the only one who wanted anything to do with her dad's business. Her siblings were living their lives to the fullest, visiting dear old dad and mom as often as they could.

Ira shed a tear when she heard. Joy filled her heart over what they had done. Before they invested, James Johnson was a widower and his only child disowned him. Now, he was a happy family man. She was beginning to understand what Sylvester wanted to do and how it would make him feel. Still, she wanted to grow on her own terms.

When James finished his story he looked hard at the three of them. "It was in the early two thousands that I realized this was the only logical explanation. I'm not sure how you did it, but it was obvious that it had been done."

James gave them the envelopes and smiled. "Also, there's this." He handed them three checks, each made out to their real names.

"What's this?" Sylvester asked.

"It's your dividends over thirty-six years. I set them aside in a savings account under my name. In the off chance that you weren't here when I arrived, I was just going to keep it. Time has been kind and this is nothing to me anymore. Each of you has earned a pretty penny." James smiled at them. "I have nothing, but thanks to you all. You've done me a great service. I was going bankrupt until you came along. You saved my life, and my marriage. Thank you."

Sylvester smiled. This was what he wanted. It was a high that never stopped, and he wanted more.

"What will you do with your newfound wealth?" James was standing to leave.

"I'm gonna travel." Tommy blurted out. Again, that flash of another person filled Tommy's face, but as with every other time it appeared, it disappeared quickly. Had anyone noticed it, they would have realized there was a dark and angry smile crossing Tommy's lips in those few seconds. He looked at Sylvester and Ira, his face once again normal. "I'm sorry guys. I know what we were plannin', but I want to see the world."

Sylvester smiled. "No need to be sorry. I'm plannin' to become a detective...who travels in time and fixes things." The idea was odd, but James had witnessed it first hand.

Ira smiled at James. "I've told Sylvester I was going to be by him, but I have other plans I haven't mentioned yet." She still smiled, but the look had an apology hidden behind it.

Sylvester wanted to smile, but the news was disturbing. James realized what the discussion had done. "I'm sorry young man. I didn't mean to cause this."

Sylvester looked at him. "Not your fault. I guess I didn't think about what they would want when we started this crazy thing."

Tommy and Ira hung their heads. They both felt ashamed, Ira more so because she hid what she really wanted. They both wanted to stay by his side, but now they had options. Ira always did. They walked James to the door. He turned one more time, smiled, and walked away.

"You're going to do what Tommy's doin'?" Sylvester asked as he closed the door.

Ira looked at Tommy, then Sylvester. "Not together, but I'm going to pay off my parents farm. Then I'm going to college and travelling. I need to experience life. I had the application for college mostly filled out before you picked me up. I was gonna ask you to come with me, but now I don't see the point."

Tommy was oddly silent. He was the only one who was given the okay to do as he pleased. The pain that Sylvester was feeling echoed across the room.

It wasn't a fight. Not anything like they experienced from their stressed families at least. It was a conversation and the end scenario was that she was leaving Denver and returning home, at least, for the time being. The money she received was the catalyst for what she wanted to do. While she loved Sylvester, she needed to broaden her horizons.

She slept in the bed that night and Sylvester took the couch. He wasn't ready to say goodbye, but she was ready to leave their world behind. The walls were closing in quickly.

The next morning they each went to their banks. Confirmation of the name change was passed to the teller for all except Ira. Their checks from James were deposited. The teller said it would take a week to verify funds. They only smiled.

Ira cried as she sat in Tommy's car. He promised to take her back safely, since he was heading to Cedar Vale to prepare his house for sale. Sylvester thought that, even though it was going to be for sale, the house would likely never be sold. He hugged Tommy and said goodbye.

"I'll be back," the man promised.

Part of Sylvester thought that maybe he wasn't just telling him what he wanted to hear. The other part knew that even if he did keep his word, Tommy would never be the same. Sylvester closed the door when Tommy sat in the Mustang and walked to the other side.

Her tears fell heavily. He only wanted what made her happy and his own tears reflected the loss they both felt. It wasn't something unexpected. Sylvester loved her in every meaning of the word, but she had things she needed to do for herself. Small town life had suffocated her experiences, and Sylvester saved her from a slow, and boring death at every turn.

She leaned close to him, pulling him into her hug while she sat in the car. The kiss lasted for a long time, the last one they would share. "This is for the best." She cried to him as she spoke.

"Maybe for you." Sylvester was angry, and he knew the words would cut like a knife.

She let go, turned to face the floor of the Mustang, and buried her face. Sylvester pulled away and closed the door. He wanted desperately to apologize, but his pride refused. The world he loved, the only people who ever mattered, disappeared as the Mustang roared to life, and drove away. The rumble of the engine disappeared in the distance and he was alone.

As he walked back inside, he cried. The bellhop and concierge tried to help him, but he said he was fine. His suite would be his residence for the foreseeable future, and it was all his.

Ding.

The doors slid open and he walked down the hall. It was wide enough for two or three people to walk side by side. His eyes were shut as he walked down the middle of the hall. When he arrived at the door, to a two-bedroom suite he no longer needed, he noticed a business card in the door.

On the front the card said Tucker Adamson PI. On the back was a note scrawled in familiar handwriting. This is the guy who'll teach you. I know you're hurtin', but trust me, it's all for the best. -S

Sylvester read the writing, then flipped it to the name. He paid no mind to it aside from stuffing it in his new, fancy wallet. Another note, again in his own handwriting, waited inside.

Also...Don't forget to return the money. I know there's a lot on your mind, but you've got plenty of money in the bank to cover it. Just make sure you get old cash, here's the place to use.

A website was written by hand underneath. Sylvester shook his head and sat. He was alone for the first time in his life. Tears flowed as he realized that it likely wouldn't be his last.

Part Two

____

Full Fledged PI

Chapter Twenty-One
Two Years Later

Tucker no longer had to have Sylvester under his wing. He was his own PI. Sylvester had only become more wealthy thanks to his stock portfolio and he was never concerned about money. Tucker suggested a cozy office south of Denver, but Sylvester eyed a large office with living quarters right in the heart of the city, like Tommy had wanted.

Tucker shook his head at the man when he told him he already purchased the building he would work from. Sylvester had to clarify that it was not just the apartment and office space, the entire building was his. It was mostly vacant, aside from some hippy living in her apartment and selling witchy cures to those who believed. Sylvester was no longer the believing type, especially after everything that had happened with the Pembertons and Ira.

His heart had been ripped out and he replaced it with cold steel. No one could break him if he only cared about facts. Tucker commended Sylvester for not holding back when a client lied to their faces, though he couldn't be sure how the kid knew.

As it was, this was the only time that Tempus had used any form of its abilities. Sylvester wanted to do nothing, but learn the full measure of being a PI. To top it off, Sylvester harbored feelings of regret toward the parasite.

Tucker was an amazing mentor, but he wasn't close enough to Sylvester to understand his big secret. Sylvester never thought the man would be that close, but Tempus knew, at some point, Sylvester would crack. Eventually, he would share the world with the man who felt more like an older brother than just a mentor.

Tempus was the only *friend* that Sylvester spoke to. Since Tommy left there was a cold silence between the men. Sylvester tried to keep in contact for a few months, but he was constantly sent to voicemail. One day Sylvester cut the cell phone off and never tried to find him again.

Ira was a similar story. They spoke every other day for a few months, then a couple of times a week, once or twice a month, and finally not at all. He killed her phone the same as Tommy's. The devices were lifelines to a life that neither person wanted, especially with him.

He considered he was being selfish, and maybe he was, but they left. Tommy's relationship with Sylvester ended quickly, but he and Ira's relationship drug out. Sylvester was the only one trying to keep them together in some form, or fashion.

Last he heard of the woman, she was at some prestigious college back east. She had new friends and a new man in her life. For all intents and purposes, she was happy.

Who needs 'em, Sylvester brooded as he sat in a car watching the outside of a retail store. What he thought he was going to be doing, versus what he actually did was far from his plans.

This client paid for evidence of his wifes spending habits. Not to see if she was cheating on him, but to see if she was spending well beyond what she was supposed to. The client was a typical chauvinist who gave the woman an allowance.

A tall woman, with long blond hair, carrying five bags walked out of the building. *Snap snap.* He watched as a man followed behind her with five more bags in each hand. The shutter closed quickly, and Sylvester rolled his eyes.

Looks like the guy was right. Sylvester shook his head. He was meant to follow the woman for the entire week. *How could this guy not see this much new product?* he questioned.

Tucker Adamson's first words of wisdom to Sylvester were that he needed to *throw what he thought was decent out the window.*

"Most of the time we're paid to take pictures so the client can go home and blackmail their wives into sleeping with 'em."

Mister Sutton was a sixty-year-old man with a wife who was in her twenties. Sutton knew, as did Sylvester, that the woman was only with him for his money. "Allowances are meant to be followed," Sutton had said with a lecherous smile covering his face.

Tucker had thrown this first case at Sylvester after he finished shadowing the man for two years. It wasn't because he felt Sylvester wouldn't make it as a PI, but because Tucker knew what Sutton really wanted.

"Word of mouth'll help bring you into the lime light though. A few high profile clients and next thing you know you're rollin' in the dough," Tucker said.

The grizzled PI had been in the business for twenty years. He was nearly fifty. When Sylvester first met the man, he was impressed with everything about him. Tucker wore a Rolex, which Sylvester had five, but was still impressed about the fact that someone else, who didn't have the same means, was able to afford.

His intellect was the next thing that really struck Sylvester. They met at a dive bar southwest of the hotel Sylvester still stayed at. Immediately the man knew who he was, and what he was worth.

Tucker took an interest in Sylvester because of his upbringing. It wasn't long before they were talking about what brought them both into the world of private investigations.

"Let me guess, you read books, or watched shows like Monk or Sherlock," Tucker said.

"I did read books, but my family didn't put much stock in TV." Sylvester drank beer during his meeting with Tucker. "My favorites were the gritty novels that took place in the thirties."

Tucker laughed. "Well I'll tell you this much, cases will never be like that. Even the big ones will be filled with you doing things for people that don't really need it."

Mister Sutton's case was definitely one of those. Over the last two years Sylvester had worked cases that felt more important than his current activities. Now, he had an entire toolbelt of skills he could bring to any important case, as well as Tempus.

As it was he could help misses Sutton by going back and giving her millions of dollars so she never had to share a bed with the pruney old man that was mister Sutton. He wouldn't though. It just wasn't worth it. Frankly, her situation wasn't his problem.

He continued to follow her as she drove back to Sutton's home. The old man was always home, but never paid attention. When she exited the car, and left the bags in the trunk, he knew she was done for the day.

Sylvester drove to the building he now resided in after two long years in a two bedroom hotel suite. It didn't cost him much to keep living in the suite, it was a fraction of what he made every year, so he didn't see the point in leaving.

The house, and farm, sold quicker than he expected. All he owned was the clothes in the closets of both rooms of the hotel suite. His office was still under construction. The office space he used was being modified. Only a small portion was going to be his office. The rest was being refurbished into apartment space with stairs heading to the upper floor of his apartment. There would be a wall of windows looking out over the city of Denver.

He pulled into the garage, swiped his access card, and drove in. The space was large enough to house hundreds of vehicles, but currently only four were parked: his, two construction vans, and Jada Jarlson's yellow Bug. He rolled his eyes as he passed the Volkswagen.

There was no reason, or desire, to kick the woman out of the building. She had been there for more than a few years, and if he was honest with himself, she was, at least, something to look at. He never agreed with her philosophies on the metaphysical realm, but he was happy to nod and smile any time they spoke of it. For all he knew, she thought he actually enjoyed it when she spoke about crystals and chakras. Really, he was just like any other man.

The elevator rode silently to the top floor where he had a desk and computer. The Sutton case was pretty cut and dry, and he didn't see the point in waiting any longer. The pictures transferred to his computer and he wrote a quick email.

Five minutes after sending the images Sutton replied back. *That was quick.* Sylvester thought.

Dear Sylvester,

Thank you for today's pictures. Am I correct in assuming, according to your email, that you feel the job is complete? I assure you it is not. I wanted five days of evidence, not a single day of pictures that only prove she left a shop with fifteen bags of God knows what. Your job isn't finished.

Sutton

Sylvester looked at the screen, debating what he would say in reply. Her allowance was smaller than what she brought out of the store. Both Sylvester and Sutton knew it.

Sutton,

There's no way that those bags cost less than her allowance. You're going to have to accept that she's overspending. I don't know what game you're playing, or what this "proof" does for you, but you have what you asked for. If you need more, the bags are in her trunk...figure it out for yourself.

Sylvester

He closed his laptop and walked to the place where he planned to have a couch...some day. His time at the hotel could have been extended, and he thought maybe it was too soon to move in. Furniture had been purchased and delivered to the basement storage area, but the construction occupied the space of both the office and the living room.

He stared from the window, looking over the sprawling metropolis that was Denver. *Why did I choose to live in the city?* A day of wasted time because an old man wanted to sleep with his young wife.

Hey, how about a show? Tempus could feel the tension built up within the man.

"Whaddya mean?" Sylvester asked.

Well, you liked that show in the eighties. I thought it was entertaining. We could go back and see it again, or see something else. The parasite really had enjoyed *Singin' in the Rain*. Often, when Sylvester was busy with other things, it hummed to the memory of that night. Since returning, they watched the movie over and over at the hotel.

What the parasite didn't understand about the situation was Sylvester felt his connection to Ira stronger in those moments. The thought of seeing it live again caused a strange gooey feeling to emanate from within.

Tempus learned to acknowledge the difference between emotions simply by the way they felt to its free floating body. Gooey was a sign that Sylvester was depressed. Light and airy, which Tempus hadn't felt since that day in eighty-six, meant Sylvester was happy. When Tempus felt pressure, much like when Sylvester travelled using Tempus's ability, Sylvester was angry.

These days Tempus felt gooey, or pressure most of the time. The parasite longed for the days when there was nothing. The feeling of weightlessness reminded it of the days it floated through space. It just wanted its host to be better, not happy, or depressed. They hadn't travelled to another time, or another place since Ira and Tommy left. The man was just not in the right head space.

"We could do something like that," Sylvester said, a spark of hope flourishing inside.

Sylvester considered everything he could do and everything he could see. Since they left, he spent most of his time reading books on his phone, or tablet. Even listening to them to kill time. The man quickly flipped through his phone and found what he was looking for.

"Alright Tempus. It's been a while since we've done this. Let's go to New York and see Les Mis." Sylvester changed clothes, opened his safe, and took a large wad of old cash from it, then vanished.

Chapter Twenty-Two
Refreshed

Three months passed for Sylvester. He spent his time seeing shows, visiting extravagant places, and bonding with people he otherwise never would have. When he popped back to the present, only minutes after he originally left, he lay back and closed his eyes with a smile on his face.

Tempus simply showed him a good time. The wad of cash he took with him lasted until he decided it was time to head back home. With his mood shifted he looked at the clock, then walked to his laptop.

Sutton,

I apologize for my previous email. I'm under a great deal of stress. I'll continue tailing her for the remainder of the week. I'll send whatever additional evidence I find to you on Friday.

S

Sutton was getting a free service. He would overlook a little abuse. Even if he complained, the people he spoke to would likely see the man for who he was and overlook Sylvester's slight.

He was as good as his word over the course of the week. Every day he took new pictures of the woman purchasing bags upon bags of only she knew what. He even tailed her to a hotel where he watched her meet up with a man, kiss him, and then disappear inside.

When he sent the pictures, Sutton only replied with a simple *Thank you.* What did Sylvester expect? At least his weekend was free and hopefully he would have a new client sooner, versus later.

Tucker sent him a text requesting a meeting at their favorite dive bar. Sylvester replied and got ready to meet the man. Driving wasn't an option, though he considered it. He was drinking, and there was nothing that would stop him from getting back to his mostly empty apartment.

Sylvester appeared in the alley behind the bar, head darting back and forth as he observed his surroundings. When he was satisfied he was in the clear, he left the alley and walked inside. He could have manifested in the bathroom, but there was always the chance the stall he chose would be occupied.

Tucker sat in their normal booth, a glass of scotch resting in his hand as he waved him over. The man smiled and looked at his watch. "You must've been headin' this way already?"

Sylvester smiled. "Maybe I was and maybe I just teleported here."

Tucker laughed and tapped the table. "This round's on me," he said.

"What's the occasion?" It was either good news, or bad. The only time that Tucker bought a round for Sylvester, it was bad news.

"You finished your first job. Don't get me wrong, I heard about your flub on Monday, but you finished it and got the old bastard more than he asked for." Tucker took a sip of the scotch.

"I just had a lot on my mind that day. I was able to see the *error* in my ways." Sylvester ordered himself a beer as soon as the waitress came up.

"You figure out the name of your agency yet?" Tucker asked.

Sylvester had been considering what it should be, but was still drawing a blank. He shook his head.

"Give it time, it'll come to you. Besides you've got all that construction work goin' on," Tucker replied.

"Should be finished by the end of next week." Sylvester smiled.

"Exactly, so you have 'til next week to figure it out." Tucker took another sip.

Sylvester caught something in the man, something he had been trained to see. "What's wrong?"

The smile remained, but Tucker's eyes looked down. "Taught you too well," he said as he took a deep breath. "My sister was hit by a car yesterday. Word is she may not make it."

"I'm sorry to hear that. Anything I can do?" Sylvester asked, though in the back of his, Tempus was already calculating effects.

"No, she'll be gone, and there's nothing I can do to stop it. She has three girls and I'm her only family. I don't know how to take care of kids." Tucker didn't see the inner conversation rolling around in Sylvester's head.

Could we stop it? he asked the parasite.

I mean it's not like we couldn't, but there's a risk that this conversation doesn't happen, therefore...well you know. Tempus had warned sylvester of situations like this. There was always the threat of erasing themselves and changing the past.

I know, but if we can stop this, we wouldn't be leaving kids with a man who's never had 'em. These situations were the reason for his desire to start the agency. *What if we brought him and he helped save her?*

Then you're definitely changing something. The important thing is that Tucker winds up here, with you, in this bar. Changing the fact that he meets with you would definitely cause things to happen.

Well that's perfect, I'm here because I finished the case. It was true that Tucker had called him there to celebrate. The pain was just a glimpse Sylvester had caught.

"When and where did it happen?" Sylvester blurted out.

"I told you, yesterday. It happened in Topeka. She was in the area for a job." Tucker downed his Scotch.

"Do you know where in Topeka and what time?" he asked.

"She was admitted to the hospital at three fifty-two yesterday afternoon. When she was hit, she was crossin' some street called

Belle Avenue." Tucker asked all the pertinent questions when the officer was on the phone with him.

"Why aren't you there?" Sylvester asked.

Tucker hung his head and looked at Sylvester earnestly. "I'm scared."

Sylvester had been to Topeka but had never to Belle Avenue. *I'm going to fix this for you,* he thought as he laid down a twenty. "Thanks for the offer, but you need to see your sister. Get outta here."

Sylvester watched Tucker leave the bar. No one was looking at him when he closed his eyes and vanished. He was standing on a random street he'd been to at some point in his life, though he couldn't remember when. Sylvester met Teresa Johns when Tucker invited him to Topeka for one of her kids birthday parties. He was always the fun uncle who spoiled the kids. That time was no exception.

"Lotsa single ladies there, I'm sure." Tucker coaxed. Teresa was a widower, losing her husband in Iraq only a year prior to the meeting. She wore a brave face when he shook her hand, but the hug was deep and filled with hurt.

Sylvester looked at his phone. It read twelve o'clock. It was a nice feature of the phone, to automatically adjust for time on the network, rather than a time that had been manually set. Still, it caused issues every now and then, but Sylvester smiled and tried calling Teresa.

"Hey Teresa, it's Sylvester Tempus. I work with your brother," he said.

"Oh hey, how've you been?" Teresa was pleasant, even though she only met the man once.

"I'm fine. Uh, I'm in town on business and I was wondering if you wouldn't mind gettin' lunch or somethin'. On me of course." Sylvester wasn't hungry, but if a meal was all it took to save her life, he would happily take some antacids and push through the meal.

There was a hesitation over the phone. "I've got an interview at four. I was going to take the bus, but if you're in town does that mean you have a car?"

"Sure do," Sylvester lied.

"Well, I'd be happy to get some food with you, if you'll take me to the interview?" Teresa asked.

"Absolutely. I'll be by your place in just a little bit." Sylvester hung up. He didn't have a car, but he could easily rent one.

A compact vehicle took no time to rent and by one thirty he was at her house. He knocked on the door and returned the sweet smile she gave him when the door opened. "Sorry I'm a bit late, but if you want there's got to be some place close to your interview where we can eat, that way it's a quick trip."

Teresa closed and locked the door behind her. "Sure thing, there's a bar and grill right next door." She turned and looked at the car. "I thought you drove somethin' nicer?" She laughed.

"I see how it is...only agreed to hang out with me because of my car," Sylvester joked. "It's in the shop, pickin' it up tomorrow."

They had a lively conversation as they ate and drank. She confessed that she was struggling with depression and the only thing helping her move past it was keeping the kids moving. Once they were in school, she had nothing and was constantly reminded of her husband.

Sylvester shared his condolences once again, resting his hand on hers and making eye contact. She smiled and brushed her hair back, looking down at her drink. When they finished the meal, Sylvester waited for the interview to finish, then drove her home.

"The girls won't be home from their after-school activities for another hour..." She looked at him, then her house. "Would you want to come in?"

Sylvester smiled. "Thank you. I would love to, but if you're thinkin' what I'm thinkin'...I'm not sure how Tucker would take it."

"I understand." She giggled and smiled at him.

It was almost five o'clock. Teresa was safe from everything that did happen to her. Sylvester made sure she was inside before he drove back to the rental place and returned the car.

Everything should go like it did from here, right?

I guess we'll see. The parasite responded as the pressure built up and Sylvester vanished.

He was back in the bar after ushering Tucker outside for a smoke. ***Mostly the same.***

"Alright kid, now it's on you the rest of the night. I'm gonna head home and crash." Tucker slapped a twenty on the table.

Not a big enough difference to change much. Tempus relaxed.

"Sounds good buddy." Sylvester stood and reached for Tucker's hand.

He looked at it, then at Sylvester. "You got a thing for my sister? And when the hell did you have time to get to Topeka?"

Sylvester dropped his hand. "I had business. The pictures I 'took' yesterday were actually from the day before. Dumb broad made multiple trips." Sylvester leaned against the booth. "As for your sister, she's a lovely woman, I just happened to have time to take her to lunch while I was there."

Tucker eyed Sylvester up and down. "I love that girl with all my heart. You do anything and I'll break your arm."

"Understood. Seriously though...her and I are just friends." Sylvester smiled.

"Alright kid. Have a good night." Tucker smiled back before he turned and walked away.

Nice thinkin' on your feet, Tempus replied.

"I s'pose it was. I've got a name for the agency now though." Sylvester smiled.

Chapter Twenty-Three
A Real Case

Another week passed and the office was finished. He had the men install a door with a window, like he remembered reading of, and seeing in, those detective novels and movies that he loved so much. Sylvester was Humphrey Bogart, minus the hat. In big bold lettering in the center of the window it read *Savior* and below that in smaller letters *Detective Agency*.

Furniture filled the office, and his apartment. There was an old-fashioned wooden desk and plush brown leather chair. A fan hung above, though unlike the novels, it was silent as it moved air across the room.

The walls were covered in wood paneling and the only thing that was new aged was the laptop sitting on the counter behind the desk. For all intents and purposes, it was a replica office from the *Big Sleep*.

Sylvester happily kicked his feet up and leaned back in the chair. Though he wasn't smoking a cigar, he was reading the paper when a woman walked in.

"Hello. I'm looking for Sylvester Tempus," she said.

"I go by Savior to my clients," he replied. At first it was strange for him, but he let the feeling pass and pulled the paper down. "How can I help you Miss?"

The woman looked at him. "Savior?" She had a look of disgust on her face.

"It's my pen name...so to speak." He put his feet down and pulled the chair closer to the desk. "Tucker send you?"

She nodded.

"I'll have to remember to tell him to call me Savior when he talks to people about me. Protects my real identity, y'know?" He gestured toward one of the overly plush chairs in front of his desk.

She sat and took the office in. Her brunette hair bounced as her head moved. Piercing blue eyes stared at him through thick rimmed glasses, eyes that stuck with Savior. Pouty lips, the brightest red imaginable, pursed.

She wore jeans, tighter than they should be, and a blue blouse with white polka dots. When she finished taking in the room, she gathered her thoughts and smiled. Sylvester returned the smile.

"Alright start from the beginnin'." A pad of paper and a pen rested in his hands.

"Well, I'm the head of security for a law firm here in Denver. Two nights ago, our company was hacked and, it seems, that I was the one who did it. It happened at nine fifty."

"Is that evenin', or in the mornin'?" Savior asked as he quickly wrote.

"Evening." She smiled sheepishly.

"Before we go much further, tell me your name." Savior shook his head. He was frustrated with himself for not asking sooner.

"Rebecca Stevens." She waited for his next question.

"Alright Miss, Misses, Stevens...?" Savior paused as he waited for the correct title.

"Miss," she said.

"Alright Miss Stevens. What was taken?" Sylvester was ready to furiously write while she spoke.

She went into detail about the electronic files that disappeared. Case logs, evidence, and months of planning. It wasn't just one case, but every case in the company database.

"Any suspects?" Savior asked.

"None," she answered as he nodded and wrote.

"Do you have an alibi?" he asked.

"I was home with my cat..." she replied.

He scribbled the note quickly. "Would you be able to get me on site to investigate the area?" Savior smiled.

"The partners are allowing me to investigate, but they gave me no money to do so. In their minds I'm the one who did it. I could get you on site, but I can't afford much." Her eyes glossed as tears started to well up.

"Calm down. Tucker knows I don't charge for my skills and expertise. That's why he sent you to me. Didn't he explain that?" Savior grabbed a tissue and handed it to her.

She shook her head. "He just told me to come see you."

"Alright. Well, here's how it works. I'm going to take this information, I'll put it in my computer over there, then we'll go see where everything happened." Savior's pen hovered over the paper, waiting for more information. "Now the big question, what do you need from me?"

She cocked her head and raised an eyebrow.

"As in photographic evidence, signed confession... what do you need to make everything right?" Savior smiled.

"Name. Photo of the person in the act. That should be enough to clear me." She dabbed her eyes.

"Alright. Is your firm workin' any big cases that someone would want to make disappear?" He watched as she hesitated.

"We're working a few big cases. One in particular is against the Irish mafia in Chicago." Her eyes never left his, though his narrowed slightly.

"Irish mob. Chicago." Micky ran across his mind. "I see. Anything else?"

"We've also got a case against the United States Government, specifically President Logan, but I can't imagine it's a government job." She shook her head. "I'm not sure beyond that."

"I don't think it's government related either." Savior felt a twang of familiarity simply with the mention of Micky's organization. "When can I come to the office?"

"We can go now, or later if you'd prefer. I have until Friday." She stood and waited for his response.

"Let me type this up, then we'll go. Feel free to take a drink from the fridge in the corner," he said as he turned and started typing. She sat back down while he hunted and pecked each letter. When he finished inputting the case file he stood up. "Your car, or mine?"

★★★

When they arrived at the office building Savior walked around the entire premises, his camera snapping quickly. "Anything on the cameras out here from before they went out?"

She shook her head.

"Cameras back up and runnin'?" he asked.

She nodded.

"You get them back up and runnin', or did they just start workin' again?" he asked, his camera pointing toward a guard walking the premises.

"They started working about an hour after they went down." Her hands were in her jeans while he worked.

He took a few more pictures and cased the area. There appeared to only be two main entrances, the lobby and a back door for employee use. "Is that where they clocked your badge?" He gestured to the door.

"It was there, but then it was a login from the computer on the sixth floor." She walked toward the door and pulled out her badge.

Hit pause Tempus. Rebecca was frozen as the card rested on the scanner. ***Good, take us back two nights, about nine forty.***

The bright sunny day suddenly lost all color and was transformed into a black, cloudy night. It was ten minutes before things supposedly happened and there was no sign of anyone outside. Sylvester waded through time and walked the perimeter.

Still, no one was there, the building was closed and quiet. Security was parked on the opposite end of the parking lot and clearly wide awake as one was in the middle of drinking from a thermos while the other flicked something away. Savior took out a smaller notepad and jotted the names of both security guards, and the company they worked for.

"Alright Temp, go ahead and move forward a minute at a time, keepin' things paused as you do." The feeling of static rushed through Savior's body. He looked at everything, seeing little change in the environment on the first minute. More obvious was the fact that the second guard was a smoker.

The second minute passed with increased static, then the third and the fourth. Savior was worried that he would miss what was happening, but on the seventh minute a van approached the end of the parking lot and pulled up next to the security patrol car. On the eighth minute, a bag was tossed in the driver side window, then the van was at the employee entrance.

There were three people in the vehicle. Savior snapped pictures of the van and its license plate. Each person was covered in black clothing and masks. He snapped a picture of their eyes, and full profile photos.

At nine fifty they entered the building and split up. One took the elevator up and two moved to the security room. Savior followed the bulky man to the elevator, riding it up to the sixth floor. He pulled out a USB device and inserted it into the computer when they entered. When the program was done the man removed it, and left.

Savior looked at the screen. It read *hard drive wiped* in green letters on a black background. Just below, it said *database cleansed*. All of the files were gone. No one had them saved anywhere. The men didn't show their identities.

"Think I could remove a mask?" he asked Tempus.

I don't know, but I doubt it. That or it would be really hard to remove.

"Alright take us back." The world changed around him again. He was back outside and behind Rebecca. He looked through the photos and was happy to find that they were all still there.

"Miss Stevens..." he said.

"Yes." She opened the door.

"I know what happened, but not who." He looked at her with a serious eye. "And we may be able to save your files."

Chapter Twenty-Four
Seeing is Believing

Rebecca Stevens looked at Savior her brow cocked in question, "How did you get these photos?" she accused.

"Calm down, there's a reason I go by Savior." He pulled her away from the building and to a bench nearby. "Look… I can travel in time and space. Anywhere in time, and anywhere that myself, or anyone else I've had physical contact with, has already been."

She looked at him and scooted away.

"Listen I know it sounds crazy, but I can prove it." Savior looked deep in her eyes.

"How?" she asked.

"I can bring you with me," he said. "The most important thing is that the files are safe right?"

She nodded.

"We can explain away your logs by maintenance. You got a notification that somethin' was wrong, or somethin' like that." He smiled. "Then you get to be the savior when you tell them the whole system was crashin', and you managed to save everything."

She smiled. "Tucker really should tell people you're crazy." She continued to back away.

"I'm not. Let me prove it. If you're not satisfied, then we call me crazy and move on with our day." He took her hand. "Please."

Whatever she saw in his eyes caused her to nod slowly. "Okay." Her tone was docile, almost like she was drugged.

"How would you like me to prove it?" he asked.

She thought and then looked at Savior with the look of a woman missing something, or someone. "Can you take me back two years to say goodbye to my mom?"

"How'd she die?" he asked, considering what he could do.

"Cancer." She covered her mouth and started sobbing. When she was able to gather herself, she cleared her throat. "We were here in Denver; I was too scared to see her in such a weakened state. Daddy was always at her side, except when he got sick near the end."

"Picture a nice, secluded place during a time when you were absolutely not at the hospital." Savior waited as Tempus scanned Rebecca's thoughts. "Got it?" Considering everything he was about to show her, his voice was as gentle as it could ever be.

She nodded.

"Close your eyes, this is gonna feel weird, and you may wanna throw up afterward." She closed her eyes, preparing to stand when he couldn't follow through. Savior closed his own eyes.

They both felt the pressure, only Savior was used to it. She opened her eyes and tumbled around a corner. Savior listened as she threw up. She finished retching and rejoined him, looking around as she wiped her mouth using her dampened blue sleeve.

Savior noticed that any time he was in a time period with cellular network his phone automatically corrected itself, displaying the correct date. "Two years and three months ago...give or take a few days." He looked at her. "Go say your goodbyes. I'll be right here. Just make sure you don't change anything too drastic."

She looked around, bewildered, but nodded. "Could you save her life?"

"Probably, but it would erase us from existence. I'll answer any questions you have after you come back." He leaned against the wall and popped a piece of gum in his mouth.

Rebecca disappeared. Somewhere in Cedar Vale a younger version of himself was still working on the farm. The Pembertons were still alive. He could go see Al and Janet, but he'd be too tempted to say something that would change their lives and his.

He thought about all of the people he could go see. He didn't look much different, though he wore a five-thousand-dollar suit, and his hair was cut slightly shorter. Aside from that, he was pretty much the same person.

Ira was likely working at the diner, paying her parents' mortgage. Tommy was off fiddle farting around with his car, or something. He shook his head and tried to pull the coldness he'd woven into his emotions over them like a parka.

Over the past weeks, since taking a vacation and no longer moping, the hardened part of him melted ever so slightly. The softening of his personal side started when he went back for three months, but the nail in the coffin was when he saved Teresa. Nothing had been erased, but he was a happier person without the burden of not caring about others. In general, he was happy about it, no longer walling himself off gave him a freedom that he hadn't experienced since they left.

Still, when it came to Ira, he wanted to forget her entirely. Even though she was who she had always been, at that moment, she was still his greatest pain. All three of them, himself included, still had months before everything would turn sour.

He looked off into the horizon, unsure if it was toward Cedar Vale, or some other random place. It didn't matter. Deep breaths escaped him as he closed his eyes. *I'm alright. Just need to breathe and calm down. That idea is a bad one.*

A sudden hand resting on his shoulder startled him and he jumped. It was Rebecca, with bloodshot red eyes. She smiled at Savior, tears falling.

"I didn't mean to startle you." She chuckled as she wiped her eyes with the opposite sleeve she wiped her mouth with.

"Sorry. Two years ago..." He reconsidered what he was saying. "Right now, I'm south of here. My girlfriend, who left me only a few months later, is there also. My best friend, who ran away from me the first chance he got, is also there."

She pulled him into a hug. "I'm sorry I brought you here." She let go. "I believe you now. We can go back and take the temptation away."

"Everything go okay?" Savior asked as he grabbed her hand.

The pressure came and went quicker this time. Neither of them had time to close their eyes. Instead, they watched as the world blurred and changed, melting all around them. This time there was no sudden urge to vomit and, when everything cleared up, she stood there, outside of the law office.

She balanced herself on Savior at first. Then she walked back to the door. "Thank you. That really meant a lot, you probably will never know how much. Now...how do we save my job and clear my name?"

Chapter Twenty-Five
Saving Grace

Savior had three more days. It was early on Tuesday. Rebecca said she had to have a programmer friend create a way to copy everything from the database. His biggest concern wasn't getting the data, however. There was a group of men who, for all intents and purposes, were going to fulfill their mission and wipe the database using Rebecca's credentials.

The van's license plate was staring at him in the clear digital beauty of a picture. He was even on the phone to a contact at one of the local precincts, though he was on hold after giving him the plate number. It was too early for the christmas jingles playing in the background, so he listened to the same three messages on repeat.

"Still there Savior?" Officer Andretti snickered on the other end.

"Andretti...you gotta laugh every time you say my alias?" he asked.

"Maybe...it's just so fresh." Andretti cleared his throat. "Alright, here's the skinny, the van is a rental owned by Thompson Rentals off west fourth ave. It's one of those shops that we all wonder just how the hell they're still open."

"Gang related?" Savior had been keeping tabs on local gang activity, just in case.

"Nah. I smell dirty money, but I'm not sure where it's coming from. They haven't done anything to warrant an investigation."

"Alright. I'm gonna check 'em out and see what I can find. Thanks again, I owe you a beer." Savior hung up the phone.

He transferred his notes to the case file on the laptop. After saving he opened a new file and called it *Micky, Mob Associate*. The first note was that Rebecca's employer had a case against the Chicago branch of the Irish mafia. Since that was all he had, aside from his parents' murders, he saved and closed the laptop.

He went to the elevator and rode it to the basement. Heels could be heard walking up to it, echoing loudly off the walls as the doors opened. A woman, five foot eight with deep brown eyes, was walking up to catch a ride. Their eyes met and her ruby red lips parted in a smile.

"Just who I was coming to see." Jada Jarlson pressed the button on her key chain as her Volkswagen squawked itself locked.

"Really should get that fixed. Sounds like your battery's gonna die. If you'll excuse me." Savior tried to exit the elevator.

"Not so fast. I have some repairs that need done. You're in charge of the building now." She placed a finger on his chest and pushed him back. "The lock isn't working as it should. The faucet is dripping in my sink. My bed is making all sorts of noise."

Savior cricked his neck. "The bed's not my responsibility. As for the lock and sink I'll get someone out first thing." He tried to push forward, but she held him in place.

"I've seen you lookin' at me." she said. "Suppose you want a taste?"

"You get right to the point, don't you?" Savior shook his head. "Yes, I find you attractive, but I'm not looking for anything more. If you want me to stop lookin', I'll gladly do so."

She smirked. "Stop lookin'? Honey why do you think I wear clothes like this?" She used her free hand to caress the curves of her body. "I just figured you wanted to take me out or somethin'. If not, that's your loss." She moved her finger. Savior stepped out of the elevator. "Don't forget about my sink and door."

It would be impossible to forget about either. A small adjustment was made to the crotch of his pants. Jada caught sight of the action and her smile broadened, though Savior was none the wiser. He unlocked his car, and sat in the driver's seat.

It was a glossy black nineteen sixty-seven Chevrolet Impala. While, he could drive whatever he wanted, this spoke to him and fulfilled all sorts of desires. The Impala was all original, except the custom dash and sound system. When he fired the engine up, it roared to life, and he quickly left the building.

Thompson Rentals was still open and attended by one employee when he arrived. Savior walked up to the building, absorbing everything he could see. Cameras covered the front, back, and sides. He looked for the van, but it was nowhere to be found.

A smile rested on Savior's face as he entered. The attendant was a goon slightly shorter than Savior with a broader chest. No smile rested on the man's face as Savior entered.

"Good afternoon," he said.

"What do you want?" The attendant's tone was overly angry.

"You sure are friendly. I need some information on one of your vans." He spouted off the license plate. "You mind helpin' me out?"

"Get lost, I don't have to answer to you." The man turned away from Savior, acting as if the conversation was over.

"Alright. I'll just go get a warrant. Bet your boss would love that." Savior turned.

"Wait. Alright, what was the plate?" The goon still wasn't smiling, but he was more malleable this time. He wasn't the smartest tool in the shed either. Savior couldn't get a warrant, he wasn't a cop. His hand hung in the air, awaiting a return shake from the attendant. With a sigh, the bulkier man shook his hand before he turned and typed the plate number in his system.

"Looks like the van was rented two nights ago, hasn't been back since. Reported it stolen, according to the notes." The goon waited.

"Alright, if it was reported stolen, when was it reported?" Savior leaned against the desk, pulling out a small notepad and jotting notes.

"The next day. Guy was supposed to return it, never did. Refused to answer our calls." The goon's eyes focused solely on the screen.

"If that's true then why don't the police know about it?" Savior tapped the pen on the counter.

The attendant's eyes shifted from side to side. "I don't know man. I just work here."

Savior shook his head. "Who rented it?"

"Tony Antonio." The goon, for the first time, smirked.

"Mind tellin' me what's so funny?" Savior was no longer smiling.

"The guy's name is basically Tony Tony." Apparently, this was too much for the guy and he rested his forehead on his arm, covering his hysterical laugh.

"Who reported the vehicle stolen?" Savior wasn't laughing.

"That's weird. It says the same thing, Tony Antonio. We ain't got a Tony that works here." He scratched his head.

"I didn't suspect you did. What's your name?" Savior asked.

"Why's that matter?" The man started sweating.

"Doesn't, but clearly somethin' shady's goin' on here, based on the way you're sweatin' and overall freakin' out." Savior waited for a response.

"John Doe." The man replied with a straight look on his face.

"Alright fine." Sylvester pulled out his phone and snapped a picture of the man before he realized what was going on. "John Doe, clever." Savior shook his head. "Let me see your cameras from the day the van was rented."

John shook his head. "Now you'll need a warrant. I'm not givin' you anything else."

"Alright I'll be back." Savior stood up and walked away, stuffing the notepad in his inner jacket pocket.

That guy don't sound suspicious at all, Tempus chimed in.

"He's probably got a warrant for his arrest," Savior said as he entered the car. "Andretti will be able to help me and looks like I'll be visitin' tonight...undercover. You got his login right?"

That and enough to know what's what, Tempus replied.

That night Savior appeared in the main office, dressed in black. Any cameras that caught him would only see a silhouette access the security room and then the camera system. He opened the files for the day in question, then watched the cameras. They saw a similar goon to the one who *helped* them earlier pull the van around front.

Three men dressed just like they had been at the office building, minus the masks shook the man's hand, handed him an envelope, then sat in the vehicle.

Savior smiled and inserted a USB drive, copying the files and then removing the drive. He had their faces, all three of them. They were all white, early to mid thirties. Two had shaggy brown hair, the other slicked his back. All men were clean shaven.

Savior didn't recognize any of them, but that wasn't saying much. He had only worked a couple dozen cases with Tucker. All of the cases did not involve any mob activity. This case, considering what he knew of the firm, was all about the mob.

He stuffed the USB in his pocket and vanished. It was too late to visit Andretti at the precinct. His fully furnished apartment appeared before him. A warm feeling of excitement coursed through his body as he realized he was finally using what Tempus had given him for the greater good. Quickly, he undressed and put on a robe and boxer briefs, then poured himself a drink.

Since starting his training with Tucker, he had slowly become accustomed to scotch. He was far from a connoisseur but learned to love the flavor. There were moments where the liquid was far too peaty, but he mustered through. The scotch he drank was a sipping scotch that he gingerly sipped as he flipped through channels.

There was a knock at his door. He stood and looked through the peephole only to find that he couldn't see anything. ***Be ready to jump if it looks like trouble.***

He placed his foot firmly behind the door and eased it open. Jada stood there, in a silk robe and high heels. ***Nevermind.*** He told the parasite. ***May want to take the night off.*** "What can I do for you miss Jarlson?" he asked exasperated.

"Honey, it's not what you can do for me, but what we can do for each other." She pushed her way into the room, untied her robe, and let it fall to the floor. A strong, sweet perfume with just a hint of citrus filled the air and Sylvester took a deep savoring breath, then closed the door.

Chapter Twenty-Six
Savior

His phone went off at nine in the morning. It was Rebecca and she had the program. Sylvester blinked multiple times and tried to clear his throat. He and Jada stayed up deep into the night, she only left an hour before, but he was already too hungover and too tired, to greet the day.

His reply to her asked that she give him a few hours. Before she could reply with an affirmative, his eyes closed and the world was no more. Sleep came back easily and the next time he woke he looked at his clock. It was nine o'one in the morning. *The hell?* he thought he slept the entire day and then some.

Then he caught the date, August fifth. He hadn't slept the day away, but instead slept for an entire minute. "Man, that felt like eight hours," he said aloud.

It was about ten. I decided to let you sleep in a paused state, Tempus replied.

"You're the best wingman ever." His accent extended and drug out over the course of a few extra seconds. He text Rebecca again and let her know that he would be ready in an hour.

She replied with a blessed emoji. Sylvester shook his head, thinking of all the texts he received with the little faces. The closest he came to using these types of messages was doodling them on a sheet of paper, before he bought his phone. The shower was hot and steaming, washing sweat from his body. He picked a suit that showed him off, then dressed and sent her a text.

Where are you?

At home.

Meet me at the office, I'll be waiting.

Sylvester shook his normal identity and put himself in character. Sylvester no longer existed, but Savior, the detective who could travel in time did. *Savior, Time Detective*. He laughed at the title. In a normal world it would be fantastical nonsense, but in his world, it was anything but.

Ten minutes passed, then, he popped into place at the office building, startling a few pigeons, but no one else. He sat on the same bench he had with Rebecca and waited. Twenty minutes later she arrived and met him, wearing all black.

Savior looked at her, his eyebrow raised. "Robbin' a bank?' he joked.

She looked quickly to each side. "No, don't say things like that," she berated.

He smiled. "Don't worry, after we're done, you'll look like a hero, not a villain."

She smiled and nodded quickly.

"Ready? We're gonna pop in just when the cameras went down. Then we'll have about ten minutes. Your friend's program gonna work that quick?" he asked.

She shrugged her shoulders. "I hope so. Seemed to do the trick in under that time, but the DB was smaller."

Savior smiled. "Well, we'll do what we can."

She took his hand. He looked around, verifying they were alone and not in camera range. "Close your eyes," he said as they disappeared. Each time he traveled, he recalled the first few times very well.

Rebecca, after three trips, no longer seemed to suffer from any of the issues travelling through space and time seemed to cause. He wondered how often he would need to explain away his powers to those who hired him. They appeared in the security room, alone.

Rebecca jumped into action, plugging the USB in and verifying the program was running. She looked at the clock on the computer, confirming they had nine minutes left as the program booted to a loading bar. She watched eagerly as it loaded as slowly as it possibly could.

Savior leaned against an open wall, not covered by the servers they were trying to save. "How far along?" he asked.

"About fifty percent," she replied.

Savior looked at his phone. They had been there five minutes. If the program was going to work, then it would just barely finish. "Any way to speed it up?"

She shook her head.

Three minutes passed and it looked like they would only be another minute. The elevator whirred to life and started descending. *Shit,* he thought as he rushed to the screen. *Ten percent, ugh.*

"I'll be right back," he said as he disappeared. When he reappeared, he was in the elevator as it neared the first floor. As the bell dinged, he had Tempus freeze time. Then he pushed all of the buttons. It would only buy them a minute, maybe two, but he crossed his fingers that it would be enough.

When the elevator opened it was empty, and the goon loaded. His face crinkled in frustration when he went to push one of the buttons, and all of them were lit. The door closed and the man slowly made his way up.

Savior reappeared and looked at the screen. *Still three percent.* He started tapping his foot.

"What'd you do?" she asked.

"Pushed all the elevator buttons." He watched eagerly as the bar moved another percent.

She smiled. When the ding could be heard two floors down, she joined Savior and started tapping her fingers across the desk. Ninety-nine percent.

"Make sure it's on the lock screen and everything is closed," Savior reminded her.

At one hundred percent the confirmation notification popped up and she yanked the USB free. Her hands clicked the mouse, closing everything, then tapped the keyboard a few times. The computer locked just as the elevator doors opened. The goon ran into the room, only a few seconds behind the original time. He plugged his own USB into the system, waited and confirmed the entire system was wiped.

Everything happened like it should have. They didn't head back to the present, but instead to an office several floors up. "Put the USB in an envelope, then make sure it's somewhere that they would overlook," he said.

She shoved the USB through a mail slot. The partner she left it with was notorious for setting things on his desk, and forgetting they existed. "Done."

"How are you going to explain why you didn't say anything?" Savior asked.

"Simple, they haven't let me speak to them since it happened and didn't let me get a word in when they were lecturing me." She smiled. "I'll blow up and finally reveal my piece of the 'truth'." Her fingers quoted in the air.

Savior smiled and grabbed her hands. "Good. Make sure you make a copy of the drive just in case this happens again." He blinked and then closed his eyes. They disappeared from the law firm and reappeared in Savior's office.

"I'd love to be there when you tell them, but that wouldn't be appropriate, I'm sure. Plus, it may look suspicious...having saved the day and all." Savior took his place behind the desk.

Rebecca's phone rang. "Hello?" She listened. "I can be there in about thirty minutes." She hung up the phone, a smile resting on her face. "That was the partner. He finally found the drive." She shook her head. "It's weird to say finally, only because it feels like it's only been a few seconds. I mean for you and me it has been."

"Time travel can be weird like that, I admit it. Just remember your cover story." He smiled. "Best get goin'."

Rebecca stood and shook his hand. "I can't thank you enough."

"Just remember...when it comes to tellin' people about me..." He put his finger to his lips and winked.

She understood the meaning and returned the wink before turning and leaving the office. Savior stood and closed the door behind her after he grabbed his morning newspaper. It was the end of his first real case and he kicked his feet up, opened his newspaper, and started reading.

Chapter Twenty-Seven
Another Case

"Doesn't seem like you did much with that one." Tucker stared at Savior across his desk. "And what's up with *Savior*?"

A smile spread across his face. "It's a great alias. So long as no one knows who I'm affiliated with, they won't know who I am."

"Don't you think you should change the name of your agency then?" Tucker had a fair point.

"Nah, I'm not worried about it really. I just like the sound of it." He smiled.

"Alright, whatever." Tucker smiled, though his voice betrayed his real feelings toward it.

"As for what I did, or did not do…well let's just say I pointed her in the right direction and…" He pulled out Rebecca's file. "I managed to get some primo pictures from that night."

Tucker flipped through the pictures. "How is this possible?" he asked.

"Trade secret." Sylvester smiled and laughed.

"No. Really…how did you get these?" Tucker slid the file across the desk. Clear concern filled him.

"I wanna tell ya, but you wouldn't believe me." Sylvester took the file and stuffed it in the empty file cabinet. It was the only physical file he had.

"There's always been somethin' strange about you. Everything I already know about you is so off. Now you show me impossible pictures. What's ya secret?" Tucker leaned in. "Between you and I."

Sylvester leaned forward and met Tucker's eyes. "I travel through space and time."

"If you ain't gonna take this seriously...don't bother." Tucker stood up quickly and moved toward the door.

"I can prove it," Sylvester said.

Tucker stopped as his hand rested on the door. "How?"

Sylvester's phone rang. "Sit down, gimme a second."

Tucker returned to his chair, still angry, but intrigued. He listened to the call. When Savior hung up the phone he rested his hand on his chin. "Another case already?"

Sylvester nodded. "Yep, and if you want proof, how about you join me on this one." An irritating smirk rested on his face.

"I don't work for free." Tucker raised a brow.

"Course you don't, but your payment this time is the proof you want so bad." The smirk transformed into a smile.

"Fine." Tucker admitted defeat without really trying.

"I'll pay ya a grand for your time. Next time try negotiatin'." Sylvester shook his head as he laughed.

"When's the client gonna be here?" The elevator down the hall dinged and Tucker turned around. "Oh."

A man in a bright blue business suit knocked on the door. The color of the suit could clearly be seen through the frosted window. Savior waved him in, a blob moving through the other side of the pane, then gestured for Tucker to sit in a corner and watch. The man took the opposite seat and looked at Tucker.

"Rebecca said you worked alone," he commented.

"Normally I do, but my associate here would like to watch me work...so to say." Savior gave a reassuring smile. "I promise that anything you say will be strictly confidential."

The man nodded. "Very well. My name is Samuel Kripke. I tried to contract the firm Rebecca works for, but their fees were too high."

Savior was writing again. "How d'ya spell Kripke?" he asked.

"K-R-I-P-K-E." The man spelled it out with a slight amount of disdain.

"Thank you. Now why were you contacting the firm?" Savior looked Samuel in the eye.

"Frankly, I'm being blackmailed." Samuel looked at Tucker again, then continued. "A few weeks back I made a stupid mistake. I invested money into what I thought was an organization that helped people who were homeless."

"Oh…" Tucker said from his corner.

Savior turned to him. "You have somethin' to add to mister Kripke's story?"

"No, but I see where this is goin'. You gave them money and they're usin' that for human trafficking." Tucker stared at Samuel.

He nodded. "I really had no idea, and I was going to sue the organization, but when I explained what was going on to the lawyer, he tripled the fee."

Savior nodded. "Do you know where they're doin' all this?"

Samuel shook his head.

"Why you?" Savior's eyes met Samuels.

"I import and export foreign goods. I have a warehouse and only use contract workers when I have a shipment. I'm not super busy so I'm usually the only one there." Samuel paused. "We ship any way we can, whether that's by air, or road."

"Is it secluded?" Savior scribbled onto his notepad.

Samuel nodded. "I'm not the only one there, but other businesses are further off."

"Lemme guess, if there was a weird shipment of, people let's say, no one would be able to tell the difference." Savior looked at Tucker, who nodded.

"Sure," Samuel said.

"And why haven't you gone to the police?" Savior asked.

"The evidence they have is really damning. I met them in a shady location and gave them cash. I didn't know they were taking pictures." Samuel leaned back.

"So, some people contact you, in some way…" Savior tapped the pencil on the paper slightly.

"They came to the office," Samuel added as Savior wrote.

"They come into your office and you, after hearing their spiel, agree to meet them in a secluded location and didn't think anything was off?" Savior raised his eyebrow.

"I should have. I didn't think that this was going to be any different than any other transaction. That stuff only happens on TV, or in the movies." Samuel shrugged.

"They asked for cash, right?" Savior smirked.

Samuel nodded, embarrassment filling him.

"A lawsuit wouldn't do much for you. What did ya think was gonna happen?" Savior set his pen down. His client's stupidity wasn't going to go in his notes.

"I just thought I was helping. This one time I was driving downtown and this woman pounds on my window when I was stopped in the middle of nowhere." Samuel smirked. "Looking back now it was a no brainer, but she seemed like she needed help, so I unlocked the car and let her in. Little did I know, she was a prostitute. I dropped her off the second I found out. That's who I am...gullible and willing to believe in the name of help."

Tucker laughed in the corner. "I'm sorry."

"It's alright, I laugh about it now and I'm just happy that I didn't get pulled over when it happened." Samuel smirked.

"Alright. So, what were you gonna accomplish when it came to suing them?" He picked up the pen again.

"All I wanted was my money back and a cease-and-desist order." Samuel shook his head, the slight mirth leaving him.

"Okay. What do you want me to do?" Savior again set the pen down.

"Rebecca said you'd likely be able to help in a way that no one else could." Samuel smiled sheepishly. Tucker raised an eyebrow.

"I can help, but I can't change what's already happened. Besides I think a bit of a reality check would do you right." Savior picked up the pen. "So, what would make this go away for ya?"

"My money back and all the evidence of the transaction erased." Samuel leaned in and waited eagerly.

Savior looked at Tucker and stared him in the eye. "How 'bout this Samuel, I'll get your money back and get rid o' all the evidence. However, I'm also gonna try to take the whole organization down. How's that sound?" Savior still stared at Tucker when he finished but turned to Samuel after.

A visible amount of shock filled Samuel's face. "That...that would be great," he admitted standing quickly and reaching his hand out. "How much will it cost?" He was eager and didn't sound like he cared too much about the price.

"I work pro bono, that way everyone is able to be helped." Savior shook the man's hand. "My cohort here, however, will be taking payment of a thousand dollars. I'll cover that, you have enough on your plate."

Samuel's eyes welled up. "Really?" He couldn't believe his luck.

"You're a small business. Every cent should go to that. Now to the nitty-gritty." He gestured for Samuel to return to his seat. "What day, and time, did the transaction take place?"

"The tenth of July and we met at five fifty in the evening." Samuel breathed a sigh of relief, his body relaxing slightly.

"Can you take us to the location? I need to see it in person." Savior looked at Samuel.

"Absolutely." A wave of relief washed over him.

"Do you still have the email?" Savior asked.

"No. About three minutes after I opened it, a virus worked its way through my computer and fried everything." Samuel rubbed the back of his head. "I'm just lucky I was on my personal computer. When I checked my inbox again, that email was completely gone. Like it didn't exist."

"Alright. Well, let's head over there." Savior stood and gestured toward the door. "Meet me in the parkin' lot, we'll take my car. I just need to make a quick phone call."

Samuel left the office. Tucker stood and grabbed his coat. "You just promised the world to that man. I'm not so sure you can actually help him." He was irritated with Sylvester.

"Just go to the car. I wasn't jokin' when I said I had to make a call." Tucker left the office and Savior dialed. "Rebecca, think you can get your programmer friend to whip up a way to completely erase a hard drive? Samuel's gonna need some help."

Chapter Twenty-Eight
Under the Overpass

The location was definitely shady, and there were plenty of places for someone to hide and snap pictures while others were unaware. Tucker walked the perimeter, aware that he wouldn't find anything. Too much time had passed.

Savior was having the client take his position. He was doing his best to recreate the scene with what little they had to go on. "Alright Samuel, there's a lot of potential here for where people coulda hidden. From what you're sayin' it was still bright enough they wouldn't need a flash either." Once Samuel was in position Savior stepped behind him. "What was the angle?"

"The pictures looked like they were from my left side." Samuel gestured toward a vast array of locations that would be great for hiding.

"Were they head on? Could they see both of you?" Savior looked off to the left.

"You could definitely see both of our faces," Samuel replied.

"Was the image exactly from the side, or was it angled to where you saw more of you, than the other guy?" Savior was trying to pinpoint a possible location where someone could have hidden.

To the left were round support columns, a few things here and there, but nothing too hidden. Unless Samuel was completely blind he would have seen someone with a camera. It wasn't adding up.

"You could definitely see more of me." Samuel stood very still.

"Did you hear anything outta the ordinary?" Savior asked. The atmosphere around them had constant noise from the highway above and could have drowned out any noise from a drone.

"No. I didn't see anything either." Samuel was annoyed.

"Tucker!" Savior yelled. "See anything over there that could be a hidin' place?"

"No!" he yelled back.

"Alright, come on over." His southern drawl hadn't lessened in two years. Instead it seemed to mature and become more dignified. While he was Savior, his voice was deeper.

When they regrouped he looked at Tucker. "I think it's time you see me in action. Do me a favor Samuel, go wait in the car, we're only gonna be a few minutes."

Samuel nodded and retreated to the Impala as they trekked over to the area they suspected the camera would have been located. Savior took a look around, searching for any sign that Tucker may have missed. When he was satisfied he nodded.

"Take my hand." He looked at Tucker, his voice once again its normal pitch.

"What?" Tucker asked.

"It's the only way I can show you. Also promise you won't have a heart attack." Sylvester held his hand out. Reluctantly, Tucker took it. "Don't think I'm crazy, and I'll explain everything when we're done. Also you might puke." He smiled at the man.

"I'm not wearin' the best suit for vomit," he nervously joked.

"Tempus, takes us back to the date and time of the incident, then pause everything once we get there." Tucker's face screwed up as he stared at Sylvester. "Close your eyes."

Tucker did, then pressure built up and released. His stomach was queasy, but he took several deep breaths, trying to counteract the action he so badly wanted to take. His hands rested on his upper thighs and he opened his eyes.

"Y'alright?" Sylvester asked.

It was eerily quiet around them. The loudness of the cars and other ancillary noises were just gone. Tucker looked around and saw several men standing where Samuel said he was. Even Samuel was there, but no one was moving.

"What the hell?" he said, realizing for the first time that everyone, but them, was frozen in time. Sylvester had let go of Tucker's hand, but rested it on the man's shoulder. "Do you still need to touch me?"

It was a fair question. "No, I don't need to, maybe I just like it." He was trying to break the tension.

"Great, get ya hand off me." Tucker wasn't mad. This was a secret worth keeping, but he thought they were close enough that he should have been in the inner circle a long time ago.

"Alright snippy. Look around, see if you can see anything." Sylvester started at the best possible angle. There was nothing in the sky hovering, or anything on the ground around them.

Tucker walked up and down, not seeing anything out of the ordinary. The fence that blocked anyone else from walking in was locked and razor wire was installed above. Green strips blocked the view. There was no way a camera could have taken any pictures through it. He looked, but nothing, and no one, was found.

"Doesn't make any sense. There should be somethin' here." Sylvester rested his hands on his hips.

"Unless the photos were doctored. Let's check over there." Tucker walked toward the group. "They ain't gonna see me are they?"

"Nah, should be fine. Just don't touch 'em. Not sure what'll happen." Sylvester walked side by side with the man. When they made it to the other side, they checked every possible location further away, then walked back.

It was inside a container, where a hole was drilled in an inconspicuous spot. Sylvester smiled. "A drone taped to the ceiling. No sound and no way he woulda seen it. These guys are pretty good."

Tucker reached out to take the drone.

"Stop. Can't change the past, just have to let it happen," Sylvester reminded him.

Tucker looked at Savior, then pulled his hand back. "You sure?"

"If we alter what happens it'll erase us from the timeline. We'll never have met Samuel and I'm not sure what would happen. A completely different you and I would take our place." Sylvester leaned against the container. "Ready for my story?" He eyed the man in the darkened metal box.

With time frozen he went into great detail about everything. His entire life was laid bare. Tucker heard everything from Sylvester's early childhood, to robbing the bank in the past, then replacing the money. He listened with great care.

"You ever used your powers around me?" Tucker asked.

"Actually, I was just gettin' to that." Sylvester smiled a pained smile. "Might even explain why I go by Savior in the business world."

"Alright, lay it on me." Tucker was leaning on the other side of the container.

"To be honest, during the Sutton case, I was havin' a hard time. I hadn't really dealt with losing Ira and Tommy...still probably haven't I suppose. I disappeared for a few months, though it was only a couple of minutes in the present. I went, saw shows, and other countries. I experienced new cultures. Hell, if I want I can take both of us to Europe in an instant now."

He paused and took a breath.

"Now when I got back I reconciled with Sutton and finished the case. We went out and celebrated, you remember?"

Tucker nodded. "Yeah I remember that. You somehow had time to have lunch with my sister." Tucker cocked his head slightly. "I guess actually this is how, eh?"

Sylvester nodded. "Yeah, and no. That's what happened in your mind. I did meet you that night. We did celebrate, but instead of you berating me over seein' your sister, you were devastated because she'd been hit by a car crossin' a street. She was dyin'."

Sylvester waited for the news to sink in. "So wait, you changed the past by takin' her to lunch?"

Sylvester smiled. "I popped over there, rented a car and drove 'er where she needed to be. She got the job, but in changin' things I may have erased the previous you." He waited for the inevitable anger.

Tucker took the news with a straight face and looked at his feet. He was silent for more than a few minutes, but when he looked up, he was smiling. "I love that girl. Ever since we were little kids. I'd've done anything for her." He sniffed and wiped his nose. "I should be mad at you for erasin' me, but I'd gladly take her place." He walked over and hugged Sylvester. "Thank you. You ever need anything, you let me know."

Sylvester hugged him back. "Alright, now get off, you're smotherin' me." They laughed.

"Well we know where the camera was," Tucker said as they separated and looked at the setup. "How do we take care of the rest?"

Chapter Twenty-Nine
The Rest

Before returning to the present Sylvester and Tucker performed a bit more magic with Sylvester' abilities. They hid and watched the scene play out with Samuel. To the relief of both detectives, Samuel looked confused at the group, as well as the request for cash.

Things proceeded and the transfer happened, then Samuel left the scene. When his car was out of sight, things moved fast. The man who handled the transfer, ensuring his face was seen by the camera, simply snapped his fingers. The rest of the men pulled everything apart quickly, as though it was never there to begin with.

"Alright this is where things are gonna get tricky." Sylvester froze time again.

They rushed to the still open van and peered inside. There was enough space for one of them to hide and Tucker was the shortest. Sylvester hemmed and hawed over this, knowing his powers would save the day if things got sticky. In the end he accepted defeat.

"You're gonna have to ride with 'em," he said.

"What d'ya mean?" Tucker asked.

"I mean get in the van, hide under some of the stuff, and share your location with me." Sylvester pulled out his phone.

A few minutes passed as Tucker manipulated his own phone, which seemed to be slowed by frozen time, then Sylvester accepted the share with the same slowness. Tucker moved a few things around. Conveniently there was a blanket on the floor next to a few small crates.

"I'll put it over you." Sylvester took the blanket.

"Is it gonna feel extra heavy on top of me?" Tucker asked.

"It's only when time's paused." Sylvester laid the blanket over the heavier set man. It was definitely a heavy fit for Tucker as he groaned when the blanket lay over him. "When I restart time, you better believe that this blanket is gonna feel light as it should. Text me when the van stops and I'll try to follow the best I can."

Sylvester planned to keep up with the van by performing a pause, teleporting close to the van, then resuming the flow of time. For the most part it worked. As he continued the practice, following them as closely as he could, he began to sweat.

Normally he didn't use his powers in such quick succession. It was usually a one off event of either pausing time or returning to the past. The fact that he was in the past didn't cause any undue strain, but the frequency of use began wearing him down. He was forced to bend over and catch his breath a few times.

You gotta slow down kid. You're wearing me out. Tempus voice had no noticeable fatigue.

"Yeah well..." Sylvester pulled a deep breath in. "We gotta keep up."

No, we don't. You've got the location. Wait 'til he says they stop, then I'll pause time. Once paused, we'll find a way to get you from here, to there...may just be walkin'.

Sylvester nodded. The light turned green, and he watched the van pull away with Tucker inside. He wanted to jump to the location but knew that Tempus was right. The ping on his phone moved further and further away from him as he walked to a sidewalk.

There was a little café with outdoor seating. He sat at one of the chairs and waited for a host to come and take his order. A large white chocolate mocha and a blackberry scone came shortly after. All the while he watched the blip on his phone move further and further away, heading to the outskirts of Denver.

A few times the blip stopped for what seemed like an obscenely large amount of time, only to start moving after his stress grew to unnatural heights. Sylvester sipped the hot drink, eagerly, watching the screen of his phone. When he finished the scone and coffee he stood and started walking toward the dot. It was miles away in an area of town that he had never really been to before.

"Pause time," he whispered.

Hours passed as he walked, eventually catching up to the blip. Sides of Denver that, for some reason, he still hadn't seen were on display as he walked. The experience was pleasant for Sylvester. Not all of the sights were pretty, but people frozen in time made the world a more peaceful place. Block after block, he made his way, walking mile after mile, only to come to the van in the process of driving down a street.

Sylvester took his place on the side of the road and released time. The van sped away, seemingly none the wiser to their additional passenger. *I wish it could have been me.* Sylvester was once again huffing and puffing, but this time from the extreme amounts of walking. Even though time was frozen, hours had passed for Sylvester.

The space in the van was perfectly suited for someone slightly taller than Tucker. Unfortunately, Sylvester hovered almost a foot over him. He shook his head.

We just need the location, then we can head back. His breath caught, and he again looked at the blip moving further away. He rolled his eyes. The phone beeped and a text came through.

They stopped and got out.

Tucker was only a few blocks away. Time froze and Sylvester ran through his physical exhaustion. The game of cat and mouse was officially over. His lungs burst with new life as he broke through the wall of fatigue, his body now charged with adrenaline.

The men had only barely stepped out of the vehicle when he arrived at the scene. "We gonna be able to open that back door?"

We can try, but I'm gonna say no.

Sylvester hid behind a dumpster and pulled his phone out. "Alright unfreeze time." He rapidly started typing as the men in the background could be heard talking to each other.

I'll be there in a few seconds.

The message went through with a *whoosh*. Both men were at the back of the van, pulling at the handles. The doors opened. They pulled crates out and disappeared behind a brick wall.

There was no stopping time for them. Sylvester simply teleported to the vehicle, threw the blanket off of Tucker, grabbed his leg and teleported them back to the dumpster. Tucker lay on the ground, staring at the sudden appearance of blue sky. His eyes blinked and he lifted his head.

"Good timin'," he whispered.

"Thanks. They say anything while you were in there?" Sylvester asked.

Tucker lifted his phone and showed Sylvester what was on his display. The entire trip had been recorded, though the quality of the audio hadn't been verified. It was a recording thirty minutes long. Time still surprised Sylvester at times and he shook his head. Tucker was confident everything they said was there.

"Smart. Gimme your hand." Sylvester took Tucker's hand and pulled the man up.

Tucker rubbed his back and then his neck. "They were not gentle." He tried to let go when Sylvester shook his head.

Time stopped again and both men stood. "We have to see where they're goin'. I want to be able to get in and then back out as quick as possible."

They followed the men's path, catching up quickly as they set boxes down. It was an industrial area and there were plenty of things to hide behind. Both hid, watching, when time resumed.

One of the men reached for a key ring on his belt, selected a gold key, then put it in the door, turning it and pulling it free. Sylvester froze time again as the man held the key ring in his open palm. He walked right up to him and examined it. The ring had four or five different keys, but the one he needed, even though it was the same as all the others, would be the one on top. Sylvester examined the cut of the key, then went back to his hiding spot.

Time once again resumed and Sylvester watched as the key went to the back of the ring, not the front. The man hung the key ring back on his belt, then picked up the crate he was carrying. Again, time stopped, and Sylvester was on the move.

He grabbed the key ring from the man's belt. It was like pulling a small lead weight. More and more effort was put in to taking the key ring. In the end, he decided he couldn't take the whole ring of keys, but he could take the one key he needed.

The key itself felt like it was magnetically clamped to the others. Slowly it pulled loose, though slower than the ring seemed to. Sylvester tried to pry the ring apart at the opening, managing to create a gap only a few millimeters wide before feeling his nail snap. He squinted from the slight shock of pain.

Reaching into his pocket and shuffling things around for a moment, he pulled his own keys out. Sylvester needed something to help pry the ring open enough to pull the key out. He managed to wedge one of his own keys in the slight opening, then pried it even further. The keys all moved slower than molasses in winter, but he made decent progress. An action that would have taken him less than ten seconds while time flowed normally, took fifteen minutes as time slowly gave way to each of his efforts.

The key rested in his hand, and he moved the others back into position at the man's hip. Sylvester reviewed his surroundings, looking at every angle, every detail. "We have to come back here Tempus. The moment after we left. Time's gotta be stopped too."

Let me worry about my job alright? You just do what you're plannin'.

Sylvester took the key and smiled. "Take me back three days ago, just outside the lumber yard."

Sylvester disappeared, then reappeared only seconds later. The original key was gold. His new key, the duplicate, was silver. He would have no trouble remembering which was his, and which belonged on the ring. The men had moved a single step in his absence, and Sylvester slowly pried the key ring open again.

He had taken the liberty of purchasing a small flat head screwdriver, the kind for repairing eyeglasses, to help with the key ring. Things moved quicker, both because of the tool and because Sylvester was holding the key when he froze time. It moved smoother than it had previously, and the entire act took him five minutes to complete thanks to the additional tool.

Once again Sylvester took his place, hiding with Tucker. Time moved forward and the men disappeared in the building. "Let's go back," Sylvester said as he put his hand on Tucker's shoulder, and they blinked from existence.

Chapter Thirty
Programmers Delight

They stood almost exactly where they were when they originally left. For Savior it had been hours of exhausting work. Tucker had experienced an hour, maybe more, but nothing exhausting.

"After you." Savior directed Tucker back to the Impala with his deeper voice.

Samuel had only just entered the car as they joined him. He looked at them both, cocking his head. Savior looked in the rearview and smiled, starting the car as the engine roared to life. Under the overpass it sounded like several cars came to life as the roar of the engine echoed around them.

"I thought you guys were going to take longer?" Samuel seemed concerned.

"We got what we needed. We'll definitely be able to help you, not to mention whoever else is being hurt by these guys." Savior pulled the car back, then stomped on the gas.

Police rarely patrolled the more deserted areas of Denver. His tires peeled across the concrete, leaving the car's signature in their wake. The wheels burned across the road for two hundred feet before gaining traction and carrying them forward.

"Well, what's the plan then?" Samuel asked as he braced himself the best he could.

"Well, to be honest, I can't tell you." Savior wove around a few cars as they entered the highway. "What I can say is that no one's ever gonna have to worry about these guys again."

Tucker turned back to the man. "I promise you, any doubt I had in this man, is gone. If he says it's gonna happen, then it's gonna happen."

They pulled into the parking garage of Savior's building, parked and each got out. Jada exited the elevator as they walked toward it. Savior nodded at the woman, his face reddening slightly. She simply passed, returning the nod with a straight face. Both Samuel and Tucker watched as she walked away.

Savior paid it no mind and rode the elevator to his office. He offered Tucker and Samuel chairs. A soft ding echoed when Savior took his place behind the desk. His lips stretched in a smile when he read the email.

"What I'm gonna need from you, once I'm all done with everything, is to be my liaison." Savior smiled.

Tucker looked at the man with a raised brow.

"How do you mean Mister Savior?" Samuel leaned forward.

"I mean..." Savior paused, raising his phone, and typing. "It's gonna be more than just you affected here. Truth is there're gonna be a lot of people, and I want you to get ahold of them and tell each one that they don't ever have to pay these guys again."

"How would I do that?" Samuel asked.

"I'll have a list of names, and phone numbers. You'll just call each one. If they don't believe you, then you just direct 'em to me, but only if they don't believe you." Savior's phone dinged again and he looked at it. "Alright I have another meeting, so if you'll excuse me."

"How will I know when everything's done?" Samuel asked as he stood up.

"I'll give you a call, expect it in the next day or two." Savior's smile was infectious. Tucker joined first, then Samuel.

"Alright, then I look forward to hearing from you," Samuel said as he exited the office, only pausing a second to look back one more time before disappearing.

"You get a choice Tucker. You can finish it up with me, or you can head on home, but I really do have a meeting to get to." Sylvester said, his voice returning to normal.

Tucker thought for a moment. "You're still payin' me right?"

Sylvester nodded.

"Then I guess I'm joinin' ya." Tucker stood up.

"Alright, but you're gonna get tired of holdin' my hand." Sylvester smiled. He stretched his hand out and waited for Tucker to take it. After a few eyerolls Tucker roughly took the man's hand. "I mean, I guess I could just grab your shoulder..." Sylvester shrugged and a second later they were gone.

★★★

They appeared miles away, outside Rebecca Stevens office. She was startled at their sudden appearance, but only slightly. Mostly she was unnerved by the additional person Sylvester had with him.

"Hello," she said timidly.

"Hey, you remember Tucker. He's helping me with this case." Sylvester looked at Tucker, who nodded to Rebecca in stern acknowledgement.

Rebecca shook Tucker's hand. "Nice to see you again." Admiration and thankfulness could be heard in her voice.

"Likewise." Tucker stepped back.

"Your programmer friend said he could help. Can I meet him?" Sylvester asked.

Rebecca came closer to Savior and whispered. "Yes, but only if I'm there when you meet him. Also, why's your voice different?"

"First, that's no problem." Sylvester smiled. "We can go now if he's ready for us. Second, well...you had Savior helpin' you before. Now, since you know so much, you get the real me."

Rebecca returned the smile. "The real you huh?" She looked at Tucker and cocked her head. "All three of us?"

"Would that make your friend uncomfortable?" Tucker asked.

Rebecca slowly nodded.

"I can wait here Syl..." Tucker smiled. "Savior."

Sylvester held his hand out. "Alright, you've been there so I'm gonna use that memory of yours to get us there. Tucker...around Rebecca, call me Sylvester."

Tucker cocked his head and rose a brow, but didn't question him beyond that.

Rebecca took his hand. Sylvester didn't notice how soft her hands were last time, but he felt it now. *Soft as Ira's,* he thought to himself, his mind slipping into the memory of his ex.

"Alright, just think of where he lives, put us in the hallway, or on his porch." Sylvester waited.

I've got it, the parasite announced.

"Alright, you remember how this feels right?" he asked.

She nodded.

"Here we go, keep a seat warm Tuck." Sylvester and Rebecca vanished before Tuckers eyes.

"I'll never get used to seein' something like that," Tucker said in a hushed tone.

Sylvester and Rebecca appeared on the porch of a little white house with dark shingles. There was a picket fence surrounding a manicured lawn. Rebecca knocked on the door three times and waited.

"Call me Savior around your friend, and my voice'll be different," he said.

It was a few minutes before the door opened, but when it did Savior was surprised. A man wearing loafers, khaki colored pants and a sweater you might see on the Cosby show, stood before them. He looked at Savior, then Rebecca, and smiled.

"Rebecca, it's good to see you." He was in his early to mid-forties. The hug he gave to Rebecca was deep and loving, almost like a brother, or father. There was only a slight acknowledgement from the man to Savior once the embrace ended. "This him?"

She nodded.

"Well come in. Please take off your shoes." He held the door open for them.

What Savior expected was a dank and musky room, or apartment. The programmer had an open floor plan, windows

190

galore, and everything was immaculately clean. As he slid his shoes off, he realized he was sitting on a solid wood bench, hand crafted by someone, and that someone was probably wearing loafers.

"This is Savior," Rebecca said as she stood. "He asked for the program."

The programmer put a finger to his lips and gestured for them to follow. They walked to a door, his office, Savior presumed. It was plain, unassuming, but had a breeze blowing underneath. When it opened there were obvious signs that this room was constructed purposefully without windows. It was the darkest and coolest room in the house, but was also filled to the brim with stuff.

The light turned on, revealing at least a dozen servers mounted on one side and two portable AC units blowing. It was warm outside, mid-eighties, but in the room it had to be in the forties. The programmer took a seat behind a desk. There were no other chairs in the room, so Savior and Rebecca stood.

"You may introduce me once the door is closed." Savior looked at the already closed door, only just realizing there was a red light above it. When it turned green he gestured to Rebecca.

"Savior this is Dylan Powell. Dylan this is Savior," she announced.

"It's a pleasure to make your acquaintance. I'm not quite sure how you made her problems go away, but I really appreciate that you did." Dylan wasn't actually looking at Savior, or Rebecca. He was focused solely on the screen in front of him.

"Where are June and the girls?" Rebecca asked.

"I sent them to a movie. Some kid thing that the girls will definitely enjoy. Junie might even have some fun." He smiled thinking of his family. The mouse was clicking furiously while the keyboard clipped and clopped with every click.

"Sure do love your privacy." She smiled.

Savior had nothing to say. He explained what he needed to Rebecca, and she relayed the information to the man sitting in front of them. The fact that Rebecca hadn't revealed his secrets to Dylan gave him reason to trust that everything would be alright.

"Rebecca tells me that you need this to wipe data from a computer while retaining things like names and phone numbers?" Dylan paused and finally took the man in.

"Yessir." Savior met his stare.

"Would you be able to elaborate on what it's going to be erasing?" A scrutinizing eye examined the suited detective.

Savior turned to Rebecca, then back to Dylan. "I'm working a case. The person who employed me is being blackmailed by people pretending to be a charity. I'm not one hundred percent sure, but I'm fairly certain there are others being blackmailed as well. I intend to get into the place where they're storing the evidence and erase it."

Dylan nodded.

"How do you know there aren't backups?" Rebecca asked.

Dylan waited, staring at the man.

"I don't. That's the thing. I only know for sure that he's being blackmailed by these guys and where they're storin' the data." Savior placed a hand on his forehead. "I shouldn't have promised that I could make it all go away."

"I haven't said it's impossible. Anything they may have digitally I can set to be destroyed. Once we have the file names I can send a virus over the net and have it destroy anything with those names and metadata. Some people may lose things unintentionally. Likely they'll have a specific naming scheme so not too many people will lose anything unrelated." Dylan began typing again. "Why do you need a list of the names and phone numbers?"

"My payment from the guy is to contact everyone on that list and let them know they're safe and to stop paying," Savior said.

"How do you know that there won't be contacts for the group in there?" Rebecca asked.

Savior hadn't considered this. His face drew a blank as he stared through the wall. The last thing he wanted was for his clients to be hurt. "I guess I'll take that responsibility," he admitted.

"Sounds right. At least I know you can handle anything thrown at you." She smiled at him.

"Alright. Give me the day. I need to make some adjustments." Dylan was ferociously typing. "The program will extract the information and gather the file names. All of the content will be destroyed locally and not so locally. The virus uploaded will look for anything plugged into an online device. Once located it will immediately eliminate the file and fry the source."

"Whatever it costs I'll pay. That sounds amazing!" Savior reached into a pocket and pulled out a roll of cash.

"No need. The first one is free, especially considering what you did for Rebecca. The next one will cost you." Dylan stared at the screen, though he wore a broad smile across his face.

"Well...thank you. Can I have your number, or however Rebecca contacts you?" he asked.

"Rebecca will give you my information." Dylan was focused solely on the screen.

Savior turned to her. "I'll give it to you outside. When that lights on, there's no outside network access. I don't think his computer's even connected to anything, but the servers." She gestured around them.

"Sounds good. Can I buy you a bottle of scotch, or take you out for dinner or somethin'?" Savior turned his attention back to Dylan.

"Sure, we'll discuss it later. For now why don't you leave. Text me so I have your number, and we'll schedule it." Dylan was almost robotic in his response. One hand lowered below his desk and quickly returned to typing.

The light changed from green to red. Savior's phone suddenly started going off in rapid succession. The vibration and dinging caused him to flush slightly. He took a cursory glance at his phone.

Tucker asking how long they were going to be. Tucker wondering why Savior wasn't responding. Tucker saying he'd be at the ice cream shop down the street.

The flush vanished. Savior smiled as he read and followed Rebecca to the door. "Thanks again," he yelled back as he put his shoes on.

Another notification came through, Rebecca sharing Dylan's contact information. "Ready when you are," she said.

"Alright. How're things at work since everything?" he asked as he put his hand on her shoulder, and they disappeared.

"I quit. Today was my last day. I don't have a plan for anything, but I'm sure I'll land on my feet," she said as they reappeared outside of the office building.

"Why'd you quit?" Sylvester asked.

"I was able to see how I was going to be treated. There was no internal help. Only politics that refused to see my side of things. I'm glad we were able to help them, but I'm done." Rebecca looked around. "Where's Tucker?"

"Some ice cream shop down the way." Sylvester gestured in a direction with his thumb. Tucker wasn't on his mind. He wanted to help Rebecca again and had an idea of how he could. "Any plans moving forward?"

"Right now I've got enough savings to make it a few months, but I'll need something before long." She shrugged.

"Ever thought of going into business for yourself?" he asked.

"Not really, I've never had a need. Not to mention no place to conduct that business. I've only really been good at what I was doing," she said.

"Have any real-world training? Like combat and stuff?" A side of his lip raised as he said *stuff*.

"Head of security. I'm trained with weapons, hand to hand, and with computers, at least slightly. Why? Are you hiring?" She laughed.

Sylvester turned to her and squinted as he stared directly in her eyes. "Maybe. How would you feel about taking on the security role at Savior Detective Agency?"

"You have a security role?" She giggled as she took a step back. Savior was still making a strange squinty face.

"No, but I think it would probably be a good idea. Besides I could have you make those calls and not stress about doin' it myself, or havin' the client do it." He stopped squinting and smiled.

"I don't think you can afford me." She turned and started walking toward the street.

"Give me a number," he said a blank expression on his face.

She stopped on the sidewalk, waiting for him to catch up. "Hundred and fifty a year, annual raises of at least three percent. Paid time off, as much as I want."

"Hell I'll even pay for the vacations," he said as he caught up. "But I don't like one fifty."

She turned around. "Well thanks anyways then."

"How 'bout two, but you have to buy better suits." A smile rested on his face.

Rebecca paused a moment, looked down at her feet, then over at the ice cream shop. Tucker was just exiting with a large cone that he was in the middle of licking. He hadn't noticed them just yet. Rebecca raised a hand, waving at the man.

"Buy me an ice cream cone and point me to the tailor and you have a deal," she said smiling as Tucker finally saw them. She signaled they were coming to him.

Sylvester laughed. "Don't want your own office, only ice cream."

"Well I'll take that too, but I just really want some ice cream." She walked across the street, checking each side to be sure no one would hit her. Sylvester followed close behind.

"Took you two long enough," Tucker said as he bit down on one of the ice cream scoops. Sylvester shuddered at the thought of biting ice cream the way Tucker did.

"We were discussin' business. Meet my new head of security." He smiled as Tucker paused mid bite. "How do you not have a brain freeze?"

Chapter Thirty-One
Game On

Dylan texted Savior when the program was finished. If they were lucky, they wouldn't have to worry about digital backups. There was concern, however, that they would have to worry about physical copies. While construction hadn't started across the hall in Rebecca's soon-to-be office, a single call to the contractor and he was pacing the floor plan. Every once in a while he would stop and note this and that.

As it was Savior gave Rebecca ten thousand dollars and told her to purchase things she either wanted or needed to fulfill her role. A smile spread across her face when he handed her cash.

"Trust me enough to know I'm not going to take off with it?" she asked.

"Well if you don't show up for work, then I'll just track you down and find out why." He smiled back.

She knew he could do it. He had been trained in the skills of detecting, but his abilities gave him an advantage no other person would have. The name he had since birth, he explained, was only to be used when clients weren't around. Rebecca understood and relished in the fact that she was close enough to know most of his secrets.

When the text from Dylan came in, Savior was alone in his office. He immediately transported to Dylan's house and knocked three times. Instead of utter silence, like last time, Savior could hear girls laughing and playing in the house.

A woman answered the door and questioned Savior's existence at her home. "Can I help you?" she asked.

"Oh I'm sorry to disturb…" he started.

"Not interested," she said as she started to close the door.

"I'm here to see Dylan," Savior quickly responded.

"Oh. I'm sorry. Thought you were one of the witnesses wandering the neighborhood." She gestured to a sign on the door. "*No Soliciting* seems to only mean everyone come to our door. Not to mention you're dressed like you are."

June wore a yellow sundress, with a white hair band holding her stick straight red hair down. She opened the door, reminded him of his shoes, then quickly closed the door behind him. "Dear you have a guest."

Dylan retreated from another room deep in the house, where the sound of the girls playing echoed all around. He wore similar clothing as the day before, but his face screwed up at the sight of Savior. When June turned her gaze to him he quickly replaced his shock with glee and reached out for Savior's hand.

"I wasn't expecting you so soon," he said. "Follow me. Hun we'll be a while."

June smiled at her husband as he led Savior away from the hall. He closed the door quickly behind the man, sat behind his desk and pressed the button. The light turned green, and his face once again resumed disbelief.

"How the hell did you get here that quickly? I only just sent you the text." He leaned back and fixated on Savior.

"I was in the neighborhood. Just a coincidence," he lied.

"I see. Let me tell you a little bit about myself. I'm an analyst at the FBI. I also work with another organization called the WHA, heard of them?" Dylan stared at Savior with a haughty air.

"No sir." Savior put his hands in his pockets.

"They handle…special people. Not my point. At my normal job I read people. So when I see someone blatantly lie to me, someone who seemed so honest just a day ago, it really makes me wonder who they are." Dylan grabbed a small flash drive and started twirling it around his fingers. "Makes me wonder if I should give this to you."

"I swear to you. I was just around the corner." Savior raised his hands in surrender.

"One last chance before I destroy this and every file in my system regarding it." He leaned toward his keyboard. "Wouldn't be the first time...."

Savior thought for a moment, watching the man, intent on knowing what he wanted to keep a secret. They stared at each other for a few moments before Savior relented and looked at his socked feet. "Fine," he said. "I'll tell you everything, but you'll want to experience it." He reached a hand out to shake with the man.

Dylan stood and grabbed Savior's hand, squeezing firmly. As the pressure built within him, his grip loosened, and he closed his eyes. Saviors grip seemed to tighten as the man tried to pull away.

When the pressure disappeared, he reopened his eyes only to find he was in an environment he wasn't familiar with. He looked around frantically as Savior slowly walked behind his desk and sat at his chair. When the man turned his attention to Savior, surprise and shock once again filled his features.

"Please have a seat," Savior said as he took his place behind his own desk.

Dylan shook as he sat, staring at Savior and clamping his mouth shut. He rested his hand on his chin before diving toward the trash can at the side of his desk. A smile spread across Savior's face as he listened to Dylan's lunch leave him.

"Sorry about that. Most the time I have the opportunity to tell someone what's about to happen. First time is usually the worst, and few get away without doin' that." Sylvester waited as Dylan hovered over the can, expecting more to come out. His voice changed into its normal, everyday voice. His secret seemed to be coming out as fast as Dylan's lunch.

When Dylan returned to his seat, he listened to Sylvester's story. Everything was explained in great detail. Dylan slowly, as the story continued, leaned back and became more comfortable. He took a tissue from the box on Sylvester's desk and wiped at his mouth.

"So you're saying that it's not something you were born with?" Dylan asked when the story concluded. He clearly believed the man, no longer doubting the kindness in Sylvester's heart.

"No sir. I'd introduce you to Tempus, but it has no way of communicating with anyone, but me. It can hear you though." Sylvester was leaning forward, looking Dylan in the eyes.

"I lied too," he said. "I do work for the FBI, but I've only followed stories about the WHA, not even sure they're real. However, I thought you would have been one of their experiments, or something."

"Someday I'd love to hear about them. For now, well, you know about me, and I've proven part of what I can do. Are we good?" Sylvester leaned back.

Dylan set the flash drive down. "When you're at the computer and have confirmed the files exist, plug this in. The program is going to start as soon as it is plugged in and will search for files needed for any computer, or operating system to run." He leaned back again.

"After it locates those it's going to mark them safe and continue searching for anything else. Once it locates any photos, or docs, it will systematically start wiping those away while retaining a file called confirmation on the drive. Do not leave the drive. It's going to contain all the information you asked for in that file. Bring it back to me and I'll extract the necessary data." Dylan finished and looked around. "Do you have a lemon-lime soda or something? To settle my stomach."

Sylvester stood up and gestured for Dylan to follow. They walked into Sylvester's two story apartment overlooking the mountains. There was a kitchen on each floor, though the upstairs was a balcony overlooking part of the downstairs area. Dylan was impressed with the posh nature of the apartment, especially when the man who owned it came from such a poor family. Sylvester hadn't gone into great detail, only said that his parents were killed by an Irish mobster named Micky.

He had the man sit at the island and reached into one of the cabinets below. Savior opened a warm Seven-Up and poured it into a glass. "I keep non-refrigerated soda for similar occasions." He smiled.

"So how many people know about this?" Dylan gestured to Sylvester.

"Well...including you..." Sylvester thought about everyone he met. "I think it's five, maybe six if we're including James. I never really told him about it, he just guessed at it, and I never confirmed with him."

"Rebecca's your head of security now?" he asked. He knew the answer, she had texted him right away.

Sylvester nodded. "What's your relationship with Rebecca?"

"I had a son about her age. He passed years back, before her mom died. She was a passerby who happened to see a lonely guy who needed someone to talk to." His voice cracked slightly. "She eventually started visiting him every time he was in the hospital. We tried to stay and spend as much time as we could. Life called and my job wouldn't let me take a leave of absence.

"It was hardest on Junie. He became more frail, and she would cry herself to sleep, eventually unable to drive the car because she was bawling so much. By the time Rebecca started seeing him we were only there once a day after work. She would always be there when we weren't." Dylan leaned forward and covered his face.

"I'm sorry to hear about your son. I wish there was something I could do to help." Sylvester came around and put his arm around the man.

"I just miss him so much. I wish I would have had more time with him, but even if I could..." Dylan stopped and leaned back, looking at Sylvester. "You could take me back, let me see him more, right?"

Sylvester nodded. "I could if that's what you really want. Thing is, it would have to be after he and Rebecca have formed their bond, and before you showed up. He would need to think nothing of the fact that you're there at that time, and later. Not to mention he would have to say nothing about it to your past self."

Dylan nodded and stood, walking to the window. "I would need to think about it."

Sylvester joined him. "Thank you for the flash drive. It's going to help a lot of people. If this is what you want for payment I'm happy to oblige."

"Thank you." A tear rolled down Dylan's face. "I could help you get some work, if you wanted. Maybe use that power for cases that have gone cold?" Dylan rested his forehead on his fist, which rested on the window.

"Let's focus on here and now." Sylvester took a drink from a cold soda. "However that would be amazing." He smiled, not at Dylan, but staring at the beautiful mountain scene before him.

Dylan nodded. "Thanks for listening."

"Not a problem. Ready to head back home?" he asked.

Again the man nodded, cautious of the potential he had for losing his lunch again.

Sylvester rested his arm across Dylan's shoulder, then the pressure once again built up and they disappeared. It was less than a second and they were back in Dylan's office. He reached below his desk and pushed the button. The light changed and they left the room.

"Any time you need me, I'll make sure I can help," Dylan said.

"If you decide to take me up on that offer let me know." Sylvester turned and shook the man's hand, grabbed his shoes, and made sure no one was around. "See ya." He vanished then and there. Leaving Dylan staring at open air.

When he reappeared in his apartment he pulled his phone out and called Tucker. It rang three times, then he picked up. "*Hello?*"

"Tuck it's me," Sylvester said.

"*Yeah, I know how caller ID works.*" Tucker laughed.

"Got the program. Ready to finish this?" he asked.

"*Absolutely.*" Tucker sounded like he was eating something.

"Well then...game on."

Chapter Thirty-Two
Overwhelming Odds

Once again Tucker and Sylvester were outside of the warehouse. It was night, and they were making sure no one was coming, or going. Each watched the empty street before walking up to the building. Sylvester received a glimpse inside, but he wasn't confident in the image in his mind.

Tempus told him that even it wasn't confident enough and they should utilize a quieter, and safer, method of entering the building. As the darkness settled, and silence continued to fill the area, Sylvester nodded. Normally they weren't petty thieves, breaking and entering at will, but was it really breaking and entering if the person was a thief in their own right?

"When I open this, they're going to be on us." Tucker was certain they had security. There would be no reason not to have security on a building that supposedly housed their nest egg. "What about freezin' time and handling things that way?"

"I'm not sure how well that'll work. I know if we do wind up opening that door while frozen it's going to be hard." Sylvester pulled out the key and handed it to Tucker. "No worries either way, I'll buzz us out if things get too hairy."

The key slid smoothly into the lock. There was a click as each tumbler lifted, and the lock turned. Tucker twisted the handle with ease. It was loose, almost as though it wasn't taken care of very well, and opened on rusty, squealing hinges.

Sylvester turned every direction, making sure no one was hidden, or that they didn't disturb anyone nearby. The area was dark, and once the squealing stopped, silence consumed everything. He smiled and looked at Tucker.

Two fingers signaled toward the warehouse. Each man walked in slowly, quiet as any mouse would have been. Tucker turned on a flashlight, trying not to unnecessarily light the area. The warehouse was filled with brown cardboard boxes. Hundreds of them covered every rack down every aisle.

"Glad we're not going through all of these," Tucker whispered.

It wasn't the plan, but they would need to inspect the contents of a few of the boxes at least. All in pitch black darkness. That made everything more difficult. Sylvester tapped Tucker on the shoulder and pointed at the box.

It was labeled with a date and seemingly random letters and numbers. Sylvester snapped a photo of the box, then pulled it from the shelf. The lid was taped down and dust half an inch thick covered it.

"Been here a long time." Though he whispered there was a slight echo. He pulled out his knife and cut the tape on the sides.

Inside were dozens of files, all with pictures. Some were clearly people they were blackmailing while others were pictures of people, beaten and bloodied. Sylvester thumbed his way through many of the files, realizing they were all evidence of the many people blackmailed for crimes they didn't commit, at least Sylvester hoped.

"All of these people," he whispered to Tucker. "I feel like we should help 'em all out."

"This is just one rack among dozens, if not hundreds. There's no way we'll be able to," Tucker said.

Sylvester nodded. "Let's find the computer and then we'll figure it out."

They walked until they found a wall, then turned and walked until they found the next. Nothing was lit. No upper windows guided them with dim lights to the place where they wanted to be. Not even an exit sign illuminated a door.

Darkness and the scale of the building made any progress they made slow. They searched an hour, every once in a while stopping to check the contents of this box, or that. All the while they grew concerned people were going to show at any moment.

Each of them had a gun holstered under their jacket. Neither wanted to use it. Sylvester returned a look that Tucker gave him in the darkness. "We can't stop even if someone does show up."

"So why don't you freeze time and give us an advantage." Tucker looked through a box as they spoke.

"Cause I don't want the excess strain from lifting seemingly weightless lids." He too was searching the contents of a box.

None of the files in the boxes had more than a few letters at the top, making it difficult to ascertain who, or what, the files contained without going through them. The numbers and letters didn't seem to make any sense. He looked through a box labeled *NB1230C50KT20.* Since the label didn't make sense he opened the file and started going through the contents.

Inside were specific details about the person, Nolan Bryan. *Must be the initials first,* he considered. The rest of the label continued to allude him. He made a mental note and once again considered how vast the warehouse was.

"What if you just go and find the room with the computers?" Tucker suggested, snapping Sylvester back to reality.

"I suppose that would be a good idea. I think the first two letters are the person they're extorting. You keep looking through here and I'll do what I can," he said as he grabbed Tucker's arm.

In an instant things felt different. A thickness that didn't exist before hung in the air. Tucker looked around, seeing no difference, but feeling the additional weight just the same. "This feels weird every time."

"Tell me about it. I've done it dozens of times, and I never feel any better about it," Sylvester said as he pushed the lid closed. "I'll find wherever they have their office, but you gotta find anything with SK as the first part of the file."

Tucker nodded and pushed a box open. It was like opening something buried in a few inches of sand. Not impossible, but definitely tough. Even pulling the files inside was like pulling magnets apart. Tucker continued sifting through boxes as Sylvester darted toward the next wall.

After reaching the final wall, he found a staircase leading up. Sylvester's flashlight swiveled to the top and then, for the first time, he saw what happened to light when time was frozen.

Up close it was just like regular light. As the light covered more and more distance it distorted in every direction. Light did reach its target, but only after creating fractured lines in the air that eventually widened so much that it covered more of the wall than it should. He was mesmerized as the lines pulsed creamy white, almost like lightning in a storm. The door was bright orange with a silver handle. It read *Office Manager*.

Sylvester waded his way up the stairs as quickly as he could. It still felt like running through a pool of water, but in a matter of seconds he was at the top and holding the knob in his hand. With the extra weight of time being held still, the handle wouldn't budge.

There were windows, but everything inside was dark and he could only see walls. The platform at the top of the stairs could fit two people easily, but it did not extend to the windows. When the warehouse was in operation, a foreman and supervisors would look over the floor, that much Sylvester was sure of.

He tried sliding the key for the entrance into the lock, but it wouldn't push in. "Well Tempus, what're we gonna do. It's gotta be in there."

Unbeknownst to Sylvester, Tempus was already considering ways to overcome this burden. It watched through Sylvester's eyes, absorbing every detail of their surroundings. ***Focus on the windows. Can you see anything that could be considered floor?***

Sylvester turned to the left side, only seeing wall past the window. The right was slightly different. It had a desk littered in papers. "How 'bout that?" he asked as he focused on it.

Crouch down and get ready. As soon as his vision lowered Tempus started the process. Seconds later Sylvester was crouching on the desk, the familiar pop signaling when he could open his eyes.

You don't always have to close your eyes, Tempus complained.

"You don't have to deal with all the strain from traveling that way. It's dizzying." Sylvester considered the one time he left his eyes open. He wasn't blind, but he saw the streaks of nothingness across his vision for a week. What he witnessed frightened him.

It was an empty expanse where existence seemed to be eradicated and time had no meaning for anyone, or anything. He made the mistake of looking at his own hands in that split second, only to realize they were nothing, yet everything all at once. It was matter in its most primal existence and it was frightening.

The office had nothing, save for the disheveled papers and desk that Sylvester crouched on. "Damn, I was sure this was it," he lamented.

Keep lookin', Tempus prodded.

The office seemed to lead to another room. At the back was a door with no windows to see through. Below the door was a faintly glowing pulsating light. It was amber for a second, then green the next. The same lights that his Ethernet connection gave when successfully connected to the network. This had to be their digital backup.

Fear overwhelmed him as he slowly walked to the door. As he expected, the door was closed and locked. He tried pushing the handle down, but it wouldn't budge. Unlike the entrance, this door was brand new. The key he copied also would not work in this door any more than the other.

Sylvester lay on his stomach, turned his head to the side, and tried to get a peek under the door. There was just a tiny gap big enough for the faint light inside to barely escape. *How in the hell do we get in there?*

Well, we're going to have to travel to a time when it was opened, Tempus announced. ***We're already here. We'll just go back to when it was in operation. Then we'll enter and shouldn't have any problems after that.***

It all seemed so simple for Tempus. Sylvester considered the problem that they actually faced. When would a door like this be open for all to enter? "How?" Was all he could muster.

We go back every year until we find it open. Won't take long.

Sylvester considered the age of some of the boxes he'd seen. While some had firm cardboard sides, others were worn down to the point that he and Tucker had been surprised they hadn't been swapped. Others had sides that were ripped or torn at some point and had only been fixed with duct tape. Inside, the files were ancient. By the look of the papers, they were from the eighties. "I guess we start in nineteen-eighty."

Chapter Thirty-Three
A Quick and Eerie Jaunt

The world seemed to fuzz and fade all around him as time snapped him back to what was quickly becoming his favorite decade. Tempus' power brought them to the year nineteen eighty. The building hadn't changed, but the feeling of the area was very different. It was almost as if it were brand new, instead of more than forty years old.

The office had several more desks than before, all with typewriters sitting on them. Several had stacks of papers, while another was completely clean. Sylvester looked at that desk, thinking that the person who once resided there no longer did, thanks to some clerical error, or other unfortunate incident.

There was an eerie calm about the building that unsettled him. Silence that surrounded him seemed unreal, and he could tell, just by the movement of his body, that time flowed like it naturally did. Still there was a pressure, like someone was watching him. He confirmed he was alone, checking the area all around.

There was an expectation that there would be a security guard inspecting the area for any wrongdoing, but, luckily, he didn't run into anyone. He turned his attention to the door and turned the golden knob. It was the typical knob you expected to find in the eighties, but unlike its counterpart in the future, this gave him access to the room.

He stepped into a small office, it was likely the owner or plant manager's office. A desk and chair were inside, and a phone sat on the desk. The office furniture barely fit in the room. Sylvester flipped the light switch. One flickering tube above the desk lit part way, only to be outshined by the other within the same ballast. It shone with a fluorescent haze, giving Sylvester enough light to absorb the room. After he was done he decided it was nothing special.

"Good enough?" he asked the parasite.

Sure, ready to head back? Tempus asked.

Sylvester paused a moment. The lingering sensation that someone was watching him still pushed at his consciousness. "Gimme a minute," he said.

Sylvester returned to the front office, looking in every corner again. His flashlight darted from desk to desk, searching for some figure that should have been there according to the nagging feeling. He shined the light through the plate glass windows. Nothing stared back at him. Still, the eyes that he couldn't find felt like they were watching his every move.

Sylvester walked to the entrance to the upper offices and opened the door. His flashlight inspected the balcony. Empty just like it was in the future. The feeling wouldn't shake, and he had all the time in the world to peruse. No security cameras of any sort could account for the sense that someone was watching him. Regardless, the building didn't seem to have any cameras hung up anywhere.

"Hey, who the hell are you!" a voice rang from somewhere in the dark below.

Sylvester turned and saw a man dressed in a traditional security guard uniform. The man's flashlight pointed at the balcony and Sylvester covered his face as he turned to walk back into the office. When he reached for the handle something blocked him. Something he couldn't see.

Everything that happened next slowed to the point that Sylvester thought Tempus was the cause. What once was an empty space, suddenly filled with a black mass that took his hand in one of its own. The other wrapped around Sylvester's neck as it pushed him toward the rail.

It was so quick he didn't realize he was falling until gravity pulled him toward the concrete below. Every foot he fell his heart raced faster and his blood pumped. His bladder was ready to empty. "Tempus!" Sylvester shouted into the air.

The world hazed again, then froze, with Sylvester inches from the carpeted ground behind the locked office door. He opened his eyes after a moment, realizing he hadn't become a blood stain on the concrete. Sylvester put his hands on the floor, then his knees.

"What the hell was that?" Sylvester asked while he shook.

Tempus was silent at first. Clearly it had thoughts coursing through its own mind. *I couldn't do anything. I couldn't use any of my powers until we were almost dead...well you were almost dead.*

"That thing nearly killed us," Sylvester complained.

It was the strangest feeling. It touched us and then...I don't even know how to describe the feeling I had. The closest thing would be like I was being shocked with electricity. You didn't feel that? The parasite was intrigued, though it's voice gave away the fear and dread it felt.

Sylvester stood and pat his body down. His pants were dry. He could move, and his neck seemed fine. It took him a second to realize that he should be concerned the black mass was waiting for him. His eyes shot to each corner of the room, expecting to see it.

"Alright let's get this done," he said when he was satisfied they were once again alone. "We'll have to do this in real time. Make sure time's flowin'."

The computer was on, the monitor lit the back of the room. It was locked, of course, but once the USB slid into the port, the lock screen disappeared. A black window opened, and lines of text started to run. Sylvester watched the process. The program first found all the files that involved pictures, or videos, then copied the names and contact details of the victims.

The process ran for thirty minutes as Sylvester texted Tucker, letting him know to be prepared. As the next lines scrolled across the screen it revealed that the program was following the data flow from the local computer to the cloud where the information was backed up.

Another few minutes passed and the door to the warehouse could be heard flying open and slamming against a rack. Sylvester shot Tucker a text, warning him to hide, or get upstairs. Tucker quickly replied with 'k' and then fell silent.

The computer finished erasing the data. A message read *Nearly Done,* then spouted dozens of lines, mostly covering the same text. The code was tracing the files to each IP address that had ever accessed the information. Sylvester wasn't sure to what extent the program would destroy the data, but he knew it would be final. Only Dylan knew the finite details of what exactly the program did to everything that accessed the data.

The door to the front part of the office opened, then closed quickly. Sylvester sat in silence, drawing his gun. Someone on the outside tried to open the door, but it was still locked. "Sylvester, it's me," Tucker whispered.

He stood up from the desk and walked to the door. "I can't unlock it from this side," he quietly replied. It was only a few seconds later when Sylvester popped next to Tucker, grabbed him, then popped back to the room. Tucker staggered as Sylvester returned to the desk. The screen had *The program is finished, your client is safe* scrawled across the screen. The drive pulled smoothly from the computer, and he put it in his pocket.

A loud crash could be heard in the outer office, followed by a key entering the lock. Sylvester rushed to Tucker's side as the door flew open. A gun pointed in the doorway, suspended in the air. The man holding the gun was none other than Micky Antonio. An angry scowl covered his face, but he didn't move.

Sylvester considered the situation. The person who murdered his parents was right in front of him and he had control over what happened next. Tucker recognized the man, just as Sylvester had. He knew the story, and he saw the look in his friend's eyes.

"He's not worth it," Tucker said.

"No one would know if we just..." He looked at Tucker. "If I just killed him."

"Another time maybe, but we've got to find a way to get rid of all the physical evidence. That's more important than what you want to do right now." Tucker rested a hand on Sylvester's shoulder.

"Alright." Sylvester shook his head. "Let's burn this place to the ground then."

Chapter Thirty-Four
Cleansing Flame

They disappeared from the building. When they reappeared, time was frozen, and both of them held two gas cans. Sylvester had no intentions of actually murdering Micky in such a cowardly way. Tucker worked on pouring the now viscous liquid over each of the racks containing the cardboard boxes.

Sylvester slowly poured the liquid over the ground. A line wound through the warehouse and out the front door. Half of his container was left when he walked back in and started pouring the gasoline over the racks and boxes on the opposite side of Tucker. The liquid poured slowly, seemingly weightless lines that rested above their intended target.

Sylvester considered the way things worked with his powers. Tempus hadn't really given him a good explanation. He knew that the only reason objects even moved while time stood still was because he had some connection to them. Simply touching the objects was enough to loosen them, but only a little.

As he walked down each aisle, watching the process, the black figure popped into his mind. *Somehow that thing has the ability to disrupt Tempus.* He didn't want to be free of the parasite. The benefits of having the creature within his mind and body far outweighed the consequences. Over the last few years, only Tempus was left.

They needed to find a way to counteract whatever it was. "Tempus, you ever hear of anything like that thing that threw me over the rail?" he asked.

Nothing. I haven't ever encountered anything like it either. Some thing has the ability to chase you to points in time. That's a real problem. Tempus paused as he considered a thought. ***To top it off, I don't know how we would counteract the effects without being face to face with it again.***

"I guess just don't put us in a dangerous situation?" Sylvester joked.

Dull echoing footsteps came closer as Tucker closed the distance between them. As they met he set down the nearly empty container, looked at Sylvester and smiled. "Left a way for those knuckleheads to get out right?"

Sylvester only nodded.

"Great then let's light this joint and get the hell outta here. You got the thumb drive?" Tucker asked.

Sylvester nodded again.

"What am I talking to a statue, did you suddenly lose your ability to speak?" Tucker smiled at him.

"No, just have a lot on my mind," Sylvester said as he and Tucker walked to the entrance.

"Y'know, I'm going to start losing weight working in these conditions." Tucker laughed.

The thick atmosphere was tough to walk through, but Sylvester didn't think that those effects would have that effect. "Oh c'mon you don't need to lose too much weight, what you really need is a wig." Sylvester jabbed his friend in the ribs.

"Can Tempus help me out with that? I'd love to have some golden locks rollin' down my back." Tucker smiled while they exited the building.

"Nope, sorry." Sylvester pulled a lighter from his pocket.

"Sprung for the spendy one eh?" Tucker smiled at the red plastic lighter resting in Sylvester's hand.

He pulled out a few wadded up newspaper pages and set them where the gas would land. "Alright Tempus let's do this," he said, ignoring Tucker's comment.

As time released the liquid fell to the ground, splashing the wads of paper. With two flicks, the lighter came to life, flame flicking back and forth in the slight breeze. The paper quickly caught and turned to balls of flame.

A trail of orange formed shortly after the paper touched it and followed along the path. Sylvester watched from the door as flame crawled up the first rack, then spread quickly to each other rack.

"What the hell's going on?" A voice rang from inside, high above the flaming debris below.

Sylvester looked at Tucker, then inside. "Sorry Tuck, I've got to do somethin'."

Before Tucker could say anything Sylvester blinked from existence. He looked inside, listening for a gunshot signaling the anger and frustration that had built for years would be over. He would never find peace and the pain would never be relieved.

The only thing Tucker actually heard though, was the sound of angry men yelling. They were trying to get down stairs that Sylvester claimed were free and easy to escape. Tucker waited.

★★★

Savior appeared in the computer room. Micky and his men were more focused on the problem they had with flames slowly crawling the old wooden stairs. Slowly and quietly Savior snuck from the room.

Micky let his men assess the situation, while he ordered them from behind. Savior smiled as he closed in on Micky's back and wrapped his hand across his mouth. He wouldn't kill Micky, not today at least, but he would leave him with a black eye in the middle of nowhere.

They both popped out of the warehouse and appeared in an empty field somewhere Savior had been. He didn't know where as he let Tempus decide where they were going, so long as it was the same day and time. The field was dark, and coyotes howled somewhere in the distance.

As soon as they arrived Savior dropped his hand and let Micky fall. The man wretched as he balled his fists. Vomit spewed from his mouth and covered the fists he'd made.

"Should stop eating so much garlic Micky," Savior mocked the man.

"Wh…" Micky tried to speak, but wave after wave of puke fountained from him.

Savior smiled. The pain and discomfort Micky was experiencing was well deserved, though not enough… not in the slightest. Savior pushed the man on to his back with his foot as he spewed bile once more. Chunks splashed over the man's face.

"You done yet?" he asked.

Micky screamed in agony and anger. The man wiped at his face, smearing the chunks across his chin and cheeks. Every swipe became more frantic, as though he couldn't stand the idea of having the dirty mix touching his face.

Savior couldn't blame him. If their roles were reversed, he would have felt the same. He laughed loudly, at times forcing the laughter out. His intention was to sound slightly insane. Micky was trying to push himself away from the cackling man.

"What do you want?" Micky finally asked. "Where are we?" The man took in his surroundings.

"I want vengeance bestowed upon you." Savior's accent grew thick with every word he spoke. Anyone who heard him would think he was a preacher, spouting to his flock. Savior was no preacher though and he reached for the man's shirt, pulling him to his feet. His hands were covered in Micky's dinner, and he rubbed the substance in Micky's hair, helping to slick it back.

"What'd I do to you?" In the dark Micky couldn't recognize the man whose picture was folded in his wallet. All he could see was a silhouette screaming at him.

"You killed people I cared about. All over a little bit of money." Savior pulled his hand back and swung with all his might.

Micky tumbled back and sprawled across the ground when he landed, grabbing his eye, and sobbing softly. "That's not helpful. You know how many people I've killed?"

"You want their names?" Savior grabbed Micky by the back of his shirt and drug him through the dirt. When the shirt finally ripped, Micky once again faced the pile of his puke. There was a telltale *schick-tch* as Savior racked the slide of his gun and rested the barrel on the back of Micky's head. "Eat it."

Micky's eyes were already wide. When the man demanded he eat his own vomit, they nearly bulged from his skull. "What?" he stalled.

"Eat your puke. Don't wretch it back up either. If you do I'm going to shoot you."

Micky hesitated. He considered pushing the gun back, but he could feel the pressure on the back of his head. If he tried, the trigger would drop, and he would die.

"NOW!" Savior yelled and fired the pistol into the ground just to the side of the pile.

Micky scooped up a handful of the vile smelling substance. He stopped just before his mouth and started to lower his hand. His stomach was already churning at the scent. "I can't," he cried back in desperation.

"Fine." The gun pushed deeper in the back of his head as Savior knelt down and took the man's hand into his own. "Open your fucking mouth," he demanded.

Another shot rang out, disappearing somewhere in the ground next to Micky and within the pile. He obliged as the barrel returned to the back of his head, the barrel burning his scalp. Micky resisted Savior at first, his muscles far less superior to that of the ex-farmhand. The pile of vomit in his hands entered his mouth and each of his nostrils. Savior smeared the rest across his face. Tears fell from Micky's face, both angry and despairing.

Savior held the hand on Micky's face, once again covering his mouth. "Swallow it," he whispered menacingly in the man's ear. There were two gulps, and Micky felt his own hand voluntarily lower to the ground and scoop another pile.

This continued until Savior was tired. He wiped the foul liquid across the back of Micky's head and shirt, cleaning his hands the best he could. The gun returned to its holster, and he kicked Micky back on to his back.

Micky was exhausted and ill. He looked like he was going to puke again but refused as he stared at the dark stranger. "What were their names?" he asked through gritted teeth.

Savior considered whether he should answer the question. He had nothing to fear from this pitiful man, but why risk revealing who he was? "I ever see you in the entire state of Colorado again, this will be the least of your worries. I'll know. My people will let me know if you're even suspected in that state." Savior smiled. "I ever see you again…this'll be the least of your worries." He reiterated to dramatic effect.

Savior stepped back and let Micky be. "What's your fucking name you piece of shit?" the gangster yelled.

Two steps was all it took for Savior to once again be in his face. He turned the flashlight of his phone on and shined it in his face. "You know who I am. You killed my parents, Al and Janet Pemberton."

Micky's face sank. He'd searched for the man in the photo for years, thinking he was the bigger threat. "I've seen your face. I'm comin' for you."

"If I even get the slightest feelin' that you're behind anything I'm investigating…" Savior smiled an evil smile. "Then the things that the rednecks in Deliverance tried to do to Burt Reynold's friends…" The smile grew wider, and Savior licked his lips. "Let's just say you'll prefer them."

To make his point, with Tempus's help, he vanished before Micky's eyes. The man was startled as he looked from side to side. Finally alone, he rolled over, and emptied his stomach once again.

★★★

It was only a few minutes for Tucker when Sylvester appeared next to him. He had been gone at least an hour, but he was safe from interrupting any timeline issues. Tucker wasn't surprised at his friend's sudden appearance, but he sniffed the air.

"I didn't kill him," Sylvester admitted.

"We should get outta here, but then tell me what happened." Tucker placed his hand on Sylvesters shoulder as Micky's men finally made it safely, if slightly singed, from the staircase. Before they exited the building, Savior and Tucker were gone, and the building was a engulfed in flame. Every box turned to ash with every second the flames grew bigger. Their contents would no longer be a viable source for anyone to profit from. The men fled the wreckage of their scheme, only realizing Micky wasn't with them when they entered their car and sped away.

Chapter Thirty-Five
Wrapping Up

They sat in Sylvester's office. The news in the background was reporting the fire they started, the one that would easily be traced, if not for Tempus's abilities. Tucker was holding in a laugh, the news not concerning him. "You really made that goombah eat his own puke?" He couldn't hold it anymore and laughed.

Sylvester blushed. He was slightly ashamed of what he did, all except the black eye he left the man with. "Yeah, well, I coulda done worse."

Tucker wiped his eyes. "I suppose that's true, but it's still funny."

"I have no idea where he is," he said.

I'll tell you that, Tempus rang out. *You remember that place we went to when you spent a few weeks in the eighties.*

"Hold on Tuck, Tempus is giving me a riddle to solve," he said as he bent his head. "Be more specific. Do you have any idea how many places we went?"

Tempus did. He understood fully how many places they visited in that time. *We took that train to Estonia and wound up in the middle of nowhere because it broke down. Remember.*

Sylvester's eyes widened. "You're tellin' me we took him to Estonia?"

Tucker broke out laughing again.

You bet. He's miles from any civilization. He's gonna be lucky if he even finds civilization. He's got his phone

though, so he'll be alright. Tempus was calm and relaxed, even jovial.

Sylvester eased and began laughing. Their mirth lasted for twenty minutes before they wiped their eyes and calmed down. They caught their breath, giggling every so often.

"What's next?" Tucker asked.

"Well, we go to Dylan, then give Rebecca the phone list." Sylvester stood up. "Then case closed as far as I'm concerned."

"No deaths reported, but the fire seems to have caused irreparable damage to the abandoned warehouse," The reporter was saying.

Sylvester smiled as he listened to the news. They hurt no one, except those who deserved it. Innocent people were going to be given their lives back, though Sylvester still wondered who the man in the photos with the victims was. He was someone connected with Micky, but it didn't matter. The man in charge was stranded thousands of miles away and knew better than to return to Colorado.

Tucker stood up. "Well brotha I've gotta get goin'." He reached a hand out to his friend. "Thank you for tellin' me and lettin' me be a part of this."

Sylvester raised a finger and pulled out his wallet. He quickly counted the bills in his head and handed a thick stack of hundred dollar bills to Tucker. "Told ya I'd pay ya," he said.

Tucker took the bills, unfolded them, and counted. "This is five grand. You said a thousand. And honestly I wasn't even gonna ask for it." Tucker smiled trying to hand the money back. "Proof was all I needed."

Sylvester shook his head. "You earned this." He smiled. "I have another offer for ya."

Tucker placed the stack of bills in the inner pocket of his coat. "What's that?"

"Move your office into my building. I'll even hire someone to build you an apartment to your specifications if you want." Sylvester walked to the door and opened it. "Get rid of that apartment you live in, that you pay thousands of dollars for, not to mention upgrade that broke down office."

Tucker stood next to Sylvester and thought. His face was serious for the first time since they arrived back in the office. "I really wanna say yes, but I don't know. That's a tremendous offer. I'd be my own separate entity?" he asked.

"Your agency wouldn't be affiliated with mine, unless you want it to." Sylvester smiled. "Or need assistance."

Tucker placed a hand over the bills in his inner pocket and looked off in the distance. "Let me think on it. I'll let you know soon." Tucker reached for Sylvester's hand again. His grip tightened when 's met his.

Sylvester pulled the man in and gave him a hug as they shook. "You decide. I'll be here. Thank you again for your help on this."

The embrace ended and they pulled apart as sounds of heels echoing down the hall followed the ding of the elevator. Jada Jarlson appeared around the corner, heading straight for Sylvester and Tucker.

"Looks like I'm about to have company," Sylvester said as he waved Tucker off. "Miss Jarlson, what can I do for ya?"

She said nothing, only placed her hand on his face and kissed him with a fire that the woman seemed to always carry in her wake. Sylvester didn't hesitate this time and met every kiss with equal passion.

They moved away from the door, Sylvester closing it as she pushed him against the wall. With a flit of his wrist the door locked, and his hand moved up and down her body. They rolled so he pressed her against the wall, then she pushed him to the floor.

She stopped and sat on top of the man. He stared at her. She wore a miniskirt and six inch heels with a white blouse sheer enough that he could see her black lacy bra. "Sure know how to make an entrance," he said.

"You haven't seen anything yet." She winked as she stood. "None of that was my intent though." She reached her other hand down, taking his empty hand, and helping him up.

"Well if that's you sayin' hello then I would love more hellos from you." He smiled as he brushed his pants down.

"Some days it is. Today I meant to ask you to dinner." Jada brushed her blouse down and straightened her hair.

"Sure, right now, or you wanna finish what we started." He was eager and definitely ready. His eyes closed slightly as he eyed her playfully.

"Oh we best do it now, cause I don't see us making dinner if we do anything else." Jada unlocked the office door and pulled him away.

Sylvester was in a good mood because of the case. Her entrance made his mood that much better. They rode the elevator down to the parking lot and drove off to a place she directed him.

★★★

The next morning he smiled as he woke with her arm resting across his chest. He moved it slowly, barely causing her to stir. Though he knew more about his tenant, it was not enough to say that she was anything more than a fling. However, he could say that she was the most fun he had in a long time, possibly even before Ira left.

His face dropped at the thought of the woman he should have been married to. She was off somewhere, doing her own thing, same as Tommy. He was still where he said he would be, using his powers mostly for good. The thought of what he did to Micky made him smile while he prepared eggs and coffee.

Jada walked out, his sheet the only thing covering her. "Why'd you leave?" she pouted slightly.

"Because we both have a long day ahead of us," he said. "Besides I thought you could use a nice breakfast after last night's endeavors."

She smiled. "Not many men treat me like this. Most of the time they throw me out as soon as they finish."

"I am not most men," he said. Disgust over what others of his sex considered *okay* filled him. "I'm gonna be honest with ya Jada, I'm not lookin' for anything serious. I'm just not ready. Anytime you need someone who's gonna listen, or whatever..." He smiled and winked at her. "I'm happy to be there for you."

He didn't expect her to smile, but she did. The kiss on his cheek was even more unexpected when she walked up to him. "Oh honey," she said. "I appreciate you and your honesty. I'm gonna be honest with you, I'm married."

The shock hit Sylvester like a woman slapping him across the face. "What?" he mustered after a moment of silence.

"He lives in Africa. He does the same thing. When he's in town it's all about us, but when he's out of town, which he is ninety-five percent of the year, our relationship is completely open." She sat at one of his barstools and watched him.

He smiled at her. "Well I guess we're on the same page then. What if I change my mind though?"

Jada's smile faded. "Don't. We can't be together for more than what we're already doing."

Sylvester nodded as he finished making her breakfast. When she finished and dressed he walked her to the door, where she kissed him, pulling him deep into it. She walked down the hall without another word.

He closed the door and showered, berating himself for letting this happen. While he wasn't ready for a relationship, he also didn't want to be part of some strange and convoluted friend with benefits...while her husband wasn't in town. His mood darkened as he dressed, only to lighten when he felt the thumb drive in his pocket.

He dialed quickly and waited until Dylan picked up. "You ready to extract the data?" he asked. "Be right there."

Sylvester disappeared from his apartment. He needed to finish his job, not to mention get away from everything that was just revealed. Once again, he stood on Dylan's porch and waited. This time Dylan answered the door and showed him inside.

He discussed the program and confirmed everything worked as it should have, but Sylvester gave only quick yes and no answers. The conversation was very one-sided as Dylan tapped his fingers quickly. Thirty minutes later Sylvester was leaving the house with a list of names on twelve sheets of paper. Front and back.

The last piece of the case was to leave Rebecca in charge of informing everyone on the list that they should be freed from their blackmailers. He called Samuel, and the call lasted all of thirty seconds. He told Samuel he was outside his warehouse, which after the call he was, thanks to Tempus.

"Mister Savior," Samuel said as he reached his hand out.

Savior shook his hand and smiled. "Just Savior."

"Ah very well. Is everything done?" he asked, shock and surprise filling him.

"Yessir. Now I was gonna make you hold up your end of the bargain," he said. "It was brought to my attention that might not be the safest thing."

Samuel cocked his head and looked at Savior.

"I have a head of security now. Someone I trust to do this. She will call all of them and we'll handle it from there. All you need to do is not fall for somethin' like this again." Savior smiled. "However, if you ever need any help again, call me, you have my number." Savior turned around. "And if you ever want me to help someone, be there to introduce me."

Samuel watched the man walk down the street. The thought of how Savior managed to get there without his car never occurred to him. Samuel returned to his warehouse and sat at his desk. He was out the money, but he was freed from the scam. For the first time in months Samuel smiled a real smile.

Chapter Thirty-Six
Mind Reader

Weeks passed with a blur after Kripke's case. Sylvester found himself more often than not roaming his building. Tucker still hadn't given him a response, other than the obligatory '*I'm still thinking about it.*'

As it was, autumn was falling upon the world and he watched as the leaves of trees turned from a fresh green to a brittle yellow, or orange. Thanksgiving used to be his favorite time of year, where he would spend time with his parents, and any family that may come from out of town. They were never invited to others' homes, since most of the Pemberton line worked dead end jobs in ghost towns that were dying just the same as Cedar Vale.

Still, he hadn't heard from any of the extended family, not even for them to attend the funerals. It was a few of the townsfolk who knew Janet and Al best and himself in attendance. It was a quiet occasion, mostly with people telling him how sorry they were for his loss. None were surprised that he planned to sell the farm, ridding himself of a home where such a heinous act occurred.

He sat on the couch, staring out of his window. There was a buzz in his head suddenly and he stood up, walking to the bathroom, and popping three Tylenol. The buzz seemed to grow in intensity and changed to a tickle over time. The pills didn't help. It was three hours of the insane buzzing that even Tempus couldn't stop.

They argued about the annoying feeling, but his only reply was **It's annoying me too** followed by a **damn dragons.** Sylvester didn't push. So they sat there and took the annoyance in stride. The buzz reached its zenith, and he wanted to claw his eyes out by the end.

He pressed a button on his phone to dim the windows to a reflective black. Even with pitch black darkness swallowing him, the buzzing never stopped, and he wrapped his arm around his face to try and nullify the pulsing pain. It was the worst thing he felt in his entire life.

Then, as abruptly as it started, it was finished. "Oh thank God," Sylvester said to himself in the dark.

Then she popped in his head. His tenant and sometimes lover. They hadn't spoken since she confessed to being married. Sylvester was certain that he didn't want to be in some strange love triangle where one person had a better advantage than he did.

He sat up and undimmed the window, revealing a darkening landscape. Weeks of no work were compounded with days of boredom and loneliness. The woman popped in his head more, and more often during those times. If only Ira were still there and still wanted to be with him. Anger washed over him the better part of the last few years. It was directed at her and Tommy, but if she were in front of him, he would gladly take her back and sweep her away to wherever, or whenever, she wanted.

Tears fell, and he quickly wiped them away. The past was a cruel mistress that he had more control over than others, but he couldn't bring himself to change how things happened between them. This was the life he wanted, she just happened to be a part of other people's lives instead of his.

Buzz...buzz...buzzzzzzzzzzzzzz.

The office doorbell rang incessantly. He wiped away hours of stress and pain, rubbing his hands across his face, and stood up. His attire did not say he was a professional. Sweatpants and a four sizes too big sweater showcasing his minor depression adorned his body. Weeks without work, still paying people for doing nothing, had worn him down.

Buzz...buzz, buzz, buzz, buzzzzzzzzzzz.

"Yeah I'm comin'," he yelled through the closed door, to the other closed office door, leading to the hallway outside.

He pulled the first door open, took four steps and paused. There were two people waiting on the other side of the frosted window. Only silhouettes of who they were, could be seen. One was taller than the other. From the figures one was a woman, darker skinned, the other a pasty white male. Both wore suits.

"I'm not really prepared for clients at the moment. Can you come back in like an hour," he asked through the door.

"We're with the NSA sir. Please open the door before we break it in," the woman said in a calm, yet demanding tone.

The man snickered.

"Shut up. Act professional," she whispered as she lectured.

"You realize I can still hear you even if the door's closed." Sylvester's hands rested on his hips as he watched them.

"Just open the door," the man said. His voice reminded Sylvester of a slightly accented southern man, possibly from Texas.

There was a click as he unlocked the door, then a slight creak as it opened. Both walked in, looked at Sylvester, then at each other. They seemed to be having a conversation, but neither spoke a word. He eyed the man first. Shorter hair, combed back and held in place with what seemed like a handful of hair gel. The tough texture of his hair reminded Sylvester of the dying leaves outside. It was dark, not quite black, but an extremely dark brown. He smiled with straight teeth and an ordinary face. By the look of him he was the senior agent between them.

Her skin was dark, her hair pulled back in a long pony tail. The sheen of her hair made him think that she had some Native American blood running through her veins. Her hair did not remind him of an African American woman's hair, as she appeared to be. It was stick straight and shined with a natural brilliance he had only seen in Native American's. Her face was thin, and she had a sincere beauty about her without even trying.

They seemed to be frozen in time as they regarded each other, a strange stare piercing the other persons eyes. Sylvester watched, and waited, for a few minutes until he couldn't take it any longer. "Alright you're in. What can I do for ya?" His accent always seemed thicker as his level of annoyance grew, his persona had not taken its place yet.

The man broke the stare, turning his attention to Sylvester, as though just realizing he was there. "My apologies. My name is Irwin Jackson, agent of the National Security Agency. This is my partner." He gestured to the slim woman.

"Agent Aiyana Evans. We need your help," she said, eyes meeting his own with a fiery heat.

"You're with the NSA. Whad'ya need my help for?" Sylvester asked as he retreated behind his desk.

"Perhaps we've been too hasty," agent Jackson said. "We can wait here if you want to go change."

Agent Evans nodded.

"Nonsense. Y'all were basically bustin' my door down. You couldn't seem to wait before, but now that you've seen me, you suddenly want to." He was perturbed.

"I told you we should have called first," Jackson whispered to Evans.

"I'm aware." She glared at him.

"Tell me what you want and then I can decide whether I want to bother, or not." Sylvester finally took on his alter ego of Savior and kicked his feet up.

Again they regarded each other. The voice change throwing them slightly. "The truth..." she started "we're hunting a monster."

For the first time since they came in, Savior broke a smile. "A monster?" He chuckled to himself. If only they knew what he could do. Then he remembered the shadowy creature he encountered while working the Kripke case. "Alright tell me about this creature." The smile remained, but his mind jumped into the serious nature of his work.

"You started this. You tell him." The man said, sitting down and crossing his arms.

"Do you want to change first? I'd rather deal with the professional detective we've heard about rather than the sickly man we're looking at." She still stood.

For the first time since opening the door Sylvester felt out of place. He looked down at himself and stood up. "Let's take this to a more comfortable location," he said, trying not to sound too creepy.

The door to his apartment opened and he showed them to his living room. "I'm gonna clean myself up. Feel free to make yourselves at home. Remote's on the table and soda and other drinks in the fridge. It's close to dinner time and I need to eat, so maybe we can make this a dinner meetin'?"

Evans and Jackson exchanged glances and then both nodded. "That's fine, it's on us if you'll just hear us out." There was a knowing look in her eyes, one that seemed to say she knew everything about him, and he knew absolutely nothing about her.

A hand waved in the air, and he retreated to his bathroom. Thirty minutes later he stepped out quietly. He could hear them discussing something below, but couldn't quite make out what it was.

The word 'parasite' and 'travel' came up, but that was all he could hear. It wasn't enough to cause him concern, many people received parasites by traveling, but the fact that they were in his home, and talking about things that implied him gave, him cause to pause. ***Be prepared Tempus,*** he spoke to the parasite.

Hushed tones met him as he walked downstairs, then silence when he arrived on the same floor as them. They stared at him, and he returned their gaze, happy to have the forty-five in its holster, but hoping he wouldn't have to use it.

"Let's not play any games. You've caught my interest, but I need to know what you know about me...and how." Savior smiled as he spoke. He pulled his suit jacket back and revealed the butt of his holstered gun.

Jackson pulled back his own jacket, placing his hand on the butt of his gun. Evans was calmer, only looking at Savior, not at her partner. A look of perturbed frustration filled the man's eyes in response to something Savior couldn't see, or hear.

She only spoke when agent Jackson's face went slack with indignant resignation. "We're not actually NSA. Our names are real, and we really are agents." She smiled at him. "We're with an organization known only by the acronym WHA."

"What's that mean?" Savior asked still resting his hand on the butt of his gun. He recalled the conversation he had with Dylan about the WHA, and how they dealt with people like him.

"World Hybrid Association," she explained. "It's a long story about who we are and how we came to be, but let's just say our job is to locate people like us and help them."

"I thought you were after a monster," he said as he lowered his hand.

"Well...technically that's not a lie. We're after a man you may have heard of. Alexander Wilson." She paused.

"He's that CEO who disappeared about a year ago." His face screwed up. "What's that got to do with me?"

"I'm a hybrid, so is Jackson." Evans admitted. "We have the ability to manipulate forces of nature. What most people would call magic." She locked eyes with him.

A smile broke his face. "You're telling me magic's real? Maybe I should check you two into the funny house." Savior laughed. "I mean c'm...." He was cut off as agent Evans held a flame with one hand, and made water dance with the other.

Jackson held three balls of water twirling and transforming before his eyes. One ball turned into a man, the middle seemed to freeze into ice and the third turned into a basketball hoop. Savior watched as the watery figure dribbled the ice ball on non-existent ground then jumped into the air and slammed the ball through the hoop. It crashed to the floor and shattered.

Savior's mouth dropped at the display.

"He's always more showy than he has to be," she said.

"So will you help us?" he asked Savior.

Savior closed his mouth and joined them at the leather couch. "You're gonna have to tell me more."

Agent Evans cleared her throat, then went into detail about who they were and why they existed. "A long time ago, tens of thousands of years, a race of beings landed on earth. They were called dragons. Well...Dragonians, but we called them dragons.

"They were peaceful at first, but soon enslaved our ancestors. There was a civil war between different factions of dragons and eventually the slaves were freed. There's a lot we still don't know, but eventually we started having children with them." Evans waited for Savior who held up a finger.

"Yer tellin' me that we slept with dragons.... Like the scaley, huge, reptiles?" Savior was in disbelief.

"She always leaves out the important part. They have the unique ability to transform into people that look exactly like us," Jackson said.

This caused Savior to stop completely. "Are one of you a dragon?"

"As I said, we're hybrids. It's possible you are too. Very few people are not." Evans seemed irritated having to explain the details further.

"What does the WHA do?" Savior asked. "Aside from help the hybrids."

"That's pretty much our whole goal. Help hybrids," Irwin responded.

Savior struggled to wrap his head around the idea of such people. He was paying attention as they wielded their so-called magic, but he still struggled.

It's true, Tempus added. *I was floatin' through space by their planet when they fled. Technically they're to blame for us meeting.*

Savior thought about this and smiled. "Well I guess I only have one question, who's drivin' to dinner? You, or me?" Savior considered revealing his own secret, but assumed that they already understood his secrets. After all, Tempus did mention dragons before they even arrived.

"You're the person most familiar with the city. Why don't you drive, and we can either ride with you, or follow," she said, relieved that she didn't have to go into any further detail.

Savior grabbed his keys and escorted them to his car. While they rode the elevator, Savior made a call and verified there was a table for three at the Guard and Grace. "For you mister Savior, always," the man said.

"Thank you, be there in ten, twenty minutes," Savior replied. "I know where we're goin' so just ride with me."

They sped off from the empty underground garage. Savior's wheels smoked and rumbled as he tore from the garage onto the lonely street. Both agents grabbed whatever they could, and Savior laughed. "There ain't nothin' to worry about. I got this."

Chapter Thirty-Seven
Another Strange Case

They sat in a private booth, not closed to the public, but no one would overhear their conversation. As it was, they hadn't said a word, the agents only gaped at the menu. "I don't charge, but I take advantage when I can." Savior smiled at them.

"Well if that's the case, have what you want. It's not like the prices are listed," Irwin replied, knowing that meant they were high. "We were expecting to pay you a few thousand at least, but this is cheaper... I think." His concerned look was replaced by a happy smile.

Aiyana sat quietly, contemplating something deep inside of her. She stared through the menu and then suddenly looked up. "We told you about us. Why haven't you told us about who you are?"

Savior smiled as he looked at the menu. "I think I'm getting the eight ounce wagyu filet mignon and some truffle mac and cheese," he replied, ignoring the question.

Aiyana gripped the table. She hated being ignored. As the waiter approached she turned to him. "We're not ready yet." Her voice was cool and calm, but held a modicum of anger.

"Speak for yerself, I'm ready," Savior announced.

"Me too," Irwin said.

Aiyana shot him a glare.

"I haven't eaten since the plane from Edinburgh. I'm starving," he replied to the look.

Savior's eyebrow raised as he turned to the waiter. "Eight ounce wagyu mignon and some of that lovely truffle mac and cheese." The waiter turned his gaze to Irwin.

"Same," he said.

"How're you from Scotland when I hear a Texas twang. Even if it is extremely slight," Savior asked as Aiyana scanned the menu and ordered.

"I was from Texas. Moved to LA, then to Edinburgh after the Alexander Wilson incident. Got married last spring." He smiled as he showed his platinum ring with several small diamonds in the center. "We have all the money we could ever need, but we still live in the same house she lived in when I met her." He shook his head.

Drinks were delivered. "Please don't disturb us for the next twenty minutes, or whenever you see me raise my hand like this," Savior said to the waiter, raising his hand and waving his fingers inward. He handed a hundred dollar bill to the man.

The waiter left and they were alone. "You already know who I am... though I'd like to know how." Savior sipped his scotch as he stared deep into Aiyana's brown eyes.

"We can read your thoughts and memories," Irwin said as he drank from his straw. The mannerisms he displayed made it feel like it was an everyday thing with him.

I suppose it is an everyday thing for them, Savior internalized.

You're not kiddin'. Musta been what that buzz was earlier. I thought it was dragons, Tempus announced.

Savior nodded.

"What'd your little friend say?" Aiyana asked as she sipped her water.

"Said you were buzzin' my mind for several hours and that musta been when you were readin' my thoughts." He took another sip of his scotch, savoring it as he swished the smoky liquid around his mouth.

Aiyana smiled. "Yeah, sometimes I like to know everything about the people I'm dealing with. It takes some time."

"You should ask permission. I thought I was dyin'." Savior shook his head.

"Next time I'll ask." She still waited for the explanation.

"So you read my mind? Why do I need to say anything about who I am and what I do?" The light caramel colored liquid swirled around the glass as he rotated it in front of him.

"You don't, but it would really show trust that we already gave to you," Irwin said. "Do we really have to wait twenty minutes for another drink?" His drink was empty. The telltale signs of his straw sucking at nothing in his glass followed his words.

"Just go get a drink at the bar." Aiyana stood to let him out. When he was gone she sat back down, then shook her head, and stared at him.

"Alright fine. I was infected years ago with a parasite I call Tempus. It's got the ability to travel through space and time, so long as it has a host." Sylvester smiled. "I wonder if you can hear 'im, if you're in my head? It's not always painful like that is it?"

"I supposed we could try, but no it's generally not. Irwin was nagging me, and I wasn't as focused as I normally am when performing." Aiyana leaned in. "Close your eyes."

The buzz returned, but on a much fainter scale. *Can you hear me Sylvester?* Aiyana's voice sounded in his head.

Loud and clear. This is crazy. Tempus can you hear her? Savior asked.

Yeah I can hear her. Also, it's Savior while he's workin' lady, Tempus replied. *You haven't earned callin' him by his real name.*

The buzzing stopped.

Savior opened his eyes and looked at Aiyana. "Why'd ya stop?"

"It sounds like it's from Jersey." Aiyana was more than a little creeped out by the random voice in Savior's head. "Let it know that I will be sure to call you Savior while working."

He smiled. "Oh it heard ya." His hand raised in the air and signaled the waiter. "Wanna do somethin' really fun?"

Aiyana's eyebrow raised. "Like what?"

"Take my hand and I'll show ya." A devious smile rested on his lips.

Aiyana hesitantly grabbed it. In an instant, time stopped around them. Savior stood, pulling Aiyana to her feet. She gaped in wonder at the frozen world around them. Since joining the WHA she had seen it all, done it all even, but this was something else.

They walked to Irwin, who was frozen mid drink. Sylvester pushed the glass up and Aiyana eyed him. "You'll see what'll happen," he said as he smiled and laughed slightly.

They stayed like this for half an hour, wandering the room, then pushing the door open and going outside. "That guy's too drunk to drive," Aiyana said as she walked over to a man who'd only just left the restaurant. He was in the middle of fumbling for his keys, searching pockets with one hand, holding the actual keys in another.

She grabbed them and pulled. It was hard to remove them from his grip. In her mind it felt like pulling them from the deep mud and muck of a swamp. They wandered back inside, the man's keys in Aiyana's hand and sat back down at the table.

Savior pointed toward Irwin. "Watch."

Time started as suddenly as it stopped. Waiters moved around at their normal pace, serving food and drinks. "Damn it," Irwin shouted, his Texas twang thicker than before.

Aiyana laughed as she watched Irwin douse himself in whatever liquor he was trying to pass off as manly. The bartender handed him a towel to dry off, shaking his head and clearly thinking Irwin was drunk. "Oh he so deserved that," she exclaimed, smiling for the first time.

"He play a lot of pranks?" Savior snickered as he spoke.

"He did when I first started with the WHA. It's been since he moved to the Edinburgh office that we've actually had the chance to work a case together." Aiyana's face dropped and the serious agent returned.

"Alright tell me about it," he said returning to his glass of scotch.

Aiyana went over the history of the WHA. She explained that the current, and only, head of the WHA was a dragon who was immortal. "Immortal is a strong word. Verschiebung can die, but she has to be physically killed," Aiyana explained.

"No one questions why the head of your organization never changes?" Savior leaned in, fascinated by the story.

Aiyana waited as their food was delivered. Irwin rejoined them somewhere in the dark ages of Verschiebung's, and the WHA's, story. She picked at her food while waiting until the waiters were far enough away.

"No one ever questions because Verschiebung can shape shift into anyone she imagines, man or woman." Aiyana smiled. "Versch is truly inspiring. Goes by Veronika right now. Jared in the past. Just depends on her mood when it's time to change."

The story continued until it got to the part where she came in. "I was a cop recruited by the WHA. We never do it like you would think. It's always some game that people like this guy put together." She gestured to Irwin. "Shortly after I finished my training with the WHA, I was put on a case that led to Wilson. He tortured me to understand who I was and how my cells would react to different stimuli. It was mostly knives cutting into my body."

"Alright so we're lookin' for a man, not an actual monster." Savior nodded as he stuffed the last of the steak into his mouth.

"No, he's an actual monster," Irwin chimed in.

"After he was done experimenting with me we went to a remote city of dragons underground. It was there that he injected himself with a serum that turned him into a beast." Aiyana looked at him. "You ever see that cartoon Gargoyle's?" she asked.

"I've heard of it, but that's as far as it goes for me. Well I guess I've seen the cover on Disney plus," Savior said.

"Imagine one of those creatures, but real, and almost a hundred feet tall, maybe more." Aiyana continued to explain what happened. "It's not like I had a measuring tape, but he was at least eight stories tall when transformed. Had it not been for the dragons, he would have killed us all."

"Then Irwin abandoned you," Savior joked.

"Hey...I was in love. I don't see why that would be considered abandoning her." Irwin was offended. "How're we getting back to your office?"

Savior smiled at Aiyana. "Well I already showed her what I can do, but not you."

Irwin's face screwed up. "When?"

Aiyana laughed. "I've only had water, I can drive."

"Nonsense." Savior's lyrical southern accent sang. "Let's settle up the tab and then we'll head outside."

Irwin took the bill and whistled. "I'm glad we're not paying you." He shook his head as he walked to the bar.

Aiyana and Savior walked out. He held the door and gestured for her to walk through. They waited in the cool air of a dying summer's night in Colorado. Tempus yelled in his head as he looked up at the stars that he'd been there, or there, definitely there. Aiyana stared as well, and as Savior observed her, he knew her story wasn't over.

"He took someone didn't he?" His gaze returned to the stars.

Tears filled her eyes for the first time. Even while telling the most harrowing and painful sections of her story, tears never came close to falling. "He took my wife."

Savior gaped at her. "I'm sorry," he said. "Do you know where he took her?"

She wiped away the tears and looked at him. "No, but I'm hoping you'll be able to find out."

Chapter Thirty-Eight
Showing Off

Irwin joined them and looked at Aiyana. "Told him about Kelly?" he asked.

Aiyana nodded.

"Well in that case give me some sleep and I'll be ready in the mornin'," Irwin said. "Where we stayin'?" he asked the woman.

As if for the first time, she realized they didn't have a room booked at any of the hotels. "Probably some sleazy motel." She shook her head.

"Y'all don't have reservations?" Savior asked.

"Apparently not." Irwin shook his head.

"I got plenty of room. You take my bed tonight and Irwin and I can rough it on the couch. Did ya at least pack clothes?" Savior asked.

"I rushed out thinking I would pick some up, then flew twelve hours to get here," Irwin said. "Only brought my wallet, badge and phone."

"I started working the case," Aiyana said.

"She gets a bit obsessed," Irwin announced.

Savior looked at his watch. "Take my hand." He raised one to each of them.

"I don't think prayer is what we need right now, a taxi maybe," Irwin said.

"Just do it." Aiyana was exasperated.

As they both grabbed his hands Savior looked around. "Shoot, we'll need to go into the alley." He noticed a camera watching the sidewalk, and in turn them.

Irwin raised an eyebrow, but Aiyana allowed Savior to drag her into the alley, still holding his hand. Irwin followed, leery of what the strange detective had in mind. "I didn't see what she saw, so I hope this isn't some fetish of yours," Irwin said.

"Just shut up and get over here." He held out his hand to Irwin once again. "You're gonna feel some pressure."

For a second they hunched over, exchanging glances. Savior, accustomed to his abilities, simply stood there, and watched their haggard reactions. When the pressure alleviated they looked around, surprised to find themselves in another alley.

"Bathrooms are around the corner." Savior pointed.

Both agents sped off and disappeared. When they reemerged five minutes later, they stood straight, bewildered at what happened. Savior smiled at them. They were in a strip mall.

"This place has all the clothes you could want, even some fancy ones. When you're ready, meet me back here and we'll get back to my place." Savior sat on a bench.

"The same way we just got here?" Irwin's eyes filled with dread.

"One and the same. If you want I could take you to your home in Cairnryan. That way you don't have to pick up clothes, but you'd have to endure the same pressure." Savior smiled.

"Maybe when we're done." Irwin exclaimed. "Not beforehand. Think I could take a Taxi back to your building?" Irwin rubbed his stomach.

"Sure, tell ya what, I'll call my buddy John Dwayne to pick you up. Real name's Mandeep Anghali, but he definitely prefers John. Can't miss him. He drives a Prius with the license plate HWDY PANR, or 'Howdy Partner'." Savior smiled. "How 'bout you Aiyana, want me to wait for you?"

"I think I'll ride with Irwin. We'll see you in an hour or two." She smiled.

Savior looked around, satisfied no one was watching, and nodded. "See you then." He vanished as soon as the words left his mouth.

He arrived at his car, hours later in Savior time, but only minutes in the real world. All of the alcohol was completely out of his system. The car started, and he drove it to his building safely. As he pulled into the garage, a woman with long smooth legs waited for him.

He parked and stared at her for a moment before exiting. "Misses Jarlson." He purposefully accentuated the word *misses*. "Odd time to be in a dim parkin' garage."

Her eyes were swollen. "I needed someone to talk to. Just talk." Her hand waved across the air as she spoke.

It was the first time he'd seen her with anything resembling a normal demeanor. Tear tracks rolled down her cheeks. Sylvester knew something was off, but couldn't pinpoint the exact reason she was so upset. He sat on his hood and stared at her for a moment.

"Alright, I'm listenin'," he said.

"Tom left me," she stated.

"I assume that's your husband?" he asked.

She nodded.

"Can't imagine why he would do that. Seems you two had the perfect setup." He didn't intend to glare at the heartbroken woman, but he did all the same.

"It wasn't perfect. We told each other about the people we slept with on a regular basis." She shook her head. "I told him about you, and it was like... he'd had enough."

Sylvester didn't feel guilty. He actually smiled at the revelation, though she didn't notice. "Well I think that serves you both right. How many people did you and he hurt by doin' what you were doin'?"

She buried her face in her hands and started sobbing. Sylvesters guilt returned as he joined her and put his arm around her shoulder, pulling her into him. She tried to push him away, but he held her even tighter then.

"I'm sorry. That was rude and uncalled for," he admitted. "I was hurt by your revelation, but that's on me, not you."

She finally submitted. He guided her to the elevator, then down the hall to her apartment. They stood outside for a while before he fumbled in her pockets for keys.

"I'm not in the mood for that," she said mistaking his actions.

He smiled. "I'm not tryin' to get you in the mood," he said as he grabbed her butt pocket. "I'm tryin' to find your keys and I figured I'd seen you naked, and more."

"It's unlocked." Her voice was flat.

Sylvester stopped groping and turned the knob. "Here, follow me," he said as he drug her inside, then to the bathroom.

He filled the tub with water, the perfect temperature, and stood up. She neither sat, nor moved while he did. "Take a bath, have some wine, which I'll go grab, and try to relax," he said as he disappeared from the room.

Moments later he returned with an empty wine glass. "You don't seem to have any wine," he said. "Just wait here and I'll go get some from my place."

Only four minutes passed as he dug through the bottles of wine, conversing with Tempus about what it was that she liked, and returning. There she was, fully clothed. Her face was once again buried in her hands.

"I brought you two bottles. They're supposed to be good years, but... I don't know for sure. Wine's never been my strong suit. I just know that they're Rieslings." He pulled the cork and poured her a glass.

She suddenly grabbed him and held him tightly. Shock froze him in the spot. Eventually, he set the bottle down on her bathroom counter, then wrapped his arm around her. "You're gonna be alright," he said as he lifted her chin. "Look at me. I promise you that everything's gonna be good."

She stared into his eyes as though she were waiting for proof. He leaned down and kissed her softly. They remained this way for what seemed like hours, him sharing his feelings for her, her accepting them. His eyes met hers when they broke the kiss.

"Promise me you'll lay in this tub, soak, and relax," he said.

She didn't speak, only nodded.

"Alright. I've got a case, and those people are stayin' with me tonight." He started to break the embrace, but she pulled him back to her.

"Stay with me tonight. Not for sex, just to be together," she pleaded.

Sylvester considered. "I can, but I have to explain to my guests that I'm gonna be here instead of there. Take your bath, drain it and warm it back up if you need to. I'll be back."

She nodded and released him.

Sylvester turned and heard the shuffling of clothing, followed by the sound of fabric falling to the floor. He returned to his apartment, confused, and concerned about a woman he was still angry with. While Ira still had hold of his heart, he wanted to be with Jada. That feeling was new, and overwhelmed his desire to remain angry.

It wasn't like she had seen her husband since they started... whatever it was they were doing. Guilt over the fact that she was married while they were doing what they did was his only reason for being angry. The knock at his door broke him free of his reveries.

Aiyana and Irwin stood at the door, bags in hand. "He didn't even charge us," Irwin said.

"I've got a revolving account with him. He picks my people up when I need him to, and I give him a couple thousand a month." Savior stepped aside, allowing them in. "Been a change of plans. I'm gonna keep a friend company tonight. She's just down the hall. Her husband just broke it all off."

Irwin smiled. "Tryin' to get in before anyone else has a chance?"

Aiyana elbowed him in the ribs. "Savior wouldn't do that."

She wasn't wrong. In any other situation, he really wouldn't do something like that. Jada Jarlson was a different story altogether. "What's the plan for this investigation?" he asked.

Aiyana looked at him. "I figured you would tell us."

"When's the last time you saw her?" Savior asked.

"Day before yesterday." Aiyana almost started crying when she thought of Kelly.

"Where?" Savior looked at her, but did not criticize her for the similar feelings Jada was struggling with down the hall.

"Los Angeles." Aiyana kept a straight face, emotion gone in an instant.

"You're in luck. I've been there. Hell you've been there. We'll make a trip tomorrow, then do some investigation my way." Savior smiled. "Aiyana, you take the bed." He stared at Irwin and grabbed a remote. "Irwin you have a choice."

He pressed a button, and three of his couches transformed into beds. One was on the landing next to his bar. The other two were downstairs. He tossed the remote to Irwin. "Blankets are in the closet here..." he pointed at a door next to the bed on the landing "and there." He pointed downstairs.

Irwin laughed. "I'll take downstairs to give her a bit more space."

"Fair 'nough." He stepped into the hall. "I'll see you two in the mornin'. After breakfast we'll get goin'. Take some Dramamine if you want to avoid the same reaction." The door closed behind him as he walked to Jada's apartment. When he reached the door he leaned his head against it. Ira once again filled his mind. *Time to let you go.* He turned the knob, and entered the apartment, wiping away a solitary tear.

Chapter Thirty-Nine
Los Angeles

He woke with Jada's arm draped across his bare chest. They were both naked under the covers. It was the first time that neither of them did anything aside from hold the other while lying in bed.

He looked at her, emotions a blur of confusion. Was he really thinking about getting into some form of relationship with this woman? His other arm draped across his forehead, and he closed his eyes.

Not what you should be worryin' about right now, Tempus announced very clearly.

I know, but it's something I'm gonna need to deal with, Sylvester sighed.

"Mornin'," Jada said, her voice thick and rough as though she smoked an entire pack of cigarettes the night before.

"How'd you sleep?" Idle chit chat he could do.

"I don't remember much, just remember being in the parking garage waiting for you. I drank a lot yesterday," she said.

Sylvester laughed slightly. "I didn't help with that. I wasn't aware you had anything. Certainly didn't smell it on ya, so I gave you more."

"Did we?" she asked, realizing they were both naked.

"No." He looked at her. "You said you weren't in the mood, so I didn't do anything, you didn't try anything either. It's not like we haven't seen each other naked, and I like sleepin' this way."

She was silent as he stared at the ceiling. It was a silence that was neither comfortable, nor uncomfortable. It just was. Emotions started bubbling as he lay there. She simply breathed.

"It was his idea," she said.

Sylvester lay there, waiting for more explanation.

"Us seeing other people. He had to move to London for business. At first it was every few weeks that he came back, then months, now it's been a year. He didn't even warn me first, just sent the papers." She was crying again. "We were only together a few years, but I should have seen the signs."

Sylvester pulled her in to him and held her. "You said it was after you told him about me."

"It was, not too long after, but still." She wiped the tears from her eyes. "I think he thought that I was in good hands. I didn't even tell him that you wanted nothing to do with me. Only that it happened."

He looked at her, and she met his gaze. "I wanted more. I was hurt that you didn't say anything so I could be ready for the eventuality of being hurt. You're the first woman since my ex left years ago."

"Explains why you didn't put up a fight that first night." She giggled through still falling tears. It was a nice sound compared to the sobbing he listened to all night.

He smiled. "We'll need to talk about this more when I'm back. I've got to go to LA for a case."

She was silent. He felt that it was due to the fact that she would be alone when she really needed him. It took him a year to get over Ira, and he wasn't sure he was fully over her. It was starting to sound like Tom and Jada's marriage lasted less than a few months under the same roof. He started to move his arm, and she stopped him.

"A few more minutes," she pleaded.

He pushed his arm back into place and she moved so she was all but lying on top of him. "I can't say I'm going to love you the way she did, but I can say, as a friend, I do love you. Even before all of this, I had an inkling that I cared for you deeper than any other fling in the past."

Well friends with benefits is somethin', Tempus said.

"Shut up," he said aloud. She was stricken and started to pull away so he did what he could and kissed her. "That was meant for me," he said after. "I really do need to get up and get dressed. Are you gonna be okay?"

She smiled. "As long as you're coming back to take me on a proper date, then I will."

See, she wants more than friends, he retorted to the parasite.

Nice save genius, Tempus laughed as he spoke.

"Sure thing. Pick a place and we'll go as soon as I'm back." He smiled and kissed her forehead.

Then he was dressed and heading to his apartment. Confusion racked him over how he felt about the woman, but he was in a better place with her. The smell of pancakes, eggs, and bacon welcomed him when he opened the door. Then, he saw Irwin cooking.

"I made enough for you too," he said, winking at Sylvester. "Have fun last night?"

"If you call holding a woman as she cried, drunkenly I might add, about her ex-husband, fun... then I guess so." Sylvester looked at Irwin. "Where's Aiyana?"

"Shower," he said.

So much for his own desire to shower right away. Still, breakfast smelled good after a long night of perpetual emotional ground control. Rather than sleep, he dozed for ten or so minutes in hour long intervals. "Coffee with that?" he asked.

"Fresh pot." Irwin gestured. "I found a nice little café not too far from here and got some of their finest grounds."

"I know the place." Sylvester smiled. "I don't know if Aiyana told you, but when we're in public, call me Savior. Right now... Sylvester is fine."

"She mentioned something about it. That's why I haven't been too name specific Sylvester." Irwin smiled. "About this case. How are you going to help here?"

"We're heading to LA today, so I hope you picked up some Dramamine like I said. It's not going to be as rough, but you'll still feel it. By the time we're done with this case, you'll be able to withstand my abilities with few problems." Sylvester returned the smile. "Also we'll be travelin' through time, but you cannot affect the past in such a way that you two never show up to meet me."

Irwin paused mid-flip. "You can travel in time?" Something clicked in his head. "That was you!" he exclaimed.

"What was?" Sylvester rose an eyebrow and looked at Irwin. His shenanigans from the previous night were buried somewhere at the back of his mind.

"My drink last night. Oh if I had your powers, I would be the worst." Irwin laughed and finished flipping the pancake.

"I forgot about that. A lot on my mind." He laughed.

"No apology?" Irwin eyed skeptically.

"Nope." Sylvester smiled back, pleased with himself. "If it makes you feel better, Aiyana approved."

"That doesn't make me feel any better, but it also doesn't surprise me." Irwin smiled as he put together a plate and handed it to Sylvester.

The eggs were scrambled, which Sylvester didn't mind, though he preferred them yolky and runny. Scrambled with seasonings, after the night he had, was perfect. Irwin's pancakes were also amazing. Soft, fluffy, and sweet, but not too sweet. Syrup was almost not needed.

"What's your secret?" Sylvester asked as he gestured to the pancakes.

A smile crossed Irwin's face, but he said nothing.

"They're so fluffy and perfect," Sylvester responded.

"He puts half heavy cream in and half sweet crème coffee creamer instead of milk. I've watched him make those a few times." Aiyana was still drying her hair with her towel.

"That was my secret to tell, if I wanted to." Irwin feigned being hurt.

"You know you were going to tell him eventually. Where's mine?" she asked.

"I don't know if you deserve them after that revelation." Irwin smiled.

"And I'm the pope," she said dryly.

"Fine." Irwin handed her a stack of pancakes, but nothing else.

They ate, no one speaking, only smiling at one another. When he finished Sylvester explained to Aiyana what he already explained to Irwin. Unlike Irwin, Aiyana looked perturbed.

"We can't just save her?" she asked.

"No." Sylvester stood up. "Any changes that don't bring you two here to hire me will cause untold damage." He walked toward the bathroom. "I'm showerin'."

An hour later they were all showered, professionally dressed, and ready to go. Irwin and Aiyana both popped a pill in their mouths, water easing the pills down their throats. They held hands and Sylvester looked at them both.

"Savior from here on, 'til we're done," he reminded. "Aiyana think of the last place you saw Kelly."

She closed her eyes, and Tempus pulled the memory from her. "Got it buddy?" Savior asked.

Almost. It's a fresh and well visited memory, but the location's hazy. Ask her where this is, Tempus said.

"Where's this memory?" Savior eyed the woman.

"At the WHA building," she replied.

"Tempus is havin' a hard time lockin' down that particular location. Almost like it exists, but at the same time doesn't," he replied.

"That's probably because in LA it's only ten-thirty," Irwin said. "The building only appears every two hours for a few minutes."

"Let's start further back then. How about your house?" Savior asked. "We'll start there, go back to the mornin' of, and see if anything is outta place."

Tempus grabbed the location when Aiyana brought the memory to the forefront of her mind. ***This one's perfect. Tell them I'd like to know how they manage that trick with their building sometime.***

"Maybe later Tempus. When you're ready, I think, we're ready," Savior said.

Again pressure built within them, the nearly unbearable weight of the world displaced around them. It lasted for seconds, but even for Savior, it felt like an eternity. When they popped back into existence the feeling wasn't as explosive, and neither of his passengers felt the urge to run inside.

"Alright. This is your house right? What time did you two leave?" he asked.

"About eight-thirty," Aiyana replied.

Still holding their hands, Savior reversed time. They were in a hidden spot, able to watch as the women prepared for their day. Irwin smirked when he saw them chatting, causing both Aiyana and Savior to direct their attention to him.

"Do you two ever get your underwear mixed up?" Irwin asked.

"Are you serious right now?" Savior replied for Aiyana.

"It was just a funny thought that popped in my head," Irwin said.

"We're about to head out of the house," Aiyana announced.

"Alright, Tempus stop time." The world froze around them the instant it was requested. "You two go look for anything out of the ordinary. Your street seems like a quiet one, is this a normal thing 'round here?"

Aiyana and Irwin let go of Savior's hands and looked around. "It does seem quieter than normal," Irwin said.

Aiyana walked to the street and looked for any vehicles that would have normally driven by, but nothing was there. "Why didn't I catch that?" she berated herself silently. When they left for work they were having a normal morning. Kelly fawned over Aiyana and Aiyana returned the feeling.

No cars on the street didn't mean much in normal circumstances. There were dozens of reasons it could happen, but there was no noticeable cause that she could see. Aiyana walked further, the nearest intersection was less than half a mile away.

While Aiyana walked away, looking for some sign of foul play, Savior and Irwin inspected the yard. Neither found anything out of the ordinary. Their house had no direct neighbors, but also nothing flat that a person, or group of people, could easily hide. Across the street was a decline, dropping roughly thirty feet.

Nothing hovered in the sky, spying on the women. There was no big and grotesque creature to be seen, so it couldn't have been Wilson directly. Savior stopped and put a hand on Irwin's shoulder.

"What can Wilson do?" he asked.

"Well, the dragons he stole DNA from have the ability to transform between human and dragon. Wilson can do the same, but his form isn't a dragon," Irwin replied.

"And he has all the same magic as Aiyana right?" Savior interrupted.

Irwin nodded.

"Think he could affect a mass of people at the same time?" Savior was trying to understand the nature and abilities of the people.

"Most definitely. I think that's why the streets so quiet," Irwin said. "We would never have noticed in real time. Coming back and seeing it first hand is something else."

Aiyana jogged back. "There's nothing. No one seems like they would have come this way at all."

"Did you see Wilson?" Savior asked.

Aiyana shook her head. "I almost thought there was a guy dressed like his troops, but that's not what he was wearing."

"How big of a radius could Wilson affect people?" Savior asked.

"Blocks. Hell, he could have put a barrier up so anyone who passes the barrier diverts another direction," Irwin replied.

Aiyana looked at both of them.

"Your place isn't being spied on. There's no car nearby that would tail you. I think the only possibility is that Wilson is usin' magic. What was the last direct communication you had with him?" Savior asked.

Aiyana put her head down and kicked at the ground. "He may have sent a message to my house," she admitted.

Irwin was taken aback. "When was this?"

"Just after you were transferred a few years ago. Nothing else ever came," she said.

"You didn't think that was important enough to share with the group, or I don't know, the WHA?" Irwin accused.

"I do now. I thought it was just a challenge and that's why I've been working as hard as I have the last few years." She was frustrated, mostly with herself.

"It's in the past. What did the message say?" Savior asked.

"It wasn't anything serious. It was a box of empty vials and a note that said he was still out there." Aiyana quietly cursed at herself.

"Empty vials?" Savior asked.

"Yeah. I thought they meant he used all of his samples on himself. I didn't think it mattered much. I wasn't living with Kelly yet, and I wasn't worried about him." She cried, but her voice never quivered.

"Alright let's see what happens after you leave." Savior said, grabbing both Irwin and Aiyana's hands. "This is going to be a bit… weird. Choppy might be a better term. I'm gonna jump ahead, still frozen, a minute or two at a time. We'll follow you until you get to the WHA."

Time stuttered and the women seemed to move from spot to spot. One second they were walking out of their door, the next they were in the car. Then the car was gone and part of the way down the street.

The whole time, nothing strange appeared. Nothing out of the ordinary seemed to be happening at all. Aiyana pulled into a parking lot attached to… nothing. The women, along with a group of other people, were standing and waiting.

Savior compared it to a group of people on a smoke break, but none of them had cigarettes. Time moved forward again and suddenly there was a building standing before them. His mouth hung open as he gawked at the structure that seemed to appear out of nowhere.

It's not out of nowhere. These yahoo's have the ability to set the building milliseconds out of sync with time itself. They think it's longer, but the truth is it's milliseconds. If it were minutes it would not appear every

two hours. Maybe every other day, but not that short of a time period, Tempus interrupted Saviors line of thought.

He let go of the other's hands and turned around. "Tempus it's not the..." He looked up and saw something. Someone was poking their head from behind a structure. Could have been a bus stop, or some place where people could smoke, but there was a head just slightly appearing from behind it. "Guys," Savior said.

Both turned and saw the head. "They weren't there before were they?" Irwin was running to see the person up close. Aiyana and Savior joined him.

"It's a woman," he announced when they arrived.

"Yeah, but look at her arm patch," Aiyana said.

"It's one of his," Irwin admitted.

"Alright so we made some progress. When did you leave?" Savior asked Aiyana.

"Mid-day. The building showed up again at three, so it must have been then." Aiyana bent down and really looked at the woman. "I wish I knew what she could do," she admitted.

"Unfortunately, that'll have to wait. Now's the tricky part. Take my hand." He took both of their hands when they reached out, and the forward momentum of time moved by a minute, then five, ten and then hours.

Aiyana left the building with others. She drove away and the woman, Hodgkins, if the tag on her jacket were to be believed, radioed someone. Five minutes passed and nothing. Another five, then five more, then they jumped to four-thirty.

The building would reappear in thirty minutes, and still, nothing had happened. Hodgkins sat cross-legged on the ground, waiting, pulling at the grass she sat on. Savior moved time five minutes, then another five.

Four black vans rushed into the parking lot and twenty men and women wearing the same clothes left appeared outside the vans. Half of them seemed to gather around the spot where the building should be. Others held automatic rifles and waited.

Hodgkins joined her comrades along with Aiyana, Irwin, and Savior. Those surrounding the building raised their hands and pointed at the space. Five minutes passed and suddenly the building appeared. In that span there also appeared to be a disruption in Savior's ability to freeze time.

"This isn't right," Aiyana said. "The building shouldn't be visible for at least twenty minutes."

I can't do much. You're gonna have to hide, Tempus announced.

"Guys we gotta get somewhere. Tempus says he can't hold time much longer," Savior said.

Each hid behind a car. Savior berated himself. There had never been issues like this in the past. *What the hell's goin' on Tempus?* His mind was furious.

Silver dragons control a lot of things. This whole building being hidden in time is their doin'. These people are castin' some spell to cancel any time manipulation, even mine. Tempus audibly struggled to maintain his abilities.

Did you know this could happen? Savior questioned.

Absolutely not. This is a first for my kind. Tempus huffed as though he were out of breath. *Best I can do is teleport us anywhere in the world, just not in time.*

The familiar tingling occurred, and Irwin jumped in. *What do we do?*

We just watch in real time, Tempus said.

For a moment Irwin was silent. "Is that Tempus?" he whispered.

It is. Aiyana chimed in. *I don't know if I can just watch Kelly be kidnapped. From this point, if I join her what happens?*

You'll be with her if you join her, even though you exist in the past. How did you know she was kidnapped? Was there any word from them? Savior asked.

There was, she admitted.

Irwin you gotta contain her. Do whatever you have to, Tempus said.

From behind a car closest to the vans, Irwin looked at Aiyana. He mouthed something she couldn't quite make out. Then eight of the ten troops that went in escorted a tall redhead from the building.

Two more followed shortly after, and the building disappeared once again.

They shoved Kelly in the back of one of the vans, then made to leave. Aiyana started to jump from behind the car, but her hand froze to the vehicle. Even her feet seemed cemented to the ground with ice. Irwin jumped up and yelled at the troops.

Aiyana worked furiously trying to melt the ice, but Irwin's hand performed soft quick movements, freezing the ice as soon as it melted. "That's my friend! What the hell are you doing!" he yelled at them.

Their guns raised and Irwin stopped everything, but the quick and purposeful movement. "Stop there and get on the ground," one of the men yelled.

Irwin complied, his hand only slightly twitching as he lay down. Two of them walked over and cuffed him. "Stop moving your hand," they demanded.

"Nervous twitch, sorry I can't stop it," he lied.

The cuffs closed and the men hauled Irwin to his feet. "Guess you're coming with us then. Any movement to use magic at all, and we'll open fire," They said as they shoved him in the back of a different van.

It was five o'clock when the vehicles loaded and each sped away. Aiyana finally broke free, but too late to do anything. She screamed in time for the building to once again appear and people looked at her.

"Aiyana." Savior jogged to meet her. "Hand," he demanded. Time froze and they followed the direction the vans sped off, trailing them as far as they drove. Time froze every few miles as they caught up.

"You could have stopped them from taking Irwin," she said as they followed.

"I could have, but then it would have been odd seeing a man simply disappear. It was too late at that point," he explained.

They followed until the vans pulled into the airport and stopped in a hangar. Kelly looked at Irwin as she was pulled from one of the vans. Her eyebrow raised in a questioning look. Time was frozen,

Aiyana walked up to Kelly, brushed hair from her face, and kissed her. "I'm coming for you," she said.

Then she stepped back and wrote something on a notepad. Savior once again skipped time ahead a few minutes, watching as they were loaded on the plane and it rolled from the hanger.

When the plane barreled down the runway and lifted to the sky Aiyana turned on Savior. "I've got the plane number. This better work, or else we're going to lose them both."

Savior nodded. Concerned over his lack of control when he needed it most. The plane flew east and disappeared behind the clouds. He put a hand on Aiyana's shoulder, looked her in the eye, and said "We will find them."

Chapter Forty
Old Fashioned Police Work

They hovered over a computer. Savior transported them back to the present, though still in California. Aiyana led Savior through the doors to the WHA headquarters, waving off security, and the receptionist's, protests. They rode a suspiciously silent elevator to the sixteenth floor and entered her office.

It wasn't protocol to bring outsiders in, especially ones who didn't have a reason to be there. Her phone rang and she ignored it, at least the first two times. On the third, she picked it up, but sat it on the desk, ignoring the person on the other end.

"Flight records say they stopped three places," she said.

"Shouldn't you be talking to whoever that is on the line?" he asked.

"No. She'll be down when she's tired of yelling at air," Aiyana replied.

"Alright. Where did the plane stop?" he asked.

"New York, I'm assuming to fill the tank because their next stop was London." Aiyana looked at the last stop. "Something I haven't told you is I'm familiar with the locations of dragon cities. They're always isolated, and they almost always exist underground."

"Where's the third stop?" Savior questioned.

"Tenzing-Hillary airport," Aiyana said.

"Don't say another word," a red haired woman demanded.

"Verschiebung?" Savior questioned Aiyana.

The door closed quickly behind her. "How dare you tell other people about my identity!" she quietly lectured.

Aiyana looked at Savior and hung her head. "He's helping on a case, and he's been more valuable than you, or anyone else in this whole building," she berated.

"Not this again." Veronika was exasperated. "I told you she simply left for the day, nothing else. Whether she came home or not, that's not something I'm concerned with. It was probably something you did." Her tone was bitter.

"I witnessed the kidnapping myself," Aiyana replied to the woman.

Savior was the one who felt awkward now. He looked between the women, and backed up. Their eyes followed him, but Veronika turned her gaze to Aiyana shortly after he leaned against a wall.

"So you're saying I'm lying?" she said.

Aiyana sat quietly for a minute. "The last troops that came out were erasing everyone's memory," she announced, her gaze still falling on Savior.

"Makes sense. Best way to cover your tracks I'd say," he agreed.

"What are you talking about?" Veronika took a seat in the chair in front of Aiyana's desk.

"He can travel through time and space at will," Aiyana confessed. "We watched as Kelly, and Irwin, were taken."

"Irwin?" Veronika leaned in. "He's in Scotland. How could they have taken him?"

"Because he was stoppin' Aiyana from doing somethin' stupid in the past," Savior chimed in. "Tell ya what, I know the times, and while it's dangerous, I can go back and show you."

Veronika's face dropped. She didn't believe him. Aiyana on the other hand perked up.

"Not you," Savior said, determined not to cause any more trouble than necessary. "Stand up," he demanded of the woman.

Reluctantly Veronika stood, watching Aiyana the entire time. She reached out, but held back. Savior grabbed her hand before she could stop him completely, and they both disappeared. Aiyana stared at empty space.

When they reappeared, Veronika was fine. She felt no sicker than she had before travelling in time. "Well you can travel through space, I'll give you that." Savior smiled and shook his head.

They were behind the bus stop and leaning against it. Savior had not removed his hand, he held on to her hand firmly. "Do not let go of my hand, no matter what you see," he demanded.

She nodded and he gestured for her to lean around the corner. The vans sat in the parking lot. Savior, Aiyana, and Irwin were following a woman in a soldiers uniform. Everything was frozen.

"Alright, just watch," he whispered.

Everything played out like it had. Veronika watched Kelly being escorted out, then Irwin surrendered to the troops. Aiyana and Savior followed the vans, never noticing the red head and other Savior hiding behind the structure.

Then, without warning, they reappeared before Aiyana, seconds after they left. She was reviewing something on her computer. "Fun trip?" she asked as she wrote something down.

"I believe you now, if that makes any difference. Where'd you find this guy?" Veronika asked.

"Colorado," Aiyana replied.

"Alright, so I have some good news," Savior announced. "Thanks to our hand holdin', I now have a much wider range of places we can travel, so long as she comes with us."

Aiyana stopped writing. "That's good, because they're heading to the dragon city in Nepal. If my calculations are correct, they'll probably arrive in just under five hours."

"I can't go to Nepal," Veronika announced.

"I'll buzz you back if I need to," Savior said.

"It's not the time, I just... I'm not allowed back in the Nepalese Dragonian city after what happened in New Stelladahn," Veronika admitted.

"You weren't even there," Aiyana announced.

"That's the problem. They know who I am and how unique I am, but they don't accept that I didn't show up to fight for them." Veronika leaned on the chair.

"They'll get over it," Savior said. "Now, get ready, we'll need to leave soon if we're gonna warn them in time."

Veronika hesitantly left the office. Savior looked at Aiyana and smiled. "That was some impressive work," he said.

"Good old fashioned police work." Aiyana smiled and stood. "Here." She opened a closet behind her desk and tossed him a heavy coat. "It's cold in Nepal from what I hear."

A few minutes later, Veronika returned, a similar coat in hand. She looked grim, though Savior was sure it was only nerves. ***It's hard to be placed in this situation unwillingly,*** Tempus advised. Then, they all held hands, and Savior took them to the dragon city of Iridian Hearth.

Chapter Forty-One
Iridian Hearth

When they arrived, they weren't on the outskirts of the city, or even the entrance. It was the home of Iridian Hearth's leader. Electricity flooded the room, and a person sat behind a dark wood desk. He jumped when they suddenly appeared before him. The dragon clutched his heart, then realized who one of the people standing before him was.

He eyed Veronika, who hung her head with shamed acceptance. The dragon looked over Savior. After a moments observation an astonished gaze rested on his face when he realized the man was responsible for this sudden disturbance, and he was neither a hybrid, nor a dragon. A smile broadened his face as he looked at Aiyana, followed quickly by a knowing grimace.

"Hello Chavy," Veronika spoke quietly, but loud enough that everyone could tell what she said.

"Verschiebung. I thought we had an agreement that you would not set foot in any Dragonian city until you were willing to fight for us." He glared at her.

"Sorry. That's my fault. I'll take her back and pop back straight away." Savior reached for Veronika's hand, but she pulled back, and looked at him, pleading.

"If I'm ever going to make up for my transgressions, I've got to start somewhere." Veronika turned to Chavy. "Wilson has kidnapped two of my people, and they appear to be heading this way. I wasn't there at New Stelladahn, but I'm here now. I'll fight."

262

"Well… then I suppose it's a good thing you brought the savior of New Stelladahn with you." Chavy stood up, walked around his desk, and embraced Aiyana. "You give my people hope that they can one day join your people."

Savior watched the proceedings, trying to make himself as small as possible. Chavy looked at him, but moved to Veronika. The staring contest between them resulted in a standoff. Suddenly Chavy broke into a smile and embraced her as well.

"What just happened?" Savior asked Aiyana.

"He's a silver. Must have scanned her mind to see if Veronika was telling the truth and spoke to her like we did," Aiyana assumed. "He scanned me, I'm sure he'll get to you."

Chavy was tall with dark skin. His black hair was thick and fell past his shoulders to the middle of his back. It reflected the light with almost blinding brilliance. The rest of his features were fine and would have made any woman blush. When he turned to Savior, the buzzing returned to his head, but even more refined than either her, or Irwin could manage.

I'm tired of you people invading our space! Tempus shouted at the dragon.

"Behave Tempus," Savior scolded.

"It's alright," Chavy said, withdrawing from Savior's inner thoughts. "I see you have a visitor within. You're okay with this?"

It was the first time anyone ever really thought to ask if he was alright with Tempus' presence. For a second he was silent, not consulting Tempus, but his own thoughts. "I would have said no a couple years back, but it has really grown on me." A wry smile crossed his face.

"Very well, then verbally," Chavy said.

"Sure, I'm an open book. 'Sides, I know you're a dragon. Only fair you know who I am." Savior reached a hand out to shake. Chavy looked at it, but never reached out. Slowly, Savior pulled his hand back.

"Not yet," Chavy acknowledged. "Sylvester is your real name, but you go by Savior while working. Your voice changes to a deeper tone when you take on this persona. Tempus, as you call it, speaks with a Northeastern American accent, but you've never thought to ask why. You're in a place where secrets are meant to be kept, is Savior how you would like to be addressed still?"

Savior nodded.

"Very well. You received Tempus as an accidental gift, correct?" Chavy had a straight face.

"Yep," Savior acknowledged.

Like hell you did, Tempus announced.

"I guess not…What do you mean Tempus?" Savior had never asked the parasite whether it was an accident. It seemed that way. Really, it was a one in a billion shot that Tempus wouldn't have wound up on the ground in Savior's mind.

The only random parts of your selection were whether the Dragonian ship that pushed me off course would do that, Tempus admitted. *Soon as it did, then it was a matter of whether I would wind up on Mars or Earth. Course then it was whether it was you or another guy, but I'm glad it was you. As for my accent… I don't know. I gleaned your mind and thought this accent was cool.*

"So it was still an accident. There were three chances where I wouldn't have been picked, not a million, sure…but three." Savior shook his head. "Did you have a choice?"

Tempus was silent, slightly embarrassed that it only now realized that it didn't have a choice, but always thought there had been some level of decision.

"Chavy what's your next question?" Savior continued as though he weren't just having a conversation with himself. A smirk rested on his face at the thought of Tempus choosing its accent.

Chavy smiled. "You two seem like a good fit. I don't have a question, but I will say this… this isn't the last time we'll meet. We will call on you and you will answer."

"Whad'ya mean?" Savior's accent was thicker as he spoke.

Chavy opened his arms and embraced Savior who returned the hug. "I mean, in the future we will require your unique gifts, and you will help. It's not because we demand it, but your fate will be connected with ours for some time to come."

Veronika looked at the pair, realization dawning. She said nothing, but smiled to herself. Chavy released Savior and looked at the trio. "We must prepare for their coming," he said.

"They'll come through the entrance that will get them here quickest. He'll likely be transformed and ready to wipe out everyone in this city," Aiyana said.

"We've had some dragons practicing with their transformed state since the attack on New Stelladahn. It was a group decision that several individuals within our society would train in the lost art." Chavy smiled. "My people have made the best progress."

Savior laughed. "I'm sure all of the other dragon cities are sayin' that."

"This is true, but I can guarantee that ours has." Chavy walked behind his desk and pressed a button.

Outside, a siren sounded, not blaring to the point of deafness, but enough to be acknowledged. Chavy raised an arm and pointed to his door. They walked from the building, on the fourth floor, to an open field at least a mile wide where seven people waited patiently.

"You'll want to see this," Chavy said, then turned to the waiting dragons. "The moment we have waited for has come."

The group standing before them seemed nervous, exchanging glances, but never shied away from the announcement. They stood at attention, awaiting the Silver dragon's orders. He inspected them, then turned to the others and pointed at Veronika.

She looked at him, then at Aiyana. "You want me to join them?" she asked.

Chavy nodded. "How long do we have before they arrive?"

Aiyana smiled. "Enough time to recover from a few transformations." She was well-versed in Dragonian transformations based on Verschiebung's writings. They would all require at least thirty minutes of rest between each. When they left LA, they still had five hours before Wilson's people should arrive.

Veronika hung her head and joined the other seven members. Each of them turned to her, questioning who she was and what kind of dragon she would be. Aiyana smiled, having seen the magnificent creatures before, as well as Verschiebung's transformation in a remote mountain range in Canada.

"Our friend Verschiebung will transform first," Chavy announced, knowing that she was the most capable when it came to transformations.

"It's been years since I've transformed," she feigned.

Gold light surrounded her body, then enveloped it entirely. It didn't grow, but instead reshaped her body into a taller figure. When the light faded a different person stood before them, a man with white hair and a white beard, still dressed in Veronika's clothes.

Chavy smiled.

Aiyana laughed.

Savior was confused.

"Not that transformation." Chavy smiled, his deep voice booming.

Verschiebung, his original form, smiled as the tension around them broke. "Oh. Sorry my nearly twelve thousand year old mind sometimes forgets." Veronika's accent remained as he spoke.

The light once again enveloped his body, consuming it and expanding. Those next to him moved quickly away as the light grew and solidified. A dragon with golden scales stood towering over everyone on the field. Aiyana smiled. She felt the same sense of joy as the previous time she saw the gold dragon stand before her.

Savior, on the other hand, was floored. His mouth hung open as he watched the beast before him. He'd always heard of dragons. Those were fairy tales where the beasts either had little intelligence and were feral, or were intelligent, but still evil.

Verschiebung did not give off those vibes. It was a beautiful beast with broad shoulders, a muscular stature, and a tail that extended the length of its body. The maw was smooth, and its eyes were golden, brighter than the scales that seemed to produce a light of their own.

It did have hair, bushels that seemed to surround the dragon's scalp. White hair that looked softer than silk, but older than creation itself. The dragon looked around at the group, waiting for their own transformations.

Everyone was frozen in awe, but as their stupor alleviated they began glowing. Some were shades instead of bright lights, but all were magnificent. Savior and Aiyana watched with their own awe as a single silver worm-like dragon appeared, then two dragons that looked almost identical, except one lacked a tail and their scales were either red or green. A large brown dragon, similar to Verschiebung's golden dragon in shape, but clearly the tallest of any other that had transformed. Two small dragons, only about ten feet larger than Savior, appeared, standing below the others.

Their bodies weren't any different than the Green, Brown, or Gold dragons. They had a tail, but looked as though they could barely stand with their thin bony appendages. Each dragon, no matter the size or shape, had claws that looked as though they could rip anyone to pieces in only a few seconds.

A booming voice escaped the Golden dragon, commanding the others to stand at attention. They assembled and faced the elder dragon, respect given entirely with no question. Chavy smiled as the dragon took charge. Clearly he was happy to be alleviated of the pains of military training when he had none himself.

They watched as Verschiebung trained the dragons. Some fizzled after half an hour, exhausted from their transformation. Others pushed the limit, preparing for the worst. Hours passed and all of them transformed at some point, except Verschiebung. The dragon only smiled as others faltered, comforting them, but pushing them to do better.

Savior watched their training from the ground, sitting with his knees to his chest and his chin resting on them. Aiyana also watched, but she was irritable. Concern raced through her mind. She didn't express her anger or annoyance with anyone in particular. Savior thought it was mainly directed at Wilson's brash decision to kidnap her wife.

He stood and walked to her. "I promise that I'll do everything in my power to help y'all."

His words were reassuring, but not enough that Aiyana was ready to calm down. "I'll be fine. I'm getting myself amped up before the fight. They'll be here in an hour, or less and Veronika is taking her sweet time training them."

"I'd be surprised if they had enough energy to keep fightin' after this," Savior said.

Aiyana paused suddenly and smiled. "How long can you keep time paused, and how many people can you bring along?"

Chapter Forty-Two
Anything To Win

It was risky. Tempus confirmed Savior could bring a dozen people with him into the void that was frozen time. Savior could even maintain it for hours, possibly days, but no more than that. It would be extremely draining with such an increased number of people, not to mention the power that Aiyana had planned to use while time was frozen.

Still, with less than an hour before the enemy would arrive, it was their only chance. Twelve people stood in a circle, staring at the only human in the bunch. Chavy joined and decided to fight in his human form, which was his true form, in his mind. Verschiebung looked deep in Savior's eyes, hope resting on his face.

Time froze. It felt no different than any other time, but it was a lot. Savior could feel the excess power draining him. Tempus hummed quietly to itself, though it too felt the draw of energy being pulled from them. Every dragon that transformed added to the flow that drained Savior's energy.

"Are you sure you're going to be alright?" Chavy asked.

"I hope so. Y'all will need me in the fight I think, even if it's just to get people outta there." Savior smiled, though his face quickly focused on the task at hand.

Chavy placed a hand on Savior's shoulder. "Would it be easier to rest, or sleep while we train?"

Probably, Tempus said.

"Y'all should train and not worry about me. Tempus is already exhausted, I can tell by his voice." Savior took off his jacket and balled it up underneath his head.

"We'll send a green over to share some energy with you in a few hours. Until then, sleep." Verschiebung's voice was tired, and a wheeze accentuated every word.

Savior closed his eyes and thought of nothing. **Hum somethin' calm,** he told the parasite.

The tune changed from the Flight of the Valkyries, or close to it at least, to a soft lullaby that came from somewhere in the depths of Savior's mind. It was calm. There were ups and downs, but they were all soft and his own breathing overrode Tempus's performance. *Just a couple of days.* Savior thought to himself. The noise from the dragons was far away, giving him peace of mind and comfort while they did their own thing.

Suddenly a warm feeling entered his body. **Oh yeah,** Tempus sounded soothed. Warmth spread all over, energizing him and causing him to no longer ache. His eyes popped open, and a beautiful woman, or dragon he supposed, hovered over him caressing his hair.

Long brown hair framed her face. Pink pouting lips met in a soft, but pleasant smile. Lime green eyes stared into his, with what appeared to be a green light reflecting from them. The light emanated from his chest and reflected in her dark hair. "Rest," a soft and peaceful voice said.

He closed his eyes again and fell in to a deep sleep. Pings of energy flew through his body though. So much energy filled him, that he felt he could take on any of the hybrids who may stand in his way. If only he could feel like this every day.

Jada popped into his mind. She really was beautiful, but her pain was so great. A picture of her formed, and it was like she was standing in front of him, smiling. *Am I really strong enough to be the person you need?* he asked himself.

As if she were answering the figure embraced him. Whether from love, or kindness, it didn't matter. It felt...good. The last time he felt this way was with Ira, not as strong, but time would grow that connection. One day, he would feel as strong for her, as she could for him.

One day.

The phrase rang through his mind. He didn't love her the same. It was love born from loneliness. In his mind, he knew it wouldn't last, then he would be Tom.

Tommy. That jerk. He left me when I needed him most. He would be dead if it wasn't for me. Savior paused and thought about the words flowing through him.

What? His thoughts were confusing. *How could he be dead? I was with him the whole time. Since we were kids.* The darkness in Tommy's eyes, that once in a while flared after Tempus joined Sylvester, popped into his mind.

I would be dead.

That thought was just as disturbing. They were thoughts he knew to be accurate, but still didn't understand their meaning. He had almost died since becoming the time traveling detective. Tommy was never there though.

Then there was a pit, and he fell. Fire exploded from every wall as he passed, brimstone slamming into his body from every angle. It was hard to breathe now. Time was running out. He would die, and Aiyana would have to save the day.

Then, another light pierced the darkness that was swallowing him. A hand reached for his. He stretched for it. As the hand closed around his own, the grip was firm. It never let go and pulled him up. His body was warm again.

Should have been warm in the fire and brimstone, he thought.

Once again energy poured into him, and he floated away from the reds and blacks, now replaced by greens and blues. A soft warm breeze blew across him as he lay on a bed of grass. Butterflies, white and fluttering through the air, surrounded him.

She would love you if you wanted to settle.

Jada was an ever present notion in his mind. He wasn't her solution, but he could be her friend. More at times, but never anything more than a friend.

Would she have you?

He thought she would. She was the one who said it after all. They were going to go on a date, but he didn't want to lead her on.

Now, he sat before her. Telling her what he needed to say. Her face sank and a gun rose in her hand. It pointed at him... at first. Then she moved it to her own head and pulled the trigger. It was quick. So quick he couldn't stop it.

His arms were nailed to the chair he sat in. Too painful and damaged to move. Tempus held time, the bullet just protruding from the chamber. A drop of blood fell from her temple, but the hole hadn't fully formed yet.

Savior cried out, begging everyone around them to stop what they were doing, and help. No one else was there. He alone had to save her.

The clock ran back, and Jada dropped the gun, her mouth running in reverse. He lied. She was free, running to him and kissing him, caressing him. She was happy, he was almost happy.

They had their first child, he aged, his hair turned white, and his face never smiled again. Their child grew, loving its mother, hating its father. Still, he toiled on, unhappily.

Once more the gun made an appearance in his own hand. Once more he cried, but this time for himself. *Not everyone can be saved, but anything to win,* he said to himself as he raised the gun. The trigger squeezed underneath his finger, happiness finding him once more, and the hammer fell.

Warmth surrounded him again. This kind of warmth he hadn't felt in years. The dragon was there, she looked at him, smiling and leaned down to kiss him. Just as their lips were about to meet, he woke up.

She was there, so was everyone else.

"We thought we lost you that time," Verschiebung said.

"How... how long?" he asked, using his voice for the first time in what seemed like eternity.

"As far as we can tell, it's been a month," Chavy replied. "We're as prepared as we can be, but we could not wake you."

I'm alright too kid. My nightmares were pretty bad, almost as bad as yours, Tempus said.

"Anything to win," Savior said to himself. "Let time go on."

It did. The others were relieved as the pressure of frozen time no longer existed. Savior had a new burden. "Can you have a few more of your people do whatever she did to me?" he asked Chavy.

The dragon nodded. "I'll get you some new clothes too." Chavy walked away. He pat Veronika on the back. Once again the beautiful red head stood there, newly transformed from the old codger who once took her place.

Savior looked at himself. Sweat, dirt, and other stains covered him. A whiff of the air told him everything he needed to know. Somehow the dragons looked different, more confident than they were when he last saw them. *At least one good thing came out of this.*

Chapter Forty-Three
Alexander Wilson

They met Wilson's troops on the surface. It was a cold, and blustery morning. The sky was a faceless grey, and it looked as though it were about to snow. Due to the inhospitable nature of the terrain, Wilson, and his people, including Irwin and Kelly, trudged through a passage surrounded by stone. At least, that's what Aiyana said.

Savior still couldn't see anyone, but she assured him, with her magical abilities, that they were coming. Savior himself was more prepared than he was while lying on the ground in Iridian Hearth. A group of Green dragons, at least, that's what he was told they were, surrounded him, and fed a green light into his body. It felt like the warmth from his dreams, and he knew this was what they did to keep them all safe while he was unconscious.

When he regained his full amount of energy, he felt renewed, as though nothing could stop him. Tempus even mentioned the surge in his abilities. When Savior woke, and they escaped frozen time, he was nothing but skin and bones. His clothes were in no better shape, they were tattered, and torn, after all his thrashing around. The only thing that survived was his coat, which rested on his shoulders as he watched an empty pass. A blue dragon cleaned the garment with magic before he put it back on. He watched as the water ran over it, then lifted dirt, and grime from the fabric.

A dragon brought him clothing, including underwear. The clothing was no different than a person would find at any store:

jeans, boxer briefs, socks, a t-shirt, and a heavy sweater. The sweater was the only article of clothing that felt different. It was soft and felt extremely fragile. He hugged the coat around him as the first black dot appeared against the grey and white background. Thirty more followed close behind.

Five minutes later, the regiment was face to face with fifty people, mostly dragons. Wilson led the pack, a wry, unyielding smile resting on his face. He looked at no one, except Aiyana.

"Somehow I knew you'd be here," he said. "Just couldn't get enough of me I take it."

"I'm sorry Aiyana. I told him everything." A battered and bruised Irwin was shoved to his knees, one arm in a sling.

"He wouldn't let me heal him, said he'd shoot Irwin if I did," Kelly yelled as she too was shoved to her knees. Her face was better off than Irwin's. A black circle, that had already begun to fade surrounded her right eye, and a skin deep cut just above her left eye was all the damage she had received. Aiyana looked at her wife, then Irwin. Rage filled her, but she did not move.

Savior wasn't in front. He waited, biding his time so he could free the hostages. To any normal observer, even those with special abilities, he was just another blip in the crowd. Aiyana would signal when it was time for him to move.

How's it lookin'? he asked Tempus.

Whatever they're doin', I have no access to time, the parasite said. ***He must have really told them everything.***

Can ya blame 'im? Look at his arm. He wasn't angry with Irwin. He likely would have caved in the same situation. ***'Sides I'm not sure he had much of a choice, that Silver dragon magic really has its advantages.***

We can still pop over there and grab 'em. Just pick the place you want to take 'em beforehand, Tempus said.

Savior decided the location. He watched as Aiyana silently looked at the man, anger still flowing through her veins. Anxiety filled her, and her body language was tight and jerky at the sight of Alexander. He was tall with thin hair. A beard, fully covered his face.

It looked as though he hadn't really taken care of his appearance for some time.

"No one deserves what you did to me," Aiyana yelled.

"It was all in the name of science," He replied, the smile never leaving his face. "Besides you agreed to it."

"I did. However you held me there with magic. I couldn't move even if I wanted to." Tears soaked her cheeks as the memories flooded back. "You cut into me, and I couldn't even scream. There were no pain killers, so I felt every cut of that blade." Her voice strained as she spoke.

Kelly's face mimicked Aiyana's, tears flowing down her own cheeks. She had been there during the recovery process. It was a year of therapy before Aiyana could sleep deep into the night, without waking to phantom aches and pains that *he* inflicted.

Aiyana's face never left Wilson's. ***When you're ready, get them outta here. Don't tell me where until it's all over.*** The thought gently touched Savior's mind.

Alright Tempus, you know the plan. The second I put my hands on their bodies get us gone. Savior looked at the space in front of Kelly and Irwin.

It happened in a blur. One second, he knelt on the ground, the next he was face to face with Kelly and Irwin. The suddenness of the entire movement caused Wilson, as well as Irwin and Kelly's guards, to stumble back in surprise.

Savior smiled, turned to Wilson, and put up his middle finger. Just as quickly, his hands moved and rested on Irwin and Kelly's shoulders. Half a second passed and they disappeared. There was pressure, Savior knew it, Irwin and Kelly both felt it to differing degrees, but then they were in Aiyana's office in LA

"I gotta get back, but you" he pointed to Kelly "need to call whatever medical services y'all have for both o' ya."

Kelly started to speak, but before a word could escape, Savior was gone. She looked at Irwin, her own medical training kicking into gear. Her hands glowed green, one rested over her queasy stomach, while the other, hovered over Irwin's broken arm.

Savior reappeared on a ridge he'd seen while waiting. Below, the fighting was really taking off. Aiyana moved like a madwoman. Her body was fluid, moving in a way that seemed impossible for any other person.

On Wilson's side a large beast was fighting two brown dragons. It was shaped like a stone man with wings. Two more of the beasts were being pushed back by the red and green dragons. People scrambled so they would not be crushed by the dragons, or the gargoyles.

Those who hadn't transformed, fought with everything they had. Some shot projectiles at Wilson's troops, others threw barriers in front of those who were busy attacking. Wilson's troops fired shell after shell from rifles. A few of them lay on the ground. More than a few of the dragons were injured, or dead, their bodies littering the ground.

Savior acted fast, popping to a place where he saw one body. They planned this before leaving the city below. He appeared next to the body and transported it to the training field. Green dragons waited to heal the injured, and red dragons waited to burn the dead.

Dragons of varying races waited, prepared to take their comrades place. As soon as he appeared with the first body, a dragon placed his hand on Savior's shoulder and disappeared onto the battlefield. Dragons, for some reason, could withstand the effects of Savior's transportation far better than humans could. Each dragon that joined him was quickly in the midst of the fight with little regard to the effects that plagued humans.

Savior performed this trick for every body that fell, and every person he saw fall. He never tired. The green dragons stopped him long enough to re-energize his body as he dropped their people off. It wasn't often that they stopped him, but each time he told himself he could last longer without their aid.

An acrid smell of burning flesh filled his nostrils while his energy was replenished with green light. The green dragon helping him cried for those they lost. Savior put a hand on his shoulder and gave him a sad smile.

"How many so far?" Savior asked.

"Not a lot, we've only had two that we could not save, but it was two that I knew personally." The dragon's hand stopped glowing. "Try to save more if you can."

Savior nodded.

He appeared back on the battlefield, prepared to take another back when he caught sight of a golden dragon being slammed to the ground. A gargoyle hand squeezed the dragon's neck, and it scrambled while other gargoyles pushed back any dragon that tried to help.

A golden light shone bright, and the golden mass disappeared below Savior's sight. "Tempus!" Savior yelled, blinking from existence as the gargoyle's foot crashed down on the body below. It raised again, prepared to crush the person once more under its massive weight, but the body was gone. It looked at the bottom of its foot confused.

"Healing now!" Savior yelled at the dragons as he reappeared with Veronika's limp and broken body.

Several hands reached out, green light flowing into the dragon's body. Savior waited, nothing else mattered to him. He put her in this position, and he was going to make sure she would return from it. Time could not be manipulated thanks to those people.

"She'll be alright, you need to go." A dragon held his shoulder. "We need to go."

Savior watched as Veronika took a breath, then nodded. They returned to the battlefield. He looked at Wilson's troops, then at the dragons unchanged numbers. They were quickly overwhelming the enemy that remained. No longer did dragons, and their people, fall at regular intervals. The gargoyles still fought, but they were running out of time, that much was clear.

They took stock of their situation. While they hadn't fallen, nearly every troop Wilson brought had. Each gargoyle's face was different. The human face on their normal body had grown and extended, changing it to meet the needs of the new size. Their bodies, however, were identical. Wilson looked around and signaled the others.

A mass of confusion followed as they grabbed at the ground, and each took to the sky. Wilson's remaining troops watched as their leader flew off, then surrendered. They lost. A triumphant cheer bellowed from every dragon standing on the battlefield. Their fatalities were few, but their injuries were great.

The dragons secured the remaining troops. They fought with everything they had, but it wasn't enough. In the end, Wilson's people raised their hands and placed them behind their heads, while they knelt on the ground. Their world would soon be different.

As Savior and the others returned to Iridian Vale, they were welcomed by cheering. It was the first time Savior had felt the excitement of his abilities in a long time. What he'd done had saved lives, and they were all appreciative.

Aiyana placed a hand on his shoulder and looked at him. "You did a good job."

Savior smiled as a tear rolled down his cheek. "Thanks. Couldn't've done it without ya."

Hundreds of dragons stared in awe of this human. A person without their abilities, yet he was able to do so much that no one else in their society could. When he peeled his eyes away from the crowd, he could see the yearning in Aiyana's eyes. "Suppose it's time to get you to Kelly huh?"

Chapter Forty-Four
Aftermath

The remaining troops were taken one by one to WHA headquarters in LA. Initially, Kelly and Irwin met them, and escorted the group to sub-level sixty-five. It was essentially a prison, meant to handle those with hybrid abilities, who needed time to process their choices. Once he was shown the prison level, Savior escorted each person directly to their cells.

When all was said and done, five prisoners were housed on sub-level sixty-five. Savior shook Irwin's hand, his arm no longer broken. Kelly pulled him in for a hug, her face no longer blemished by bruise or cut.

"Thank you for everything," she said. "I should say more, I know thank you is just not enough."

Savior smiled. "Y'all don't need to thank me. I got a pretty good meal out of it."

Kelly laughed and shook her head. "You really are something else."

He disappeared and reappeared in Chavy's office, the dragon sat behind the desk where Aiyana, and Veronika waited. Chavy smiled at the man as he appeared. It had been an interesting few days.

"That's all of 'em," Savior said.

"Thank you," Chavy replied. "You have done a lot for us. Things could have been far worse."

"What were the totals?" Savior asked.

"Only three were killed. The rest were all injuries," Veronika replied. "All in all, it could have been much worse."

"You're forgetting that one of the dragons is missing. We don't know whether he's alive, or dead, just that he's missing," Aiyana said. "We can't even use his powers to find out."

Chavy shook his head. "Do not worry. All will be well. If that dragon is dead, we do need to find him, more so if he lives."

"It'll be the WHA's top priority." Veronika stood. "Speaking of, I'd like to propose something and hope you'll hear me out." Her attention was focused on Chavy.

"You have been redeemed. I'm only sorry you almost died to earn redemption." Chavy leaned back in his chair and waited.

"You really do have the most well trained dragons now. Twelve to be precise, at least one from each race. Well you know what I mean." Veronika leaned down. "I want half of them to join the WHA. The other half I would like to have you send to each dragon city. Train their people so we're prepared for Wilson's next move."

Chavy smiled. "I was thinking nearly the same thing. I wasn't considering the WHA's acclimation of my people, but I was considering the other part of your request."

"Can I chime in," Savior asked.

"After what you've done, I would take your advice anytime it is given," Chavy replied.

"It's important that the WHA, and Dragonians, get along. Your people working within the organization would go a long way to ensuring peace between your groups. Not to mention, I'm sure it would help with training on both sides." Savior looked at Aiyana. "What do you think?"

Aiyana sat quietly while they were talking, she had little to say in the matter, but looked at Savior and smiled. "I think ambassadors would be amazing. Had New Stelladahn had these defenses, we would have stopped him as soon as he arrived. I think the WHA would only benefit from dragons joining. I say, let the dragons have the choice. Either way they're moving from what they know, and going to places they've never been."

"It could be years before any even have a chance to return. If ever." Savior finished Aiyana's sentence. "Let them choose."

Chavy nodded.

"That's true. We don't want to force anyone into it," Veronika agreed. "Chavy, you of course, will stay behind. You need to lead your people."

"We'll let them decide," Chavy said.

They met with the group of dragons an hour later. The choice of leaving, or staying, was given and each was eager to see the world, not just the city they lived in. Then the next choice was given by Veronika.

She offered five of the dragons, each from a different race, positions within the WHA. They would be trained in matters of the surface world, and would be given homes of their own, with the freedom to do as they pleased.

One dragon from each race took her offer, so long as they were still allowed to travel. "With the WHA you travel a lot," Aiyana announced. "You'll see the world before too long." She smiled at them.

"Pack your things and meet us here. Those travelling to New Stelladahn will be transported first with me," Veronika announced. "The rest of you will travel to your new home in Los Angeles with Aiyana. She'll take care of you until I return. I have to make a world tour of my own and announce the other's arrivals." She nodded to those that were to join her. "Go say your goodbyes as well."

Savior transported the dragons to New Stelladahn, saying his goodbyes to Veronika. She hugged him and whispered in his ear. "Expect an envelope from the WHA, as well as a call from the dragons in the future," she said.

"I look forward to workin' with y'all again." He dipped his hat to her, then disappeared.

When he dropped Aiyana in her office he smiled. "I thought you were trouble when I first met you." He laughed. "Turns out I was right." He smiled at her, then laughed.

Aiyana chuckled, then looked him in the eye. "Here's my number. Call me anytime. We're friends now and I couldn't ask for a better one." She smiled.

"Mine too," Irwin offered. "Also, mind poppin' me home? Wife's ready for me to be there and I miss her somethin' fierce."

Savior smiled, hugged Aiyana and took Irwin's hand. "Right outside your house," he said as they disappeared.

Irwin bent over and took a deep breath. "Nothin' beats the salty sea air of Scotland," Irwin said as he stood up.

Savior took a deep breath, and smiled. "It is pretty nice. Have a good one Irwin. Call me anytime. I'll shoot the breeze with ya, or we can go have a pint...so long as I meet you here." Savior smiled again and disappeared as quickly as he and Irwin appeared. The man smiled and walked into the house. The blue paneled door closed behind him with a satisfying thud and a woman screamed with glee at the sight of her husband.

★★★

Sylvester reclined in his overstuffed chair. Work had been quiet since being introduced to the WHA. Then again, it had been quiet before the WHA. He was the only person in the building now. Jada left after they talked. They both agreed that friends was best for now, but she needed to center herself and find who she really was, and wanted to be.

Sylvester hugged her, after one last night together, and kissed her goodbye. He couldn't love her as she deserved, but she was his friend, and he wanted her to know that. She smiled at him as they parted, and handed him the keys to her empty apartment and shop.

He watched her leave, sad to see her go, but he was happy that she would eventually find what she truly wanted. *Besides with Alexander Wilson in my life, there's no way she'd be safe*. At least, his secrets were his own. He returned to his office, and that's where he waited for his next client.

The knock at the door was far from unexpected. His office door had frosted glass after all, and he could still see shapes and silhouettes very clearly. He also recognized the shape that waited outside the door.

"Come on in Veronika," he said.

The small, framed woman sheepishly walked in. "I was going to leave it, but you're here so I'll hand it to you directly. Please don't open it until after I leave?"

Sylvester smiled. "Can't be that embarrassin'." He took the envelope and set it on his desk. "Just finishin' up your Dragonian city tour?" he asked.

"Aye. I made a personal stop to the Edinburgh office and visited Irwin. I handled that envelope as well. Have you been to Edinburgh?" she asked, taking a seat in front of him.

"I've been to Scotland. Edinburgh, Loch Ness, had to see if Nessie was real, a few other places." Sylvester leaned back and eyed her. "I'm glad you're alright. Sorry I couldn't get there sooner."

The dragon smiled. "You saved my life. You have nothing to apologize for. I thank you in that letter, for everything you did for me."

"Some people probably wouldn't have gone out of their way, but I wasn't raised that way. The people who called me son, who I called Ma and Pa, would have been devastated if I didn't do everything I could to help." Sylvester's eyes glossed.

"Well, either way, you're truly a gentleman, regardless of your accent." She smiled. "I would not mind having a conversation about you joining my team."

Sylvester smiled. "I would, but I kinda like having my own business. Although, it would be nice to be busier." He shook his head and leaned forward. "Anytime y'all need me though, I'll be there. Now that I know where y'all operate from, I can buzz in and out at will."

"How do you do that?" she asked.

"Well, once Tempus figured it, out he just plugged the calculations in and... voila." Sylvester looked at his watch. "It's already six? You got dinner plans?"

She smiled. "I had planned to get on a plane and head home."

Sylvester smiled. "I'll make it easy on ya. Let's go get a meal. Anywhere in the world, at any time, that either one of us has been. Then I'll pop ya back to your office whad'ya say?"

Veronika smiled. "Of course, I say yes! Suppose the only question is, do we want breakfast or dinner?"

Sylvester laughed. They decided on breakfast, and popped away to a bistro in Switzerland, not only jumping to a different place, but a few hours in the future. They ate, laughed, and got to know each other. When they finished Sylvester took them back to the present and he left her at the WHA building, in Aiyana's office. The woman was still working when they both popped in from nowhere.

Instead of explaining, Sylvester tipped his hat, and disappeared once more. Tommy and Ira were gone, maybe he would see them again, maybe not, but Aiyana, Veronika and the rest of the WHA would be there if he needed them. When he arrived back in his office, he looked at the envelope, and picked it up. It tapped a few times on the palm of his hand before he opened it and read the letter.

Savior, or Sylvester,

Words can't express what your actions have meant to myself, and the dragon community as a whole. I would not be here if it weren't for you, nor would the people of Iridian Hearth. Alexander Wilson would have destroyed them, and gone on to decimate the world.

Those actions alone would have been enough to earn you a place within the WHA. We'll be there anytime you need us, but I fear that you'll be called upon by us, before you'll have a need. I believe it will also be the end of this separation that the dragons, and the humans, have. It also may be my death. If it is, it will be worth it to ensure that my people live on in some fashion, or another.

When that time comes I ask that you help Aiyana lead the WHA into the future. I'm not saying join us, just be there for her. She will need it. There are two threats from the Dragonian world,

Alexander Wilson is only the first to show themselves. A hero will arrive to stop them both. He'll need you too.

Since I'm sure you're declining my request to join the WHA, included with this letter is a check for a large sum. When you see the number, don't worry, it doesn't even begin to chip away at the financial means of the WHA. Honestly, we make that in a few hours with everything we're doing. Don't tear it up, don't look at it as a bribe, just know that we are thankful, and it is on behalf of myself, the Dragonians, and the WHA.

Truly yours,

Veronika Johnson
Head of the WHA.
Also Known As Verschiebung

PS: It's tax free, don't worry about claiming it. I've paid the taxes personally as a thank you for my continued existence.

Sylvester smiled again and filed away the letter in his filing cabinet. He found a folder called *Thank Yous*, and dropped it there. This was his way of remembering the deeds he'd done right, so anytime he wanted, he could review the thanks he'd received. The check lay face down on the desk, and he contemplated.

Money really wasn't a concern for him. The financial backing his accounts held would hold him over for decades to come. He would deal with the deficit when he needed to. Still, he knew it wouldn't be a bad thing to add to his coffers.

He flipped the check over, and his mouth fell open. Fifty million dollars. *That's a drop in the bucket?* he thought to himself.

Apparently to them, but they do have magic and who knows what they can do with that, Tempus chimed in.

Sylvester leaned back in his chair again and stared at the check. He had more than that, but it was a generous gift, one that he would deposit and cherish. At least, until it was gone. He smiled and closed his eyes before gathering his jacket, and leaving the building.

Part Three

____

All good things...

Kenneth L Powell

Chapter Forty-Five
An Offer He Can't Refuse

Sylvester lounged in his office chair, watching the news as he attended his open hours. He wore a three-piece suit. His jacket was hanging on a coat rack by the door below his hat. The president was on the news again, the world forever changed because of his historic acclimation of Canada and Mexico. It was no longer a deal being worked for years, the nations were now officially part of the United States.

The men that knocked on the door waited patiently as he turned the TV off, then asked them to enter in his southern drawl. There were three, he had only seen two, but the third was nestled behind the others. One of the men had a standard issue government haircut and sunglasses to match. His dark hair streaked with grey, and he wore a windbreaker that read *FBI*.

The other men wore fine black suits. One was bald with brown eyes and a permanent tan. Their partner, had brown hair cut short on the sides, yet long up top. They took the seats in front of Savior, still not saying a word. Windbreaker held a file as he walked over to the detective.

"You're Sylvester Pemberton," he stated flatly.

Savior nodded. "Most folks these days call me Savior."

"We've heard good things about you from the NSA, and we'd like to hire you," the bald man said as he brushed something from the fabric of his pants.

"I don't work for a paycheck. I only work for the cause. If I like the case I'll consider takin' it. Y'all know me, but I don't know you." Savior looked at the men and waited. Windbreaker sat the file on his desk and took his place behind the other men.

They exchanged glances. "Agent Hernandez," the bald man said.

"Agent Smith." Savior smirked slightly, but kept his composure with the agent.

"Agent Sudeikis," windbreaker said.

"Who at the NSA recommended you hire me?" Savior asked.

"We were contacted by an agent Aiyana Evans," Sudeikis said. "She recommended you for this case. I personally think you're too close to it."

Savior raised an eyebrow and looked at the file. *Tony "Micky" Antonio – Chicago, IL.* He stared at the name for longer than he realized. They all watched his expression closely.

"You want my help to bring down Micky?" he asked. "Sorry... I'm just shocked is all. I considered takin' on this case myself. That was before I found out y'all were workin' it."

"We're glad you didn't mister Pemberton..."Agent Sudeikis said.

"Savior, I wasn't jokin'," he interrupted.

"As agent Sudeikis was saying, had you done so I wouldn't be surprised if you messed the case up for us completely," Hernandez replied.

"I don't care about any of that." He watched the men exchange glances. "What I care about is justice. Whad'ya need from me?"

"We've hit a dead-end. Your parents' murder wasn't the first, and definitely wasn't the last. Micky is ruthless and has debts he's been collecting since long before that day mister Savior," Smith said.

"If only my name were Anderson." Savior shook his head.

"You're not the first to make that joke, can we move on?" Smith replied with an irritation that told Savior it had been a regular practice.

Savior raised his hands. "I surrender. You still haven't gotten to what you need from me."

"After we were informed about you we did some digging. You've actually been messing with Micky's organization since you started working. Your employee, Rebecca Stevens, had a run in with the mob and somehow you managed to help her find footage of the act in progress," Sudeikis explained.

"And?" he replied. "I got lucky."

"So lucky that a man named Samuel Kripke, who was being blackmailed by another arm of Micky's organization, was freed from that debt and the entire operation in Denver was shut down?" Hernandez leaned in, a broad smile on his face. "Don't mistake my tone for displeasure. I'm thrilled that dirtbag is getting his own ass handed to him."

"You also helped the NSA with their own problem. It was never made clear what that problem was, but you came highly recommended," Smith finished.

"Alright so it's more than luck." Savior shrugged.

"We need evidence to convict Micky and put him away forever." Sudeikis looked around the room. "Stevens monitoring?"

A single camera looked into the room, installed recently by Rebecca herself. There was a knock on the glass and Rebecca opened the door. "Of course, I'm monitoring."

"Good, cause you're gonna be a part of this," Smith said.

"Only if Savior wants me to," she replied, staring at him.

"You won't be in the field, you'll just help with equipment. Your government demands it, and in exchange a nice little bonus for each of you." Hernandez leaned back.

"Again... I don't do it for the money. Ms. Stevens gets paid a pretty salary. I'll tell you what, I don't want anything, but if I manage to get you evidence of my parents' murder, or any other crimes he's committed himself, y'all pay her triple her yearly salary and ensure its tax free." Savior smiled and thumbed the file open.

The agents exchanged looks. "Could pull it from the black budget," Smith said.

"Nah they're throwin' that to the CIA," Hernandez rebuffed.

"Look Savior, most we can do without getting the brass involved is half her salary. I can pull some strings and get her, and you, a tax holiday for the next three years. Save you some money," Sudeikis replied.

"I can't even do that," Hernandez said.

"I can. I've been here longer and greased the right wheels in most departments." Sudeikis smiled smugly.

Savior looked at Smith.

"I'm new compared to these guys. Don't look at me," he said.

"Tell ya what, we'll let Rebecca decide," Savior said.

She looked at the detective, smiled and rolled her eyes, then looked at the agents. "Three quarters my salary and five years tax free for the both of us."

"Done," Sudeikis replied.

"You have equipment to make this happen?" she asked.

"State of the art. What do you think you'll need?" Hernandez replied.

Rebecca looked at Savior. "I've got lots of ideas runnin' through my head, but let's get this guy to the crime scenes you want evidence from. Except... well you know."

They did know. He didn't need to see his parents' murder again. If he had his way then he really wouldn't. Savior would let Rebecca watch that one, once they had evidence. Now it was time to plan.

Chapter Forty-Six
All The Crime In The World

They drove with Agent Sudeikis. He was the senior agent on the case, and the best resource for each incident. If Micky was physically involved in a crime scene himself, he had been there. There weren't cases many tied directly to Micky. Aside from Savior's parents, Micky had not been seen at any other location, though he was suspected to have been at three more.

"The evidence has to be legit," Sudeikis said. "We need to see Micky's face, hear his voice and witness the act."

"If I get you evidence, it'll be legit. I won't even need to see him myself," Savior said.

Rebecca nudged him.

"That is, I won't need to be put in a situation, where you'll need to put a wire on me," Savior corrected.

"That's good because we're not going to do that either way. Too many factors to worry about and the department doesn't know we've hired an outside contractor." Sudeikis put his blinker on, and they turned left.

He pulled into a parking lot. "This is one of the locations where a body was found and Micky may, or may not have, been here."

"Mind showing us exactly where things went down?" Rebecca asked.

"Sure, follow me." Sudeikis got out of the car and walked them to a large open area.

Rebecca and Savior held back. "I got you two microphones and two cameras. She handed him two cubes barely large enough to look like they housed a camera, let alone a recording device and two flash drives. "This switch will turn it on. They can record for eight hours, so try to put them in place close to the time he's there."

"Comin'?" Sudeikis rushed.

"Sorry 'bout that," Savior said.

"Like I was sayin' the body was found here at nine p.m. and, according to the autopsy report, it should have happened around four," Sudeikis cited the report from memory.

Savior looked around the area for places to hide the audio devices. "When was it?"

"January fifteenth two thousand eight," Sudeikis answered.

Savior looked at Rebecca and winked. Time stood still. "You heard him Tempus, take me back." The world warped around Savior, moving in reverse. It was all a blur.

His vision cleared and time was still frozen. The body was already there. "Go back every ten minutes," he said.

Ten minutes earlier, the body was still there. Another ten minutes, then another, and another. The autopsy report seemed extremely off, but time continued rolling back.

Then the body was gone. Savior stopped Tempus and looked around. No one was there. He walked toward the street and looked, but there were too many vehicles to pinpoint which one he was looking for.

"Minute at a time buddy," Savior said.

Yessir oh master sir, Tempus chided.

Each minute rolled forward, cars passed with no sign that the area was interesting. Suddenly, a small pickup truck stopped, and backed up to the entrance. Two men got out of the vehicle, clad in white hazmat suits. The tailgate fell, and the body was dragged out and dropped.

"Alright Tempus, we're goin' for a ride." He hopped in the pickup truck and let the parasite reverse time every few seconds. It was like living in a slow-motion movie.

The truck drove backward to the scene of the crime, an office building. Savior followed the men inside, rode the elevator a few flights, then smiled when he saw the man sitting in the office chair. Micky, covered in blood, stood up and met the men who stood holding the lifeless body.

The face started to move of its own volition, eyes darting wildly as Micky pushed a bloody bowie knife into the man, then pulled the knife free. It was clean with no wound to be seen. The man's face was battered and bruised, but he could have survived.

He watched the man, as every few punches seemed to heal his wounds. Then there was just a clean shaven guy, held by two goons, fear filling his face. The world continued to rewind as Savior watched him drug from the room in reverse. Micky left for a few minutes, then came back.

"That's the spot," Savior announced.

Tempus moved time forward to the moment when the office was empty, then froze it. Savior examined the area, holding his hands up, thumbs touching, and index fingers extended as though he were setting the camera for a movie. He placed the first camera in a location where it would be clear that Micky was the one taking his aggressions out on the victim. A tenacious grouping of papers lay on Micky's desk. It was an easy enough place to hide one of the microphones, and he lay it under a few pieces of paper. One of the other camera's took footage of the crime from the opposite side of the room.

He wanted to be sure he could capture the best possible audio. Each microphone was the size of a small USB flash drive. He thought about putting the second mic directly on Micky. It wouldn't be too hard, and the mobster would be too busy to realize it was on him.

Then he considered all of the jostling Micky would be doing. As the man pummeled his victim, he did not hold back. His goons wore thin shirts, nothing that could easily hide anything small or large. Even the victim couldn't be used. Not only was he going to be the one beaten up, but he would also be stabbed.

Savior settled for a side table near the scene. Close enough that it should pick up the voices, but it would sit in the open, obvious to anyone paying attention. Savior looked at the microphone, then at the table. The stain was dark enough that he may get lucky, and the mic would blend.

I just hope it isn't spotted, Savior thought.

Soon as it's over we'll grab that one, Tempus said as he attempted to alleviate any concern. *The other one can wait until Micky leaves.*

The scene played out once more, though moving forward in time. Savior watched as the man was brutalized, then murdered. They could have simply moved to the right moment in time, but Savior wanted to be sure that no one caught sight of his equipment.

Micky never even looked in the direction of the table. When it was over and the men were gone, Micky examined himself, said something, then left the room. It was done.

Savior collected the devices before teleporting back to the dumping ground. He took his original position. *Ready,* he said.

"I'm not sure what you'll be able to do here," Sudeikis remarked.

"Was there any blood on the ground?" Savior asked, staring directly at Rebecca.

"Yeah, but it didn't match any patterns for a knife wound, or the brutal beating he took." The agent replied.

"Were there any cameras on the streets at that time? Did anyone see anything at all?" Savior asked.

"No." Sudeikis shook his head, thinking he may have hired someone who thought the FBI were incompetent.

"I don't think Micky was here. Looking at the photos and actually seeing this place today, it just doesn't make sense. Why would Micky risk exposing himself to the public?" Savior still looked at Rebecca. "If I were the FBI, I would have looked at any buildings that Micky was associated with at the time, but that's just me," he mocked.

Sudeikis took a deep breath. "We did that," he said as calmly as he could.

"Would you mind letting my associate and I have a brief moment alone?" Savior asked.

Sudeikis raised his hands and walked away. His gait showed the frustration he clearly felt. A smirk graced Savior's lips, but only briefly.

"I've got everything we'll need for this one. It didn't happen here. Happened at an office building of all places." Savior handed her the equipment. "Can you connect to these with your phone?"

Rebecca smiled. "Give me two minutes and we'll see how well these worked."

"And check the records of his known addresses and associated buildings while I go talk to this 'agent'." Savior air quoted, raising his voice enough so Sudeikis would hear him mock the man and his profession.

"What buildings did you look at? Secluded ones that he would have been at... maybe?" Savior asked when he joined the man.

Another deep breath escaped Sudeikis. "We looked at warehouses nearby, as well as any alleys along the way just in case there was a blood trail we missed."

"Didja try office buildings? Homes? Any of that personal stuff?" Savior looked at the man. "I'm only askin' 'cause the man's a hothead."

"We figured that would have been too on the nose, and he wouldn't have wanted to be in the public eye when he murdered someone." Sudeikis continued to stare at Savior with a blank face.

"Savior," Rebecca yelled.

"Excuse me." Savior walked away slowly. When he didn't hear footsteps following he joined Rebecca.

"This the building?" she asked, pointing to her phone.

"Sure looks like it," he said.

"Micky didn't own it, nor was it associated with him in anyway. However, the victim was leasing an office on the...."

"Fourth floor." Savior shook his head. "Killed him in his own place. Bet they didn't think to look there."

"Wouldn't have mattered. The audio was crisp and clear. Video too. He ordered a cleanup crew when he finished the job." Rebecca tossed one of the cubes in the air. "This thing is amazing."

"You didn't try it first?" he asked.

"I did, just nice to know it works in the field," she replied.

Sudeikis was walking toward them. "Are you ready to move on to the next place?" he asked.

Savior raised a finger and leaned down to speak into Rebecca's ear. "The next location is the last one in Denver, start compiling what you can while we drive."

"You're in luck," she whispered. "I brought my laptop."

Chapter Forty-Seven
Just One Hitch

The last crime scene in Denver was much the same as the first. Savior followed the body from where it was found to a random building where Micky, once again, slew the victim. Every image and soundbite was captured perfectly. Complacency at how easy the case was overwhelmed Savior.

He felt a bit bad that he was treating Sudeikis like an incompetent agent. Sudeikis had not been part of most of the crime scenes in Denver. Case files were the base of his knowledge, and once he became aware of the involvement, Sudeikis had the lead walk him through every detail. Overall, he seemed like a good guy. Someone the detective would enjoy spending time with outside of work.

There were two crime scenes in Kansas where Micky was suspected to be involved. Of course, one was his parents' murder only a few years earlier. The other, was another farm house, but this time the entire family was slain. It happened only a couple of years before the events at his own farmhouse.

Savior thought there had to be too much media presence to continue operating in the state. Kansas was boring. For those, like himself, who grew up on a farm in a flat state whose main claim to fame was farming and transportation equipment, the state wasn't exciting in the slightest. When a murder happened, it was blasted across the state, and became nearly national news.

When the Henderson's were murdered, husband, wife, fifteen year old daughter, ten year old son, and six year old son, it was the only thing people talked about. After the media coverage died down, and the authorities were baffled, things went quiet. No one thought that, just a couple years later, another gruesome set of murders would occur.

The media, again, immediately latched on to the crime. They tried to interview a son who seemed to have disappeared entirely. For the authorities, the connection was made, the Bureau was called in, and someone let leak that the Henderson and Pemberton murders were connected. It had only just died down once again, leaving those to wonder what happened, how it happened, and whether the culprit was still at large.

Rebecca, Sudeikis, and Savior sat down to lunch, and discussed the case. "I'm confident I can get you some real evidence. Not just something you have to make happen by luring him into a trap." Savior dunked a fry in ketchup and ate it.

"How can you be that confident?" Sudeikis asked.

"Just trust me. Maybe one day I'll tell you in on the how, and why of it all. That day is not today." Savior waved him off.

"He helped me. I can't tell you how, but I promise you, he'll give you everything you need." Rebecca placed her hand on the overwhelmed agents. "After all... you've seen my file."

"What I give you at the end of this will need a lot of explaining, and I will explain it eventually. We can even turn it in as anonymous evidence if you want. I wanna be there when you take that bastard down." Savior leaned in. "I want him to look in my eyes, so I can tell him, I was the one who brought him down, even if it's just a whisper. He has to know who I am." Savior was angry. The others knew it wasn't with them, but Micky.

Rebecca leaned back, silent.

"Alright. As long as you'll tell me how... someday," Sudeikis said.

The smile spread across Saviors face. "Sure thing."

"We'll get to the house in a bit. It's still there, completely abandoned." Sudeikis took a sip of his coffee.

"Sure." Savior looked at Rebecca who gave him a half-hearted smile. "Sudeikis... I'm sorry."

The agent looked at him. "What for?"

"To be honest, I've been ribbin' ya hard. You don't deserve that. You do a damn good job as an FBI agent." Savior nodded at the man.

Sudeikis flushed slightly. "Well... thank you for the apology. I'll wait to accept it until I understand how you do what you do."

"Fair 'nough," Savior said.

They finished their lunch and drove another three hours to Dighton, Kansas, then another forty minutes to a farm south of town. For Savior, it was like going home. The farmhouse was almost identical to his parents, though mister Henderson had far less land than Pa Pemberton ever did.

They walked inside the farmhouse, and stopped in the living room. The nearest neighbor would never have heard the screams of the children or the parents as Micky slaughtered each of them. Savior wasted no time. He ordered Tempus to take him back. They knew the date, and time. All residents in Kansas did. It was six years ago. Savior watched the incident unfold like laundry in the wind. His equipment recorded all the while. Micky placed the entire family in stiff dining chairs and bound their hands and feet.

He gagged each member of the family and pulled out a knife. The little boy started crying, then everyone else joined. Micky yelled something. Savior could only hear echoes of it, as though the words reverberated off of distant canyon walls. It didn't matter, they would have audio soon enough.

Micky started with the little boy, slapping him hard, then punching the little face. The mother struggled frantically, and yelled through her gag. The gangster moved to her. He punched her so many times that Savior lost count, and her head lulled in the end. His knife sat on the hearth. It was clear that this was the same one he used in Denver.

Micky reached for it and cut the woman's throat. She didn't move at the feeling of the blade. Micky had beaten her to death. The knife ran across the daughter's bared arm as he wiped her mother's blood from the blade. The girl sobbed through the gag, tears falling. Savior assumed that the remaining members of the family, were a loud cacophony of gagged wails and sobs.

Micky said something to one of his men who turned the father's chair. The fat man fondled the girl, rubbing her all over as he watched the man's face. Depression and rage filled the father at first, then Micky smiled, and he smacked the girl. Fear overwhelmed Mister Henderson as he struggled with all his might to move. All he wanted, was to break free and save those who still breathed.

Savior cried a lot. He was heartbroken that he couldn't change this one thing without causing untold damage to the timeline. Every fiber of his being wanted to stop it. Tempus held him back with words of comfort and justice. All Savior could think was how unfair the situation was.

Micky started punching the girl, first in the stomach then the face. He laughed maniacally as he did, though all Savior could see was the physical laugh. Sound wasn't always an echo. When the girl cried hysterically Micky leaned in and licked the blood mixed tears from her face. The tip of the blade rested in front of one of her open eyes. He wanted her to see what was coming.

She panicked and struggled more than she had the entire time. Micky pointed the knife at her left eye and pushed the blade in. Her screams reached a fever pitch that even Savior in his place out of time could hear. The detective moved forward to stop Micky.

This has to happen, Tempus' voice cracked.

Savior stopped and watched as the girl's eye was ground away as he twisted the knife within the socket. Then Micky ended her suffering by pulling the knife from her skull, looking at Mister Henderson, and plunging the blade directly into her heart. He sobbed and rolled his head.

Savior caught something he hadn't before. One of Micky's eyes was different. The color was only slightly off, but it was different. Scars where a knife fell into his eye ran from each lid. It seemed so familiar, but he couldn't place why, not exactly.

Micky indulged himself with the middle child, performing similar acts, except for the groping. When the boy was dead Micky looked at the smallest child, still crying and shaking. He said something to the father, then stabbed the boy in the heart as well.

Savior shook his head as he watched everything else. The tape covering the father's mouth was ripped away. He said something Savior couldn't hear. The man's lips formed the words *'just kill me'*. Savior didn't need to hear what the broken man said.

Micky leaned down, and, instead of stabbing him, pulled his hair. He looked at the men he brought, said something and waited for them to laugh. Clearly, they were uncomfortable, but after a second they joined in. Pleased with himself, Micky laughed louder as he scalped the man. His screams matched that of his daughter's and Savior could hear the eerie echo in his place out of time.

Micky didn't stop there. One of the ears was cut off, then Micky sawed at his nose. The last thing he did was pull the man's tongue out, not to cut, but to physically rip it away from his mouth. The knife disappeared into a bag and Micky left the house.

His men moved around, wiping away anything that may have linked the crime to Micky. Saliva was cleaned away from the girl's face. Savior didn't need that evidence, he had video and audio.

His stomach turned as he froze time and gathered the equipment. The cameras fell into the pocket of his jacket, which he zipped closed afterward. No sense losing the evidence when he had to endure seeing such a gruesome crime.

"Alright Tempus," he quaked.

Nothing happened.

"Tempus?"

From out of nowhere a force shoved him into the wall. Savior looked around, but nothing could be seen. He stood up, and looked the room over. Just as suddenly as before, he was shoved toward the kitchen, crashing into the dining table.

"... saved them..." A voice echoed with no distinction of whether it was male, or female.

Savior whipped around in time to see the shadowy creature rush toward him. This time, he couldn't even communicate with Tempus, let alone have the parasite use its powers. Savior ran to the door and ripped it open only to come face to face with Micky.

Chapter Forty-Eight
The Name Of The Game

Micky, and his goons, strapped Savior to another chair. Excitement covered the boss's face. "Saw everything didn't ya?"

The goons didn't pat him down, so they didn't find the cameras, or audio equipment. Neither did they see the shadowy figure hovering behind their boss. Micky didn't feel it, or see it. Only Savior could. The mob boss looked at him, some form of recognition covering his face.

"This is the fuckin' guy," Micky said.

"What guy boss?" one of the mostly identical goons asked.

"This is the guy who gave me my glass eye!" Micky pointed at the scarred eye lid.

Savior looked at him. He had never seen the man before he killed Al and Janet. "I don't know who you are," Savior lied.

"Then what the hell're you doin here?" Micky growled.

Savior said nothing else.

Micky smiled. "That's okay. I like it when they don't talk."

The first hit felt like a brick to the side of his face. Micky went for the gut next. For fun, he raised his foot, and stomped between Savior's legs. Every hit caused the detective to scream in agony. The kick to his groin increased the pitch and volume of his scream. Those listening could easily mistake it for howling.

The shadow figure behind Micky swirled differing colors of red, green, blue, black and silver. It liked what it was seeing. Savior watched the creature through tears and gasping breaths.

Tempus, I really need ya buddy, he yelled in his mind.

Bright lights blurred his vision as another punch met the other side of his face. A tooth came loose, and flew across the room, landing somewhere Savior couldn't see. Another cracked and shattered.

"Who do you work for?" Micky yelled.

"You want the knife boss?" a goon asked.

Micky paused. He seemed to be weighing his options. As he did, he leaned on the chair. "Nah. If I do I'll kill him. You know how I like to do this." Micky closed his fists and dropped them on Savior's skull with all of his weight.

Red blurred his sight, but he could still see the shadowy creature violently changing shape. Spots filled his vision as Micky hit him again. This time his nose bent at a weird angle.

The creature's shape changed from manlike to an amorphous blob. Then, it stretched toward the ceiling, from the ground. It seemed to be struggling, and Savior hoped this was a good sign for him.

Another few punches landed, then Micky balled his fists together again and slammed them into Savior's chest. His breath caught and wouldn't release while the subtle beats of his heart seemed to stop. Fear took hold. He was going to die.

"Think you killed 'im boss," one of the men said.

"Damn, and I was just gettin' into it." Micky laughed.

The creature froze too. It seemed to be looking at Savior and acknowledging his presence. Savior raised his head slowly, and looked at the creature. What he could see of it vanished as his vision turned to pins and needles in an ever darkening tunnel.

Kid are you alright? Tempus was yelling in his head.

Savior couldn't even get a thought out before the world blurred around him. For the first time in years he felt the pressure of moving from one place in time to another. It was unbearable with his wounds, but he couldn't scream. He couldn't even think beyond the pain.

Tempus worked hard inside Savior's body, trying to put the man back together. When they landed at the same spot they left, Sudeikis and Rebecca stared at the man who was suddenly strapped to a chair and looked as though he were dead. ***Call the emergency line you morons,*** Tempus yelled, though none could hear the parasite.

"Get an ambulance here," Rebecca yelled at Sudeikis. The agent was in shock. He had never seen a man change from standing to strapped in a chair in an instant. It wasn't a subtle change, and it broke his resolve.

Rebecca pulled out her own phone and dialed the number as she frantically tried to untie Savior. "I've got an emergency, my boss was beaten, or fell. I don't know, but he looks like he's going to die. Get an ambulance here.... Use my GPS, I'm at the Henderson farm." The operator acknowledged the location.

Rebecca stood, and smacked Sudeikis. "I'll tell you everything, and show you what he's been doing, but you have to pull yourself together." She shook him.

Slowly Sudeikis came to. He acknowledged the scene, then looked at her. "How?" he asked.

"Right now it doesn't matter. He needs our help, and we have to get our stories straight. We came in and found him like this... right?" she asked, though it was more like a demand.

Sudeikis only nodded.

Rebecca took a deep breath and knelt back down. "He's got a pulse. Let's hope he keeps it until they get here."

Sudeikis knelt next to the battered and broken man. "Will he be alright with you telling me everything?"

"I don't think that's what matters right now," Rebecca said resting a hand on Savior. Everything seemed to finally hit her, and she started crying. Sudeikis wrapped his arm around her, and held her while they waited.

Chapter Forty-Nine
Recovery

Three weeks passed. Savior was in and out of consciousness the entire time. Tempus, while able to boast about keeping the man well, could only do so much. Rebecca was at her boss's side when she could be. The hospital only allowed so much when it came to visiting someone who wasn't a relative.

After spending his initial time in a Kansan hospital, he was transferred closer to home. Christmas was only two weeks away and Denver received a thin blanket of snow. It wasn't the first snowfall they had, but it had been a couple of weeks since snow fell, and melted away. The weather was abnormal for what they typically saw.

Agent Sudeikis visited regularly. He also knew why Savior was able to get what he was. "I still don't understand why he doesn't just go back to when Micky was born and off 'im." The agent shook his head.

"As I've said a dozen or more times over the last few weeks, it would alter the timeline. He's who he is because of Micky," Rebecca said as she sipped her coffee.

"I just don't understand how he could sit there and film those things without reacting," Sudeikis said.

"Because if I change things, the world changes so much, I no longer exist. Your whole career changes completely," Savior said. These moments of consciousness grew increasingly common. "Tempus says hello," he said.

Rebecca smiled. "Tell that thing that it needs to figure out how not to be so useless when it comes to whatever the shadow is." She giggled to ease Savior's mind.

Savior didn't smile, or laugh. He communicated the incident to her, and Sudeikis, the first time he came to. He agreed wholeheartedly with Rebecca, not in a joking manner, but with real fire in his thoughts. The first time it showed up he would have been severely injured, this time he was on the brink of death.

"Rebecca showed me what you have. It's great, almost enough to convict. No jury is going to believe that he was there and allowing people to film him," Sudeikis admitted. "We know it was him. That's all we have. I knew it was him before then."

"You had a hunch, not confirmed evidence," Savior replied, his voice strained. "He never stopped using that same knife. I could snag it from him at the most recent crime scene."

"Only when you're better. He has no idea that we have this much on him," Rebecca said.

"She's not wrong. The longer we wait the harder it'll be. We know where he is right now, but if he gets spooked for any reason, he's gone with the wind," Sudeikis said. "He's visiting his daughter now, like he does every Christmas. We need to take him down before he leaves."

"If it weren't for the random times that I pass out, I would definitely finish this now. I just need to see the others," Savior said.

"Doctors said they found the reason for that and have made plans to fix it," Rebecca replied.

"Or I could finish this beforehand. Just bring one of you with me." Savior shrugged.

Are you crazy? You couldn't do anything while I was incapacitated. If that thing shows up again they're in just as much danger as you and me, Tempus replied.

"Surgery happens in the next few days. If you come out of it, and you're not passing out anymore, then I would gladly join you," Sudeikis said. "Until then, let's make a plan."

"I need to get footage of my parents' murder. Then we need some physical evidence. The knife," Savior said.

"The knife only works if it's still covered in blood. If you take it out of the equation too soon won't that ruin the timeline just as much as if you took Micky out?" Sudeikis responded.

"Seems like I already have tried." Savior mumbled.

"What do you mean?" Rebecca asked.

"When I was back there, he recognized me. Said I gave him the scars, and the glass eye. I've never seen him before their murder, but that's what he says." Savior closed his eyes and grabbed his head.

"Relax. It's okay. Go to sleep and don't stress about this," Rebecca said.

Savior leaned back, and was instantly gone. Sudeikis looked at him. "Poor kid. Has all this power and can't do what I would be dying to do."

"Well, not everyone can follow through with murder," Rebecca replied.

"Got the glass eye from a kid in an alley," Sudeikis said. "Claimed that the kid was in a hospital gown, and that he just vanished before his eyes."

"Who knows what happened, but it sounds like Savior before he really understood what he was doing," Rebecca said. "Maybe he was trying to stop Micky from doing something." Rebecca leaned forward. "Maybe Micky was the reason he was in a hospital gown?"

"Doesn't matter how it happened, or really if it was Savior who did it," Sudeikis walked to the door. "I've gotta get back to Chicago. Let me know if he comes out of this."

Rebecca smiled. "Will do."

Sudeikis left and Rebecca opened her laptop. If Savior never came out of his condition the footage would have to be enough. She looked at the man lying there. *If he doesn't come out of this I'm out of a job.*

Chapter Fifty
Picking Up The Pieces

A week later Sylvester was back on his feet. Any concerns that he would lose consciousness at random times, were alleviated. When he left the hospital, Rebecca helped him to her car, drove him home, and put him on his couch. Thankful for her help, he still complained that he'd had enough of laying around.

"You have two options, cause you're still not fit to do your job," Rebecca said. "Either recover in real time, and spend the next two months lazing around, and learning to do what you already knew how to do again, or do your time thing."

"Tempus said he could stop time, and allow my recovery that way, but that's gonna be hard and so borin'." Sylvester took a breath.

"If you want to finish this case, you'll need to do it that way," she replied.

The thought of Micky getting away with everything he'd done irked him. He didn't want to fail to solve any case, but this one hit hardest, and closest to home. "Fine." He submitted after thinking about it a while. "Do me a favor, and go pick up some books for me. Dime store detective novels, fantasy novels also. Big thick ones if you can."

Rebecca smiled. "I'll be back in a couple of hours."

"Food too, bottles of water. Really anything that I can easily eat without cookin' it," Sylvester finished.

"Alright. Make it four or five hours then." She waved a hand at him as she left his apartment.

Sylvester turned on the TV and flipped through the channels. What else could he do while he waited? News, cartoons, movies… none of it had any appeal. He opened the Audible app on his phone, and flipped through different books. He could manipulate his phone, and the battery still drained, but he could always charge it so long as he touched the outlet in some way.

By the time Rebecca returned Sylvester had purchased every available Stephen King book, and dozens of Fantasy books on the app. Two months in a state where time was frozen would fly by with each of the books that he now had access to.

"Alright. I've got a bunch of jerky for you. Not the healthiest meal for anyone to eat, but it'll do for what you need I suppose." She set one bag down at his side. It was filled to overflowing with different bags of jerky.

"I'm gonna get fat," Sylvester joked.

"I didn't know how milk would fair, so I bought you a gallon and a variety of cereals. I'll get you more if you need it." Another bag was set down next to him, then two more. All filled with varying cereals.

"I bought some fruits, oranges, apples, and berries. No sense in giving you scurvy while you try to heal." She set yet another bag on the floor next to him. "Also a couple of loaves of bread, a couple of jars of peanut butter, and jam."

"Well… I guess this'll do," he said.

"If you need more at any point, unfreeze time again, and let me know. I'll even cook something for you," she said.

"Thank you Rebecca. I know you won't be here for more than a few minutes, but I appreciate ya doin' everything you're doin'."

She plopped down on the couch next to him. "Well, I won't get my tax free five years until you finish this case, so… hurry up." She smiled and nudged him playfully. Sylvester froze time while she smiled at him.

Two months would be a long time, and a friendly face was always a good thing. He turned on Stephen King's *It* and listened to the narrators voice until he was tired sixteen hours later. Sleep took him until his body decided it was ready to be awake.

At least a day had passed, and the milk held its coolness. It even tasted fresh, as though it hadn't sat on the floor all night. ***You're going to want to let that sit outside of frozen time. It'll still spoil if you don't,*** Tempus said.

"What? I just tell you to freeze and unfreeze it?" Sylvester asked.

Still learnin' after all these years. Almost brings a tear to my eye, Tempus jokingly replied.

"Alright I get it. Well do your thing then, I got enough for now." He set the jug of milk down and it looked no different than when he picked it up. "You sure that worked?"

Absolutely, now get back to the story. Tempus enjoyed the tale of the evil clown. By the time Sylvester was ready to go back to sleep, the book had finished, and he was thinking.

What's the matter? Tempus asked.

"The preteen orgy at the end. That's what's the matter. Great book, except for that." Sylvester scrolled through his phone, looking for the next book to listen to.

Just go to sleep, pick another when you wake up, Tempus demanded.

Sylvester agreed, and retired to his room. That's how it went for the next fifty days. Sometimes he did unfreeze time, but only when he was low on food, or needed a decent shower. It was the only way he could actually shower, without having to hold the pipe so water would flow.

At day fifty two, he felt normal. There was no strain on his body when he moved. He unfroze time for the last time during his recovery. For Rebecca, only a couple of hours had passed and she wasn't that lonely, but for Sylvester it was nice to have someone to talk to aloud, whenever he wanted.

"Sixty days?" she asked.

"Fifty two. I feel great though." He shrugged. "Close enough I think."

"Well, I guess it'll have to do. Pickin' up where you left off tomorrow?" she asked.

"Yeah. My parents' murder," he said in a sullen and soft voice.

"I'm going with you," she assured him. "Just in case that thing shows up. At least it's two against one in that situation." She smiled. "Tomorrow at eight we'll head to Kansas."

Chapter Fifty-One
Nightmares

Rebecca arrived the next morning with ten minutes to spare and inspected him. Sylvester looked older, not much, but enough that she noticed. He smiled weakly at her, and accepted the cameras and audio devices.

"I'm a bit nervous," he said.

"Because of the creature, or the place we're going?" she asked.

"Both I guess." His hand was shaking, though he placed the other on top to physically stop it.

"I'll be there with you. If you don't want to be in the basement at all, I'll set everything up while you wait upstairs," Rebecca offered.

"Can't do that," he said.

She looked at him.

"I blocked the door so I can't just walk up the stairs and go to the kitchen." Sylvester stared at her.

Rebecca placed a hand on his shoulder. "Just get us there, and turn around. I'll deal with the rest."

He nodded.

"Ready?"

He shook his head, but took her hand and smiled. "Not in the slightest."

The pressure that built up was still new for her. She hadn't traveled with Sylvester since he helped her. When they stopped in a basement, darker than the night of a Colorado winter, she lurched. Dry heaving was all that came from it.

After she repeated the motion a few times, she stopped and stood up straight. Sylvester rested a hand on her shoulder, and rubbed lightly. "Gonna be alright?" he asked.

She nodded. "Sorry. I forgot how this whole thing makes you feel."

He smiled, and looked around. "I brought us to a couple hours before it all went down." He walked to the hidden room. "This is where Ma is, likely countin' money." He pulled out the cameras, and handed her one.

It took him no time to explain the way Micky was facing, then how his parents were facing and where he hid. She walked around the basement and found a decent spot for the first camera. Sylvester looked around and placed the second while also placing both microphones. One sat in an obscure spot just under the stairs. The other sat on an open ledge between one of the eight-by-eight weight bearing columns and the bracket that held it in place.

When all was said and done, the man held out his hand and Rebecca grabbed it. "Neither one of us'll have to watch this," he said. "Not 'til later at least."

He moved them through time, which was less straining on Rebecca. They stopped just after he left originally. Their bodies sat in the chairs. The Pembertons' were dead, blood pooling below them. Sylvester closed his eyes, and asked Rebecca to gather the equipment. A few minutes later she returned and took his hand.

They disappeared from the place he once called home, and arrived back in his apartment. "Go ahead and go through that, make sure it's good enough," he sighed, eyes still firmly shut.

She set the cameras and the microphones down, then grabbed the tall man and hugged him. She said nothing, only held him as he cried warm salty tears. After twenty minutes she let go, and looked up at him. "We're gonna take him down," she said.

He nodded, but said nothing in return.

Rebecca took the equipment and disappeared into his office, then through the office door leading to the hall. Depression set in. Tempus tried to speak to Sylvester, but the man firmly ignored it. At some point, he ran a bath. A full bottle of scotch and a glass joined him as he eased himself into the tub.

He poured a little into the cup, then a lot. Eventually the bottle tipped up and into his mouth. Every time he started to cry, he sat the bottle down, and dunked his head until it stopped. By the time he was ready to get out, the water was ice cold. Sylvester swayed as he left the bathroom without a towel, water pooling with each step.

He poured himself into bed. The sheets soaked up the freezing droplets that still clung to his body. Consciousness left him.

The world seemed to spin behind a black veil, and his stomach grew nauseous. Quickly, he opened his eyes to counteract the spin, but found himself tied to a chair. No scream could leave him, a gag filled his mouth.

Micky stood in front of him again, joined by the black shape lording over the unsuspecting mobster. Once again the man hit him, and he felt it just as strongly as when it happened before. The shape seemed to raise above Micky and hover. As the man turned to see what Sylvester stared, at he froze.

Micky actually saw the shadow creature as it descended upon him. At first, he stood there, silent and no more violent than a kitten. Then the man turned around, and his face morphed into someone he would never forget.

Ira stood there. Beautiful as ever. He smiled, though his jaw still ached from Micky's fist. She did not return the smile. Micky's fist raised again and punched him between his legs with all of the large gangsters weight. The pain reverberated, and Sylvester wanted to throw up. Micky-Ira turned around again and stood there while Sylvester fought the reaction.

Al's face stared back at him when he recovered. He yelled at Sylvester, accusing him of not saving them. All the power in the world resided at his fingertips, but still he refused to stop their murder.

The world swam and reformed. He was still strapped to a chair, but this time, he was in the middle of a field. All around him people watched Sylvester struggle. They held knives, or batons, ready to beat, or cut him at any moment.

Tommy stepped up to the bound man, leaned down, and looked him in the eye. His best friend for so long, yet he held the largest knife. Sylvester begged Tommy to cut him free and let him go.

The knife rose in the air, signaling for the crowd to begin their work. One by one everyone from his past stepped up. If they had a knife they used it. Each was only allowed one use of the blade. If they had a baton it crashed against his body. Everyone was there. Everyone except Tucker, Rebecca, and Jada.

When the last person took their turn, Tommy stepped up to the bashed, broken, and bloodied man. He walked behind Sylvester, finally cutting his arms free and pushing him forward. The detective lay face down on the ground, trying to move.

Tommy stepped over him, kneeling on Sylvester's back side. His knife rose more, then plunged into Sylvester's spinal cord at an angle. He could no longer move, or breathe.

Sylvester jerked out of bed and looked around at his room, then his sheets. Blood covered them, Rebecca's blood. The woman hung from the ceiling, her wrists and throat slashed by her own knife. A smile rested on her face.

Sylvester woke again. This time he looked up, and nothing was there. He was alone with drenched sheets and drying hair. When he stood, he fell right back down. The scotch hadn't worn off.

His phone was nowhere nearby. The urge to call every number he had, and make sure everyone was safe, overwhelmed him. He rolled off his bed, and started crawling to the bathroom, hoping the device was there.

No luck.

Slowly, he crawled toward the living room, looking all over for it. When he went to the bathroom with the scotch he stripped as he walked. Every piece of clothing that he threw willy-nilly, wherever he wanted, was empty.

He made it to the couch and finally found it. His head spun, and every time he tried to push a contact to call, he missed. The first number rang, and Tucker answered.

"Hello?" the voice sounded tired.

"Oh good... you're alive," he hung up and scrolled through the numbers again.

"Who is this?" another voice sounded.

"Jada! You're okay..." Sylvester partially sobbed.

"Sylvest..."

He hung up and quickly scrolled to the next contact.

"Sylvester? Everything okay?' Rebecca answered.

He simply cried over the phone and pulled it away from his ear. He did not hang up. *They're okay,* he balled.

Not long after Rebecca, Tucker and Jada stared at his naked form curled in the fetal position. Jada went to his room, found the soaked bed, then brought him a throw blanket that somehow managed to stay dry.

Tucker and Rebecca lifted him off the ground, and onto the couch. Afterward, Jada covered him. Tucker wandered, looking for signs of what happened. The empty bottle of scotch standing straight up was his first clue. Rebecca hadn't said anything to Tucker about their current case.

Tucker decided to take Sylvester up on his offer, and was weeks away from moving into the building, waiting for his current lease to end. He hadn't seen Sylvester since Thanksgiving. A text every now and then was sent, but nothing more. Tucker's practice was just too busy for personal time.

Jada hadn't spoken to Sylvester since she moved. She thought about texting him, but he was the one who said he would love her only as a friend. His head rested in her lap, and she stroked his hair.

"What's he working on these days?" Tucker asked Rebecca.

She eyed Jada, who ignored them for the most part. Rebecca signaled for him to join her in the office. The door firmly closed behind them, and she told him everything.

Tucker was awe struck. "You say that his friend Aiyana sent the feds to him?"

"That's what Sudeikis said," she replied.

"Doesn't sound right. She would know more than anyone else that he would have trouble with this case." Tucker leaned on the desk. "He's too close to it."

"I tried to take the brunt of the pain for him with his parents. It was too much. I've never seen him cry like that," she replied.

A sudden scream came from the apartment. Tucker and Rebecca rushed inside and found Jada, eyes wide, hair disheveled, and tear tracks where her makeup ran. "What happened to you?" Tucker asked.

She sat in shock. "Tornado," she replied.

"Tornado?" Tucker looked at Rebecca, then noticed Sylvester. He was on the floor with cuts and bruises across his body.

"He wouldn't have..." Tucker said looking at Rebecca. She simply shrugged.

Chapter Fifty-Two
Friends

Jada sat on the other side of the room. All three watched as Sylvester would disappear, then reappear later, his body either better, or worse than it was when he left. Once he disappeared, white and pasty, and returned tanned from time in the sun.

This happened several times, until Sylvester finally drug himself out of his drunken stupor. He looked around. Jada, and her chaotic appearance, Tucker sitting straight across from him, and Rebecca standing across the room. All stared at the man. Then he realized what he was, or in this case wasn't, wearing. The blanket wrapped around him, and he darted up the stairs without saying a word.

"What the..." he could be heard saying.

A short time later he reemerged, shorts and a t-shirt on. All three sat on the couch. Rebecca had her arm around Jada, attempting to comfort her.

"What the hell happened?" he asked.

Tucker looked at the others, then stood up. "Buddy, you drank a whole bottle of scotch. What do you remember about last night?"

A grimace covered his face. He remembered his parents' bodies once again staring at him. His session of crying into Rebecca's shoulder came to mind, but that was it. He shook his head.

"Let me put it out there for ya. You drank a bottle of scotch, called all of us, happy we were alive, then passed out down there." He pointed to the ground. "Rebecca and I got ya on the couch, then we went to talk about what you were up to these days. Jada starts screamin' sayin' Tornado, then you started poppin' in and out."

Sylvester looked at Jada, then Rebecca. "I'm sorry," he said quietly. "I would have told you, but I didn't think you needed to know."

"Is that why you gave up on a chance at something with me?" Jada asked. "You thought I wouldn't understand?"

Sylvester shook his head. "I told you the truth. I'm still in love with Ira."

Jada blinked.

"What the hell happened?" Rebecca asked. "Does this happen every time you get this drunk?"

Sylvester shrugged. "I haven't been this drunk since before Tempus came around."

"Say your apologies to Jada, but I want to talk to you about this case you're workin'," Tucker said.

Sylvester looked at him, then walked to Jada. Rebecca stood as he put his hand on her knee. He stared her in the eyes. "I never meant for you to find out this way. I guess I never meant for you to find out, but here we are. I didn't continue things with us because I knew that you deserved better than me. Tom should've known you were worth more of his time than he gave."

She put her hands on her face.

Tucker signaled for Rebecca to join him in the office. "When you're done we'll be in here."

"I do love you, but I love Ira too, and I don't think I can get over that," he took her hands from her face and held them. She stared into his eyes.

They were almost in sync. He pulled her up from the couch and into a deep hug. "I'm still messed up from everything that's happened to me," he started sobbing again.

Jada, still shocked, held him as his grip grew tighter. She didn't know what she expected of the man, but this was not it. A late night rendezvous potentially, but this was deeper. It was on an emotional level she wasn't sure he was ready for. Deeper than Tom had ever revealed to her.

"I love you. I'm willing to try, but you can't hold these secrets back." She leaned back and pulled his head so she could meet his eyes.

He studied her, then kissed her. "Let me finish what I'm doin', then we can talk about this. I'm hopin' I'll be in a better place after."

She smiled. "Just consider it."

He nodded.

She took out a piece of paper, wrote an address down, and handed it to him. "This is where I live now. Come see me when it's all done. Hopefully before Christmas."

He walked her to his apartment door, but held her hand in place. "One more kiss for strength?" he asked, his eyes bigger than she had ever seen them.

She obliged and they kissed. It was passionate, and she didn't want to let go. He didn't want to let her go either, but he did. "Before Christmas," he repeated, watching her as she walked down the hall.

Once she was gone, he walked into his office, and sat down. Both Rebecca and Tucker stared, waiting for him to speak. He had no idea what to say, so he just stared back, shrugging his shoulders.

"This case doesn't add up," Tucker started.

"What about it doesn't?" Sylvester said.

"Your friend Aiyana would never have given your name to them. Someone's settin' you up," Tucker said.

"Aiyana's cover is for the NSA, they specifically pointed that out," Sylvester rebutted.

"She knew how close you would be to this. How much you would get hurt." Tucker looked at Rebecca. "I think the shadow creature gave your name to them, under the guise of Aiyana Evans."

Sylvester leaned back. "You think that thing is intelligent? It's stupid. Never says a word, just tries to kill, or hurt me."

"I would never tell the people leading an investigation into your parents' death, that you would be able to solve all their problems," Tucker said, then looked at Rebecca.

"It makes sense Sylvester." She leaned in. "You said she read your mind. Aiyana would know everything about you, including that bit about the shadow creature. She wouldn't risk you going into something like this alone."

"Okay, but the shadow creature... really?" Sylvester shook his head. "I'd believe it was Alexander Wilson before that thing."

"You're in it now. That's what matters. Finish it so you can move on with your life," Tucker said. "I want to be there for the rest of it though. I'll have your back."

"Me too," Rebecca agreed.

"You bring me on any trips to the past, or another location. I'll make sure that thing gets what it deserves." Tucker stood up, and put out his hand. "Shake on it."

Sylvester smiled. "Fine. I still say it couldn't be that damn creature." He stood and shook Tucker's hand.

"Alright, where do we go from here?" Tucker asked.

"We get Sudeikis in on this and then we get the rest of the evidence, even the knife."

Chapter Fifty-Three
Check And Mate

Savior gathered the rest of the video and audio evidence they needed. It was easier than he thought, especially with Tucker and Rebecca helping him. The only downside for them, was that they had to witness the same atrocities he did.

Savior watched twice more as Micky devastated the people he tortured. They were beaten to a pulp, then all of his potential evidence was wiped away by the cleaning crew who joined him for every murder. Bleach was their best friend, using it to wipe away blood on the ground, as well as any potential physical evidence Micky's violent streak left behind.

The mob boss didn't care how big or small his victim was. He performed the same act, time and again. No witnesses ever came forward because, if they saw anything, they became a victim as well. That was the case during the last trip to the past, merely three weeks ago.

An innocent bystander was doing his job, and stumbled on Micky in the middle of beating one of the victims. His boys quickly pulled the man into the room and secured him. Savior watched the knife stab, and cut, while Micky laughed.

When they came back to the present, Agent Sudeikis waited patiently in a chair. For him it was only a few seconds, but when they arrived, all three were exhausted. They were in an office building in Chicago. The last victim was a CEO who got hooked on drugs that Micky's people were pushing across the city.

"You guys already done?" Sudeikis asked.

Savior nodded.

"It'll take some time, but I should be able to put the evidence together," Rebecca replied.

"All with two days to spare." Tucker smiled. "Savior's got a date." He eyed the man.

It was true that he made plans to talk to Jada before Christmas, but this was still his priority. His love life could wait. Savior shuffled his feet. "I guess," he said.

"What about the knife?" Sudeikis reminded.

"Not yet. I'm not sure whether it'll change anything. We may need to wait until he commits some other crime with it." Savior shook his head. "You've got enough to get things goin' right?"

Sudeikis nodded. "Holes can be poked in the footage and audio. Biggest question will be how the hell he would let someone film him? I think the D.A. should be able to get the warrant without the knife."

"Still, that knife may be the only thing that makes it stick," Tucker replied.

"Gimme a second," Savior said, grabbing Rebecca's hand. They disappeared, then reappeared in Rebecca's office. "Get to work on compilin' everything. We'll worry about the knife later." He didn't give her a chance to respond and simply disappeared again.

When he arrived back at the office, both men still stared at the disappearing trick. He was ready. "I don't want Rebecca to be seen," he said.

"But I'm okay?" Tucker laughed.

"You can handle yourself. Besides, when they arrest him, I want to be front and center. If I could slap those cuffs on him I would." Savior shook his head. "I just wish I could testify. I did get the snot beaten out of me after all."

"Again, you can't. You were there, and vanished. You went to the hospital, and are supposed to be recovering for the next month and a half," Sudeikis reminded.

"That's alright. So long as I get to look 'im in the eye and say my piece. I'll be alright." Savior looked at Tucker. "If you want you can go home. Feds are gonna wanna search for the knife first either way." He looked at Sudeikis. "When can we go?"

"Hernandez and Smith are watching Micky and his family." Sudeikis started dialing a number. "When can you get me the evidence?" he asked.

"A day," Savior replied.

"Hey Watkins. Can you get me a warrant for Tony Antonio?" he spoke into his phone. "I got plenty of evidence, it'll be compiled tomorrow." His face turned red. "Look it's video evidence of him committing a crime, audio too." Sudeikis looked at Savior. "My source is reliable. I'll have it tomorrow."

"He's gonna wanna wait," Savior whispered to Tucker.

Sudeikis waved a hand at him. "I'll try to get it tonight." He hung up the phone. "He'll get the warrant, but he needs to see the evidence first. Not sure what he's going to want to know, but you may have to explain everything to him."

"Not happenin'. Only reason you know is because of the incident." Savior's face was stern.

"Well, he won't get the warrant until he sees the evidence for himself. It's going to raise questions." Sudeikis looked at his phone again. "Get to Rebecca, and try to light a fire under her."

Savior nodded, put his hand on Tucker's shoulder, then disappeared. They arrived in Savior's office and Tucker sat down. "I thought you were gonna go after the knife?"

"Make them do some work. We've done more than enough," Sylvester said.

Tucker nodded.

"I was thinking about grabbing it after he pulled it from that guy, but Tempus told me it needed to stay." Sylvester shook his head. "Not sure I made the right choice, but if he says leave it, I leave it."

"Better talk to Rebecca," Tucker said. "What are you gonna do if you do have to reveal all to this Watkins guy?"

Sylvester stood and walked to the door, shrugging as he passed Tucker. "Deal with it when I need to." He left the office, joining Rebecca who was already hard at work editing the evidence.

She looked up and smiled. "Shouldn't have a problem getting this done tonight."

"That's good. I've gotta deliver it to Sudeikis." He leaned over her shoulder and reviewed the footage. "This was a great angle." He pointed at a camera that faced Micky. His features were plain, and you could see the scars from the incident Micky blamed him for.

"I'll have this ready in an hour, just need to cut the non-important stuff." She dug in.

"Need anything?" Sylvester asked.

"Coffee and some snacks would be fantastic," She replied as she buried her nose further into the screen.

Savior returned to Sudeikis two hours later. He handed a yellow envelope to the agent and waited as he called Watkins again. Another hour passed, and they were in an old building in the heart of Chicago. Walls glistened from the recently lacquered dark woods adorning them. Savior looked at the scaffolding in the halls, realizing that they were renovating the building. Sudeikis knocked on a solid wood six panel door and waited.

A tall man, with orange hair, opened. He was in his late thirties, maybe early forties. "Sudeikis, glad to see you." He opened the door, escorting them in. "Who's this?"

"This is the guy who gathered the evidence," Sudeikis said, handing the envelope to Watkins.

"Very good, let's see it." He popped the drive into his laptop. Watkins' smile fell as he watched the brutal slayings taking place. He reached for his stomach, then stopped the footage. "Excuse me." Watkins quickly left the room, and disappeared down the hall.

"Some people can't handle it," Sudeikis said.

"I guess not," Savior replied.

They waited until he returned, paler than before. A stare rested on his face, first looking at Sudeikis, but then, for a long and hard time, at Savior. His hands brushed over his shirt, and he straightened his tie, as he composed himself and sat back down at his desk. The whole time he eyed the stranger in the trench coat.

"How?" he shook his head.

Sudeikis looked to Savior for the explanation. "Let's just say that this footage is genuine. It was taken from the places where these murders were committed."

"Micky isn't that stupid." Watkins leaned in. "There's no way this is authentic."

"I assure you it is," Savior confirmed.

"So what, you're rattin' your boss out?" Watkins replied.

"Far from it. I want to take him down." Savior leaned over the orange haired man.

"What's in it for you?" Watkins asked, meeting Savior's stare.

"Justice," Savior replied in a deep tone through gritted teeth.

"Tell him who you are." Sudeikis looked at the attorney.

"My real name is Sylvester Pemberton. There's a file on that drive of my parents' being murdered by Micky." Savior looked at him.

"I see," Watkins replied.

"Can you make the evidence work in court?" Savior asked, irritation accentuating every word.

"It's hard to say. Like I said, Micky isn't stupid. He would never have done this in front of a camera." Watkins looked at the image on his laptop. "For these people though, I'm willing to put it in front of a judge, assuming physical evidence can be found?"

Sudeikis smiled. "Get me that warrant, and I'll find that evidence. Worst case he'll find it."

There was a vague look from the man, but he nodded. "Alright. You've got your warrant. Find that evidence, I don't want this footage to come back and bite me in the ass without a backup plan."

Sudeikis smiled.

"I'll get ahold of a judge and send it to your office as soon as I can." Watkins picked up his phone and started talking.

Sudeikis escorted Savior to the hall. "If you really want to be here for this, then I suggest you come back to my office and wait."

Savior nodded, and expressed interest in eating. He hadn't been hungry, not like normal. Seeing all of the blood and gore, the constant strain, and stress of the creature appearing when he least expected, and the strains of his love life were finally taking a toll.

Deep in the night the warrant came through. Sudeikis, Savior, and a group of officers loaded into vehicles. It was a thirty minute drive at ten o'clock on a Tuesday. Traffic was light, and they arrived, lights blaring, but sirens turned off.

Hernandez and Smith joined them as they busted the door in, guns at the ready. Every light in the house lit up, as a dozen federal agents stormed in. Savior waited at the vehicles, leaning against the hood. The detective was surprisingly patient.

Profanities could be heard as the home was secured. Savior was eager for what was coming. He knew this was going to be the best night he had since Al and Janet's deaths changed his own life forever. Sure, he had money now. He was successful and there was a woman waiting for him, but this was the single most exhilarating experience he ever had.

What remained of Micky's hair stood up at varying angles, lipstick covering his face and neck, as he was escorted from the home. He yelled and screamed as Hernandez and Smith walked him to the man leaning against the hood of the vehicle. Micky's face went stark white when he realized who he was.

"Long time Micky," Savior snarled at the man.

"It's you," Micky whispered.

"Do you know who I am?" Savior asked.

There was a vague sense of realization, but Micky refused to speak.

"I'm Al and Janet Pemberton's son. You killed my parents, and I watched the whole thing. You're gettin' what you deserve, and if they free you..." Savior leaned in and whispered into the man's ear. "I'll drop you in the sun. You know I can. You saw how I disappeared."

Micky looked at Savior as he leaned back on the hood. "Get this guy away from me," Micky said as they moved him from the home, and into the back of a car.

"Micky." Savior sang as he smiled. "Just remember, all of this... was me." His smile faded, replaced by the same menacing snarl.

They shoved Micky into the back of the car and slammed the door. Hernandez and Smith waited for Sudeikis. The agent was still in the house, yelling at two women who argued about the intrusion. He shoved papers in their faces, and walked away.

"Feel better?" he asked.

Savior smiled. "Give me twenty minutes with him and he'll tell you exactly where that knife is."

"From this point forward, unless we can't find it, you're a civilian." Sudeikis held his hand out.

Savior took the hand, and shook it vigorously. "Don't hesitate to call me if someone breaks him out, or he's set free. Three life sentences at least. His fortune... his empire... should go to the families of his victims."

"Not my call. All I do is get 'em off the streets. It's up to the judge and jury at that point." Sudeikis smiled. "Tell Rebecca there will be a check in the mail with her name on it, as well as documents to submit with all of your taxes. I even added Tucker to the list. He's a good guy and he did help."

"Thank you Sudeikis." Savior looked him in the eyes, his own starting to tear up. "Really... I couldn't have done this without you." He wiped away the tears. "Well I could have, but I wouldn't have been so easy on that beast."

Savior walked away from the scene. "Where ya goin'?" Sudeikis yelled.

"Home. Then to see that girl." He waved goodbye to the agent then disappeared down an alley.

Chapter Fifty-Four
And Then...

Sylvester rested on his couch while he read the newspaper. The front page had Micky's face plastered across it. *Infamous Mob Boss Convicted* the headline read. He smiled.

The FBI recovered ten knives from ten different murders. Micky kept them, dried blood and all, in boxes labeled with the victims' names. Trophies and signs of the madness that enveloped the man for forty years.

Jada leaned on his shoulder, arm wrapped around him. She dozed in his apartment after a long night of celebration. Sylvester arrived at her house on Christmas day, a gift in hand. He apologized to her for the way he acted, and for not giving them a chance.

She smiled at the door to her apartment and ushered him inside. Since then, Sylvester hadn't taken any cases, and he took her out every night. It was weeks of wining and dining, and Sylvester, for the first time in years, was at peace.

Ira still popped into his head from time to time, but Jada quickly replaced her, and Sylvester was slowly starting to forget Ira's face. With everything in the open, Jada was treated to trips anywhere she wanted to go, though never on a plane if Sylvester could help it. They went to shows in the past. Some nights they dined at the top of the Eiffel Tower. Sylvester rented the entirety of the restaurant so they could take their time and enjoy the view.

Tucker moved into the building, expressing enthusiasm for the lack of taxes he would have to pay for the next few years. He asked for advice from Sylvester, though the man was far more intelligent when it came to detective work. Most of the time with those cases, it was just a quick jaunt back to see what actually happened. Tucker still lived elsewhere, not wanting to live and work in the same building, but he was there every day.

Rebecca was given a vacation for as long as she wanted. She travelled, the traditional way, across the globe. The check she received from Sudeikis was enough for her to be gone an entire year. That was her plan at least, seeing every place she possibly could, and never worrying about going back to work. Sylvester told her to come back when she was ready and gifted her another year's salary.

He put the newspaper down and looked outside. Snow fell on the roofs of the buildings his apartment overlooked. Jada grumbled next to him, and he leaned down to kiss her on the forehead. "I love you," he whispered so not even she could hear.

There was still time, and he wasn't quite ready for those words in a more than friends manner. It was a big phrase, and only Ira had ever heard him say it in this capacity. Voicing it to Jada, as more than friends, would make it permanent. It wasn't that he wanted things to change, but he just wanted to be sure it was the right time.

A knock echoed from the office, barely audible through the apartment door. He eased away from Jada, laying her gently down on the couch, then walked to answer it. Two people stood outside. "Look I'm not really workin' right now, I'm takin' some time off. Come back in March, or somethin'," he said as he opened the door.

A blonde woman, shorter than him, stood there and smiled at him. The man next to her had darker hair, though he didn't smile. Ira and Tommy both stared at him.

She was dressed as though she had money, which of course she did. He hadn't seen her in years, and his heart ripped and tore at the sight. Deep red lipstick made her lips pop, and her glasses were gone.

Tommy wore what he always did. Jeans, a t-shirt, and a black jacket. He was strangely silent, not saying anything, only walking into the office and sitting down. Sylvester stepped aside for Ira, and offered her the seat next to Tommy.

"Long time," he said as he took his seat behind the desk.

"Yeah it has been." Ira smiled.

Tommy nodded silently. There was a quick twitch of his lips that Sylvester caught.

"What brings ya to town?" he asked.

"We saw on the news that they got him," Ira said. "I wanted to see you, and tell you how happy I am for you. Tommy said he wanted to come too."

"So you two have kept in touch?" Sylvester asked.

Ira's face blushed. "We dated a while," she admitted sheepishly.

He looked from Ira to Tommy, then nodded as though he accepted it. "I see."

"It was right after we left. We stayed together, traveled a while, and it just kind of happened," she explained. "We've not been together for years though."

As if that makes up for abandoning you in one of your worst moments, Tempus said.

Sylvester said nothing. He stared blankly through the woman he once loved. "Well... thanks for comin' and seein' me," he spoke with a flat tone. "I'll show ya out."

Ira looked down, embarrassed. "We weren't together anymore."

"Not because that's what I wanted. That's what you wanted. I wanted to live happily ever after with you," Sylvester said, the wound freshly reopened. "I wanted you, at my side." He gestured to Tommy.

Tommy still remained quiet.

"All you did, was abandon me when I really needed you. I'm startin' to put my life back together now. I met someone and she's in there, and we're happy," he finished.

Ira's eyes welled up with tears, and she started crying. The apartment door opened, and Jada, rubbing her eyes, looked in. "Everything okay hun?" she asked. Then she noticed Tommy. "What're you doin' here Tom?"

Sylvester looked at Jada, then Tommy. "You're her Tom?" For the first time he really took his old friends face in. It was different. He was Tommy, but the smile, and the eyes, didn't seem to be his.

"You bet I am," Tommy said, a wicked smile suddenly covering his face.

"I had no idea. It doesn't matter because you left her to go off on an adventure," Sylvester berated.

"I was also pluggin' your girlfriend at the same time too." Tommy smiled. "And you know what... it felt so good knowing that it would hurt you."

Sylvester stood up. "I think it's time for both of you to leave."

Tommy stood, though Ira still sat. "No. I think it's time to come clean." One second Tommy stood in front of the chair, then suddenly, he was pulling Sylvester's chair from behind him.

"The hell?" Sylvester exclaimed as Tommy threw him to the ground. Jada ran to cover him with her body.

"Oh don't you worry Jada, you're goin' with him." Tommy cackled, disappeared and suddenly reappeared, hovering over them. His hand lowered to the woman.

Just as suddenly as he appeared, he was smashed through Sylvester's apartment door. Ira, furious over what had been said, blocked both Sylvester and Jada. "Leave 'em alone!" she screamed.

Tommy stood, laughing. "You don't need to exist either." Tommy's form shifted and he became the black shadow creature.

Sylvester stood, and stepped in front of both women. "This is between you and me. Leave them outta this!" He held his arms out trying to protect them from Tommy.

A terrible sound escaped the creature. Sylvester thought it might be laughter. "You did this to me." The creature reached for him.

At the creature's touch, memories flooded Sylvester's mind. Tommy, that night in the field. Tommy in a wheelchair. Tommy dead. Tommy absorbing all of it into this version of himself.

When he let go of Sylvester, he stepped back. Sylvester fell to his knees and looked at his friend. "What was that?" He sounded as though he were in pain.

"That was how I became what I am." The creature walked forward.

The women crowded closer, trying to block what was once Tommy. Each touched Sylvester and the creature smiled. "Like I said, you don't need to exist either." He vanished, then reappeared behind them. With a single touch, Sylvester felt the world ripping apart around him.

The creature reverted to Tommy. "Too bad. I liked you both. You were... fun." He smiled as Sylvester cried out... and they were gone.

Tommy walked to Sylvester's desk, now his, and took the seat. He put his hands behind his head and reclined in Sylvester's chair. Tucker rushed in, having only just heard the commotion.

"What happened Tommy?" he said.

"Don't worry about it Tuck, everything is just fine." Tommy laughed as Tucker put away his gun and sat down.

"Had me worried. What case we workin' today?" Tucker asked.

"Any case we want."

Author Bio

Kenneth L. Powell, a dedicated system support engineer, has always aspired to transcend the ordinary. In his formative years, he dreamed of becoming a Rockstar, Author, and Chef—someone celebrated, someone unforgettable. While the dream of being a household name hasn't changed, the focus has sharpened: authorhood is now his sole pursuit.

A lifelong explorer of fantastical realms, Kenneth has never wavered in his belief that he could build worlds worth getting lost in. That belief manifested with the publication of his debut novel *Dawn of Prophecy*, the first entry in the sprawling *Dragonkind* saga. What followed was a momentum of creativity: *Herald of Heresy* expanded the series, *Scholar of Duplicity* prepares to deepen it, and *The Wolf's Dragon* promises to upend expectations.

But Kenneth doesn't just dwell in one universe. *The Hybrids* introduced readers to a gritty, speculative tale of transformation, while *Savior Time Detective* launched a new series that blends temporal mystery with raw emotion. These stories—distinct yet interconnected—reflect his growing literary multiverse.

With more than two decades of storytelling under his belt, Kenneth's vision remains ambitious. The *Dragonkind* series was only the beginning of a legacy in the making—one that's designed to evolve, expand, and endure with *The Hybrids* and *Savior*.